THE *Lady* MEETS HER *Match*

GINA CONKLE

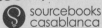

sourcebooks
casablanca

Published by Sourcebooks Casablanca, an imprint of Sourcebooks, Inc.
P.O. Box 4410, Naperville, Illinois 60567-4410
(630) 961-3900
Fax: (630) 961-2168
www.sourcebooks.com

Printed and bound in Canada
MBP 10 9 8 7 6 5 4 3 2 1

This one's for you, Mom.

*Thanks for introducing me to "The Highwayman"
and Cinderella, but most of all for pushing
through hard times years ago. Together we
learned a thing or two about perseverance.*

One

London, 1768

No mask like open truth to cover lies,
As to go naked is the best disguise.

William Congreve, *The Double Dealer*

A WOMAN ON THE VERGE OF MORAL DOWNFALL OUGHT to be well dressed. Claire's particular transgression was gartered to her thigh, a paper hidden by yards of silk. She walked through the empty alley, confident in one comforting truth: no one dared ask a lady what her skirts concealed.

She glanced down at her small bosom, where soft moonlight splashed a distracting display of flesh. "And no one will be alarmed by what's revealed there, not that any will see me."

The sparkling blue-and-silver creation would be off soon, after midnight. The ball gown was worn just in case, a costume of sorts to fit into a place she didn't belong. Despite each well-planned detail, damp palms proved her outward calm a hoax. She'd always been a good girl—minus a slip in judgment some years ago.

What she was about to do trumped her past error. In spades.

That is, if someone catches me.

A deep breath failed to stop a tiny hiccup. Looking at the grand house ahead, this evening's ruse proved one thing: a woman's independence came at a price. If she wanted a different path, everything hinged on tonight's success.

She hooked her plain cloak on a fence post. Wetness swathed cobblestones from a recent summer shower, wafting scents of washed earth. Nice for this part of London...so different from her Cornhill section of Town.

She stepped off Vigo Lane into the mews of one Cyrus Ryland, the King of Commerce. England's celebrated commoner and landlord for much of midtown had something she wanted—his signature. Somewhere in his palatial West End sprawl of a home she'd find it, forge it, and disappear back into the late August night.

The well-laid plan sounded reasonable.

Why then did the sheer size of Mr. Ryland's home put a lump in her throat?

"There you are," Abigail said, pots and pans banging behind her. She passed through the kitchen doorway with a busy woman's stride. "Didn't see you earlier. Thought you'd lost your nerve."

Abigail Green, housekeeper of Ryland House, jingled a set of keys. She searched out the right one as she moved along the limestone edifice toward the servants' quarters. Overhead, brass candle lanterns chased off the night where two of Mr. Ryland's hulking carriages claimed much space in the mews.

"Lost my nerve? No." Claire adjusted her beaded mask. "But I admit, I'm holding on to my last ounce of courage."

An iron key slid home in the lock. Abigail turned it with a quiet snap, but she kept one hand on the knob, her mobcap casting shadows over serious features.

"If you're having a change of heart, now's the time to say so."

Claire looked at the key nestled in the lock. "No. I'm going through with this."

The door clicked open to a stark, whitewashed hall stretching ahead. Both women marched through the lonely quarters, their footfalls echoing.

"Understand, I'll lead you to his study, but I won't stay with you." Abigail opened another door, this one broad paneled and crafted to blend into the wall. "The house is in an uproar what with being two footmen plus a maid short and this grand ball going on."

The portal offered entry into another world, the kind of place spun in fairy tales told for lesser mortals. People talked of Ryland House's grandeur, and now Claire stood, an openmouthed witness.

Massive chandeliers cast tiny rainbow prisms high on pale walls trimmed with elaborate boiseries. For the hall to be so well lit... Were there people in this section of the house? She couldn't imagine letting candles burn for no reason.

Lush murals of pastoral bliss covered ceiling panels, creating a wonderland. The artful display unfolded overhead like delightful pages of a child's picture book, stretching the length of the hallway.

Abigail pushed the door shut and pocketed the keys, a dark, weighty clump in her apron. "I'm only helping you because of what you did for my sister, but if you're caught, don't say my name. I'll deny everything."

There was finality in those pale blue eyes, so like Annie's.

"I'm only copying his signature." A quelling hand rested on her midsection. "Then I'll take my leave as quickly as I've come."

Saying her crime aloud brought to mind awful images of Newgate, but anyone of a reasonable mind would agree tonight's dubious errand wasn't the same as stealing money. She was a grown woman who wished to run an honest business, have a coffee shop of her own. The intractable Mr. Ryland wouldn't allow an unmarried woman the privilege.

Mr. Pentree, one of Ryland's agents, rang in her head: *"Sorry, Miss Mayhew. Mr. Ryland's most insistent. It's one of his rules. A husband, father, or brother must be on the lease, or I can't give you the key to the property."*

In other words, she needed a man.

She didn't have one in hand. Nor did she want one.

Mr. Pentree had pushed up his spectacles, informing her with all gentleness, *"Your only recourse is to see Mr. Ryland in person. Plead your case. Get his approving signature."*

Approving signature, indeed. A grown woman beseeching a man for the right to conduct lawful business? Yet, even there, she'd tried.

One probably had better luck setting an appointment with King George. There was a four-month wait for a spot of Mr. Ryland's time. Former housekeepers didn't rate high enough to gain entry on his calendar. One of his secretaries always responded with the same polite refusals and delays. Claire was done petitioning.

She had snatched back the document from Mr. Pentree that day, informing him she'd find a way to get the signature from the lofty Mr. Ryland, even if it meant accosting him on London's streets.

It was time she took matters into her own hands.

Now, Claire walked with Abigail through Mr. Ryland's elegant beige hallway, her bravado floating away, lost in the expensive chandeliers overhead.

She'd been in grand homes before, but the lights shined…differently here. What made this place so extraordinary?

Graceful orchestral notes drifted everywhere. Conversation and laughter threaded with music, weaving the kind of noise that turned a large ball into an impersonal entertainment, yet easy for a body to get lost in the crowd. The housekeeper nodded to where lights gleamed brightest.

"Go that away, and you'll find yourself in the ball. But if you turn left at that plant," she said, pointing at frothy greenery in blue ceramic pots, "you'll be in the kitchen hallway. Wait there when you're ready to leave."

"You don't think that's a bad idea? Meeting you in such a visible location?" Claire frowned. "Someone might see me and wonder."

"Did you get a good look at yourself?" Abigail's voice notched higher. "You're lovely. Same as any of those fine Society ladies with their gowns and such. You could easily be one of them."

Be one of them?

The glittering gown made all the difference. Tomorrow, she'd don her practical, starched gray broadcloth, and her conscience could lock away tonight's aberration in judgment.

They moved down the hallway and the house-keeper turned and pushed open an elaborately carved door set in an alcove. A dark room. The study. Claire stepped inside the modest space, high ceilinged but small and unexceptional when one considered England's King of Commerce transacted half the realm's business here.

It was said Ryland owned every warehouse from Manchester to London. Northern goods sat in one of his buildings waiting for a ride to London's harbor on one of his canals.

And this humble-sized room is where he labored?

"Remember, you must be out before the unmask-ing," Abigail warned.

And she shut the door.

The latch clicked like a pistol cocked at her back. Claire's fingernails dug into her palms while her vision adjusted to the dark. She dare not light a candle.

Her objective, Mr. Ryland's desk, claimed a spot by the window where moonlight spilled through open curtains. She raised voluminous skirts and slipped the folded signature page from her garter. The paper, warm from her leg, crinkled in her grip.

She moved with care, a sweet thrill shooting through her. The prize sat atop the middle stack of papers: the bold scrawl of Cyrus Ryland.

Silk skirts brushed leather, a murmur of sound, when she slid onto his seat. A brass clock ticked a steady cadence, and she concentrated on the bold *C* and *R* dominating the page, her fingers picking at her gown's lace.

Ryland's signature slurred across the bottom as though he couldn't be bothered to form the remaining letters.

"Audacious man," she said under her breath and grabbed a quill.

Keeping the nib dry, she traced her quarry's name on foolscap, scratching the paper again and again. To convince Mr. Pentree, this had to be an excellent facsimile. Yet, within the quiet, the bold name she copied called to her.

Her hand slowed. Ink blurred, ceasing to be lines on a page.

Those lines turned into a name…a person.

Cyrus.

Her brows knit together, brushing the inside of her mask. Could a signature reveal much about a man?

What she was about to do wasn't simply copying a signature, nor was she on the path of faceless transgression. She set out to deceive a man, a man who was someone's brother, someone's son, and deception could turn ugly, as well she knew.

The moon's telling light washed over Ryland's black signature, the lettering strong to the point of arrogance. Yes, arrogant and unstoppable and barely educated. A man quite like her father. She stumbled over that impression, letting the inkling sink deeper.

No one will get hurt.

Her thumb pressed a new wrinkle on the foolscap. "This is just a case of nerves."

Really, if Mr. Ryland hadn't been so difficult about leasing his properties to an unmarried woman, she wouldn't be in this predicament.

Why did men get to decide these things anyway?

She slid the original signature behind the document to be forged, paper brushing paper. Vexation dissolved into what was truly the heart of the matter: the longing for a place of her own, to make her own way in the world—a new path made possible by the single stroke of a quill.

At the moment, her success hinged on one man, or at least on stealing his name. Lips curving in a wry smile, she dipped the nib in ink and, with surprising ease, copied over faint lines.

The result produced a stunning imitation.

Once the signature was sanded, she leaned back in Ryland's chair, her thumb and forefinger pinching the aquamarine stone hanging from her neck. Footsteps crunched on gravel outside. A carriage rolled past the study window. Voices came closer. Louder and more of them.

She peered around the chair. Footmen loitered by the window, the tops of their white periwigs visible at the bottom. If one man angled his head just so, he'd spy her at Ryland's desk.

Slipping from the chair, she sought the room's lone settee, a safe harbor in the shadows. She sunk down, squashing her skirts like some rustic cousin new to Town. Her head lolled against the back cushion, finding needful support.

Who knew committing a crime could be so draining?

One. More. Minute.

Then, she'd be free.

The signature page nestled on her lap. Let the form get good and dry before tucking away the incriminating piece, but behind her, the door clicked. She jerked upright and faced the door.

A bright beam of light sliced the blackness.

A man stepped forward, his silhouette tall and well dressed. She blinked at the blinding glow. Every muscle seized with the want to flee. Her fingernails dug into chintz upholstery. The commanding figure shut the door, head bent as though lost in thought. He placed a single brass candleholder on a table, oblivious to her presence.

The study's late-night visitor took a step in her direction, tense lines bracketing his mouth. Immense shoulders shrugged off a fine velvet coat in slow, distracted fashion, the fabric rustling its intimate hush in the dark.

Excuses flew through her mind. *She was looking for the lady's retiring room…she got lost—*

"Who are you?" The coat stopped halfway down sizable arms.

Claire tried a fortifying breath, but her lungs refused to cooperate while her mind absorbed a new fact: she faced Cyrus Ryland. He loomed large, waiting in the silence.

Masculine brows shot up when her lack of response stretched too long.

"I'm Claire." The truth burst out, and she cringed as much from the social slip of blurting her Christian name as from revealing her identity.

His eyes flared, likely from her blunder of manners, but she hadn't thought of a false identity. Mr. Ryland took his sweet time removing his coat. His unhurried gaze traced her hair, the mask, finally settling on her plunging bodice with thorough consideration.

"Just Claire?" he asked. "Not *Lady* Claire Something-or-other?"

"For a masked ball"—she attempted a lighthearted smile—"just Claire."

He retrieved the candle, his granite-hard features severe behind the guttering flame. Mr. Ryland put his coat and the lone taper on a small table beside the settee. Her smile wobbled the closer he came, caught as she was in a neat trap of her own design.

Big hands spun his jabot's lacy fall around to his nape and went to work on the knot under his chin. Glued to the seat, she couldn't stop from staring. Little scabs marred his knuckles. She lingered on those marks before her vision drifted upward to confident gray eyes watching her. His powerful presence made the idea of him being anyone's victim laughable.

The cushion dipped beside her, and her stomach dropped. They'd crossed paths once at Greenwich Park, when she was in service there. Would he have any recollection of her? One hand touched her mask, and she remembered: her face was half-covered in a dimly lit room.

She was safe. For now.

Mr. Ryland faced the wall, more concerned with his neckwear than the stranger in his study.

"Let me guess," he drawled. "You'll remain anonymous until midnight, when all will be revealed."

"Typical of these entertainments, don't you think?"

"Lovely as you are, being in here isn't a good idea. I'm not the type to marry because I'm alone with a lady."

Mr. Ryland assumed she'd come here to entrap him? She wanted to laugh at the absurdity. The evening's ironic twist was too delicious.

"Oh, I'm no lady, Mr. Ryland."

His keen stare slanted her way.

"And I promise not to accost you, sir."

What possessed her to toss out those forward morsels? She may as well have dropped a succulent lure to a hungry fish.

There was a snick of sound, velvet rubbing on chintz from his body shifting toward her.

She sat taller, drawing on reserves of coolness. Armed with enticing anonymity, her hand eased its grip on the settee. There had to be a way to extract herself from this predicament, but his inflated belief that she sought to snare him needed an adjustment.

"You may find this hard to believe, but not every woman in England wants marriage to you or any other man."

"Is that so?"

"Yes," she said, smoothing her skirts. "Some women want independence, the chance to forge their own path."

His stare locked on her. "An interesting consideration."

But her skirt-smoothing fingers missed something. *The signature sheet.*

Her heart lurched. The page must have slipped from her lap when she'd turned around on the settee. Her hands hunted for the paper, subtle movements over her gown and the seat beside her, but she found only air and cloth. At the bottom of her vision, the page lay on the floor, a fallen soldier in the evening's covert skirmish.

The toe of her shoe inched the damning evidence closer to her hem, all the while she faced him and held the facade of a woman at leisure. Under the circumstances, diverting small talk wouldn't be out of the ordinary.

"I see you've unmasked already."

"It was off long ago…strap broke." Ryland winced, yanking on the ties. "Waste of fabric."

"The mask? Or the jabot you're about to strangle yourself with?"

A smile touched his lips. "Both, I suppose."

His hands eased their grip on the neckwear and rested on his thighs.

"I'm guessing the evening's been a trial, and you'd rather be elsewhere," Claire went on, looking across the room where the door marked her escape. "That makes two of us."

He followed her sight line. "And what could possibly drive a woman of independence to hide in my study? A man?"

She balked at his amused suggestion, her fingers tugging a loose silver thread on her bodice.

"In a manner of speaking, yes. It's been a most unusual evening."

The thread snapped, a tiny sound in the quiet study. Mr. Ryland's attention dropped to her waist.

"Rest easy. You're safe with me."

Her busy fingers fell to her lap. She believed him. His broad-shouldered presence was like facing a nicely dressed bulwark. How gallant that he offered his protection without question. The man was sparing with his words, but his deep voice soothed her.

His eyes narrowed a fraction on her mask.

"If you're not a lady, are you a courtesan?"

Her arms clamped under her bosom, laughter bubbling up sharply. "Rather blunt, are you?"

His stare dipped to the soft, white flesh pillowing from her low-cut bodice. Her arms went stiff, and air kissed her cleavage. Despite his bold attention, she would *not* move her arms.

"A fair question," he ventured. "A man can only wonder when he finds a pretty woman waiting in the dark. And I prefer getting to the point."

"And this assumption of yours, is it because you divide women neatly into marriageable and *un*marriageable types, and you're not sure where to put me?"

"Never believed I thought of women quite like that," he said, the corners of his mouth twitching. "But you could be onto something."

She peered at him, glad for the anonymity of her mask. The harsh bracket lines around his mouth were gone, replaced by the semblance of a smile. The changes made her want to lean closer for a better look at what else might happen. Were these subtle shifts because Mr. Ryland fed on candid conversation? She was certain he wasn't at all put off by her tart tongue.

"Did it ever occur to you there's more to the fairer sex?"

"No, but Lucinda likes to argue a similar point."

"Lucinda?"

"My sister. The ball honors her birthday. This evening's part of my *blunt* attempt to get her wed." His tone dropped with dangerous softness. "But you'd know it's her birthday if you went through the receiving line."

She lowered her lashes, avoiding his questing stare. He likely suspected a man sneaked her into the festivities. Now she was caught. Her status was akin to a mouse trapped in an audience with a lion. She tensed, ready to spring. The door was not too far.

"Relax," he said. "You're welcome to stay if you free me from this noose. Bothered me all night."

"You mean untie your jabot?"

Such a personal request, but then he believed her to be a woman who removed lots of male clothing. Freeing him of neckwear was modest by comparison.

"You did say you wouldn't accost me." His chin tipped high, giving her access to his neck.

Claire scooted nearer to Mr. Ryland, keeping her spine properly rigid. The change in proximity spread a flush of warmth across her bare skin; probably shared body heat was all. The way he sat, assuming trust, muddled her.

She raised stiff arms, inching into unfamiliar closeness. A marionette master could be maneuvering her, so stilted were her hands. Mr. Ryland's sheer size dominated the settee, and his lopsided smile stayed in place.

"I see you're entertained."

"More like glad to be in your company…a woman speaking her mind."

"Oh." He took the starch right out of her, stoking her curiosity. Faint aromas of smoke and a woman's perfume clung to him, but another indefinable essence about the man played on her wits.

"We've just met, but you're not put off by me."

His deep voice sent a pleasant tickle down her spine.

"Should I be?"

"No."

Her hands worked the jabot's knot. Sitting this close, his chest gave the impression of solid armor plates beneath his burgundy silk waistcoat. Nothing could knock him down. Rumors had spread concerning his youth as a farmhand. Many said he worked as a laborer, digging ditches in the early days of the Bridgewater Canal Company.

How could a man like that rise to become a major stakeholder?

His soft chuckle drew her attention upward. "I grew up with seven sisters. Never got through a meal without my ears blistered by unshakable female opinions." His ribs expanded from a deep breath. "Something I never thought aristocratic women would lack."

"Perhaps you haven't met the right ones." She concentrated on the knot, surprised at wanting more conversation with him.

"I've met plenty."

His accent was decidedly lacking the crisp syllables of Town, more Midlands or Manchester by the way he honored vowels over consonants with every word.

"I think I understand. You fear a future of dull dinners with a woman who says what she thinks you want to hear. But aren't you courting a duke's daughter?"

Ryland's chin dipped, his stare pinning her.

"Since you like bluntness," she said, giving him a pert smile. "Besides, we are virtual strangers in a dark room."

"As in, strangers with the freedom to say anything."

His leg moved, his knee gently bumping hers. The contact was obvious despite layers of silk skirts.

"Something like that," she murmured, keeping her knee against his.

Her focus went back to the knot, but the undercurrent shifted between them. Mr. Ryland's warm breath mingled with hers. The simple task of unloosening a tie threatened to dismantle her thinly veiled composure. She had caused herself enough turmoil by sneaking into his house to steal his signature on the incriminating document half-exposed under her hem.

And now she added this unexpected element to the mix? Matters weren't helped by the man's intense scrutiny either.

"Is that part of your occupational talent? Listening… to men."

His voice rumbled strong and sure above her head. She licked her lips, concentrating on the balled fabric.

This is sheer madness.

How long since the headiness of attraction last touched her? Her throat thickened on notions of tenderness and men. She'd locked away those parts, hiding them in a safe place. Tonight, one man cracked open flirtation's door, and she was ready to skip happily forward.

No matter that Mr. Ryland thought her a woman of loose morals. She couldn't deny the charged atmosphere sparking between them.

The tip of her finger nudged his chin higher, lingering there. "I need you looking up."

He obliged her, and the air warmed from the faint touch.

She coaxed free a loop of cloth, the slow slide of cotton against cotton matching the tenor of her voice. "I have lots of talents, Mr. Ryland. Listening is only one of them."

His breath hitched. Her words, as potent as her tone, offered shameless encouragement. She played with fire, but she liked how Mr. Ryland was just as taken with the unusual interlude. And in the unspoken balance of power, the scales tipped gently in her favor.

He kept his head back, eyelids closed as though shutting away the world, save the two of them.

"Since we're speaking freely, the duke's daughter… the Lady Elizabeth Churchill. I'm not officially courting her. Nor do I want to." His words flowed in the lax way of a wearied man. "But that doesn't stop her determined mother from pressing the matter."

"I see." Claire inched closer. "And by the way, her perfume's all over your clothes. Lady Churchill's resorting to desperate measures to gain your attention."

Ryland's hands fisted on his thighs. "The perfume belongs to another woman."

Who? Her eyebrows shot up, brushing the inside of her silk mask.

"Well, at least you're honest. For a man who doesn't appreciate aristocratic women, you certainly have your share of their attentions."

"And yet, here I sit, seeking refuge in my study."

With me.

The uninvited thought slipped past her defenses.

Their conversation took a peculiar turn on this already peculiar evening. Ryland's rules of business were unconscionable to her, but his directness gave an unexpected delight. She asked forthright questions; he gave forthright answers.

She adjusted her hold on the jabot, the backs of her hands brushing his neck and under his chin. Burgeoning whiskers and warm, male flesh grazed her skin.

"Careful," he teased. "A body might think you're trying to accost a vulnerable man after all."

She laughed softly, dipping her head closer to his chest. "Something tells me, Mr. Ryland, you're vulnerable to no one."

"Cyrus," he said. "At least in here…call me Cyrus."

Was there a hint of longing in his voice?

She studied him under the veil of her lashes. England's stalwart King of Commerce, a man said to own almost every warehouse from Manchester to London, proved to have a vulnerable side.

"Aren't you on the marriage hunt for yourself?" she asked, adding quickly, "For a noblewoman, I mean."

"No."

The steel-hard quality in his voice brooked no further discussion. Mr. Ryland was a riddle to unfold, an attractive one at that. The lone candle flickered behind him, outlining powerful shoulders, tempting solidness she wanted to test.

"But an evening of harmless flirtation isn't out of the question."

His gaze fixed on her. "I'd welcome an evening free of complications."

Did he just proposition her?

Her legs relaxed under her skirts, his overture pushing open closed places. Tonight an element more dangerous than her forgery lurked. She uncurled his fist resting on his thigh and placed the bothersome neckwear in his hand.

"And now you're free," she said softly.

His shirt's neckline opened, the cotton seams bunching and wrinkling enough to reveal the tempting flesh of his upper chest. Sitting this close, interesting details like a minute cut on his jaw drew her attention. The split marked the center of a maroon bruise the size of a ha'penny.

A hard force must've struck this strapping man to leave the deep cut. Near that mark, a cleft dented the center of his strong chin. Before she could stop herself, her fingertip touched the small cleft, then slid along his jaw to circle the bruise.

"Battles with your valet?"

He grabbed her hand, holding her fingers in his warm grip. Ryland suspended his hold midair before slowly lowering her hand to her knee.

"My turn for questions."

They sat closer than propriety allowed, with his warm hand possessing hers. This strange meeting blurred Society's rules, but to Mr. Ryland, she was a woman of easy virtue sitting alone with him in a dark room. In these circumstances, both parties set their own boundaries, didn't they? Though he had no idea who she was, she sensed they sat as equals.

How freeing.

She sat up straighter, aware this shared power was of a sensual nature only; there'd be no parity outside the bedroom with Mr. Ryland. He was a man who led, expecting others, especially the gentler sex, to follow. Yet his strong-boned face would appeal to most women, women who'd forgive his overbearing ways and find his rough magnetism and substantial fortune qualities of great consideration.

His riches didn't interest her. His inviting mouth did.

A thin guise of civility covered this brute of a man who, through will or wealth, got his way. But his brotherly admission of listening to, even *liking*, his sisters' opinions turned her on end—not at all what she expected. How extraordinary to be in the company of a difficult man and discover he's not so…difficult.

She leaned back for mind-clearing space. "What do you want to know?"

He let go of her hand and stretched his arm along the back of the settee. "Who's your protector?"

"Perhaps I'm a woman of independent means. An honest businesswoman."

Cyrus laughed, a full sound radiating from his chest. "Sounds dangerous."

With fluid movement, he stood up and walked across the room to his desk. She turned around on the settee, watching his broad back.

"You don't think a woman should live a life of independence?"

"An invitation for trouble, if you ask me. Women need a man's guiding hand. Been that way since the beginning of time. Why change what already works?" He picked up the brass clock from the corner of his desk. "What about those baubles around your neck? Made of paste?"

Her hand shot up, touching the necklace. By his inflection, she caught Ryland's assumption that the jewels were a gift from a man. He'd be right. Her fingers rolled the largest stone, evidence of a past mistake.

"They're real," she said, her tone flat. "But I mean to sell them."

"Not sentimental jewelry, then?"

"No." She'd give no more on the necklace.

Her shoe pressed the floor, ready to grind stinging memories underfoot, when something crunched beneath her heel. *The signature sheet.* How could she let rampant flirtation muddle her mind and make her forget the very reason for being here?

Mr. Ryland angled the clock's face toward the moonlight. "Midnight approaches."

Midnight. The unmasking hour. She was supposed to meet Abigail. Her glance dropped to the sheet, shot to the door, and ricocheted back to the man by the moonlit desk. Was he going to suggest she go into the ball with him?

How was she going to get out?

She bent down, the air squishing out her lungs from whalebone stays poking and prodding—her corset and false hips made touching the floor nigh on impossible. Nimble fingers folded the paper into quarters, then once more, all done in time to quick, shallow breaths.

Stuffing the incriminating piece down her cleavage, her eyes shut for a split second.

The shop, her plans…all were within reach.

The necklace swung forward at the bottom of her vision, a pendulum of sparkling aquamarine, reminding her it was time to move on with her new life. Out of the corner of her eye, polished black shoes came into view.

"You've got to give me more about yourself before the unmasking—" He slipped on his coat and started to bend low. "Is something wrong?"

"Fine. I'm fine," she said, breath huffing and moving upright again. "My hem needed fixing."

Mellow candlelight touched Ryland's brown hair, the queue restrained in a black silk wrapped ribbon. He adjusted his sleeves, and the bottom seam of his fine waistcoat skimmed well-formed thighs. The man was granite hard without an ounce of excess. She stroked a white-blond lock of hair curling against the top of her left breast. The coy move was unintentional, but caught his eye all the same.

She could be any woman she wanted to be tonight.

Wasn't she doing that already?

Free, masked, unknown—a woman once in service, now wearing a ball gown, playing a part she'd never play again. What woman didn't want a taste of the forbidden at least once in her life? The chance to masquerade as someone else if only for a night?

And then she'd leave, escape as harmlessly as she

came. No one would be hurt. What better place to slip away unnoticed than in a crowded ballroom? Tomorrow would bring the beginnings of her more reliable adventure as midtown proprietress of a humble coffee shop.

"What were you saying?" she asked, champagne-like giddiness pouring over her.

She'd sipped the stuff twice in her life, and tonight's victory made her feel as though she had consumed the sweet, golden nectar again.

Growing up a steward's daughter on the grand Greenwich estate afforded her many opportunities. But life changed one fateful night, a reminder of who and what she was. Since then, she labored hard, building calluses anew on her hands and heart, all in an effort to fall into a deep sleep every night and forget what had happened years ago. Many more years of hard work stretched ahead of her.

Why not sip champagne once more?

What harm could come of that?

$\mathcal{T}wo$

Music has charms to soothe a savage breast,
To soften rocks, or bend a knotted oak.

William Congreve, *The Mourning Bride*

NO MAN COURTED A FINE WOMAN'S FAVOR WITHOUT paying a price. Alluring women always demanded their due in one form or another. Cyrus understood this, even ran his life on a constant balance sheet of costs and rewards, whether in his head or on paper. But women? He didn't fully understand them. What man did?

This masked blond with her bold tongue equaled a wealth of trouble. She wasn't a prudent candidate to become Mrs. Ryland, but he wasn't looking for anyone to fill the role. Claire's undeniable hint of mystery and playful daring touched him like welcome caresses in all the right places.

And an evening of hot flirtation that could lead anywhere? A timely reprieve.

He liked that his mystery guest wasn't intimidated

by him, but he couldn't say if she *was* or *was not* after money. Such were the limits of trying to read a woman in a dimly lit room.

And he had to admit, he wasn't thinking entirely with his head.

But if she wasn't chasing gold guineas, what was she in search of?

In recent years, he'd met his share of courtesans, and his enigmatic guest struck him as too proper and too pert to be a refined lightskirt. Could she be a newly fallen woman exploring that mode of employ?

When they touched on the subject of women and independence, his guest became tart tongued and emphatic, meeting him word for word, qualities that stoked his interest, among other parts clamoring for better acquaintance with her.

He would know more of the secretive beauty named Claire, if that was her true name, and there was no better way to coax the fair sex into openness than a festive atmosphere. Women thrived on entertainments.

"We ought to return to the ball."

"So soon? And here I thought you wanted a reprieve from the crowd."

"True," he said, offering his arm. "But the evening's improved considerably."

Claire's fingertips rested lightly on his sleeve, her silk skirts stirring a seductive sound as she stood up. Glittering silver embroidery drew his attention to cream-white curves moving with the strong ebb and flow of her breathing.

"And I'd like to further our conversation in the light."

The curl on her breast swayed from her gentle laughter.

"The light has no bearing on our conversation," she asserted, making a point of dipping her head to restore eye contact with him. "I'd venture to say the lack of it has been freeing."

He grinned like a lad caught ogling a tavern maid.

"If I said I'd like to dance with you, would that make a difference?"

Her charmed smile was his reward. He strained to see Claire's eye color, but couldn't. Candlelight sparkled off the beads around her eyes. Her visible features rounded with pure merriment.

"Since you put it that way, how can I resist?" She reached over and lifted the jabot off the settee. "You'll need this."

He turned around and crouched low for her to retie the bothersome neckwear. "Please be kind with the knot. My valet is new and was overanxious when preparing me for tonight."

She leaned close to his ear. "I'll do my best."

Cotton skimmed his neck, and her nearness tantalized him…her warmth at his back, the allure of her gown brushing his legs. Agile hands worked efficiently at his nape, tying the jabot, and he couldn't help the wicked thought: *Why don't men hire women as valets?*

The air cooled behind him and he rose to full height. Claire was at his side, setting her hand on his arm.

"Shall we?"

They made their way out of the study's intimate atmosphere, into the bright hallway.

Standing on the royal-blue carpet, light shocked his system. His fair-haired guest looked to him, waiting for him to lead the way no doubt, but his limbs locked.

Her lustrous white-blond hair appeared that unique shade by nature, not artifice of paste or powder. Her face, though covered with a demi-mask, promised symmetry of the kind poets waxed on about. His breath caught on the singular yet insufficient word *beautiful*.

"Beg pardon?" Her head tilted, artful and feminine. "What did you say?"

Did he say the word out loud?

One corner of his mouth curled up. He wasn't smooth with words, nor was he the fawning type.

Clearing his throat, he led their amble to the ball. "I was wondering how the evening progresses."

His constitution needed balance on this already off-kilter night since ahead lay the battle zone of a London ball. He wasn't bred on these events the way others lived and breathed the social whirl.

Why the gluttonous need for grand entertainments? Do London's refined citizens exist under a constant cloud of boredom?

His teeth clenched in the manner he suspected a soldier's would as he bore down in battle. He could hardly tolerate these things, but one footfall after the other led them to the blast of festivities.

An explosion of unsavory odors pummeled him, the result of too many hot bodies together for too many hours. The orchestra plied their skills with frenzied vigor for throngs of colorful dancers. Discordant laughter jangled through the room. Most of the guests had been dipping rather deep in the free flow of his wine.

A perspiring earl, his bagwig askew, spun past. The man squired a masked, guffawing woman through a fast-paced courante, her face paint streaking down one cheek. Layers of pomp and dignity had long ago deserted the tipsy crowd.

He wanted to wipe the room clean and finish a quiet evening in his home, but that wouldn't aid his quest to find a fine place in Society for Lucinda. He needed the good graces of these people to arrange the most advantageous marriage for her—and someday for himself.

His sister, masked in purple silk, chatted amiably with two of Society's matriarchs at the far end of the hall; her cheerful composure showed she was none the worse from the evening's earlier drama.

A ravaged refreshment table provided breathing room near double doors flung open, allowing cool air to reach the perimeter of the ballroom. Empty glasses littered the table. Clusters of grapes had been devoured, leaving skeletal vines poking up from a silver tray. Only a small bowl of luscious red berries remained untouched, tempting the eye.

"Oh, strawberries. How lovely," his mystery guest cooed. "My favorite."

He made sure to steer closer to the succulent fruit, ready to engage his guest in private conversation. But as they approached the table, so did his good friend, the Marquis of Northampton, with his younger brother, Lord Marcus Bowles, at his side. The pair stepped through the open doorway from the back courtyard, North scowling his displeasure.

Out of sorts from Lucinda's refusal of his marriage proposal? Or taxed by the burden of rescuing his half-sprung brother yet again? Lord Bowles's walk was steady, but his queue was near undone. A crumpled, brown silk mask dangled from his fingers, and the man reeked of whiskey. The former soldier's brash stare, however, lost no time settling on Claire.

"Ryland. Wondered where you went." Lord Bowles's voice dropped with suggestion. "But I see what's occupied your time."

Cyrus's mouth firmed at the younger man's encroachment. North moved closer to his brother as though proximity could bring the younger man to heel. A pair of dancers, loose with laughter, bumped the marquis's silk-clad arm.

"As it is, we're on our way home." Within his black silk mask, the marquis's dark, assessing stare moved from Claire to Cyrus. "I'd hoped to speak to you, but the evening's deteriorated, an—"

"And he's got to run home with his tail between his legs." The younger man cut in, directing his last words to Claire. "That, and make sure I don't cause trouble in exalted circles."

North's frown stretched. If Cyrus were a betting man, he'd have laid odds on the sibling being the thorn in his friend's side, not Lucinda's rejection. The brothers together often made a powder keg waiting to explode.

"We'll talk tomorrow," Cyrus promised North and began to steer away from the table.

"What?" Lord Bowles stood taller, smoothing the

front of his brown silk waistcoat. "Dismissed without so much as an introduction to this tempting armful?"

"Marcus," North snapped. "You forget yourself."

The former soldier perused the flaxen-haired woman, lazy eyed and curious. Most women found the irreverent second son appealing, no matter that he lacked two pence to rub together. He offered little more than dashing looks and the occasional witty remark, yet ladies flocked to him.

Cyrus placed a possessive hand atop the feminine fingers resting on his arm. Lord Bowles's hazel eyes caught the maneuver, one corner of his mouth curling up. Though in his cups, the man read the universal message, one man to another.

She belongs with me.

Lord Bowles's daring, heavy-lidded gaze drifted from the claiming grip to meet Cyrus's rigid stare. The reprobate raised a challenging eyebrow. The former soldier liked to push the limits, especially under the influence of strong drink.

When would the evening's absurdity end?

Cyrus wasn't getting any closer to uncovering more about the mystery of the woman at his side. In those jarring seconds, Bowles must've reassessed his position. He backed down, ceding with the barest of nods. Cyrus wanted the fair lady to himself, but he grudgingly accepted good manners meant introductions were in order.

"Gentlemen, I forget my manners. Please allow me to introduce Miss…Miss…" He stalled, his brows slamming together.

Bad enough he reemerged with his jabot loose. He

couldn't introduce a woman as *Miss Claire*—to do so would all but put her in the worst possible light.

"Miss Claire Tottenham," she interjected, pinching her skirts and dipping low.

North nodded at the pretty curtsy, but his brother's eyes kindled with shrewd assessment. Unfazed, his *Miss Tottenham* held her head high, sidling closer to the strawberries.

Cyrus motioned to his friend. "This is Lord Northampton, the Most Honorable Marquis of Northampton." His eyes narrowed. "And his brother, Lord Bowles, formerly an officer of the Eightieth Regiment of Light-Armed Foot."

Both men bowed. Lord Bowles placed his crushed mask over his heart, the reprobate's stare hovering indecently on Miss Tottenham's neckline.

"I live only for peaceful pursuits now. My latest heroic service is rescuing damsels in distress."

"When I find myself in dire need, I shall call upon you, sir." She gave them both a bright smile and plucked a ripe red berry from the bowl. "And is this a family endeavor, your rescuing damsels in distress?"

"You mean me and Lord Perfect here?" Lord Bowles angled his head at his brother. "No. Gabriel's too busy saving the family to bother with life's finer pursuits. I'm your best bet."

The marquis stiffened when his Christian name was bandied about, but Miss Tottenham smoothed his ruffled feathers with another glowing smile before looking again to Lord Bowles.

"Then your brother's the archangel to your... darker heavenly being."

Cyrus's jaw ticked at the soft tempo of her voice. This flirtatious back and forth between the two served little to get him closer to the enigmatic woman. And simply put, *he* wanted to be the sole recipient of her smiles and soft, playful words.

The former soldier's eyes darkened with keen interest. His voice, rough from smoke and liquor, dropped to an intimate note. "Wherever did Ryland find you?"

"I'm afraid that will have to stay our secret."

The saucy Miss Tottenham slipped the strawberry into her delectable mouth, all the while looking at Cyrus. His thigh muscles tensed inside the velvet prison of his breeches. Hot pleasure shot through his body at the sight of the red berry slipping through her lips. Adding to his misery, a spurt of juice from the tender morsel painted her bottom lip red. He nearly groaned.

Tradition named the apple as the fruit of man's downfall, but tonight he'd argue mightily for the dangers of a ripe strawberry on a certain woman's lips.

Lord Bowles laughed, his face alight with fascination. "I like this one, Cy. She'll keep you hopping."

Cyrus's body hummed between charmed interest and the sharp edge of frustration. He had more than hopping in mind where Miss Tottenham was concerned.

With perfect timing, the first notes of an allemande played, and the dance floor thickened with new revelers full of laughter. The allemande was the last dance before the midnight unmasking, a decadent rout, allowing some close contact between partners—something he wouldn't miss.

He set a firm hand on Miss Tottenham's elbow. "I plan to, starting with this dance."

"But you don't like to dance." The startled admission came from North in the middle of pulling off his mask.

"I do tonight." He bade them farewell and steered his guest away from the younger man's poaching stare.

No doubt Bowles would pounce on any opportunity to assert himself with the fair lady. Tonight, however, Cyrus was the hunter who would claim Miss Tottenham. He drew her as close as her wide skirts allowed, finding pleasure in her graceful sway. He maneuvered through the crowd, nearer to the open, cooling doors, where partners pranced the allemande.

He positioned himself beside Miss Tottenham, and with a light handhold, they ventured into their first steps. Bodies pressed everywhere, the hot, noisy swarm expanding and contracting. But his lovely guest caught the joy, laughing with delight. His every sense went on high alert, honing in on *her*: her scent, her feel, her sound. He hungered for details of this woman, but words of a hot nature sprang out first.

"Are you always a flirt?"

Her eyes sparkled within the demi-mask. "Flirting, you say? I take it you refer to the conversation with the marquis and his brother?"

"Exactly." Miss Tottenham's fingertips moved across his palm. The tantalizing connection quieted him, bringing to mind a cool breeze soothing overheated skin. What she did was correct for the dance, but on the fringe of propriety with so much fleshly contact.

"I like to think I helped calm obviously stormy waters between those two. Simply another one of my talents, if you will." Her head tilted, revealing a flirtatious stretch of her neck. "And I am dancing with *you*."

The procession stopped, and Miss Tottenham twirled under his upraised arm, smiling at him over her shoulder. Her reminder of the obvious calmed the covetous beast within. Miss Tottenham glowed, a mix of the coquette and a woman lost in the fluid freedom of dance. Dark blue-green eyes trifled with him, vibrant within her mask. Now he knew their color.

"Is it true?" she asked over the loud hum of music. "You don't like to dance?"

Their hands switched for another rotation. Her silk skirts brushed against him, sending a thrum of pleasure across his legs.

"I don't. Usually," he admitted. "Never had the occasion until coming to London last year. And then I had to learn."

She came out from under the arc of their arms, her body moving in time to the music. "Then I should feel especially honored."

He bent his head, all the better to hear her, but it was her scent he craved. He tried breathing in her skin's perfume. Instead, Miss Tottenham circled away, her unique fragrance eluding him.

His body quickened when her lithe form spun around in front of him with both hands overhead. Her gown's false hips kept her from coming too close. The way Miss Tottenham's eyes shined, she grasped very well her maddening effect.

Two could play this game.

He wasn't good with words. Never had been. Nor was he ever the handsomest man in the room or the ugliest. His well-muscled size drew as many of the fair sex to him as repelled them. Yet he understood the power of the right stroke with a woman. Where flowery words failed him, touch succeeded.

They swayed together, their hands joining in a high arc. One hand slipped free and slid under the sack portion of her gown. The cloth draped high from her shoulders to the ground, hiding his calculated move. Throughout the room, partners paraded side by side…one, two, three. Behind the swath of fabric, he caressed the contours of her back, her sweet warmth flowing from the bodice.

Her torso stiffened under his hand. She kept their forward progress at his side, but jeweled eyes slanted his way, glittering brighter than the beads on her mask. Her pink-red lips opened a fraction as though she needed more air.

His veins drummed an insistent rhythm. The flat of his palm brushed a slow, meandering trail down her spine, finding small, silken ties. The single row cinched her bodice shut, each fascinating X softly abrading his fingers.

He imagined loosening each lace…one by one…all the better to explore the tender landscape of her body.

The move lured him into deeper enchantment. His vision went hazy on Miss Tottenham's blue-and-silver bodice. They turned and faced each other, their bodies closer than other dancers around the room. He didn't care. His limbs hummed with sizzling awareness.

He leaned in and whispered, "Tonight, with you, has been the best conversation with clothes on."

Her pink-red mouth opened. "Because it's something of a sexual nature when clothes are off, Mr. Ryland."

He stumbled, missing a dance step. His phallus clenched. Hard.

Recovering, he chuckled. "Indeed, it is."

Miss Tottenham circled slowly for the dance, her skirts rubbing him, and glad he was for the longer, concealing waistcoat. His mysterious guest grasped well the game he played, giving better than she got.

His lungs expanded, drinking in much-needed air. There seemed to be so little of it in the room. He wanted to be alone with her in his dark study again. He hungered for connection with the woman beneath maddening layers of cloth, something physical and yet…something else.

Then, she took a deep breath, her small breasts straining the lace of her plunging neckline. The simple movement snared his vision.

Was she just as affected?

He itched to test the smoothness of her pearl-colored skin, and not only the plump parts about to spring free. He wanted to test her shoulders, her back, the legs hidden by voluminous skirts. Would the rest of her feel as soft as she looked?

Chattering dancers took two steps forward. He slipped his hand again under the sack and splayed his fingers across the small of her back. The silk gown slid against his skin. The scandalous move was lost in the crowd, but her dark lashes fluttered low within her mask.

"Should I worry you'll take advantage of me, sir?"

"Something tells me that doesn't happen easily with you," he said, eyeing a lock of her hair falling loose.

His hand traced her spine to her shoulder, finding the warm flesh where the white-blond curl settled on her collarbone. Her body quivered, and the tender reaction shook him. Another arrow of heat shot to his groin at the image of his mouth planting a hot kiss where the curl met skin.

Miss Tottenham's blue-green stare reached his, dark and liquid. Her lips parted for him and him alone.

Across the room, violins sought soaring notes. Music stretched. Strained rhythms reached for high peaks, as taut as Cyrus was from head to heel. His abdomen squeezed behind the placket of his breeches.

Miss Tottenham's mouth was accessible...tempting. His head bent lower. The small, dark space between enticing pink lips captivated him—lips that said saucy things, lips that needed kissing. Her warm breath came faster, brushing his chin.

He inched closer. Ever so slowly, her mouth softened, opening more. His lids drooped. A fraction of space separated her lips from his.

A baron's booming laughter blasted them apart. The man spun by, his elbow hitting Cyrus.

He jerked his head upright, taking a half step backward. The oblivious man saved him from doing the unthinkable—kissing a woman for all to see in the middle of a ball.

Blood rushed his ears. He tugged his jabot, his body hot and constrained. His impulses galloped near out of control, running roughshod over rational thought. He stretched his neck and blinked at the ceiling, sucking

in more air. The crowd of dancers pressed them.
Everywhere light and noise jangled his singed nerves,
and he lost the allemande's movements.

They weren't in a wharf-side tavern, nor was his
dance partner a woman of coarse manners to be kissed
in public display.

"Miss Tottenham…I…" His voice trailed off, his
mouth pressing into a sober line.

She surprised him, taking a half step nearer to begin
the next intricate turn. "Don't."

She looked to where their hands joined for the
dance, curling her fingers intimately with his. This was
no delicate crossing of fingertips, but holding hands.
Her simple, affectionate act wrapped around him.

Violins and voices, noise of a hundred shoes scraping the floor enveloped them, but Miss Tottenham's
breath came heavier too, moving the inviting flesh
plumped high from her bodice. She was just as caught
up in the moment as he, yet offered tender forgiveness.

Her smile was part country maid and pure temptress.

"Of course, a woman could just as easily take
advantage of a man, couldn't she?"

Her voice came low and warmly textured to his ears.
Was she trying to take back some semblance of control? Encourage more blatant behavior? He grinned,
ready to cede the night to the beguiling enchantress
and find his way to the nearest bed with her.

His pulse throbbed. Flirtation spiraled in the
space of one dance, turning the ground beneath
his feet into hot and perilous quicksand. And he
liked it. Each step invited another curious touch,
another flirtatious move. He wasn't sure who had the

advantage, but he wasn't about to back away from his intrepid exploration.

Short of kissing her now, how far could he go?

Emboldened, Cyrus traced one finger over the architecture of her collarbone. Her body twitched with a delicate shiver; a faint flush painted the upper curves of her breasts. Within the silken mask, her dark-fringed eyes turned a deeper hue.

They raised their joined hands for a new arc, all part of the dance, but they pushed the limits of contact that polite Society allowed. Intimacy shrouded them. He dipped his head close to hers, his breath fanning flaxen wisps of hair.

"If I had to trust a woman…let her have the advantage," he murmured, "I'd choose you."

Miss Tottenham gasped. Her lashes shuttered her eyes and she turned her face from him.

Is she in pain?

"Mr. Ryland," she whispered. "Please…"

His head jolted at the sudden change. Gone was the coy, confident woman. She slipped away in spirit as did her unfinished plea. In those few seconds, hot flirtation cooled. Rapidly. The rest of his body, however, hadn't gotten the message, his bollocks clenching with painful want.

Miss Tottenham looked beyond the doors into the black night, withdrawing from him though their bodies engaged in the dance.

The sensual hunt was over.

What happened?

They made another rotation, this time in silence. Miss Tottenham twirled, coming back to him with a smile pasted on her face. An unseen wall erected itself between them.

Why couldn't he make the pieces to this puzzling woman fit?

Courtesan or not, he was certain the potent attraction was mutual. Equally diverting was his ease with her, an instant comfort. He wanted more.

Had he played his hand too much? Come on too strong? Or did something else vex her? Women were complex creatures, requiring a deft hand. Was her change because he'd been too forward in so public a place? Or because he said words of a more personal nature?

His limbs moved stiffly, compensating for the ache inside his breeches, but he'd take his time, alter his strategy. And that took him back to his original plan: learn more about his elusive guest.

"By looks and speech, you're a woman who can hold her own. But other than your name, hair color, and eyes, I know next to nothing of you." They stepped together again, and he grinned at her. "Even a hunter gets a scent of the prey."

"Want to sniff me, do you? I suppose that makes me the fox to your hound."

She'd snapped out of her brief fracture of distance, but his fair-haired guest was decidedly cooler, despite the flush touching the exposed parts of her cheeks. Her life vein throbbed low on her neck. His stare fixed on the inviting spot, a spot in need of much kissing. He'd find a way to warm Miss Tottenham up again. Tonight. The first moment they were alone.

Their bodies brushed together. He breathed her

in, or tried to. All of him knotted with want and frustration, causing his legs to move with sluggish determination through the allemande's steps. Patience, he needed patience.

"You've got to give me something before the unmasking. It's only fair."

"Fair?" she asked, her eyes flaring. "Is that word in your vocabulary?"

Maybe she had him there. His gaze locked onto her lips and the tempting, creamy skin not covered by the mask. Miss Tottenham's skin…her softly angled jaw, her slender neck, down to her small breasts pressed upward—all of her glowed.

She vibrated with life and something indefinable he couldn't name. Around them the music swelled, reaching for another crescendo. This time the turn of her body was not the practiced move of a flirt, simply the loose flow of a graceful woman.

"Very well. I can toss a tidbit." She looked to where her fingertips crossed politely with his. "See that?" She tipped her head at their hands. "The scar near my thumb?"

He turned his attention to their hands, the allemande's final notes drifting over them. His fingers curled under her hand, cupping her loosely.

She angled her thumb to give him a better view, and he honed in on the star-shaped scar. Dancers jostled around them, bumping her closer. Little more than an inch of space separated them. More loose blond wisps fell from their pins, framing her dance-flushed cheeks. With each breath, her body made contact with his.

His thumb stroked the unusual pink mark at the base of her thumb, and then slipped around to massage her palm. When she looked into his eyes, another shock went through him. Miss Tottenham's strawberry-painted mouth opened a fraction with definite invitation. Again. His mouth curved triumphantly: he was regaining lost sensual territory.

"You're very thorough in your study, Mr. Ryland," she said, breathy and soft. "I don't think my hand's ever had such tender attention."

Her skirts caressed the length of his legs. The music stopped. They weren't moving, but he held her close as though the dance would continue, her breath's rhythm melding with his. The floor thronged with men and women, revelers laughing and mingling. Many removed their masks.

Surrounded as they were, he settled in a private world with Miss Tottenham.

He liked having her in his thrall, just deserts for the way she tempted him. Long brown lashes rimmed her darkened eyes. He searched her face, the small tip of her nose; her mouth curved and open.

"The scar," he reminded her. "You were telling me about it."

"The scar?" The pink-red flesh of her lips rounded gently.

Was she as lost in the moment as he? He squeezed her hand, and one finger tapped the star-shaped mark. She dipped her head, cheeks flushing anew, but when Miss Tottenham looked at him again, her tender smile was open.

"When I was seventeen, I cut my hand climbing a

tree." Her body brushed his, but her small, rounded chin snared him, the pert feature tipping up. "And despite the scar, I've no regrets. That day was wonderful. A woman who seeks to look and be perfect like some doll on a shelf hasn't lived."

"A bold proclamation," he said, warming to her haughtiness. "But I'll have to bow to your wisdom about dolls on a shelf. Never bothered with them."

Her laugh whorled between them. The white tips of Miss Tottenham's teeth nipped her lower lip. He glanced at her hand again, his thumb rubbing careful circles over the mark.

A scar. Women weren't supposed to have them. They were supposed to be soft-skinned, elevated creatures with men mucking through the hard places. But life left marks, those seen and unseen.

Of all the things she could have said, Miss Tottenham shared an imperfection, a flaw over an accomplishment, which made her all the more fascinating. The picture of a proper young woman teetering between girlhood and the demands of maturity warmed him. He savored the image of her laughing in a tree, and he wanted more of the grown woman before him.

His eyes narrowed on her demi-mask. "It's midnight. Time for the unmasking." He was done with the flimsy barrier. It was time he saw her.

All of her, if he had his way tonight.

Her hands jerked free of his and bracketed her face. "The unmasking..."

Visible parts of Miss Tottenham paled. She took a half step away from him, backing into a laughing lady.

"Beg pardon…" she said, giving the reflexive courtesy.

Moving backward, her hands framed her mask. Did she plan to keep the disguise in place?

Around them, the crowd of dancers thinned. The colorful horde made a slow exodus around Miss Tottenham, drawn to midnight's cooler air on the back courtyard. Outside, a row of footmen stood sentinel with trays of champagne at the ready.

Lucinda's birthday.

A twinge struck him. There were duties to attend as brother and as host, duties he'd tossed aside in favor of getting lost for a time with a certain woman. Cyrus scoured the room for his sister, aware that a toast was expected. He turned back, reaching for Miss Tottenham.

"Stay with me."

But another feminine voice reached his ears. "Mr. Ryland."

Cyrus twisted around, looking into hazel-green eyes framed by a bronze silk mask. The young woman facing him equaled the pinnacle of London's pursuit of perfection, her auburn tresses and good manners pinned properly in place.

"Lady Churchill." He bowed.

He was certain no saucy retort ever left her lips.

"If I may have a moment of your time," she said, her light touch slipping from his arm. "I wanted to speak with you about what happened in the garden."

His neck and shoulders tensed, constricting him better than any wretched jabot. "No need. I'm the one who should apologize. That you were subject to my unsavory exchange with Lady—"

"No, Mr. Ryland." She lowered her voice, a needless thing with all the noise. "You have always been a gentleman with me. I wanted you to know—"

Lady Churchill quashed her words upon seeing her mother's approach. The Duchess of Marlborough's perceptive eyes took measure of the loose jabot. The grande dame frowned fiercely, skirts swirling about her ankles in her forward press.

Lucinda walked a pace behind the duchess, mouthing *I'm sorry*.

There was no escaping the requirement of social parley with a duchess once she had a man in her sights. His feet were rooted to the floor, and he was ready for the inevitable.

He scanned the herd of people over his shoulder, finding Miss Tottenham melting into the mass beyond the open doors.

"Miss Tottenham?" he called, but she didn't answer.

The mask stayed on. She wasn't looking at him. With movements less graceful, her focus went beyond him as if he weren't there.

A new line of footmen marched by from the kitchens, bearing more trays of champagne. His masked guest skirted the orderly servants, skimming the wall and potted plants on the other side of the room. Where was she going?

His body tensed, his every instinct for the chase, when a fan thumped his shoulder.

"Mis-ter Ryland."

His mouth firmed, but he turned around and bowed low from the waist. "Your Grace."

"There are proprieties to be observed." The

Duchess of Marlborough's stiff, imperious voice demanded attention.

He glowered at the ivory fan, which the grand dame wielded like a scepter. She had the good sense to tuck the offending item into the folds of her skirt. His patience hung threadbare over what would be another attempt to foist her daughter on him. He had run out of gentlemanly refusals and was about to say as much.

Lady Churchill studied the lace flaring from her elbows, tugging on impeccable threadwork. Her mouth drooped such that he guessed she was less than enthusiastic about this meeting. For that reason alone, Cyrus held his tongue from the unwise lashing he wanted to give; the young lady couldn't be held accountable for her overbearing mother.

"You're right. There are proprieties to observe when a brother celebrates his sister's birthday." He gave his sister a tight smile and motioned to the courtyard. "Lucinda, why not take our guests outside where it's cooler? We'll raise a glass in your honor as soon as everyone's gathered."

From his peripheral vision, a lithe form in pale blue and silver silk exited the ballroom for the main hall. He bowed again.

"Please enjoy the courtyard. I've something to attend, but I'll be out shortly."

His body moved of its own accord, pursuing Miss Tottenham. The duchess blustered at his retreating back, but her complaints were lost in the ballroom chatter. He went on alert, hunting down his mystery woman. Alarms of concern went off inside him. Did someone scare her?

The man she hid from earlier?

Was that the reason for her strange turn when they danced? His heels slammed the floor with his hasty exit. Protective instincts surged. He would take care of her.

"Miss Tottenham." His voice rose above the din.

Heads turned. Cyrus threaded past those guests. Ahead of him, Miss Tottenham took brisk strides through the long, wide entry hall. She looked over her shoulder and slammed into a plant pedestal.

Frantic hands saved the fern from falling over, but verdant fronds caught her hair. A cascade of snowy tresses fell loose. She swiped the leaves free and continued her rapid progress, greenery swaying in her wake. Two guests moved across his path, wanting some of his time, but the woman he wanted was slipping away.

"Claire?" he called out again, raising a hand to hail her. "Claire, wait." His voice boomed in the cavernous hall. He didn't care that he broke cardinal rules of social protocol right then.

Didn't she know he would protect her?

Miss Tottenham jolted to a stop. Pale blue skirts swirled wide when she faced him. She raised a hand as though she would push him away.

"No." The single word bounced off the high ceiling.

Her eyes, cool and remote, froze him, every muscle locked by the icy refusal. In the blink of an eye, she grabbed handfuls of her skirts and ran.

She sprinted as though the very devil nipped her heels, racing for the open front door. Her footfalls echoed. Guests mingling in the entry hall paused to witness the unfolding tableau, their hushed murmurs and curious stares following the minor drama. Two footmen milled near the open door, but when Miss Tottenham sped their way, both servants snapped to attention.

And she ran headlong into midnight, the darkness swallowing her whole.

He blinked at the empty doorway.

The drive to chase her loosened his limbs, but what followed came in nightmarish seconds.

Belker moved into the hall, the butler's stern forehead wrinkling. The man said something, but Cyrus failed to hear words in his rush to the doorway. Blood hummed in his ears. He had to reach her.

There was movement…a servant coming around a large support column. Then chaos struck.

Cyrus collided with a footman bearing a full tray. The wide salver tipped, dumping the contents. Champagne showered Cyrus. Glassware splintered everywhere. The silver tray crashed on marble tiles, ringing a loud, metallic spin. Mouths gaped. Guests were shocked to silence at the display.

"Sir, my apologies…sir…" the footman stammered.

Cyrus checked the footman and himself. No cuts. His heart pumped hard but not from fear of glass splitting a vein.

"No harm done." His body ran hot but his voice was cold.

She had vanished. He'd lost her.

Disbelief twisted into another blazing emotion. The acrid taste of having hosted a pretty deceiver settled over him: the mysterious Miss Tottenham had played him for a fool. Oh, she was good; he'd give her that. He fell—and fell rather hard—for the ploys of an artisan of flirtation.

His lips pressed into a grim line. Had she marked him as an easy target, the Midlands rustic fairly new to Town?

Her practiced seduction had him panting after her in his own home no less. An ugly, guttural laugh rumbled from him when he pictured moments ago how he'd raced after her like some besotted swain.

He picked up the chase again, this time with measured steps. Glass crunched underfoot. No, he'd not find a trace of her, but that didn't stop him from moving past gawking men and women gathered in his hall, all witnesses to his folly.

He needed to check the obvious for himself.

Behind him, Belker issued terse commands and profuse apologies that fell on deaf ears. Cyrus stepped through his open doorway, scanning the night. Clouds covered the moon, casting darkness everywhere.

Liquid clung to his lashes, and he became aware of how much he'd been doused. Cold champagne soaked his waistcoat and shirt. He swiped wetness from his face and shook the excess from his fingers. The nectar seeped into the corners of his mouth but failed to sweeten him.

Carriages lined his driveway; many more waited on Piccadilly. Their candle lanterns dotted the blackness with yellow points of light. Somewhere out there, London hid a lone woman on the escape. His fists curled at his sides. He would hunt down the vixen and find out what game she played.

She hadn't run from another man tonight. She ran from him. *Him*. Why?

A coachman cleared his throat on the bottom step, clutching a brown object to his chest.

"Beggin' yer pardon, sir." The man tipped his head in deference to Cyrus and held up a shoe. "The lady who just ran out left this."

Cyrus moved down the steps. The coachman stretched out his hands, offering a brown leather shoe of middling quality—a commoner's shoe, not a silk slipper.

"The lady wore this?" He turned the flat-heeled footwear in his hands, examining scuffed leather and a broken tin buckle.

"Fell off her foot on this spot, it did." The coachman nodded with conviction. "Saw it meself. So'd Harry over there." He jabbed a thumb at another coachman who bobbed his head in agreement.

"She came flyin' out yer house wearin' a blue gown." Harry spoke into the fray, waggling his finger at the bottom step. "Right there, the lady almost tripped. Then she ran that away." The coachman tipped his head toward the east.

Cyrus stared blankly in that direction. On ground level, much was obscured by the black shapes of carriages and horses.

"Thank you," he said, nodding curtly to the men.

He climbed the stairs one slow step at a time, twin hazes of anger and bafflement battling in his mind. His fingers slipped inside the shoe, meeting grainy leather warm from her foot. He turned the shoe with its ruined buckle over in his hands, hunting for evasive clues but finding none. The cobbler's imprint had been worn down, the impression unreadable.

What did he know of women's shoes? Their footwear had never fascinated him, but he held an important key to the secret life of one Miss Claire Tottenham.

More like he burned to get his hands on her.

To do what? Shake her? Kiss her? He scoffed aloud and the two coachmen glanced his way. Yes, he wanted to test her lips—claim them was more like it—if only for the satisfaction to take what she brazenly offered when they danced. Any tenderness was crushed the moment Miss Tottenham looked at him, aloof and rejecting, before running away. He needed to find out why she played him falsely, for that was most assuredly what went on tonight.

Her words rang in his head: *Of course, a woman could just as easily take advantage of a man, couldn't she?*

He turned, facing London's midnight sky. Cool night air caressed his champagne-soaked skin. His flaxen-haired guest shunned silk slippers under her skirts...an interesting choice for a courtesan. One surprising question pushed hard, a question he was certain contained the answers he needed.

Why would a woman wear common brown shoes under a ball gown?

"I'll hunt you down," he vowed under his breath. "Whoever you are, wherever you are, I'll find you."

Three

A little disdain is not amiss…

William Congreve, *The Way of the World*

"WOMEN MAKE THE CLEVEREST ADVERSARIES, MR. Ryland," Sir John Fielding said, rubbing his flaccid chin. "Much more difficult to capture than men."

"It's been more than a fortnight." His words came clipped and forceful. This was his third visit to Number Four Bow Street. "You say your men have not a single clue as to the woman's whereabouts? How many blonds of that hair color can there be in London?"

The wooden chair creaked under Fielding's form.

"A woman's toilet is a delicate matter. We cannot accost every flaxen-haired woman in London, asking how she achieves that shade." His slack waist jiggled with his chuckle. "My men would meet with more slaps in the face than answers."

The magistrate's eyelids fluttered low under the black ribbon tied across his forehead, the sign announcing his blindness.

"Your masked lady doesn't match any descriptions of the women in my gazette. Her unique hair color aside, what we have is a brown leather shoe lacking a cobbler's imprint, and some silver threads…threads you say match the lace on her dress. The scar on her hand is the best identifying mark we have."

The Blind Beak of Bow Street, as he was known, turned his ear toward Cyrus. "You're welcome to look through the gazettes again, but I must counsel patience."

Cyrus had witnessed Sir John's odd habit often in their meetings. The older man caught details from sound alone—a scratch of the ear lobe, the cant of his head a few degrees, all telling signs the magistrate was digging deeper. Did Sir John seek something from *him*? Cyrus bristled in his seat, disliking the awful sense of being bare-arse naked before the Blind Beak.

He breathed in deeply, seeking the advised forbearance but not finding any. Rumors claimed Fielding could identify over a thousand criminal voices with his practiced ear. But Sir John likely hadn't heard Miss Claire Tottenham speak. Nothing about her fit the typical housebreaker.

"None matched her description the first time around," he said, eyeing the row of paltry evidence on the desk and trying for a different tack. "But if I increase the reward…five hundred guineas—"

"Ho there, Mr. Ryland." Sir John leaned forward. "Much as I welcome fair payment, let's not be hasty. Justice moves at her own pace. Tossing money around won't make her appear any faster."

"Justice? Or Miss Tottenham?" Cyrus gripped the woolen bundle in his lap.

Beside Sir John, Jack Emerson, the tall thief taker who patrolled the West End on horseback, crossed his arms, bunching his poorly cut coat.

"That's a fine bit of reward, Mr. Ryland," Emerson said. "A lot of gold to offer for a thief who hasn't stolen anything. Begs the question: What exactly is your interest in the woman?"

"She stole *something.*"

Across the desk, Emerson's eyes narrowed. He no doubt gleaned Cyrus's intent and had already passed judgment. The man stood in a wide-legged stance, which probably intimidated most people. Not Cyrus. A wicked slash bisected Emerson's left brow and cheek down to his jaw, making him all the more threatening. Both men came from rougher places, survived rougher times.

Cyrus squared his shoulders, determined to have his due. Truth be told, the thief taker wasn't far from the mark. To have Miss Claire Tottenham in his grasp would gratify him to no end. But that was his business. Apprehending thieves was the magistrate's.

Every nuance of the masked ball had etched itself on his memory, playing in his mind on a daily basis. Only in rare moments did his brain prod him with meddlesome moral questions: Did he go too far? Should he use his power and wealth to seek what amounted to vengeance over an embarrassment?

"Do your job and find her." He gave a curt nod. "I'll worry about the rest."

"Gentlemen, please." Sir John's visionless stare

drifted over the desk. "Mr. Ryland, you said you have more evidence to add to our collection."

Cyrus took the folded cloak from his lap and set the dark wool with the other items brought out for discussion.

"This woman's half cloak was found on a fence post behind Ryland House. The butler kept it, thinking the cloak belonged to a forgetful maid, but none claimed it. He brought it to my attention this morning." Cyrus pointed to a single thread of white-blond hair caught on the fabric. "And there's a strand of hair… matches hers."

"Behind the house. The mews." Emerson placed the cloak in Sir John's waiting hands. "The lady might've entered through a back door, maybe the servants' quarters. I'd like to interview your household staff again"—he smirked at Cyrus, a hand fisted on his hip—"that is, with your permission, of course."

The cocky thief taker would do as he pleased, whether officially showing up at Ryland House or tracking down the servants on their half days.

"Do what you must," he said. "I expected you'd be more adept at finding one simple woman."

"You mean the simple woman who sneaked into your house and duped *you*?"

Emerson's jibe failed to cow him.

"Let's keep to the matter at hand." The magistrate's hands rubbed the cloak's fabric, searching the seams. "A half cloak of decent quality but not a fine weave, likely worn by a woman of the merchant class…or she's in service, an upper servant perhaps."

Sir John set the rumpled cloak on the desk, and one finger circled the air, a habit signaling he was recounting facts.

"You say she wore a ball gown with a jeweled necklace…one appearing to be real, not paste. Yet you didn't see earbobs, gloves, or a fan anywhere on her person."

"None that I can recall."

He'd wanted to kiss her ear lobes, not admire jewelry that might dangle from them. The canny magistrate pushed him at their first meeting to picture Miss Tottenham again. Those hazy, insignificant details trickled from him, and he gave Fielding due respect for capturing subtle, telling facts.

"And she wore common, brown leather shoes with a ball gown," Sir John said, his voice slowing as though he weighed the facts. "Yet, after three weeks, you still report nothing's gone missing, not so much as a pence from the money box in your desk."

"Correct."

"I'm less inclined to think your masked lady is a courtesan." The magistrate leaned back in his chair. "Perhaps the question we ought to ask is: What else did she want from you?"

❦

The carriage trundled through London's teeming afternoon streets. Cyrus sat cocooned in butter-smooth leather, the new squab in his new carriage lending to the aroma of success. But the back of his head banged the high cushioning. First-rate carriage wheels hit the same ruts in second-rate roads.

He rubbed his aching neck. Had he gone soft living in Town this past year?

Life sped by too fast, and he couldn't shake the sense that he was going…nowhere.

Strange notion for a man with so much.

He leaned an elbow on the armrest, staring out the window, looking but not seeing. His skull throbbed from recalling every nuance of the fateful evening three weeks past. But his shoulders and back? Those muscles bore welcome soreness from recent labors, reminding him of where he'd come from.

The magistrate had insisted they revisit the disastrous evening once more. He asked again about each person Cyrus spoke to that night, digging all the deeper into the nature of each relationship.

Some questions were harmless. Some answers were not.

The interview shed light on tetchy corners Cyrus would rather not revisit. He'd sat stone-still through the miserable process, spilling information with Emerson scratching names and notes on paper. Cyrus didn't flinch once, despite the inner pummeling he took. Retelling the debacle when his former mistress crossed paths with Lady Elizabeth Churchill offered more fodder for the thief taker to look up from his pad and smirk anew.

Nothing had gone smoothly that night.

Cyrus had excused himself from the ball's mind-numbing noise in need of quiet. He went to his study and, instead, found *her*.

His carriage rocked down Cornhill, his memory lulling over the agreeable parts of the evening. The pleasurable image of her untying his jabot, speaking her mind, and yes, their dance floor flirtation played in his mind. Other parts of him unhampered by Miss Tottenham's deception savored the memory when he was alone, clenching with delight. Her specter invaded his quiet and solitude, those two rare commodities in his life, and it wouldn't let go. Her words, her smiles teased him, reaching places long dormant.

His breath fogged the carriage window, creating a blur as unclear as the answers he sought. With Miss Tottenham, a questionable woman at best, he devoted much time and energy hunting her. He wanted more from the woman, but exactly what that meant eluded him.

He touched the window's cold glass, dragging his fingers across the flat cloud his breath created. Beyond the haze, the Royal Exchange's arcade came into view, freeing him from the very male quandary of females.

The carriage rolled to a stop and a welcome phantom weight settled on his shoulders—the mantle of responsibility found in the world of commerce, his comfortable world of existence. Outside his window, the Cornhill streets bustled with shoppers.

North lounged under one of the Exchange's outer arches. Hat tucked under his arm, the marquis removed his watch from his waistcoat. He walked up to the carriage, sunshine bouncing off his gold watch.

"You're late for today's meeting," North admonished, tucking away the timepiece while Cyrus exited the carriage. "Or we could say you're very early for next week's."

Cyrus dismissed the carriage with a clipped command, but upon turning around, North's brows shot up.

"And by the look on your face, the day's not been good to you either."

"I'm at a standstill on something." Cyrus jammed his tricorne on his head.

"So things didn't go well at Bow Street," North speculated, tapping his walking stick on the ground. "I can't say the Lloyd's meeting was much better—at least for some of us."

Cyrus eyed the brass and ebon stick, an item he associated with the foppish and the aged, yet the male ornament hid a wicked blade that'd snap out the end with the push of a lever. His friend was a man not to be taken lightly, though too many did.

He glanced beyond the trim, stone arches, trying to divine the inner workings of the appointment he missed.

"Was the meeting that bad?"

"Not if your name's Ryland," North said wryly. "Your coffers runneth over, my friend, to the tune of a princely sum according to the clerk's report." He peered at the sky, shoulders drooping under his frock coat. "I'll never understand business."

"Play the percentages to your advantage."

He shifted his feet into a wider stance. Most of life could be worked out with numbers—a belief he held firmly since words bedeviled him. He was about to tell his friend that he spent too much of his income, but his face tightened in a pained way.

North wasn't up for talk of business strategy any

more than he wanted to be interrogated about personal matters. Stark news must be ahead for his friend. The marquis needed cash flow in a bad way; his estate bled money, from his ne're-do-well brother causing one costly scrape or another to a flighty sister who didn't marry well, yet considered requests for funds from her brother the marquis a standard answer to her problems.

"You could try courting Lucinda again," he suggested. "Some women need persuading."

"Let a man keep his pride, will you?" North brushed away a speck from his sleeve. "Neither my impeccable manners nor my lofty title convinced your sister we'd make a good match." He settled his hat on his head, smiling blandly. "Let's face facts. She doesn't want to be the next Marchioness of Northampton."

"Lucinda doesn't know what's best for her."

North snorted. "And you do?"

"Women need a man's strong, guiding hand." He clamped his hands behind his back and tipped his head at four glossy-coated bays pulling a fine carriage. "Like those beautiful steppers. Give them limits, point them in the right direction, and they perform as nature intended."

"Such wisdom." His friend chuckled, shaking his head. "And yet you still manage to keep company with some of London's finest ladies."

Cyrus squinted at the street humming with life. "I'm not daft. There's a right time and a right way to guide a woman…let her know what's in her best interest."

North tugged his ear, appearing to digest that male wisdom. Both men had their successes and failures with the fair sex. Cyrus settled on the firm belief women were like beautiful jewels: treat them right, put them in the best setting, and they shined.

To his dismay, he found a man might also reach for a woman he finds fascinating only to discover sharp edges. With Cyrus's luck of late, his friend was better off ignoring his advice.

North scanned the environs. "Right now it's in my best interest to have some kind of refreshment." He pointed his walking stick to the left. "Over there...the White Lyon Tavern and the Nagshead. Of course, we might run into Marcus. And that'd ruin this glorious day for everyone."

"What's the problem with your brother now?"

Wind ruffled Cyrus's coattails. Early autumn breezes had already turned brisk in London, carrying the Thames's grimy scent. He considered their options to the right. Drapers, silversmiths, cabinetmakers, and the like all lined either side of the Exchange. Midtown merchants of every stripe sought coveted space close to the heart of London's commerce.

"I'm about to send him packing, but let's save that news for later." North looked to the establishments lining the other side of the road. "How about a coffee in one of those fine shops? You own most of them, the buildings anyway. And you can tell me again why you insist on this odd pursuit of yours."

Those words hit him like a jab to a fresh bruise. Cyrus stepped onto the wide Cornhill road, dodging a steaming pile. "You mean my hunt for a certain woman."

"Yes. Why look for a woman who doesn't want

to be found?" North spoke over the road's clamor. "When others like the lovely Lady Isabella Foster move conveniently in your path?"

"My connection with her ended."

"You could pursue Lady Churchill," North suggested. "A young woman who by all appearances would shed her lofty position to be joined with you."

"You mean stoop low enough to marry the likes of me?" Cyrus growled.

"You know what I mean."

Yet North couldn't look him in the eye.

Cyrus shrugged off the unintended insult, looking to the shops ahead. "I'm not stirred to move beyond the surface I've already scratched with Lady Churchill or Lady Foster. And I'm not on the hunt for a wife."

"But you are on the hunt for a certain mystery woman."

He was sure his friend wanted to pick at the fresh wound that was Miss Tottenham. He couldn't answer what he didn't fully understand.

There was wanting her, yes, but what would he do if he found her?

Lascivious ideas aside, did he plan to give the lady her shoe back? Chastise her for sneaking into his house and stealing a dance? For that, so far, was her gravest wrongdoing. In the bright light of day, evidence pointed at no true crime having been committed, save the damage to his pride.

No, he couldn't stop his hunt.

Beside him, North hefted high his walking stick, pointing at a blue-lettered sign: The New Union Coffeehouse.

"Let's try that one. Opened over a week ago. Heard some at the Exchange raving over the pastries. That is, of course, if you don't mind the raucous crowd."

His friend preferred the stately formality of expensive gentlemen's clubs. Cyrus hardly frequented coffeehouses, but he wasn't bothered by the prospect of the noisy, common crowd. Coffeehouses were London's hubs of equality, a gathering place for men to share a mug and share their views, no matter their rank.

The Royal Exchange banned common traders for being too loud and disruptive, rabble-rousers in the ever-shifting world of high commerce. A chosen few commoners received special permission from the Crown to conduct business within the Exchange. Cyrus was one of them. The rest milled about the wharfs or hunkered down in midtown taverns and coffee shops to ply their trades through runners delivering messages.

On the other side of the shop's mullioned window, merchants and traders gossiped and debated, the wavy panes distorting their animated faces. Every subject fell under their jurisdiction, from politics to the price of wool and cotton, all the while waiting for messengers to come with fresh news, news to be posted on the chalkboards found in London's coffee shops.

Passing through the doorway, they were greeted with the hot, earthy aromas of strong coffee mingled with cinnamon apple. A smart proprietor ought to leave the door open, all the better to lure the casual pedestrian inside.

"Ahh, fresh-baked apple tarts." North tipped his

nose up, breathing deep. "You get a table, and I'll ask about the pastries."

Patrons occupied black lacquered tables and chairs scattered around the long room. High-backed benches, shining from a recent coat of onyx paint, lined both sides of the establishment's brick walls. A tall lad of eighteen or nineteen years poured coffee into a pair of white mugs behind the counter.

Cyrus sought a table near the window, keeping his back to the bench for a better view of the place. He dropped his hat beside him, catching sight of a man slouched nearby. The man sat alone, his black tricorne pulled low over his eyes, but he recognized him.

Lord Marcus Bowles.

Black boots, scraped and muddied, sprawled before him. His stained shirt opened at the neck. The brown-and-green-striped waistcoat he wore gapped from missing buttons, the fabric moving up and down in the relaxed flow of a man fast asleep.

North came to the table, his hat and walking stick clamped under his arm while bearing two white mugs of steaming brew. A black stencil proclaimed *The New Union Coffeehouse* on the sturdy stoneware.

"Fresh tarts will be out of the oven soon," he said, settling himself in a chair.

Cyrus motioned to Bowles. "Looks like he's not at the Nagshead or the White Lyon."

North glanced across the bench, his mouth a flat line. "At least I know he's not smashing up taverns." He shifted to rise, but Cyrus stopped him.

"Let him sleep. He's not causing trouble...as long as the proprietor doesn't mind." He hooked his finger through the mug's handle, looking around for the man in charge.

Right then, two lads ran panting into the shop, papers crushed in their fists. One gangly youth delivered his notes to a round, florid-faced trader wearing a gray yarn wig. The trader dug out a farthing for payment and read aloud the news to five men sitting with him. An energetic debate on the price of wheat ensued.

The other lad went to a chalkboard, pondering the note in his hand. Cyrus scanned more of the coffee shop, his study catching a slender woman emerging from a passageway near the counter. She balanced a wide tray of pastries. A larger than normal mobcap covered her hair, but something about her…the glimpse of her face made him look twice.

He craned his neck, but the shopgirl set the wide tray on the counter and turned her back to him. She stretched for a coffee grinder from a high shelf, her willow-slim body a pleasant sight.

"Nate…more coals on the fire…" She spoke over her shoulder to the tall youth at the counter.

She curled her hands in her apron, wiping them as she looked to the lad at the chalkboard. Her profile struck Cyrus oddly, but the mobcap's frill obscured her face. Some women pinned a small scrap of cloth to their heads in the name of propriety, but this shopgirl covered every strand of hair.

He watched her while North relayed his brother's latest exploits. Something about the shopgirl teased his memory like a pleasant taste he couldn't recall. Was she from his home village of Stretford? Cyrus sipped his coffee, keeping vigil on the woman in his periphery.

She set a tender hand on the shoulder of the older boy standing at the chalkboard, whispering something to him. The lad passed paper and chalk to her and disappeared into a doorway leading to what must be the kitchen. One slim arm covered in plain gray broadcloth cuffed past her elbow moved over the blackboard. She wrote neat lines, her skirts swaying with her movement.

Light gray fabric draped her slender bottom. The white bow of her apron cinched her small waist, the ties fluttering down her gentle curves. No large hip roll masked her shape.

He grinned at a simple truth: working women tolerated no taxing fashion. They wore simpler hip rolls. Practical demands of their everyday world required maneuverability such as the woman at the chalkboard carrying on with grace.

And he was worse than a stripling lad the way he ogled her.

But something about her reminded him of...*home*?

She finished listing ships and goods docked off Tower Wharf and dusted her hands of chalk. Men clustered behind her to read the news, beginning lively discussions on *The Grosvenor*'s cargo of indigo and saltpeter, but under the table, a shoe nudged his shin.

"Go to the counter. You'll get a better look." North folded his arms across his chest, bunching Greek-patterned embroidery on a fine waistcoat.

"It's not what you think," he said. "I recognize her...think she's from Stretford."

"Then while you're figuring it out, why not get us some tarts?"

A pair of macaronies entered the shop, mincing their way to the counter in high-heeled shoes painted garish shades of green and yellow to match equally revolting coats and breeches. At the counter, the young fops dawdled, discussing the merits of one pastry over another.

Rising from the table, his body loosened. The shopgirl could be exactly what he needed. He warmed to the idea of a pleasant diversion with a less-complicated woman.

Between the high-wigged macaronies and the woman's oversized mobcap, he couldn't get a good view of her face. The fops paid for their pastries and moved on, their heels clicking on plank floors. Right as Cyrus ambled to the counter, the lady dipped out of sight. The lad, Nate, plunked a bucket of coal on the floor and wiped his hands with his apron.

"Sir, can I get ye something?"

Cyrus tried to see over the block counter but earned little more than glimpses of her gray-skirted bottom. She crouched on the floor, appearing to lean into what must be shelves underneath.

Another time.

He glanced at the tall youth. "Two apple tarts."

Nate set two plates on the counter, cocking his head. "Don't I know you from somewhere?"

He had a pretty good idea the source of the lad's recollection. The tall, gangly youth had the look of an East Ender about him, but what the shop boy likely knew was something Cyrus would rather not have bandied about in midtown.

"Don't think so." Cyrus averted his eyes to the chalkboard, rubbing the sore spot on his neck.

The shopgirl made lots of noise rummaging through goods. He drew out coins for payment. Nate scooped the tarts onto two plates, all the while studying Cyrus behind a black forelock hanging over his eyes. Young though he was, the lad wore cleverness about him the way others wore wealth and position.

On the other side of the counter, the woman spoke up from the floor, louder this time.

"Nate, have you seen a cherrywood box with a heart carved on the lid? It's long and narrow"—there was more rustling—"about this big."

That voice.

The small hairs on his neck bristled.

Images of a laughing, blond coquette in a low-cut gown teased him. The voice went with the lithe body dancing through his memory these past weeks. He set a claiming hand on the countertop, staring at the gray-skirted bottom coming in and out of view.

The lad picked up the plates, his green eyes hard slits on Cyrus. "No, Miss Mayhew, haven't see it."

The youth idled, puffing out his chest. Protective of the woman, was he?

"To the table by the window, if you please." Cyrus kept his voice firm and the lad moved with sullen steps.

Stoneware clanked. The shopgirl set a steadying hand on the counter—a hand good at untying things, a hand with a pink, star-shaped scar.

A hefty brawler could've knocked him in the gut for the way his stomach muscles clenched. Behind him, the shop burst with male laughter and boisterous boasts. Life went on as usual for everyone else, but where he stood, stormy silence swirled.

"Excuse me. I might have what you're looking for...*Miss Tottenham.*"

The gray skirt ceased moving.

Cyrus wasn't a hunter, not in the conventional sense. But he recognized the moment when prey froze, clinging to a split second of freedom while deciding: fight or flight. And he waited, his pulse quickening. She hadn't seen him standing there, but she heard him.

The vixen remembered his voice.

A thrill coursed through him, sharpening his wits. What would she do when she faced him?

His quarry set her other hand, dusted with flour, on the plank counter. She rose to full height and pretty blue-green eyes met his with cool challenge.

"Thank you, but you have no idea what I want."

Her chin tipped high and a long tendril fluttered against her cheek.

That show of bravado roused him, stoking his fire for her. He *liked* that she looked him in the eye. A lot of men wouldn't do as much.

There was probably some deeper meaning in her words, but satisfaction at having snared her settled in bone deep. The weight of power was his. One corner of his brain counseled caution: an oversized, angry man could never be easy for a woman to face.

No matter. The flirt would get no quarter from him.

"How nice to see you again, *Miss Tottenham.*" He smiled, lacking all warmth. "Are you looking for your shoe?"

Four

There is in true beauty, as in courage, something which narrow souls cannot dare to admire.

William Congreve, *The Old Bachelor*

CLAIRE ACKNOWLEDGED AN UNDENIABLE TRUTH: A man always, always, always played a part in a woman's downfall. Though, not to put too fine a point on it, *her* own disastrous decisions created the shaky ground on which she currently stood. She couldn't avoid the painful truth of her circumstances any more than she could avoid Mr. Cyrus Ryland standing in front of her.

Nor was the matter helped by childhood biblical lessons booming in her head, all meant to rain down fresh guilt. If those storied reminders didn't keep a woman in line, she faced a sizable man ready to pour his brand of fire and brimstone inside her humble shop.

At least that's what she assumed by the sparks shooting from Mr. Ryland's hard, gray eyes. Unsteady nerves tied her legs in knots, but she'd defend her small slice of independence.

"How nice to see you again, Mr. Ryland," she said, lobbing a brazen volley. "And thank you, but you can keep the shoe."

The cold, masculine smile stayed in place, but his eyebrows moved a fraction higher.

Did he expect her to grovel?

She kept both hands on the counter. The way they stood, both could be squaring off over the same hotly contested territory. A spurt of pride bolstered her, despite the awful squeeze to her chest. Provoking the angry brute was not a good idea, but neither would she show fear.

Her brain ticked with the best solution to rid her shop of his presence: demonstrate proper success. Didn't the New Union Coffeehouse reflect midtown prosperity? England's King of Commerce understood one thing well: money. She was about to impress him with her freshly minted business skills when Mr. Ryland furnished his own announcement.

"That's good about your shoe, because it's with the magistrate." His arms crossed, straining a fine black coat over broad shoulders.

"The magistrate?" Her voice thinned. "Why?"

"Let's see…an unknown woman sneaks into my home, hides in my study, only to flee suddenly at midnight." He paused, and his voice turned brusque. "Of course I went to the magistrate. I was certain you stole something."

She leaned against the counter, needing support. The sharp corner dug into her midsection with welcome pressure. Running off the way she did must've caused more of a stir than she had imagined.

She had truly believed he would brush off their chance encounter.

"There's no need to involve Bow Street. I didn't steal anything. I assure you, I meant no harm."

"Something in your practiced flirtation made me think otherwise."

"Practiced flirtation?" A shrill laugh escaped her. "I'm nothing of the sort. What you see is an honest woman, an honest woman of *business*...just as I told you."

"Then who was that woman rubbing against me while we danced?"

He asked the startling question with nonchalance, but her cheeks singed from the crude reminder. Mr. Ryland perused her pale gray workaday dress cinched with black ties from her waist to the modest, square neckline, where a neckerchief covered her skin. She didn't dress the part of a temptress.

Behind her, a commotion inserted a welcome break in her crisis. Jocular voices, laughter, and the footsteps of young men sounded from her kitchen. Ryland cocked his head at the disturbance.

"It's the messengers finishing up their stew," she explained.

"Busy place."

"Good for business, don't you think?" She managed a small smile, glad for the distraction.

Half a dozen young men, all on the verge of manhood, filed out of the kitchen, setting their Dutch caps on their heads. A few swiped their coat sleeves across their mouths, laughing and talking. But the roughly dressed youths chorused their appreciation for the meal. One of them, Sharp Eddie as he was called, snapped to attention on seeing Mr. Ryland, his hawk-like eyes taking special interest in her patron.

"Thanks, Miss Mayhew, we'll be off." Sharp Eddie veered close to the counter, staring at Ryland.

The odd attention bordered on rude, but she had other things to attend than to puzzle over the lad's lack of manners. Two more men entered the shop, footmen enjoying their half day in search of coffee and macaroons. She obliged them, relieved to see to business rather than appeasement of an angry male. Mr. Ryland moved out of the way so she could tend her counter.

But he didn't leave.

That would make things too easy. Instead, arms still crossed, he leaned a hip against the counter and kept close vigil on her every move. Her jittery hands managed to pour two steaming cups for the men and scoop up the pence they left on the counter. With impish mischief, she noted Mr. Ryland wore less complicated neckwear today, but to comment on such would not be wise. She dropped the coins into her till box, her lips clamping shut.

Beneath the till, on the bottom shelf, a basket of clean linens cried for attention. Keeping busy offered an antidote to her upset. She reached for a newly laundered cleaning rag, glad for something to occupy her hands.

Mr. Ryland looked at the open archway leading to the kitchen. "The messengers, are they any relation to you?"

"I have no brothers and sisters or cousins for that matter." She started folding the cloth, unsure how to adroitly remove his presence from her counter.

"A father?"

"Alive and well," she said, making a tidy crease. "A land steward on the Greenwich Estate."

Mr. Ryland's stony stare roved the shop, finally landing on the kitchen's entry. His gaze drifted up the narrow stairs, taut lines framing his mouth. She lived above those stairs.

"A husband, perhaps?"

She took a deep breath, her fingers fixing a messy corner. "I'm not married."

Her shoulders were achingly rigid while finishing the cloth, a pristine square her final product. The cloth reflected order—order that failed to reach her jumbled senses. When she looked up, Mr. Ryland's mouth curved into a cool, discerning smile.

"I see what this is about. *You're* the letter writer. The one who pestered me for months to relax my rule requiring a man on the lease."

She snapped straight another rag in want of a good folding, all the better to keep her from doing or saying the wrong thing.

"I am," she admitted, her movement brittle.

Her hands made rapid progress, turning the cloth into a square identical to the first. Then, she grabbed a cheesecloth requiring order and whipped straight that linen, but erupting emotions bubbled higher, refusing to be bottled. Her ruin came in mere seconds—wasn't that always the case for a woman?—when words spouted with a life of their own.

"I'll have you know, I tried doing everything the right way"—she gave him a pointed look, the cheese-cloth crumpling in her grip—"but you are impossible."

"Is that so?"

"I find it hard to believe I'm the first woman to shed light on that particular corner of your character."

She whipped the cheesecloth straight, and he moved off the counter, staying silent.

"I told Mr. Pentree I accosted you on the street outside your home and you signed the lease."

"You...accosted me," he repeated with some amusement.

"Yes. You may as well know I copied your signature that night in your study." Her voice shook. "Your agent manages so many properties for you. I thought my shop would escape your notice."

His eyes narrowed as facts must've settled in. She'd heard he was all about lists of numbers over lists of names.

"You mean you *lied* to Mr. Pentree." A harsh, dry chuckle loosened him. "And since I signed no such document, we can add forgery to your list of crimes. Now I understand why you gave me a false name."

"It was for a good end, I tell you." She professed brave words, but her mouth went dry.

Swallowing became hard. Forgery of any kind guaranteed years of imprisonment but most often the offense won a quick trip to Tyburn gallows.

Surely he doesn't want that?

Ryland set both hands far apart on her counter, gaining her full attention. He leaned forward, his unbuttoned coat flapping open.

"Forgery's beyond Bow Street, miss. That's a crime

against the Crown, a ticket to Tyburn. Have you any idea the trouble you'd be in if you faced another man right now?" He lowered his voice. "Or what that man might demand of you?"

Her knees weakened, making the floor like shifting quicksand beneath her. She scrambled to digest all the pieces of information coming at her. He didn't say he'd report the forgery, and he wasn't any other man: he was Cyrus Ryland. And she was completely ensnared in a neat trap of her own making with nowhere to go and no way out.

"If you don't report it, no one will know."

"*That* was your plan?" His head jolted, eyes spreading wide. "Hope I'd stay silent?"

"I didn't have a plan." She inched closer, all the better to keep their conversation private. "I didn't think I'd be caught. Merchants here told me you come to the Exchange once or twice a month, if that. They said you never set foot in Cornhill shops."

"I did today, didn't I?"

Her shoulders crumpled under an unseen weight. "I didn't expect to see you again."

Something flickered in his eyes. Had Mr. Ryland *wanted* to see her again?

She checked the shop beyond him. No one noticed them save Nate, who was sweeping the doorway, and the marquis and his brother looking with keen interest from a table near the window. She clamped the white cloth in both hands, the very picture of a supplicant beginning her appeal.

"It's in your best interest if I stay here. I'll make more money for you, working to pay the rent."

"That's what this is about?" he snapped. "Money?"

A cold, ugly shiver touched her from her scalp to her feet. She never expected her actions would lead to disastrous consequences. Why would a man with so many properties stretching from the Midlands to London care about one little shop?

"Well, yes...isn't that what impels you?" Claire blinked, pulling back more, needing some space. "I thought money's what's most important to you. You are a man of business after all."

Ryland scowled at her, the faint lines around his mouth deepening. Somehow, she'd touched a raw nerve. Yet she couldn't fathom why he'd be so bothered. He was England's man of the moment, the King of Commerce. Whatever caused his odd turn, Mr. Ryland kept it a secret.

Claire shifted her feet, relieving some of the pressure. She'd been on them all day, but this was not the time to let down her guard and rest.

"Now you've found me out, sir. What can I do to convince you to let me be?"

The quiet question hung between them when Annie emerged from the kitchen with a tray of custard tarts. She was dressed like Claire, in a dove-gray dress, save the sticky smears of egg yolk and butter on her apron. Her pale blue eyes lit with delight at the dozen tempting delectables on the tray before her.

"Look, Claire, I did it." Annie flashed a gleeful grin at Claire, then addressed Mr. Ryland. "After many burnt offerings, I finally master her recipe."

"They look perfect." Claire's brows pressed with

concern. "We've an hour or two to sell them before our doors close for the day, but I'm sure we will."

This wasn't the right time to tamp down the woman's enthusiasm with worries over selling late-day goods. Her cook beamed, rosy cheeked from the baking victory; mastering the custard *was* a hard-won accomplishment for Annie.

With cloths in her grip to protect her hands, Annie levered the metal tray, sliding the fresh-baked pastries, dusted liberally with nutmeg, onto a display platter. She made a mental note to remind Annie to use a sparing hand with the costly spice. She'd say something tomorrow. Annie deserved this small victory today.

She checked Ryland's reaction to Annie's face. Pink marks mottled her cook's skin where she healed from a terrible beating. One could surmise she had survived something horrid. Mr. Ryland kept his anger at bay and tipped his well-groomed head with thoughtful gentleman's decorum to Annie.

"They look and smell excellent. I'll buy three of them, one for my coachman and two for the footmen attending my carriage."

Annie's mouth flopped open. "Why that's right kind of you, sir." She winked at Claire and nudged her with an elbow. "Now, there's a *very nice* man. I'd let him dawdle at the counter, if I was you."

With a firm nod, Annie walked back into the kitchen, singing a bawdy tune. The corners of Mr. Ryland's mouth curled with satisfaction, no doubt from her approving words. His pewter-colored stare ranged over Claire again.

"And do many men dawdle at your counter, Miss Mayhew?"

He asked the question, but his deep-Midlands accent turned the query into flirtation. She brushed her hands down her apron, meeting his bold perusal.

"A few," she acknowledged and tipped her head at the fresh custards. "Did you mean it? About buying three tarts for the men attending you?"

"I wouldn't have said it if I didn't mean it." He eyed the display platter and waved a hand over the dozen. "In fact, I'll take them all. I'd be obliged if you wrapped them for me."

All dozen of them? Her jaw dropped momentarily, but she recovered, silently placing plain brown paper on the counter, grateful for his generosity. How could one stay upset in the face of such thoughtfulness as to purchase pastries for the people attending him? She knew how to respond to the man who fit neatly into the brutish, intractable mold she had cast for him, but Mr. Ryland chipped away at those set notions.

She stacked the tarts, sneaking quick looks at him from under her mobcap's ruffle. She couldn't bring herself to fully trust this shift of charity. What was he up to?

Her landlord pulled out a considerable coin pouch from a pocket inside his coat. He stood stoic and businesslike, placing the bag on the counter. No, her being here wasn't about money—his or anyone else's. Her little shop was about much more than that. Surely a man with so much wouldn't begrudge her the opportunity to make her own way in the world? But this wasn't something to explain with tempers barely cooled.

Mr. Ryland kept one hand on the counter and twisted around, looking to his friends sitting by the window. Setting the last tart in place, she guessed him to be close to a decade older than her. Waning daylight and polished metal candle sconces brightened the shop, highlighting a few silver threads glinting in his brown hair.

The texture looked soft and touchable, not coarse and wiry or sparse and absent, like some men's hair. A black silk ribbon wrapped around his queue's length, the silk line trailing down the middle of his back. A silly flutter in her chest kept time with her visual exploration of Mr. Ryland's wide shoulders.

Her lashes dropped low when he faced her again. "Thank you…about the custards," she said, calm but wrung dry. "They're a pence each."

They were at a standstill. He could be naught more than a male patron lingering at her counter for friendly conversation—except for the heated words they'd exchanged earlier. The little interruptions of the messengers, other patrons, and Annie's sweet praise had defused hot tempers, but Claire didn't fool herself. Matters were far from resolved with Mr. Ryland.

She made quick business tying the wrapped tarts with twine and stretched out her hand to accept payment. He set two shillings in her hand, his fingertips brushing her palm. The brief touch tickled her skin. Claire hadn't forgotten the play of attraction the night of the masked ball, but she was not that woman: neither a woman of pleasure nor a woman of substantial means with idle hours for flirting.

The mask and gown made a ruse; her gray broadcloth and apron were real. Best she left their sensual conversation, the midnight dance, and, yes, provocative flirtation behind. The coins dropped with a clink in the till box, and she rubbed her palms slowly down her apron as though she could wipe away his tantalizing touch.

"What do I need to do to convince you?" she asked. "About the shop?"

He tucked his coin pouch in his coat. "Meet me at Ryland House—"

"I'll do no such thing," she blurted.

His hand paused inside his coat, amused gray eyes pinning her. "—because I conduct business there with my secretaries. And I keep financial records in my study."

"Oh." Claire shut her eyes.

She wasn't sure what mortified her most: that her mind pounced first on the idea of a sensual meeting, or that Mr. Ryland meant no such thing yet was amused by *her* lascivious presumption.

He laughed, a low and pleasant rumble, the first sound of genuine amusement since seeing her again.

"I don't mix sex with business, Miss Mayhew." His Midlands accent dropped to an intimate note. "But I'll admit, I want to see your…accounts *in full*."

Her gaze snapped open, meeting his. Sparks flew between them, hot and hard as a hammer hitting iron. Mr. Ryland leaned close, but his voice playing with those words messed with her senses. He sounded exactly the way he had in the study, when he had asked about her talents. With men.

"My accounts, sir, are private. And as such, will stay that way."

Mirth faded from his eyes—eyes that glimmered dark and hot. "I'm not mistaken about our mutual interest the night of the ball, am I?"

Her skin tingled everywhere at the memory, and he knew very well the answer to his question. Never had she flirted as boldly with a man as she had with him at the masked ball. Of course, he wouldn't know that. To reignite their mutual interest would be a dangerous path to tread with a man like him. A woman could lose herself and everything she wanted if she said yes to Mr. Ryland.

To what end? Mindless sensual pleasure?

What woman in her right mind would sacrifice independence for that?

She linked her fingers together, adopting the same prim stance she did with footmen who had made the unwise choice of flirting with her when she had been the housekeeper at Greenwich Park.

"You ask a question, Mr. Ryland, yet from you, it sounds curiously like a statement. This seems to be a habit of yours."

"Then answer the question." His voice could be iron wrapped in velvet.

"My answer." She paused, resting her clasped hands on the counter.

Somehow facing him was nothing like taking an errant footman to task. Mr. Ryland was not a man a woman could easily bend to her bidding.

She took a measured breath. "That evening was a singular event, never to be repeated. We are landlord and proprietress. Ours is a business partnership, if you'll allow it. Anything else would be most unsuitable…in fact, simply forbidden."

"Like forbidden fruit?" He smiled at her, a tolerant turn of his lips. "But if you returned to your home in Greenwich Park and lived with your father—"

"Out of the question. I'm a grown woman of twenty-six. I'll not hang on my father's sleeve." She spread her arms wide. "*This* is what I want. Is that so hard for you to imagine?"

Mr. Ryland stood up straight, his shoulders blocking her view of the shop—no, he filled her view. She couldn't read his shuttered expression, but he nodded slow acknowledgment.

"Very well. I need to understand your finances then, before I take a risk and change my leasing rules. I have considerable doubts about a woman operating a business by herself, especially in London." He frowned at the stairs. "Nor should a woman live alone in Town. It's not safe."

Her finances?

"My accounts are a stack of notes to pay and the till you saw me drop coins into. I pay Nate and Annie from the till."

"You don't keep any books? No record of income and expenses?"

She winced at the scattered mess of notes due at the end of next week, all jammed under the counter. Perhaps she shouldn't have revealed so much information?

She wasn't about to add more fuel to his argument that she was out of her depth running a business.

She understood how to make appetizing pastries and how to create a warm, inviting shop, but she kept no account books—not yet anyway.

There'd been so much to do to open the New Union Coffeehouse. She worked alongside Nate and Annie, giving a hand to most tasks. Between roasting green coffee beans to the right shade of brown, tending her counter, and helping in the kitchen, her days had been filled with exhausting, but pleasurable, tasks. By evening, fiddling with columns of numbers had held the same appeal as cleaning chamber pots.

Thankfully, Nate approached just then with the broom in hand, saving her from having to respond.

"Everything all right, Miss Mayhew?"

The dear lad squared his shoulders, glowering at Mr. Ryland, but she couldn't take another confrontation at her counter. She needed to sit down and figure her way through this muddle, something she couldn't do with an imposing male examining her every move. Nate's courage was contagious, heartening her.

"We're fine, Nate." She picked up the wrapped package and handed it to him. "Deliver this to Mr. Ryland's carriage, if you please, and tell the coachman Mr. Ryland's ready to leave."

One eyebrow arched high at her bold dismissal, but her oversized patron told Nate where to find the carriage. Her deft assertiveness met with quiet, gray-eyed assessment absent of male bluster and indignation. *Interesting.*

Mr. Ryland's mouth curled with bemusement. "You and I have unfinished business."

Claire's body sparked with warmth. Under her

plain garb, her stays teased sensitive skin, brushing her breasts with an agonizing reminder of how long it had been since a man last touched her. She wrapped a protective arm across her waist, not wanting to absorb the strong attraction simmering between them. Silence was her best ally.

"I'll grant you this," he said. "Want a chance to prove your mettle? Rents for this quarter are due end of next week. That'll be your first test."

She gave him the first easy smile since he had walked through her door. "I'll make the rent. You can be sure of it."

From under the counter, she pulled out a heavy, earthen jar. She removed the lid and the aroma of dark-roasted coffee swelled from the plain vessel, the most pleasant perfume.

"I may not keep excellent records," she said, cheerfully scooping coffee beans. "But I have my own surety."

Mr. Ryland crossed his arms, following her every move. Did he spy the aquamarine stones sparkling among the roasted beans? She couldn't be sure. The heavy earthen jar provided the best hiding place for the necklace; she alone handled the coffee beans. The irony was she valued the savory coffee more than glittering jewels.

She dumped beans into the grinder on the counter. Going about her work, she tried to ignore him, but the effort was futile.

His presence made breathing a little harder. Or was that because she cranked the coffee grinder? She sneaked quick peeks at him under her lashes. He looked tired. Faint shadows fell under his eyes, and he rubbed his shoulder as though the spot ached. She wanted to ask him how he fared, enjoy small talk the same as when they had sat together in his study. But they couldn't be two more different people. His garb alone could pay her rent for a year.

A large sapphire the size of a small egg pinned his shirt together high on his chest. The stone shined the same dark blue shade as his fine waistcoat, a garment embroidered with scarlet-and-gold threads, all marks of success.

A black carriage rolled up to her shop's front window. The thing was as big as a mail coach and as brutish in size as the man who owned it. The stark conveyance boasted no flourishes and no noble crest on the door but gleamed everywhere with rich, burnished-brass fittings and trim: door hinges, elaborate handle, and fine candle lamps for evening rides. Even the wheel hubs and spokes gleamed with brass trim.

Her hand slowed its rotations on the grinder, meeting with less resistance. Maybe things would go smoother for her? Ryland moved off the counter, his guarded stare roving her cap, her face.

He set his hand over his heart and tipped in a bow. "You can be sure I'll pay close attention to this business experiment."

∽⌒∾

Cyrus leaned a shoulder on the window sash, his hands jammed in his pockets. Behind him was the rich world of London's finer gentleman's clubs, though not the finest. This one accepted commoners. Leather seating arrangements ensconced the elite within a dark-paneled citadel for men. North and his scoundrel of a brother sat enthroned in a cluster of four armchairs, waiting for another acquaintance to join them.

Conversations stayed at a murmur; even the footmen whispered. Yet, beyond the glass square, Cyrus glimpsed men and women walking and talking, enjoying twilight. How easily the sexes mixed from where he stood. Would that ever happen for him?

He breathed in, convinced he could smell sugared apples and cinnamon, the aroma of one very determined woman's coffee shop. The taste was something he could savor for a long time—like a taste of her.

Or was she smooth like custard?

One corner of his mouth curled at his not-so-innocent thoughts.

Miss Mayhew aroused him, yet beyond the obvious surface attraction, he couldn't figure out why. Was his fervent interest because she stood her ground, facing him like some fine-boned fighter in a skirt?

Or was this entirely about parts hidden by said skirt?

He took his seat with the brothers. At least bothersome questions were answered, questions that had pestered him since the woman had invaded his home. But, as with most things in life, when one question was answered, several more demanded gratification like an itch refusing to go away.

Bowles lounged in his chair, stretching his legs and flexing one booted foot before crossing it over the other. His heavy-lidded smile a sure sign trouble brewed.

"The coffee shop used to be Tottenham's," he said. "But of course, you knew that, owning the property and all."

"He owns so many," North countered, accepting a message a footman delivered on a silver tray. "One can't expect him to pay attention to the signage of each establishment."

Bowles linked his hands in his lap, his stare speculative. "Odd how she was Miss Tottenham at the ball, but today she's Miss Mayhew."

Cyrus gripped the chair's arms, the need to protect Miss Mayhew surging.

"Sneaking a lightskirt into a proper ball...and here I thought you were all work," Bowles went on. "Bold move on your part."

"She's *not* a lightskirt," he stressed.

North stuffed his message into his coat pocket, glaring at his brother. "As if you'd be one to counsel him on what's proper."

"Guilty as charged." Bowles grinned and faced Cyrus. "You did know your pretty shopgirl used to be in service...housekeeper to the Earl of Greenwich?"

Cyrus snapped his fingers. "That's where I've seen her. Last winter. I visited the earl over a patent question."

Was the reclusive earl the one who gifted her with the fine necklace? And what had she given in return? Whatever was done in the past was no more. The prickly Earl of Greenwich was supposed to be famously in love with his new countess.

"If you wanted to find your masked lady, you should've come to me," Bowles said. "I'd find her a lot faster than Bow Street for half the reward."

Cyrus glanced at North, who sat mute and properly rigid, brushing off an invisible speck from his breeches. Cyrus bristled at his private matter becoming fodder for discussion between the brothers. He'd confided in North about his hunt for the mysterious woman in confidence.

"You've known about her long?" Cyrus asked Bowles.

"Awhile. Saw her open shop one morning. Hadn't put her mobcap on yet. Hair that color's rare. Then I saw the old Tottenham sign come down and strolled in for a coffee." The former soldier's voice dropped with suggestion. "And who can forget her mouth, her form…though she tries to hide the goods."

Bowles knew her whereabouts and kept the news to himself. Cyrus's jaw ticked as much from that knowledge as the miscreant's provocative words. A decade ago, he would've reacted in a bad way, but not now. Time had tempered him, and he'd not give the man the satisfaction of witnessing his agitation.

Bowles chuckled, a hoarse sound from too little sleep and too much liquor. "Planning on the shopgirl replacing Lady Isabella Foster? A real step down for you, going West End to midtown."

"You speak as if these women are commodities he trades…one for another," North said.

"Isn't that what he does? Moves things and people around to suit his purpose?" Bowles answered, his bloodshot stare sweeping from his brother to Cyrus. "Seems to me there was a lot of effort to find one woman."

"So he wanted to know what she was about…her

sneaking into his home and running off the way she did. Can't blame a man for wanting an attractive woman."

"There's wanting a woman and then there's remembering a woman." Bowles's head lolled against the chair. "Question is which one applies to Cyrus and his shopgirl?"

Breath snagged in Cyrus's chest. *His shopgirl.*

He turned his attention to the window, his muscles tensing with the want to strike. He tolerated the scoundrel because he was North's younger brother. This time, Bowles went too far.

"The shopgirl has a name," Cyrus insisted. "Miss Mayhew. You would do well to remember it, though I doubt you've tarried long enough with any woman to learn her name."

Nor did he want the miscreant tarrying with Miss Mayhew.

"A coffee shop, not your usual haunt," North said to his brother.

Bowles withdrew a tarnished metal flagon from inside his coat. "Man cannot live by ale and tavern wenches alone. Coffee and the company of an upstanding woman could be what a degenerate like me needs." He grinned at Cyrus, something wolfish and sly. "Former housekeepers must know how to clean a man's nook and crannies. I wonder about her thighs—"

"Marcus…" North cautioned.

Cyrus's back came off the leather.

"Stay away from her," he snapped. "There's enough *other* women's thighs in London. Or have you exhausted the Town supply of lightskirts?"

Murmuring ceased nearby. Two heads turned their way, a middle-aged baron in an oversized wig and the footman attending him. One look at Cyrus's scowl and the two averted their attention.

"Touchy about this one, aren't you?" Bowles took a quick swig.

"If you know what's best, you'll leave her alone." The scoundrel's bloodshot eyes opened wider.

"So that's how it is?" Bowles rubbed his jaw, heavy with whiskers. "Then you must like them hard to get, Cy. Because if I read things right in the shop, the pretty blond doesn't want anything to do with you." He raised his flask in mock salute. "Here's to your merry chase."

Bowles took another quick draught and returned the flask to his inside pocket. He pushed off the chair, saying something about seeing a friend across the room.

The familiar rush of attack filled Cyrus's veins. He looked at his lap where his fist ground into his thigh. His reaction was as startling as it was defining. Miss Mayhew was of particularly powerful interest. At the same time, he couldn't help but think the sly Lord Marcus did some neat scouting with his provoking words.

North's gaze beetled from his brother's retreating back to Cyrus.

"Rare is the day I agree with my brother, but have you asked yourself why you're so focused on this one woman? Is this because you want her in some carnal way and she doesn't want you?"

Forbidden fruit.

Cyrus smiled at nothing in particular, recalling his

innuendo about wanting to see her accounts in full and the pretty flush that had colored her cheeks.

"This is about business. About what's best for a woman alone in London." Cyrus crossed his arms loosely over his chest, satisfied with that sliver of truth. "I feel a sense of responsibility."

Was his interest in Miss Mayhew purely about the age-old pursuit? He didn't understand all the facets, but he wouldn't reveal any more about her, especially her forgery. Such dangerous information would stay between him and Miss Mayhew, because he wanted to…protect her.

From men who'd prey on her like Bowles?

Or from *himself*?

Equally vexing was Bowles's accurate observation: *The pretty blond doesn't want anything to do with you.*

What was he going to do about that?

Five

Wit must be foiled with wit; cut a diamond with a diamond.

William Congreve, *The Double Dealer*

A few days later...

"WOMEN GO POSITIVELY WEAK KNEED OVER A FEW things in life." Lucinda stretched forward for an eyeful of the wooden box on his lap. "At least I'm guessing the receiver is a woman by the rather large and pretty red bow."

Cyrus set his hand over the incriminating box. His other hand kept time against his knee, as though he could tap the distance to their destination and make the carriage go faster. All morning, his body had itched with the want to be in motion. The contents of the box put him on a cliff of uncalculated risk, an uneasy place for a man to be when matters pertained to a woman.

His sister sighed loudly. Lucinda wanted to wrench secrets from him as much as she wanted his full attention, and normally he would have lavished attention on her, but today was different... All because of a flaxen-haired woman who had left her shoe on his front steps.

"In my estimation, a surprise gift tops the list of ways to capture a woman's heart," she said, intruding on his thoughts.

Capture her heart?

Cyrus slid a finger inside his neckline, tugging on his cravat. Capturing Miss Mayhew's heart wasn't top on his list of wants.

Was it?

Lucinda fidgeted on the seat, her dark brows arching. "It is a surprise, isn't it?"

"The box is none of your concern, Luce." The words came out with regrettable sharpness.

Her eyes rounded with feigned shock. "So that's the way it is?"

She bounced back against the squabs, but her impish smile told him she wasn't put off in the slightest. Lucinda had fished all morning for information since he had told her to cancel her plans and then been vague about his.

He kept words at a minimum where Miss Mayhew was concerned, wanting no poking or prodding as to his intent. Let events unfold as they will. The proprietress had haunted him body and soul since he last visited her shop.

The bold idea in his lap had struck last evening, a decidedly harmless way to walk into the New Union Coffeehouse as patron rather than landlord, but the exposed parts of the suggestive red ribbon taunted him.

Not *completely* harmless.

The secretive package containing provocative contents had left him pushing his breakfast around his plate. The audacious red bow might've been too much, but his carriage sped toward Cornhill with all the inevitable force of a storm. His course was set. Too late to turn back now.

He had one goal in mind today: smooth things over with Miss Mayhew. He hadn't left under the best of circumstances after his first visit to her coffee shop days ago. One glance at his sister, and he shifted the box on his lap. If the gift failed him, Lucinda wouldn't. She unwittingly played into his strategy this morning. Time he laid some of the groundwork.

"Think of the War Widows Betterment Society. That's why I'm bringing you with me today."

"No you're not." She laughed, her chestnut curls bouncing. "You hardly give my work a second thought. You're up to something. That overbearing tone of yours gives you away." Her mischievous gape lit on the package. "*And* the box with a shiny red bow."

His sister crossed her hands in her lap, looking like a satisfied schoolgirl who had stumbled on the answer to a vexing riddle ahead of other students.

"You want something, Cyrus." Her thin lips worked to restrain a smile. "Badly, I think."

His breath caught on her last words. He was a man in his third decade, well beyond the years of a youth mooning over a maid. Yet Lucinda's simply stated truth proved sharp, cutting to the heart of a matter. He lifted his hand, hoping he hadn't crushed the bow. Too late. Faint wrinkles marred the glossy ribbon.

"Perhaps I'm mending my ways." One finger tugged a red coil back to life. "About your work, I mean."

She snorted a very unfeminine kind of sound. Lucinda had gone through years of instruction to gain her current comportment and polish, but part of their modest roots stayed in her bones. The same was true for him.

"Of course you are…a leopard changing his·spots all of a sudden." She smiled, but then her brightness dimmed. "Wait a minute. You're not trying to force the Marquis of Northampton on me again? I'll marry when I'm good and ready to a man of my choosing. And it *won't* be a business arrangement to a friend of yours."

Cyrus smiled benignly, acknowledging her upset at the debacle with North. His youngest sister *would* marry well, but next time, matters needed finessing.

Her shoulders slumped under her velvet cloak. "You haven't dropped your plans to marry me off to some title, have you?"

"Of course not. A Ryland will marry a peer of the realm. And since you're the only unmarried sister I have, you're the logical candidate."

"Why don't *you* marry into the aristocracy, since it matters so much?"

"I will. Someday," he said, breathing easy. "But it's not the same for me. A man doesn't gain a title by marriage, as you well know. A woman can. If even one of us makes that kind of connection, all of our family, our sisters and their husbands, and our nieces and nephews will benefit."

His sister sat across from him in all her finery, a

beautiful purple gown, her favorite color. Her cheeks boasted healthy color now. In years past, those same cheeks had worn a sickly pallor. Too often he'd held a young Lucinda wheezing for breath, seized by coughing fits, attacks he was helpless to stop. Everything changed when he could afford the exotic, bitter yellow tea that gave her blessed relief.

"I don't understand." Lucinda flounced on the seat, looking equal parts spoiled and sweet. "Why do you press so much?"

Pictures of the past spun before him, particular moments reminding him that, through will or wealth, he would provide one thing without fail for his sisters and their families.

"Security."

His shoulders squared, ready to carry any burden for the ones he loved. Lucinda was not so old that their days as freehold farmers escaped her memory, a time when he was not yet a man trying to be a man at the head of their farm. After his father's death, Cyrus failed miserably at the task.

At the untried age of sixteen, he'd struggled wearing the mantle of authority, looking to the care of his mother and sisters. The costly mistakes he made sometimes left the larder bare and caused his long-suffering mother to take in laundry among a mountain of other labors she did. The memory of one hungry season hung heavy, causing Cyrus's mouth to harden as he stared out the carriage window at nothing in particular.

No man delighted in reliving his failure, no matter how youthful the error.

Lucinda plucked the yellow trim on her velvet skirt. "I'm sorry, Cyrus."

Her small-voiced apology wrenched him. "No need to apologize, minx."

He was supposed to be the solver of all problems, provider of all things necessary to his sisters and his mother, when she'd been alive. This was the stamp his father had impressed on him since he had strapped on his first pair of boots, the way of a man with the weaker sex.

"*Take care of them*," his father would always say.

"But this meeting today, we aren't going to see Lady Foster, are we?" Lucinda's brows pressed in a dark line. "I thought your…connection with her was done."

He frowned at her choice of words, but she waved off the disapproval. His sister was an interesting jumble of innocence and burgeoning awareness. Lucinda tolerated the self-assured, sharp-tongued Isabella in part because Cyrus spent time with the lady and because the lady lent a generous hand to Lucinda's newly formed War Widows Betterment Society.

"Really, Cyrus," she chided. "It's no secret she was your lady-bird. I did just turn twenty-three. I'm not a babe anymore."

"I won't ask where you acquired such a colorful phrase as *lady-bird*, but you *will* refrain from using it in the future."

She gave a mutinous shrug and stared out her window. Cyrus guessed the war widows she'd begun to help in recent months were more than forthcoming with information to Lucinda's boundless, inquisitive nature. But the carriage rolling to a stop prevented reminders of decorum.

"A coffee shop." Her brown eyes glinted with a troublemaker's light. "You're taking me to a coffee shop? Rather daring of you with my reputation, since proper West End ladies don't visit them."

"Today we make an exception, all for the war widows. The pastries here'd make an excellent addition to your next luncheon."

They exited the carriage, tasting fall's late-morning fog. Gray skies and the Thames's metallic, briny aroma hung heavy. The change of season—autumn's quarterly rents were due in five days.

Would Miss Mayhew meet the first requirement?

Overhead, the shop's new sign boasted bright blue letters carved in relief with a mug and curling steam at the bottom, all outlined in fresh black paint...a costly choice. Many sturdy midtown shingles honored the tried-and-true flat standard, keeping to traditions of the business name with a simple picture of what the shop purveyed.

Between the fine stencils on her mugs and the showy signage, Miss Mayhew was a tad flashy for a woman fond of staid gray broadcloth and matronly mobcaps. Did she exhibit such daring in other places?

He dismissed the carriage and the rest of midtown came into view. Laborers toiled up and down Cornhill, slower of purpose this cold morning.

"Pastries for the War Widows Betterment Society?" His sister folded demure hands against her skirt. "We're here for no other reason?"

Of course, she would figure out the lay of things soon enough, but no need to present all the facts yet.

"And to meet Mr. Pentree," he said, searching one

side of the street for his employee. "He's providing a report on a damaged cistern from a property on Lombard Street."

"Mr. Pentree. He's your new employee. The one with the spectacles. He's meeting us here?"

She glanced at the shop's facade, her cheeks staining red. Nate, the raven-haired lad, stood out front cleaning the window. The shop boy nodded his greeting, his hand slowing its rotation on the glass.

"Good morning, sir, miss."

The young man focused on Cyrus with keen interest. They exchanged morning pleasantries, and Lucinda pinched her skirts, moving into the shop. He followed his sister and was about to step through the doorway when a few choice words stopped him cold.

"I know who ye are," Nate called out. "Ye're the Stretford—"

He gave the shop boy a hard look, sufficient to make the lad clamp his mouth shut. The East Ender had figured him out, had he? Cyrus turned casually around, holding the box in one hand. The young man glanced at the fluttering red ribbon, his smile sly beyond his years.

"And I know why ye're here," he said, crossing his arms over his thin chest. "Ye think ye're the only one to go sniffin' around Miss Mayhew? May as well get in line if ye want her to give ye the time o' day."

Cyrus stepped closer to Nate, but his boots could have been filled with lead.

How *much* did the lad know?

Moments like these, small intersections in a man's life, tested his character. A man's secrets never truly left him alone. Nate's youthful, bewhiskered jaw worked—likely he was near bursting with certain knowledge about Cyrus and his past.

Beside them, midtown's music played. Harnesses clinked. Horse hooves trotted on hard-packed earth, adding to the daily rhythm that was Cornhill.

"What's your name?" he asked quietly. "Your full name."

"Nathaniel Fincher." His black forelock fell across one eye. "What's it to ye?"

Mr. Fincher's sullenness returned, part of the armor that must've saved his hide more than once. Cyrus grasped full well the youth's position. Hadn't he been there before?

"Because when I meet a good man, I want to know his name."

Nate's jaw dropped. The grind of a young man scraping to survive in an unforgiving place wrote *survivor* all over the lad. The East Ender must've clawed his way out of some hellacious hole, landing in the respectable, midtown employ of one pretty, kindhearted Miss Mayhew. Not a bad spot to be.

He glared at Cyrus. "Why'd ye say that?"

"Because a good man looks after a woman, takes care of her, be that woman his mother, sister, wife"— Cyrus looked to the mullioned window—"or his employer. We are their protectors. *That's* the measure of a real man."

Nate brushed back unruly hair, his brows pressing together. Behind Cyrus, Lucinda's voice beckoned from the shop doorway.

"Cyrus, aren't you coming?"

"In a minute," he said over his shoulder, keeping a careful eye on Nate. "Go ahead to the counter. Take a look at the pastries."

He waited until the rustle of her skirts faded. Through the wavy, diamond-shaped panes, he spied her moving through the shop. Satisfied she was out of earshot, Cyrus tucked the box under his arm.

"Let me give you some advice."

Mr. Fincher clamped his arms across his chest again, fingers gripping his biceps. The conversation couldn't be going as he'd expected, a fact that pleased Cyrus. His father had been dead a few years by the time he was Nate's age. He remembered the daily mix of fear and bravado when forced to navigate life without an older, wiser man offering guidance. Was the lad adrift without family?

Nate cocked his head. "Go ahead."

"The mark of a good man"—Cyrus slipped his hand inside his coat pocket—"his word is gold."

Like a magician at a summer fair, he produced a gold guinea, holding up the coin between his thumb and fore-finger. Nate's eyes brightened on seeing the shiny metal.

Cyrus tipped the guinea at the youth. "Keep your mouth shut about the Stretford business. I don't want Miss Mayhew to know."

Cyrus suspected the young man harbored more than brotherly affections for his fair-haired employer. All the more reason depending on Nate to keep a confidence put him on edge.

But the needful want of gold dropped a potent lure, more enticing than the power of spilling information.

"It won't matter none to Miss Mayhew, but"—the

youth licked his lips and reached for the coveted coin—"I won't say a word."

Cyrus passed him the guinea, and Nate rubbed the piece across his sleeve. He held up the coin, admiring King George's imprint before pocketing it.

"Keep your mouth shut, and I give you my word to help you in the future," Cyrus said, nodding. "Do we have a bargain?"

Nate nodded, his green eyes wary. "I won't say a thing. And, Mr. Ryland, here's some advice I can pass yer way: ye'd best come by more often." The lad grinned. "Lord Bowles stops in for coffee. Every day. Flirts a lot with Miss Mayhew."

Cyrus's upper lip curled against his teeth, but he nodded his thanks, moving to the doorway. Flirt with Miss Mayhew? Bollocks. Bowles was a master of the skill. Cyrus wasn't about that today.

This was business and…

The wooden box pressed against his ribs, evidence to the contrary. He hitched the package higher under his arm. The provocative contents came as close to flirting as he'd get. And Lord Bowles? He spied the miscreant currently leaning against the counter as relaxed as you please with a harem of five females in his thrall.

An ember of hotness seared him square in the chest at the sight of the younger man's encroachment. He longed to give Bowles the boot. Miss Mayhew stood at her counter, her mouth turned in an effort to suppress laughter at the scoundrel's anecdote. The shop buzzed with patrons sipping dark brew and scraping forks across their plates while they discussed the day's business.

Cyrus removed his hat, his insides raw over his bold risk, but he looked to the counter again. Miss Mayhew dipped her head, laughing with the other women, when her body stilled. Her jeweled gaze met his across the shop, touching him with something soft and secretive.

His spine straightened, and he met her gaze across the distance. The others laughed around her, but Miss Mayhew's lips opened with a gentle gap. For him. The invitation was the same as when they almost kissed at the ball, and her small, unspoken welcome seeped through bone and sinew, sealing his purpose.

She was temptation today, an Eve garbed in a dark blue dress hugging her slender body. White ties laced back and forth up the center of her bodice, cinching Miss Mayhew into her worker woman's dress. His stare followed the pale lacing against dark blue; the white ties were like lines on a map, marking the way to feminine delights.

Her chin dipped and one feminine hand reached up, grazing her collarbone where a linen neckerchief curved sedately over her shoulders. She touched the exposed sliver of white skin all the while looking at him across her shop.

A quiet, rusty chuckle moved in his chest.

You can run, Miss Mayhew, but you cannot hide.

Baser parts of Cyrus clenched inside his breeches, wanting this enticement—a man on the chase of a woman.

The claiming was only a matter of time and a matter of ridding the field of poachers, one being Lord

Bowles, who stood, hip cocked against the counter, regaling the women, Lucinda among them, with a colorful tale. Putting one boot in front of the other, he walked with steady confidence, arriving in time to hear Lord Marcus finish with a quip.

"My money's on the heir, dresses better."

The bevy of females tittered, but within the group, a woman with stygian-black hair spied Cyrus and brazenly arched her neck for a better view of him around Lord Bowles. Her coal-dark eyes measured him from head to boot, alighting with interest on the beribboned box under his arm. Lush lips curved in a moue, emitting a final *humph* before her curious, carnal stare drifted away with well-practiced disinterest.

On the other side of the counter, Miss Mayhew brushed away flaxen wisps, tucking them into her mobcap only to have them fall around her face again. Her cheeks colored nicely when he drew near. Had her thoughts slipped to something less than virginal?

"Good morning, Mr. Ryland," she said, glancing at the box, her voice crisp and efficient. "May I get you some coffee?"

"Good morning, ladies." He gave the cursory greeting to all, pausing on Lord Marcus. "Bowles."

"Ryland." Lord Marcus stood to full height and took note of the box.

With his jaw freshly shaved, boots polished to a shine, and a new black tricorne on his head, Bowles had cleaned up for this morning's midtown visit. Cyrus put his hat on the counter, claiming more space.

"Yes, a cup and a moment of your time, if you please…for a business proposition." He gave polite attention to the women lingering at the counter, avoiding Bowles. "When you're not too busy, that is."

Miss Mayhew paused in the act of reaching for a mug, her brows furrowing. "What kind of business proposition?"

"We'd like you to provide a variety of pastries and desserts for a special luncheon next Saturday," Lucinda spoke in a rush. "I'm hosting a meeting for the War Widows Betterment Society. Cyrus raved to me about your baked goods."

"Did he now?" The words rolled off Lord Marcus's tongue, ripe with suggestion. "Only the baked goods?"

Miss Mayhew ignored Bowles and poured coffee from a heavy pewter pot she grabbed from a squat corner stove.

"I hadn't thought of that, selling my baked goods in such magnitude. I'd only take on such an order if I could do the job well." She set the mug in front of him with care, her blue-green stare probing Cyrus. "Though…unexpected…it shouldn't be impossible."

Was there a message in her words?

The way Miss Mayhew studied him, absorbed and pensive, he could only guess she tried to read his intent. Why shouldn't she? Days ago, he'd laid out his doubts regarding her abilities to conduct business without a man to shepherd her. His mind wasn't changed on that score, but she deserved the promised chance to prove herself.

Cyrus reached inside his coat for the required pence to pay for his coffee, keeping eye contact with Miss Mayhew. This close, he couldn't help but notice faint shadows under her eyes. More pale tendrils fell in disarray around her face today and a spot of coal dust smudged her chin. Was something wearing her down?

"'Course we can." Annie spoke up from her position beside Claire. "And what better place to come to than a business of women to help other women in need?"

Annie's pale blue eyes glowed, as if Cyrus were a warrior hero of old come to save the day; he stood stiffly accepting their praise, his conscience pinching him miserably. Beside him, Lord Marcus crossed his arms in that loose-jointed way of his. His face, a mask of well-defined features, turned shrewd and calculating on Cyrus.

"Big supporter of women in commerce now?"

Cyrus gave Bowles a close-lipped smile. The dark-haired woman beside Lord Bowles set a delicate hand on the woman next to her. Both had to be cut from the same familial cloth: though their coloring was different, their slender noses and lush lips marked them as sisters.

"Come, Elise, we dare not keep Claire from her work." Her words came in the lavish way of a woman born to another tongue. French by the look and sound.

She faced Lucinda, tipping her chin in a most expressive way. "But, Miss Ryland, should you crave gowns of original design, my door is open to you."

The Frenchwoman's feline gaze reached out to Cyrus before returning to Lucinda.

"I'd be delighted to visit your shop, Miss Sauveterre, but I forget my manners." Lucinda touched Cyrus's arm. "Allow me to introduce my brother, Mr. Cyrus Ryland." Lucinda motioned to the woman with obsidian eyes. "Miss Juliette Sauveterre, a mantua-maker ánd her sister, Miss Elise Sauveterre." She grinned at Cyrus. "Friends of Miss Mayhew. Their shop is around the corner on Birchin Lane."

"*Je suis enchanté*, Mr. Ryland." The sisters parroted the greeting in near unison.

Cyrus tipped a bow, and Miss Elise Sauveterre, a lighter, wistful version of her sister, smiled at him open and warm, giving an altogether different greeting than her sister. She dressed simpler, but her elegant comportment came from having been born in Society's highest places. Her hands touched, fingertips to fingertips, at her waist. The way she carried herself, the more serious Miss Sauveterre could be conversing in a fine salon rather than a midtown coffee shop.

"Your sister has been telling us about the Betterment Society. What you do helping these widows, this is a good thing." Her graceful, Gallic accent was smooth as amber port. "I wish only for you to cast your net a little wider, Mr. Ryland, and help more women in need. But perhaps in due time, with someone of your unique position to champion the likes of us, much can be changed."

Cyrus tucked one hand behind his back. "My thanks for your generous words, Miss Sauveterre."

Then he averted his gaze lest he burn to ashes from the undeserved admiration shining from Miss Sauveterre's and Annie's eyes. *Champion of working women?* He shifted the load under his other arm, the gift turning more burdensome by the second.

Bowles smoothed the front of his waistcoat. "That's Cyrus, quite the dragon slayer. Always helpful to women in need."

"Come, Lord Bowles, my sister and I require your safe escort back to our shop." Miss Juliette Sauveterre slipped her hand over his sleeve, and the other Miss Sauveterre followed suit on his other sleeve. The darker Miss Sauveterre's onyx eyes settled on Cyrus. "Cornhill abounds with dangerous men these days."

Claire flashed a reproving glance at the departing Juliette. "Dangerous men, indeed," she said under her breath.

Of course the Sauveterre sisters didn't need an escort to walk around the corner. The wily Frenchwoman returned the chiding look with a dismissive shrug.

Her friend would return tonight, once the business day was done. They'd close the New Union's door, share a cup of velvety chocolate, and discuss their day. With Juliette, men always topped the list of conversation, and Mr. Cyrus Ryland made himself the prime candidate with this morning's appearance.

She regarded him with interest stoked by, of all things, a business proposition. The man was full of surprises—enough to throw a woman off balance. She wanted a day free of complications, but his appearance today added a new twist.

The shop's bustling demands brought her back to the present. Annie carried a cup of chocolate for

Miss Ryland, chattering as she walked with her to an open table. With the exodus of the others from her counter, she stood alone with a stoic Mr. Ryland. Again. He watched her quietly with a curious box under his arm.

Scooping up the coins for his coffee and his sister's chocolate, she couldn't help but *feel* his presence touching her. Her underskirts brushed sensitive thighs, as though she scandalously wore no drawers. A warm glow poured through her at being near him again. Even the heavy wooden counter made a flimsy barrier between them, failing to stop this dismaying pulse thrumming inside her.

She dropped the coins in her till, her slow exhale stirring bothersome wisps of hair gone loose from their pins. Did his attendance this morning mean he came to offer his full consent to her proprietorship of the New Union Coffeehouse, after all?

Beyond the legality of signature sheets, his nod of approval meant a great deal to her. For some reason, she wanted his complete support, and a business proposition sounded like an endorsement.

"Has this section of Cornhill become a hazardous place?" His rich voice reached her, and her face angled to meet his.

"You mean what Miss Sauveterre said?" She wiped her clean, dry hands on her apron, since she didn't have anything better to do with them. "In case you haven't noticed, my friend has a flair for the dramatic. I vow she left on the arm of the most dangerous man to lurk in midtown."

Mr. Ryland smiled at her, the corners of his eyes

crinkling nicely. "Then I'm honored that you feel safe and secure in my company."

Her heart expanded twice in size. His beautiful male smile was a shared connection for her alone, restoring the unusual familiarity they'd shared in his study. She stood taller, breathing in this vitality bouncing between them.

"Secure…" Her voice quavered faintly. "Yes, you'd protect me to the death like some gallant knight of old. I'm sure of it."

His shoulders squared under the unusual praise, and potent male satisfaction glowed from his eyes.

"But safe?" She shook her head. "Mr. Ryland, your nearness messes with my sense of purpose, causing me to stand on treacherous ground whenever I see you. You, sir, are anything but safe."

If possible, his face opened with a wider smile. He could be made of sun and stone the way his strength and authority intensified the space around them. With his large hands, large frame, and nose that had been broken a time or two, he'd never match the fine-featured appeal of Lord Bowles or men like him.

Her landlord was *not* the kind of man who attracted her. He couldn't be. He was a formidable, rough-edged man who'd come up in the world the hard way.

One look from his gray eyes, a subtle smile on those fine lips, and long-dormant parts of her stirred to life. Her body sung its own tune, persuading her to toss reason to the four winds when Cyrus Ryland stood close by. And she rather appreciated his neat, silk-wrapped queue in need of unraveling, and the shape of his sculpted mouth, a mouth that moved, speaking words…

"Miss Mayhew?" His brows pinched together. "Did you hear me?"

She blinked, snapping to attention, all the more a fool for getting lost in her musings. "Oh, I...I wasn't paying attention."

He'd been speaking to her, and she gaped at him, eyes glazed and assessing like some doxy sizing up a freshly scrubbed sailor.

"Why don't we sit down and discuss the luncheon?" He motioned to the table where his sister waited. "Surely even a busy proprietress can take a moment to sit?"

She took a bracing breath and grabbed a clean mug. "Of course."

Steady hands poured her coffee. She hoped for a moment alone before sitting down at a table with him, all the better to reorder her rampant senses.

Her morning, like the last few days, had been full of surprises, most of them unpleasant. A moment to collect herself was what she needed before shifting into this most unexpected meeting, but the dratted Mr. Ryland waited, his nearness absorbing all the air around her.

She moved around the counter, and Mr. Ryland jammed his hat under his other arm, waiting for her. His pewter eyes creased again in the corners, his warm hand enveloping hers to take the steaming stoneware. On the short walk through her narrow shop, he carried her mug and his like some attentive beau. She could carry the coffee on her own. She served multiple mugs at once throughout the day, but any protest died on her lips.

He was winning a charm battle today, she'd give him that.

She slid onto the shiny black bench, her hands curling around her cup, the singeing heat waking her mind from a numbing fog, and, oh, to sit down was heavenly. Beside her, Miss Ryland set down her chocolate, ready to take on the business at hand.

"Annie was telling me what happened to her. I can't imagine a man promising marriage, then trapping a woman into prostitution." Miss Ryland's chocolate-tinged lips made a small O.

This was good—a diverting subject that caused her to face Lucinda rather than the mind-muddling man across from her.

"It's true. There's a man in Stepney…done that to more than a few country girls. He brings them here under the guise of marriage, but the marriage certificate turns out to be false."

Mr. Ryland sat square shouldered, consuming much of the space across from her. He set the box tied with a red silk bow on the table and sipped his coffee, his eyes on her over the white rim of his cup. Surely he was aware such things went on?

She dare not divulge every detail. Miss Ryland looked to be a few years younger than her, but the young woman's manner was that of someone who lived a sheltered existence. Claire rubbed her thumb across her mug's New Union stencil, choosing her words with care.

"Annie managed to escape, but not before he gave her an awful beating," she said, keeping her voice low. "I hadn't been in London very long. I was looking to obtain a shop—" She shifted on the bench and her knee touched Mr. Ryland's. "Needless to say Annie and I found each other, and now she has honest employment here."

Mr. Ryland's gray eyes flickered—from the contact under the table?—yet he kept quiet. Her skin warmed everywhere, the attention as soft as the feel of the sun on a summer day.

Miss Ryland planted her hand on the table. "All the more reason we should serve your pastries at my luncheon, *and* I insist you attend the gathering as my honored guest."

Honored guest at Ryland House? Meaning I will walk deliberately back into the lion's den...at least one particular lion?

Claire licked her lips and of all things, Mr. Ryland's cambric cravat came into her sight line, if only for a second, before her gaze shot up to meet his. The corners of his mouth turned with hidden humor, lighting his face in the subtle way of a shared secret.

Did he see her looking at his neckwear?

"You would be most welcome." His eyes sparked with provocation.

"Of course you would," Miss Ryland echoed the sentiment, seemingly oblivious to the current flowing between Claire and her brother. "Why not talk about the hardships of women you've met? That'd make the ladies who usually attend the meetings understand this isn't about delivering baskets of jam."

Claire tapped the side of her mug. Miss Ryland was full of youthful verve. Her compassionate heart had to be sizable to want to help struggling women. Lucinda

Ryland wasn't pretty, but she sparkled with life. Thin lips and a nose too much like her brother's dominated her face, but her dark hair and vivacious manner made her distinct.

"The ladies who participate in the War Widows Betterment Society do so because they or their families seek connection with my brother, not out of any desire to help the less fortunate"—she grimaced at her brother, who took a breath, appearing ready to protest, but didn't—"and you know I speak the truth."

Miss Ryland touched Claire's arm. "But if you could share Annie's story, make them understand that these terrible things happen right here in Town."

"Crimes of all sort go on in London, wouldn't you agree, Miss Mayhew?" Mr. Ryland posed the question, his voice taciturn to his sister's energy.

Claire tucked her elbows close to her side, aware that he wasn't letting her off so easily for sneaking into his house after all. Why the veiled reference to her forgery? Why make an appearance in her shop today as though he offered his support? The well-intentioned Miss Ryland spoke in her emphatic, youthful rush, unaware of the tension.

"And just think, your baked goods served at the meeting could only be good for business…" Miss Ryland mused aloud about the menu and numbers of guests.

Under the small table, a male leg stretched, skimming Claire's skirt. She forced her attention on Miss Ryland, but from her side vision, she noticed him. Couldn't help it. He watched her like a hawk does a sparrow. Then his booted foot planted itself very close to her leg.

A spangle of awareness shot up her legs, causing her bottom to fidget on hard wood. Despite layers of underskirts, she couldn't shake the feeling of sitting before him in naught but her drawers. She nodded amicably at Miss Ryland, sipping her coffee. Was he staking territory? Goading her to accept?

His foot moved closer.

She regarded him across the table, one brow raising in challenge to his leg pressing hers. She stayed politely stiff. A masculine brow arched in response.

"I would be pleased to attend," she blurted. "And I'm happy to provide an assortment of baked goods for your luncheon. This Saturday, you say?"

Her chest and neck warmed with a flush. The bold move tossed more complications her way, among them her lack of appropriate attire for a luncheon at Ryland House. But she'd not be cowed. The meeting could be exactly what the New Union needed.

The shop door opened, and Mr. Pentree entered with a few more patrons behind him. The agent approached the table, tucking his plain black tricorne under his arm.

"It's always a pleasure to walk past your door, Miss Mayhew, if only to get a whiff of the wonderful aromas inside," he said with his customary cheer. "A sure sign of success, wouldn't you agree, Mr. Ryland?"

"To Miss Mayhew's success." Her landlord raised his mug in salute, his deep-voiced words a provocation.

Claire shot up from her seat, clutching her cup close. "Mr. Pentree, please take my seat."

Across the shop by the chalkboard, Nate jabbed Sharp Eddie on the chest. The two leaned in close, as though menacing each other. Claire rubbed her nape and walked toward the lads. She didn't want to interfere, but this was a place of business, her business. She couldn't afford to look bad with Mr. Ryland on the premises.

Nate bared his teeth at his friend. This was the second incident between the two in as many days. Thankfully, the shop's din absorbed most of their argument.

"Gentlemen, please," she admonished. "This is not the time or place."

Eddie's head whipped around, his lips curled in an ugly snarl. Claire halted mid-step. The lad from St. Giles could be a cornered beast. His breath came heavy…from rage or running from the docks, she couldn't say, but he thrust a wrinkled page at her.

"Here. News from Tower Wharf." Eddie jammed his cap on unruly hair. "I'll come back later to collect my ha'pennies."

The youth banged a chair in his hasty departure, and Nate skulked into the kitchen.

Outside, a tempest of a different kind blustered; gentlemen walked past her window gripping their coats. A storm was coming. Her day held enough turmoil; she need not get between Nate and Eddie.

Claire set down her mug and smoothed the foolscap. Unexpected troubles came of late…conflict between the runners…a late delivery of flour…bad sugar… spoiled coffee beans she had to toss and then purchase more at a higher price…a basket of eggs crashed on the floor twice this week…and the cost of spices…

She rubbed her neck, a dull ache forming there and

in her shoulders. Doubts crept in, sometimes crashing over her, leaving her pummeled and bruised despite her best efforts.

"Trouble with the lads?"

She whirled around, her hand still on her neck.

Her unwavering landlord stood there, hat and box in hand.

"I'm sure it's nothing," she said, her tone over-bright. "Things are going along quite well here."

"I could see that by the way Mr. Fincher's friend stormed out of here."

She chafed at his droll tone, yet for a long second wanted to lean on him, test those capable shoulders. Would that make her less competent, finding shelter in a man, if only for a moment? She was strong of mind and body. She stood on her own two feet, but part of her craved rest from the tedium that wore a soul down to the nub.

Her hands slipped into her apron pockets, and she decided against any naked admission of need.

"Mr. Ryland, on your first visit to my shop, you questioned my accounts. Now do you plan to inspect how I manage the messengers?" She was being a little tetchy, but that assessment of his touched a sore spot. "As long as I pay my rent come Friday, whatever else happens is no concern of yours."

He cracked a smile. "Not afraid to put me in my place, are you?"

"As in reminding you that you're my landlord and you've no business giving me such commentary? I'm happy to. I doubt you share your opinions with the *male* proprietors who rent from you."

Frayed nerves and a morning fraught with mishaps put her on edge. To admit this to him would be akin to acknowledging a chink in her shopkeeper's armor. She wasn't choosing her words with care but let them flow nonetheless.

"Duly noted, Miss Mayhew. I admit I haven't changed my mind on this venture of yours," he asserted. "At the table, even you acknowledged the dangers preying on women in London. At least my sister's business proposition must prove some goodwill during this trial period."

She heard him, but her vision caught on the curious red ribbon. Ryland glanced at the box under his arm, his stance relaxing.

"This is the other reason for my visit today," he said quietly, holding out the wooden box. "It's for you."

Her gaze snapped up to his. "For me?"

Claire reached out, accepting the gift with cautious hands. She hefted the box gingerly up and down, checking the sides.

He chuckled. "I promise there's no viper inside."

"You bought me a ledger, didn't you?" Her tone lacked all enthusiasm. A rectangular account book could fit inside the box. So would a shoe.

"If I did, you must agree a ledger would do you good." His brows slammed together, a small vertical line forming above his nose. "But you won't know until you open it."

Claire took a step closer, clutching the box between them. She could never stand nose to nose with him— her head reached him mid-chest—but something about being in Mr. Ryland's presence enlivened her. She welcomed whatever he offered, same as she welcomed the small revelations that came to her about this man.

Wasn't a gift of an account book a step in the right direction? She should be grateful, but looking again at the coming storm outside her shop opened her to a new notion.

"I thank you for the gift, Mr. Ryland, but it'd be more truthful to say I think I've just figured you out."

"Have you, now?"

"Yes." She nodded, warming up to her discovery. "You actually enjoy telling women what to do, giving them the full weight of your opinion."

Ryland clasped his hands behind his back, appearing to ponder what she said. "The full weight of my opinion."

"Oh, yes. Some men bluster on about duty, issuing orders to their wives, daughters, or sisters"—she dropped her voice and gave him a pointed look—"their mistresses. But you, *you* take joy in the task."

"And what if I do?" he drawled. "Is it bad to want to take care of a woman?"

"Take care of a woman?" Light laughter bubbled up from her. "Therein lies our dilemma: how you and I define what that means."

Her body quickened, invigorating every limb. Standing up to him, speaking her mind, freed her, almost erasing the rough morning. But his reaction baffled her. He didn't bristle at all from her pronouncement. Rather, unsettling, natural power emanated from his eyes, as deep a gray as calm winter seas.

Did Mr. Ryland feed off their exchange?

She wouldn't find the answer because the caustic smell of burning baked goods reached her nose.

"Oh, the tarts," Annie cried and sprinted from her place behind the counter.

Weight settled again on Claire's shoulders, reminding her she was a woman of business, not leisure. Beyond her front window, a black conveyance fitted with polished brass trim came to a halt. The demands of the day pulled her in one direction, taking Mr. Ryland in another.

"Your carriage," she said, looking past him to the front window. "It's here."

He put on his hat. "Yes, there's a cistern that apparently needs the full weight of my opinion this morning."

A hiccup of laughter escaped her, and Mr. Ryland's mouth twitched with restrained humor. Claire's hand dropped to her side, tautness setting in as she looked from her empty chalkboard to the kitchen.

"And the morning news will have to wait, since there's a dilemma in my kitchen."

Ever the gentleman, Mr. Ryland bowed his leave.

"Until we meet again, Miss Mayhew." He glanced at the gift she held. "Please. Don't wait long to open the box."

Six

They are at the end of the gallery, retired to their tea and scandal, according to their ancient custom...

William Congreve, *The Double Dealer*

TURBULENCE HAD ARRIVED AT THE NEW UNION Coffeehouse in the form of man and nature. Outside, a quilt of clouds covered midtown skies. Seated at her humble table, Claire witnessed these changes through a small window in her room above the shop where she sat with the unopened gift.

Throughout the day, Mr. Ryland's broad-shouldered presence had taunted her every time she glanced at the box. Now the workday was done, and her excuses for not opening his gift dwindled to none. She wanted a quiet evening free of the tumult of men and mistakes, but the glossy red ribbon incited a tempest.

She liked storms, welcomed the thrilling feel of them. Her father had instilled a love for seasonal rhythms; rain quenched nature's thirst and washed the land clean. Their shared connection, a love for the beauty of the outdoors, was something she missed.

Her fall from grace had disappointed her exacting father, as did her recent bid for independence. Some women grew up with spirited backbones from birth. Claire, however, was late to blossom, developing her strong spine after tripping over the consequences of a poor choice. In time, she learned standing up for oneself, while freeing, came at a cost.

She wiped the cloudy mist off her small window as Juliette came through the doorway. Her friend dropped her pattens, the outer shoes worn to protect her leather shoes from Cornhill's mud and mire. The Frenchwoman came bearing gifts of fresh baked bread, the floury sweet aroma filling the garret.

"Elise will not join us this night. She wishes again to read about ancient dead men." She adjusted her black-and-gold shawl. "The *belle lettres, non*? All very refined and intelligent, I'm sure."

The twist of Juliette's lips showed her distaste for an evening alone with fine, intelligent literature.

Claire wrapped her hands around her mug. "And you cannot wait to sink your teeth into talk about live men."

"Such as your Mr. Ryland," Juliette said, sauntering across the room, a basket dangling from her fingers. "I'd heard he was big, but I did not know he was an *appealing* man to behold."

Claire frowned, not liking the twinge of discomfort at her friend's interest in Mr. Ryland. "I thought you only entertained thoughts of titled gentlemen?"

Juliette shrugged off the question, her dark eyes

lighting with pleasure on the cup of chocolate
awaiting her on the table. She stood beside Claire
and pulled back the cloth cover on the basket,
revealing a loaf of gold-brown bread and a variety
of cheeses.

"My sister and her fascination with men of intel-
lect…be they dead or not. Why waste time on a man
who can do nothing for a woman?" She set the basket
on the floor and folded herself into the opposite chair,
shivering like a child tasting a bad lemon. "Nor do
I understand how you like these storms as you do.
London is so cold and damp."

Juliette curled one leg beneath her, revealing a neat
ankle under the hems of plush silk underskirts. Black
and gold rosettes scattered across the shimmering
fabric, connected by twisting green vines.

"Scarlet underskirts today?" Claire sipped her
chocolate, her gaze skimming Juliette's demure outer
charcoal gown. "I'm sure you could wear something
brighter than your current mode, something to match
your underskirts."

As a nod to her old life, the Frenchwoman
wore fine petticoats and the latest cuts in fashion,
but she dressed in drab colors when women came
for fittings.

"And expect to keep my midtown clientele?
Humph. These midtown Englishwomen. They are…"
Her tapered fingers fluttered. "What is the word I
seek? *Boring*?"

Claire grinned. "*Somber* or *of sober character* would
be better."

The stylish Miss Sauveterre had not mastered the

King's English with quite the same talent as her well-read older sister.

Juliette rolled her eyes. "I *know* boring. That is the right word, but as you say the *somber* matrons of midtown would not like their mantua-maker dressed so provocatively." Her brows rose with suggestion. "Such as the blue-and-silver creation I restored for you...would gain too much male attention, *non*?"

"That was a courtesan's gown that you altered for me," she said, biting back laughter. "My breasts almost fell out."

"Of course they would." Juliette slapped the table, laughing. "That is the idea. All the better to lure a man. A certain man, in fact, who dresses well for a rustic."

Obsidian eyes sparkled at Claire. Juliette embraced life with passion despite her darker circumstances of recent years. Her quick expanse of emotions could be startling at times, which made her skill with needle and thread all the more stunning. The work she did exhibited patient, detailed talent few possessed.

Juliette tapped the box pushed against the window. "And the fact of a gift appearing from a certain man tells me my gown worked some kind of magic." Lush, Gallic lips pressed together before she added with less enthusiasm, "And you are very lovely too. There is that."

Claire stifled a smile at the grudging compliment. Juliette Sauveterre preferred to be the most desired woman in any room, but her unexpected friendship was supportive and true, sometimes even zealous the way she prodded Claire to be daring.

She had conspired with Claire about sneaking into the masked ball and forging Mr. Ryland's signature. The Frenchwoman went as far as to orchestrate certain details, waiting patiently at midnight for Claire in a hack off Piccadilly that fated night.

"If I had known the nature of Mr. Ryland's appeal, I would have volunteered to seek his signature myself." Juliette's accent curled around each word. "And we would not have emerged from his study for days."

"He could still evict me, and here you are concerned with matters of a sensual nature."

"*Exactement.*" Juliette sighed, putting the cup's rim to her bottom lip, hiding half her wicked smile. "Makes me wish my shop sat on Cornhill instead of Birchin Lane. But he is taken with you. This much is true."

Taken with me?

She wanted to dig into that idea, but Juliette set her stoneware on the table with a decisive knock on wood.

"And his gift would've been opened long ago if I were you."

Juliette slid the box to the center of the table, her eyes glinting with curiosity when a clamor sounded from below. Claire's narrow door was wide open. She rose from her chair, her shoe heels tapping bare plank floors. Standing in the doorway, she looked downstairs where soft light glowed from the kitchen.

"Nate? Is anything wrong?" she called.

There was a quiet pause, a scrape of wood against wood, footsteps.

"Knocked over a chair's all. 'Bout done with the mopping, then I'll take my leave." Nate's voice carried across the shop. "Miss Mayhew, be sure to lock up after me."

He didn't poke his head around the corner from the kitchen. He had to be near the shop's front door, ready to toss out the old mop water. Nate wouldn't want to walk across wet floors he'd just cleaned.

"Very well. See you in the morning." She grinned at his admonishing tone.

Threatening rain clouds drove most souls indoors. The door's lock would be attended to later. Besides, damp air meant the floors would dry slowly, and Juliette's inviting bread and cheese—fine fare for the unmarried women of midtown—needed some attention first.

An icy draft wrapped around her ankles, all the more reason to shut the door and put coals on the grate to warm her small abode. Juliette chattered on about one of the ladies she had fitted today, and Claire tried to focus but only half listened. She scooped out the porous black chunks from a bucket with a small shovel, careful to seek the smallest pieces, saving the larger ones for cooking and heating the shop tomorrow.

"Are you digging for gold?" Juliette's fingers drummed the table.

Claire lifted her dark blue shawl from a wall peg and wrapped the wool around her shoulders. As tempting as the box was, other, weightier issues played in her mind.

Money. Or the lack of it.

"There's something I need to tell you." She sat across from Juliette again, leaning her elbows on the table. "I have to sell my necklace—tomorrow—if I'm going to make Friday's rent *and* pay all the notes due. I don't think I have enough with what I've made each day."

"Already?" Juliette gasped. "It's the cabinetmaker, *non*? The thief charged you twice what he should for tables and benches. You should never have given him a rush request."

"It's not that." Claire pulled her shawl tighter. "I haven't kept close attention to my spending. The bad coffee beans…the cost of spices has gone up, Annie's taking longer to master the recipes, burning too many baked goods…" Her voice trailed off. "Everything has added up to be more than I expected."

"These troubles are why you were so"— Juliette's face clouded a brief second—"ah…*distracted* today?" Her lips pursed. "Then it is good you have the necklace."

"Yes, except I thought I wouldn't need to sell it this soon. Mr. Ryland was right on one score," she said archly. "I do need to track my funds better."

Juliette nudged the box closer to Claire. "Or perhaps he has something for you, something that will solve all your problems."

Claire examined the wood grain of the simple box, his gift to her. "I don't want a man to solve my problems."

"But a dalliance would do you good. Put color in your cheeks."

"I find it amusing, Miss Sauveterre, how you have

no problem mastering English words alluding to sexual congress," she teased. "And a man putting color in my cheeks got me into considerable trouble in the past, remember?"

That earned her a disapproving moue. Juliette waved her hand dramatically.

"So, your Mr. Ryland wants to get under your skirts. Getting lost in mindless sensual pleasure? *Humph*. What a hardship." Dark eyes flashed at Claire. "Just open it."

"I'm guessing he gave me an account book." Claire pulled on the red silk. "Or could be he's returning my shoe in some grand gesture."

She unwound the ribbon and let the silk drop to the table. Her fingers caressed the box's smooth wood—walnut, by the grain and soft brown color. Someone had lovingly crafted the small chest. Was this a jewelry box? Juliette's dark head bent close, but Claire turned the hinged side toward her friend. She wished suddenly to open the box in private. Too late for that now.

The last gift she opened from a man was the necklace from Jonathan, then heir to the Greenwich earldom. His gift was a form of penance…payment, for taking her virginity with the false promise of marriage.

And then deserting her to attend ladies who made better candidates to be his wife.

Yet, for all the pain of her past, she couldn't imagine Cyrus Ryland giving a woman false promises. He was too blunt for that.

And then she raised the lid.

She gasped. One hand touched her lips. "Strawberries," she said, her voice featherlight.

Bright red, the tempting flesh, shiny and plump with tiny, vivid green leaves. Inside, a folded missive rested atop the pile of luscious fruit.

"Strawberries?" Juliette angled her head for a better view.

Juliette studied her and the red berries likely trying to gauge Claire's reaction to the unusual gift. Her friend must have expected something hard and glittering, stones of the expensive variety, not something soft and temporal, or unique and personal as a favored fruit.

Claire lifted a single, plump strawberry to her nose, smelling the sweet fragrance; satisfaction filled her, as desirable as the delicious aroma. Taking a slow bite, she savored the crunch of what had to be the product of Mr. Ryland's hothouse, since strawberry season was over for the rest of England.

Juice squished, and she licked her lips. Most of the berries were intact, with a few slightly damaged from their sojourn to her table.

What this meant went far beyond a box of fruit.

The ball. Her delight at the bowl of strawberries.

He remembered.

For a man to carry with him a small, personal detail of a woman's happiness and then act on it?

One hand touched the exposed skin below her collarbone. Those storm-gray eyes of his saw too much. She pulled her shawl tighter about her shoulders, but no amount of cloth could cover her from being bared to him. What other intimate details did Cyrus Ryland store away about her?

Her spirits lightened with this startling revelation, but Juliette flopped back in her chair, bemused.

"There is a note. A billet-doux, perhaps," Juliette suggested, pointing at the small folded paper. "Aren't you going to read it?"

Claire set down the half-eaten berry and unfolded the note. Outside, light rain dropped from the heavens, tapping her window. The words on paper were few and personal and as devastating as the surprise of the strawberries.

"Oh my," she murmured, holding the paper close for privacy.

She didn't expect flowery, poetic language, but his words reached out, brushing tender, feminine places with shocking, seductive intent. She read and reread the brief missive to make sure she hadn't missed his meaning. But with Cyrus Ryland, blunt was best.

"Aren't you going to let me see?" Juliette's voice pitched higher.

Claire set the sheet on the table so both could view the note's single line. Juliette's lips moved while she read the message under her breath.

I find your forbidden fruit most desirable of all.

Cyrus

Seven

Uncertainty and expectation are the joys of life. Security is an insipid thing.

William Congreve, *Love for Love*

THE NECKLACE WAS GONE.

Claire rubbed her forehead, pushing back her mobcap. This had to be a mistake. She missed the baubles somewhere amongst the roasted coffee beans.

Look again.

She stood on tiptoe at her counter, digging deeper in the ceramic jar. Hard, roasted coffee beans trickled through her fingers, but the pale aquamarine stones failed to show. She looked wildly around the shop, not more than a dozen patrons sat within the brick walls, sipping their midday brew.

Did someone take them?

Frantic hands dumped the weighty, earthen vessel upside down. Brown beans clattered across the counter and some fell to the floor.

Inside the jar? Nothing.

Numb, she stared into the distance, grateful for the counter holding her up. Rain blew across Cornhill, squalls of wetness smearing the front window. Outside, a few brave souls traversed midtown, hunched blurs holding down their hats as they passed her shop.

The front window. Yesterday.

Nate and Mr. Ryland. The flash of a gold coin passed between them.

Did Mr. Ryland pay Nate to steal her necklace?

She inhaled, a sharp hiss of breath. Last night…the noise below stairs. Was that when Nate searched for her modest jewels? Her pile of bad news kept growing. Everything turned bleaker without the necklace to pay her rent, the notes due. How would she secure her future?

A harsh laugh caught in her throat. Her future wouldn't matter if she ended up languishing in debtor's prison.

Her mind bounced between encroaching fear and mounting evidence. A tumble of facts buzzed around her head, working to lay themselves in a neat but unforgiving line.

Nate failed to show up today. Noon had come and gone. Where was he?

He'd mentioned a time or two a life of thievery in St. Giles, "small and insignificant thefts" he'd called them, the kind where no one ever got hurt. Recalling those words, she laughed darkly. A few patrons turned their heads her way before going back to their conversations.

Could such a thing be true? Crimes done, transgressions committed…and no one gets hurt?

But the dear lad had started *here*, working hard, making a new life for himself. Claire rubbed her forehead, her face crumpling when she looked to her rain-splattered window.

"Oh, Nate, how could you?" she whispered.

An aching throb started where her fingers made slow circles. Everything hit her, a spin of too much to absorb all at once. But she had to. And top among her problems? Nate's theft. His betrayal of her trust hurt just as much as the knowledge that he'd gone back to his old life.

And the cascade of thoughts kept pouring over her.

Her forgery.

Mr. Ryland's staunch belief an unmarried woman had no business being in business, putting out her own shingle.

Her mouth twisted. And there was his wish to get under her skirts.

Did Mr. Ryland use his money and influence with Nate? Did he think he'd back her into a corner? And in a desperate state she'd say yes to anything he asked of her?

If she put the parts together correctly, her landlord lured a young man scraping by, striving for a better life. Of course the temptation would be too much.

She didn't know what hurt worse: bitter disappointment in finding Mr. Ryland to be dishonorable or Nate breaking her heart by choosing to return to his old way of life.

Oh, the choice words she'd have for Mr. Ryland.

"I say, Miss Mayhew, are you well?" a male voice spoke, pulling her from the fog.

Claire blinked, refocusing on the space in front of her. A florid face framed by an outdated, gray yarn wig, the wig of her most steady patron.

"Mr. Cogsworth," she said, brushing coffee beans away from the counter's edge.

"Having a fit of the vapors?" His hoary brows twitched. "Perhaps a rest would do you good."

Dear Mr. Cogsworth, a good man and an energetic trader, married almost thirty years and raised five daughters. He'd likely seen the vapors a time or two, but this wasn't a fainting spell about to happen.

"Thank you, sir, but I'm fine." She gave him a brittle smile.

Mr. Cogsworth's slack eyelids drooped all the more. The dear man didn't believe her one second, but he nodded briskly, allowing her false assurance.

"Then let me help clean this up." He scooped beans back into the container, flashing wary looks at her now and then.

His smile, marked by a gap between front teeth, had become a welcome sight every day. Some men could be counted on in life, sturdy and dependable. Men like Mr. Cogsworth. Together, they had most of the counter cleaned when Annie appeared from the kitchen with a large plate of warm biscuits. Her shoes crunched beans on the floor.

"Gor, Miss Mayhew, what happened here?" Annie put the plate down and grabbed the broom leaning against the brick wall.

Claire poured a fresh cup of coffee for Mr. Cogsworth, her mind spinning with what to do next. The stack of notes was due at the end of the week…

three days from now. What was she going to do about that? She had no clue, but one small act of kindness deserved another, thus she slipped biscuits on a plate for her most faithful patron.

"For your thoughtful assistance, Mr. Cogsworth."

"If there's anything I can do for you, Miss Mayhew," he said, balancing his plate and mug in both hands.

Mr. Cogsworth lingered, his heavy jowls clenching and unclenching as though he wanted to say more. She turned her attention to the road outside her shop, stone-like resolve forming a plan.

"There is one thing," she said, her voice level. "I need a hack. Would you fetch one for me? I've an urgent errand."

Mr. Cogsworth cast a hesitating glance at the storm beyond the front window. He mumbled something placating but did her bidding and set his mug and plate on his table. The trader girded himself against the storm, his stare beetling from her to the turbulence outside before he sought the door. Claire whipped her cloak off its peg and wrapped herself inside thin wool, insufficient armor against the tempest, but it would have to do.

Annie swept the coffee bean mess into a tidy pile. Her pale blue eyes bulged under her mobcap when Claire scooped a handful of coins from the till and dumped them in her apron pocket.

She nearly cleaned out her funds.

Then, she produced an iron key from her other pocket.

"Annie, I need you to mind the shop." The key

dangled by a makeshift cheesecloth ribbon. "I don't know how long I'll be."

She fixed the hood on her head, preparing for the turmoil ahead.

❧

The hack sped through London, pressing full force against the storm. Last night's friendly clouds had turned angry, dousing those brave souls who dared to march against the watery tumult. Claire was mutinous enough to set her face against the gray wind and wet. She would save her shop, her independence, and if she could, she'd rescue one errant, green-eyed lad who'd won a soft spot in her heart.

How these tasks would be accomplished was the murky dilemma she hadn't quite worked out yet.

The ride to the West End was perilous through near-empty streets, but less so than what would happen once she arrived at her destination. Number Four Bow Street was conveniently situated for her needs, but that wasn't her first stop.

A certain residence in Piccadilly was first on her order of business.

The hack's wheels had barely rolled to a stop in the horseshoe drive when she sprung from the seat and paid the driver. In front of her, the ashlar edifice of Ryland House matched its stone-hearted owner: each limestone piece had been cut and stacked into rigid, unbending lines, creating an unshakable structure.

Time someone changed that.

Her upset had failed to cool on the long wet ride; rather, the journey from midtown to Ryland House firmed her resolve all the more to hold fast to what was hers. Claire charged up the steps, stomping through puddles.

She pounded the brass lion's head knocker three times, wind and rain whipping her skirts. Impatient, she curled her fist and banged thrice on the heavy wooden door for good measure. Pain bit her knuckles. The sting could be a slap on the hand, reminding her what happens to women who put their trust in the wrong man, a man who promised to give her a fair chance.

How many times would she repeat this lesson?

Today, she'd fight back.

Fist poised to smite the portal again, the indigo-lacquered door opened. The butler's staid eyes narrowed at the sight of sodden, furious female on his master's doorstep. Belker. She knew of him from her days in service.

"Yes?" The implacable butler's mouth drooped.

"I'm here to see Mr. Ryland. Now," she said, cool rain dripping down her cheeks.

"Mr. Ryland's indisposed to unannounced guests at the moment, I'm afraid…" His sonorous voice trailed off when she pushed past him.

"Then he ought to *dispose* himself rather quickly, or I shall have his friends from Bow Street on his heels."

At the mention of the thief takers, Belker's lax eyes rounded. Aside from impudence and interruptions, the only thing a man in his position despised more in life was a whiff of scandal settling its odorous cloud over the house he served. His status put him squarely as the first line of defense.

Claire's heels struck the marble floor with

determined snaps. She raced to the far end of the entry hall, her head turning from one set of double doors to another. The well-lit Ryland house wasted too many candles in her opinion: light underscored each door. She cocked her ear, catching the hum of Mr. Ryland's voice layered among others somewhere in the vicinity.

"Where is he?" She whipped around, her hood falling back. "Are you going to tell me, Belker, or do I have to open every door to find him?"

"Miss Mayhew," the butler's stern voice rose. "As someone once in service, you know very well this impudence of yours is poorly done."

Belker stared at her as though she'd lost her mind, his polished shoes rooted to the floor.

So he knew of her.

There'd been gossip from other servants who patronized the New Union Coffeehouse. Some admired her, but others viewed her as an upstart, a female leaving the secure world of servitude not for stabilizing matrimony but for an independent life in business. The butler's appeal to the common bond upper household servants shared wouldn't work.

She shot off toward one set of double doors and flung them wide open to find a team of footmen setting a long table with the utmost care. Each man was a study in pristine, blue-and-white livery topped with blinding-white periwigs. A few of them patronized her coffee shop on their half days.

"Thomas, would you be so kind as to tell me where Mr. Ryland is?"

He blinked at her, straightening from the waist. "He's entertaining guests in the royal drawing room."

His white-gloved hand pointed the direction. "Let me take you, miss."

"You will do no such thing, Thomas." Belker spoke in her periphery. "See Miss Mayhew to the door before she causes further disruption."

But the butler's nervous glance at a certain pair of gilt-edged doors flanked by effusive ferns gave the secret away. Before the ever polite Thomas got any closer, she sped to those doors and yanked them wide open.

A beautiful assemblage filled the well-appointed drawing room, sitting in clustered tableaus of color and perfection. One by one, their faces turned her way, all conversation fading. Her labored breaths made a conspicuous sound in the cavernous room.

She was an earthly rebel invading a gathering at Mount Olympus.

A dark-haired, violet-eyed goddess held court in the middle, her plum skirts spread wide. The lady spied Claire, her eyes turning to feline slits, but the Marquis of Northampton, who sat beside her, gaped.

A small, older man spoke to two young men of university age. His eyes were cold and colorless under the bob wig framing a thin face. The two younger men he spoke with bore the stamp of Ryland lineage. One of them smiled at Claire, his mouth curling in the same arrogant way as Mr. Ryland's.

Apparently not all of Olympus resented her intrusion.

Lucinda Ryland held a dish of tea aloft, her mouth a perfect O. Miss Ryland briefly gawked at Claire, and then turned to look at the opposite end of the room.

Claire followed the young woman's line of vision to the commanding form standing with another broad-shouldered young man by the windows.

Cyrus.

Heaven help her, she didn't need anyone to alert her to him. She'd find that man the way desperate sailors seek a lighthouse. Despite the storm, afternoon light haloed him like some sort of Greek god come down to trifle with mere mortals. With those infernal broad shoulders and glowing, slate-gray eyes, Cyrus Ryland dominated her senses, touching her most feminine places.

His nostrils flared. Was he scenting her? The notion was ridiculous, given their distance and the circumstances, but Claire settled a hand on her stomach, quashing the flutter.

He could very well have said aloud to the silent room: *She belongs with me.*

And his dangerous draw turned her legs, her resolve to jelly. She was woefully out of her depth, swimming in waters she had no business being in.

Mr. Ryland strode toward the open doors, confident as ever, greeting her like a tardy guest, not some rain-drenched, midtown proprietress with flour dusting her skirt.

"Miss Mayhew, a pleasure to see you." He came an inch closer than courtesy dictated, blocking out the others behind him. "You will join us."

He spoke in an authoritative tone, his close-lipped smile as smooth as you please. Standing this close, she took her fill of his tantalizing, clean smell. Plain soap must've earlier lathered his freshly shaved jaw, where a new thumbprint-sized bruise marked him.

She pushed wet hair off her face. "I will not, unless you care to include your friends from Bow Street." Her trembling voice dropped lower. "I'm sure they'd like to know about *your* thievery."

Belker and a pair of footmen hovered outside the doorway. "I'm very sorry, sir—"

Mr. Ryland raised a halting hand to the butler, his eyes narrowing on her. "What are you talking about?"

She opened her mouth to respond, but the quick-thinking host clamped her elbow, steering her firmly from the doorway into the entry hall. Mr. Ryland looked to the butler and tipped his head toward the drawing room.

"Luncheon. Take care of it."

Those words were sufficient. The servants flew into action, which made Claire wonder: Did Ryland House receive distraught females on a regular basis?

There'd be no time to delve into that question. He guided her across the entry hall and down the royal-blue hallway, toward his familiar study. When they entered, she got a daytime eyeful of his study.

Few books lined the shelves of the plain blue-and-gray room. Worn-out folios, the spines cracked and losing color, lined shelves built into the wall. The room thankfully was well lit and warm, with enticing charcoal embers glowing from the hearth.

He led her straight to the familiar chintz-covered settee, but his gaze swept her from head to toe.

"You're drenched."

"A very astute observation since I traveled here in a storm."

His brows slammed together at her sarcasm, causing a

small, vertical line above his nose, but he bent his powerful frame, pulling one side of the settee close to the grate.
Mr. Ryland adjusted the heavy furniture as easily as one
might move a small chair. Then he pointed to the seat.

"You'll want to sit here, closest to the heat."

She looked from the inviting spot back to him. Oh,
no, the greater heat frothed between them.

"I shall stand, thank you."

"Don't be ridiculous." The lines around his mouth
tightened. "And give me your cloak. We'll hang it
here to dry."

She was about to tell Mr. Ryland the purpose of her
unannounced visit when a chill snaked up her skirts,
reminding her not to be a fool. With a rain-splattered
cloak and her soaked hems plastered to her ankles,
practical wisdom won. The cloak came off.

"I'm not staying long." She stretched out her arm,
keeping their proximity to a minimum.

Male lips curved, suppressing a smile at her staunch
effort to maintain some distance. Mr. Ryland accepted
the cloak, his warm, dry hands covering her icy fingers
in the exchange.

His gray stare fixed on her. "Now, what's this
thievery you're talking about?"

He hooked the cloak's hood on a stone carving
sitting atop the mantel. The comfortable seat beckoned her to sit by the orange and amber coals. What
needed saying could be done as much in comfort as
discomfort. Why be miserable in the process?

Claire sidled over to the proffered accommodation,
and waves of cozy warmth touched her frigid ankles,
going bone deep. A sigh of satisfaction slipped.

"I speak of my necklace. Stolen." She inched her puddle-soaked shoes closer to the hearth. "By you."

"Steal your necklace?" He set one hand at his waist and chuckled, a rasping, ill-humored noise. "You forget. Between the two of us, *you're* the criminal here."

She winced at the undeniable fact but pressed on, meeting his hard examination. The man would not run roughshod over her today. She scooted to the edge of the seat, her chin tipping higher.

"What you did was, was the lowest...the vilest thing."

"I repeat: I did not steal your necklace." His arms spread wide. "I don't need it."

Ryland spoke in even, practical tones. His calmness and straightforward demeanor chipped away at her certainty.

"Of course you don't *need* a necklace," she retorted. "But you'd take it. Just to prove your point. To make sure a woman alone doesn't succeed in business."

"I'm not hard-pressed to prove my point." His voice was dry as sand. "Nor do I spend my days pondering the activities of proprietors who rent from me. Either they succeed or they don't. You have the same opportunity as everyone else."

She smarted from his words. Was everything so decided with him? The way he studied her, she guessed her landlord worked the facts in his head, calculating fluidly from one scenario to another.

"Let's take this one step at a time, shall we?" He hefted around a wide leather chair and sat down, facing her. "I don't want your necklace, Miss Mayhew. I want you."

Pleasure skittered over her, the sensation like tiny pebbles skipping softly down her body.

Those simple three words—*I want you*—suspended clear thinking. A drop of water trickled down the side of her cheek. She swiped her hand over her face if for no other reason than a reprieve from an intent male.

"If I can't sell the necklace, paying my notes, the rent…" Her voice trailed off.

"Do you understand? If I wanted to coerce you into my bed, I would've pushed the matter of the forgery." He leaned his forearms on his thighs, meeting her at her eye level. "But I didn't."

Her courage burst, sinking underfoot from his honest words. And of all things, another flare of attraction sparked, seesawing with her present dilemma. Mr. Ryland spoke in the confident way of a man used to being taken at his word. Clear, gray eyes opened wide to her. Nor did he wax long, attempting to convince her of his innocence.

Why should he?

He told her the truth. She knew it in her bones.

Her chin dropped to her chest. The devil she knew seemed manageable, but the alternative carried starker, more dismal consequences. Uncertainty shifted the earth. She braced her hands on the cushion on both sides of her hips.

"I didn't want to believe Nate would steal from me. I thought you paid him to take the necklace for your own purposes." She looked up at him again, small-voiced worry sucking the air out of her lungs. "Yesterday…the gold coin you gave him…"

Ryland's eyes flickered at the mention of the gold

coin, but he said nothing. She rushed on, explaining Nate's odd absence, his hints of past thievery, but Mr. Ryland listened, emotionless as one gathering information. He didn't react at all when she mentioned Nate's scurrilous youth in St. Giles.

And he listened, truly listened, to everything she had to say.

"Circumstances may point to Mr. Fincher as the culprit, but I don't believe he stole from you. There has to be some other explanation." Large, warm hands reached for hers. Mr. Ryland cosseted her frigid fingers, rubbing away the cold. "But the more important issue, you aren't safe there. A woman alone above a shop. You can't stay—"

"I'll be fine." Her hands pulled free, and she started rocking on her seat.

There was no time to debate with him what a woman should or shouldn't do. Her problems were bigger than that. She looked around the room, blinking hard.

"But the shop...I have to pay the cabinetmakers seven pounds by Friday, the potter two pounds for the cups and plates, Annie still needs her wages..." She tugged the bothersome mobcap off her head. "And the rent..."

Hairpins dropped to the cushion, and more blond strands fell loose around her face. Her hair had become a bedraggled mess, its damp weight hanging on her neck. Quick fingers worked the flimsy mobcap into a ball while outside a rumble of thunder sounded.

Mr. Ryland plucked the cap from her. "I'll waive this quarter's rent and give you a loan for the rest."

Her gaze shot up to meet his. The light played stronger on one side of his face, casting a shadow on the other.

"And you expect nothing in return?"

Mr. Ryland's bluntness must've rubbed off on her.

His head tipped with minute acknowledgment. "There are many things I want, but when you come to me, it will be of your own free will. Money will not be something between us."

She couldn't help the sharp burst of laughter. "A bit sure of yourself, Mr. Ryland. What makes you think I'll come to you?"

His modulated tone told her one thing: the notion of holding something over her head to get what he wanted had crossed his mind, at least with her forgery.

"In here, it's Cyrus, remember?" His deep voice was smooth and assured. "And I'm confident because you're the one fighting our obvious attraction."

Small tremors of pleasure shook her. Her body, it would seem, had already turned mutinous, ready to set sail for the deep, gray waters of the unwavering Cyrus Ryland.

"Then you have a long time to wait." But her words held no bite.

She hugged herself, rubbing her hands up and down her arms. This spot by the fire would be a perfect place to curl into a tight ball and block out the day's troubles.

Cyrus removed his fine blue coat, the slide of cloth on cloth an inviting sound to her benumbed senses.

"You're not warming up sufficiently." He leaned in and wrapped his coat over her shoulders, his deep voice like an intimate connection. "Someone needs to take care of you."

She shuddered when his breath tickled her ear. His warmth and nearness was just as heavenly as what he draped around her. She could tell he found her refusal more amusing than deterring. Cyrus closed the coat in front of her, his body heat palpable inside. The collar's woven broadcloth brushed her rain-misted cheeks, his pleasant scent on the cloth. The coat was part of an expensive, well-tailored ditto suit: identical blue fabric with spare gold trim on the coat, waistcoat, and breeches.

"I'll ruin part of a perfectly good suit." But she pulled the coat tighter, greedy for the snug feel.

He added more coal to the blaze. The inferno's orange light danced across white cotton stretched over his shoulders. Muscles moved under the fabric, mesmerizing her while he built a hotter fire. And then there was his offer to waive her rent and give her a loan, an offer apparently free of *unique* requirements. His act of generosity pinched her conscience.

How dare he be so...nice.

"About the rent, the loan, I cannot accept your kind offer." She cleared her throat, trying to sound competent. "I'll find a way."

Ryland glanced at her but said nothing to counter her refusal. Instead, he dropped to the floor, kneeling before her. Without asking her leave, he removed one shoe and then the other, and set the soaked footwear against the hearth's ash pan.

"What are you doing?" Her words, like her body, went slack, all of her too worn down.

His head bent close to her knee. One hand, large and warm, curled around her ankle, rubbing life back into her foot. A big, masculine palm moved under the arch, creating delightful friction. She pressed her lips together, holding back a moan of pleasure.

"I would think a land steward's daughter would know wet clothes are hazardous for one's health." He flashed a devilish grin. "You ought to remove your wet clothes, cover yourself with something warm and dry."

Such as covering myself with you.

The way the corners of his eyes creased, she was certain what crossed her mind crossed his, but the tantalizing attention to her foot wore down her resolve.

Why argue with a man delivering such mind-melting attention?

Her laughter was skittish. "You're the only hazard to my existence, Mr. Ryland. And thank you, but my clothes will stay right where they are."

"Cyrus," he reminded her, but his playfulness morphed into concern. "At least, we need to get these wet stockings off. Your lips are quivering."

Could that be from you touching me in this most agreeable way?

Her body slunk lower on the cushion, becoming pliable clay under his expert attentions. His fingers sapped the strength from her with each gentle circle on her foot. But he must've decided more of her needed warming, for Cyrus set one hand on her leg, just under her hem. He rested her foot on his rock-hard thigh as though he would slip a shoe on it, testing its size on her. Large, capable hands massaged her ankle and another shudder skipped along her spine.

Never had she thought of her ankle as a pleasure spot, but her skin tingled.

And those gray eyes of his asked permission to venture higher.

She didn't move, lest he stop the ministrations. Even her lips relaxed, opening softly. She wouldn't let him go higher up her leg, but his hands rubbing her ankle did things to her, made her want him to reach secret places.

And then there was her other errand: Nate. Her leg shifted, part of an attempt to regain control of a situation slipping perilously into parts unexpected.

"If you remove my stocking, that means I stay longer." She gave him a feeble smile. "I can't. Nate. I must find him."

His hand wrapped around her calf, inching higher with convincing caresses. "Nate's a grown lad. He can take of himself. Been doing it a very long time."

"But he must be in some kind of trouble. I need to find him—"

"And where exactly do you plan to look for him?" Those expert fingertips drew tender circles on her stocking-covered shin. "Do you know where he lives?"

How was she supposed to respond with those hands stroking coherent thought right out of her? His touch prevented her from stringing the appropriate syllables together.

She gripped the broadcloth coat encasing her, her plans faltering under the weight of practical questions and the persuasive hands working a slow trail up her leg.

Her shoulders slumped. "I don't know where he lives." Looking down at her foot settled on his thigh, she nodded tacit approval. "Go ahead, my stockings. Take them off."

His hands slipped higher, more efficient in movement than seductive. Wet locks fell forward as she watched him work. His genuine concern about her welfare touched her, bringing messy wants and emotions.

A lonely ache settled on her like sand sinking to the bottom of a water-filled jar.

He peeled down one stocking and laid the black wool across the hearth. He set to work on the other leg, propping her foot on his thigh. She leaned closer, studying him with rapt fascination.

Dark brown lashes fanned stone-cut cheeks, and within his brown hair, those few silver threads glinted. Black silk wrapped around the length of his queue, a thick cylinder of hair down his back.

Why not one touch?

She reached out and touched the back of his head. His hair was fine as silk against her palm.

Masculine hands stilled in the act of removing her stocking. One stroke to the back of his head was all she wanted to discover the texture of his hair. That forbidden place was harmless and hardly sexual, yet so personal.

"I notice you like to wear your hair this way. And no wig," she said, wistful in her exploration.

Emboldened, her hand wrapped around the thick

coil trailing past his shoulders. She slid her loose grip down the span of black silk twisted around his hair.

Cyrus kept his head bent. The wide line of his powerful shoulders barely moved. He could be a lion, bowing for a fine lady stroking his mane. There had to be an ancient tale of such, but her muddled mind couldn't recall the story.

His fingers encircled her calf with beguiling contact. The un-gartered stocking slid to her ankle, the undergarment dropping in collusion with the talented male fingers going up her leg.

He caressed her cool, bare skin, the effect devastating. Fingertips swirled over her shin with the lightest touch, sending hot spangles of pleasure everywhere.

Her breath stalled when he reached the tender flesh behind her knee. She let go of his queue, needing a stabilizing grip on his shoulder. Her fingers couldn't span the width of his rock solid shoulders.

"I've no need for a wig, nor do I like them," he said, rasping his delayed response.

She'd forgotten their thread of conversation, lost in the spell of his comforting hands. Cyrus looked up, his pewter eyes darkening.

His fine mouth held her attention. Light played with his resolute jawline, where the bruise she noticed earlier bloomed purple on his skin. She ought to ask about that, but her mind was a jumble of senses, not sensibility.

Nothing about this day was going as expected. Would a kiss from Cyrus Ryland be the same? Her one hand held the inside of his coat for dear life, the other grasping his shoulder. His hand slipped out from under her hem, leaving her riotous flesh singed.

She inhaled sharply, mourning the loss. "Your hand…"

"I've another place for it," he murmured, his breath soft as down on her cheek.

He curved his fingers around her hair-mussed nape and pulled her close. Cyrus's forehead touched hers, his silky hair brushing her face. She shut her eyes, seeking the security of darkness. If she didn't see him, she'd keep a safe distance from the threatening torrent of emotions.

Could she give in to him and will her body alone to feel, erasing her heart from the equation?

Firm, talented fingers massaged her skin beneath her hair's tangled knot, guiding her closer to him one inch at a time.

And their lips touched.

Her breath quickened. Oh, how she liked his lips on hers.

Cyrus coaxed her, his mouth stroking hers in a lingering kiss. He wooed her, tender flesh meeting tender flesh in a burst of heat and…yearning. His mouth moved over hers, a gentle brush of lips to lips, of longing and want, so astonishing, this persuasive tug on her mouth and heart.

He pulled a whisper's distance away from her. His mouth swept hers as though she was a thing to be treasured. Cold, wet tresses dangled on her cheeks as more hair came loose. Cyrus's mouth tugged gingerly on the flesh of her upper lip. Each velvet kiss lured her, reaching deep inside.

She kissed him back, finding new ways to explore the curves and planes of his mouth.

How could a man of brutish size be so careful?

One corner of her brain wanted to place Cyrus neatly on a shelf categorized as *arrogant and overbearing*, the kind of man who demanded and took, giving little in return. The kind of man she could ignore. This surprising part of Cyrus washed sensation after sensation over her, drowning all thought.

Her knees fell wide open under the trap of her skirts. She inched closer, needing him. His gifted, agile mouth sought hers in a delicate dance of lips stroking lips. Cyrus angled his head sideways to hers, as though he wanted to test a new position, his tongue flirting with the seam of her mouth.

He didn't invade. He beckoned. He teased and he tasted, seeking her.

His kisses weren't the claiming kind; his kisses sought connection. And this made Cyrus all the more dangerous. A tremor shook her body, and Claire loosed her hold on the enveloping coat, all the better to press closer.

She needed to rub against him.

Her mouth opened, and she tasted him back. Cyrus was warm and desirable. More than desirable. *Heart softening.* Her hands moved over mountainous shoulders that required exploring. Needy palms stroked the broad, heavily muscled span she'd itched to discover the first night they sat together, but what she found disturbed her more than settled her.

She wanted more, not less. She wanted clothes off. Now.

She didn't know how long they sat as they did, lost in thorough kisses. Cyrus separated himself from her, a thing not to her liking. He pulled back and she leaned forward into him, mewling soft, deprived sounds when cool air touched her face.

Her hand touched her mouth. The best kind of kisses numbed the mind, leaving a body floating between heaven and earth. She wasn't ready to touch ground yet. But there were voices in the hall outside the study door. None came knocking. Were those voices what made him stop?

She opened heavy-lidded eyes, and the room glowed. With careful fingers, Cyrus brushed back the wet tendrils plastered to her cheek.

"You look like a wanton," he said, breathing hard.

"Only because you kiss like one. We don't have to stop, you know."

"And you speak like a wanton." A hoarse laugh rumbled from his chest. "But this is not the time nor the place for what I have in mind for you."

His Midlands accent was stronger, and Claire gripped the cushion to keep herself from jumping into his arms like a bawd. She was starved for him.

"I wouldn't be opposed to a small sampling."

He chuckled, grazing his fingers over her cheek.

She glanced down at herself, registering the shameless changes Cyrus had wrought. She practically thrust her breasts at him. Within her skirts, her legs spread wide, ready to welcome him into the fold of her body. Her drawer's seam tucked between her legs was slicked with warm wetness.

How mortifying. She tucked her knees together and inched back on the seat, the first move to return to her regular, un-wanton self.

If not for those bothersome voices beyond the door, what fine use would they have made of the settee?

Her hands fussed with her disheveled hair, needing something functional and proper to do. Practical thoughts formed, reminding her that as wonderful as kissing Cyrus felt, their situation and her circumstances were changed not at all.

"I really should go." Her voice hadn't recovered, still scraping deeper notes.

"Stay. Please."

He'd moved around the other side of the tall chair, his hands high on the backrest. Though the chair hid more than half his body, the visible fabric of his waistcoat stretched with each deep breath he took. Did Cyrus Ryland need protection from their soul-shattering kisses too?

"I know I ask a lot, but I want you to wait here for me." His gaze swept over her attire, the terribly mussed hair. "It would be an honor to have you sit at my table, but even I know it's not in your best interest to attend a luncheon with the Duke and Duchess of Marlborough garbed as you are." His lips pressed in a flat line. "That is…I don't want *you* to be uncomfortable."

Was there a touch of longing in his eyes? She understood his meaning, but disappointment jabbed her, causing her lashes to flutter low. His intentions were perfect, but she wasn't dressed right. He wanted to spare her the discomfort of being ill prepared for such an event. But there was more to this than mere social separation.

He was a man who would someday marry into nobility, something she was not.

She gathered her pins, now sprinkled around the settee, and smiled, trying for humor. "I don't think I'll ever be in a dining room with the Duke and Duchess of Marlborough unless it's to serve them."

Her upraised hands removed the few remaining pins clinging in her hair and let the tresses cascade in an uncombed mess. She finger combed dampened hair as well as she could and began to recoil the knot. The simple act calmed the chaos of her flesh and nerves.

Arms raised, she was about to push a pin into place when she hesitated. Cyrus watched her hungrily, his fingertips whitening on the chair. A magic charmer could've claimed his soul, mesmerizing him the way he stood stock-still.

"I could watch you pin and unpin your hair... again and again and never get tired of the view," he marveled.

Her heart thumped faster. If she wasn't careful, this potent thing between them could dissolve rapidly again, with more than hairpins scattered across the settee. And to what painful end?

"I really must go," she said softly and finished her task.

It'd be easy to say yes to anything he asked right then. She leaned over and grabbed her shoes. Cyrus's glassy-eyed stare ranged over her, drinking in her face, her untidy hair, tracing her movements as she slipped one bare foot into a water-stained shoe.

"You won't stay to meet my nephews?"

She gathered her limp stockings and stuffed them in her apron pockets. "Those young men in the drawing room?"

"Yes, Peter, Zachariah, and Simon," he said, eyes shining at their names. "My older sisters have a bent for biblical names."

The corner of his mouth quirked when he gave the last tidbit of information. Claire picked up the second shoe, listening attentively. This reprieve washed over them, giving their lust-strung bodies a chance to recover.

"I'm proud of them," he said, moving around the chair. "They've worked hard at their studies, and now Simon's on his way to becoming a physician, and Peter and Zach will soon become barristers. The duke is helping them to land in some high places." His smile stretched but failed to light his eyes. "Not bad for a family of freehold farmers from Stretford."

He wanted them to keep talking; she could tell as much by the way his voice, his gaze lingered. His tone was as tender as it was humble, playing on her heart… all the more reason for her to be gone. Conversation bred hope.

Cyrus trod a very different path from her. The want to reach higher and take more from life was common ground they shared, but their lives diverged from there.

Sluggish hands slipped on her second shoe, practical brown leather, same as she always wore.

"Those are wonderful achievements for your nephews," she said.

Her fingers rubbed a smudge on the buckle of her shoe, hollowness growing inside her. The scuffed footwear illustrated with perfect clarity what needed saying.

"As a girl, I always wanted pretty silk slippers."

She raised her hems and tapped the worn leather toes together. "I spent my childhood with the Greenwich family, a companion to Lady Jane, the earl's sister. She let me wear her silk shoes, but by nightfall it was time for me to go home where I belonged...the humble land steward's cottage."

Cyrus didn't move.

"Don't you see? They weren't mine. I had to give them back." Her voice turned soft and pensive. "I never had pretty shoes of my own."

He stood statue still, his dark lashes dropping over his eyes.

She released her skirts and sat up tall. "If I let this go too far with you, I'd be that girl wearing silk shoes for a time, pretending to live a life that isn't hers. Eventually things would end."

"It doesn't have to be that way. I would take care of you."

"You mean like a mistress?"

"That's not what I mean."

"But that's what would happen." With measured care, she stood up and passed him his coat, her tone level. "I like who I am and what I have...my life as it is."

Cyrus slipped on his fine blue coat, fixing his shirt-sleeves at the wrists. "Is there more to your message? Speak plainly."

His jaw was rigid, a small muscle ticking on his cheek. This rejection hurt them both, but she would not let this thing between them consume her. She retrieved her cloak hanging from the mantel. The wool became the armor she wrapped around her.

"Everybody in London knows you'll someday marry a woman of high social standing, and that's something I'm not." Claire lifted her hood. "To embark on something with you would be folly. I don't belong here. I tried mixing with a man not of my station once, and…"

"The necklace," he demanded. "Who gave it to you?"

She stared past Cyrus and exhaled a long, soul-cleansing breath.

"Jonathan," she said. "He taught me to climb trees, helped me laugh again after I lost my mother. He was the giver of my first kiss, receiver of my virginity, and heir to the Greenwich earldom." She paused, biting her lower lip. "He's the only man I've ever loved, and the only man to break my heart."

"You speak of the deceased Lord Jonathan Greenwich."

"Yes, he led me to believe we'd marry, deceived me really. Once his mother discovered what went on between us, she made sure he found the companionship of more suitable women, while I was shamed in my home village." Her voice was faint. "And in return, Jonathan gifted me with a necklace."

His mouth's hard line softened with her painful revelation. Did he understand the push-pull of being part of one stratum while existing in another? Repeating the old news stung her less, but not so the truth she gained from it.

Her false smile thinned. "I will not seek the companionship of a man of position."

Square shouldered, his arms made solid lines at his side. "But I'm a commoner."

"You are the King of Commerce, an uncommon commoner, a man who seeks high places." With heavy hands, she tied her cloak under her chin. "Your wealth will get you there."

And she needed to get back to her life, her accomplishments, and her problems—all of them, from the notes due, to Nate…if she could ever locate him.

"I'd be obliged if you had one of your men fetch a hack for me. Then I can leave almost as quietly as I came." She grinned, trying for a spark of humor again, but the flare didn't catch.

Cyrus stayed shuttered and distant. Her shoulders drooped with lagging spirits. She had been wrung dry on this wet day.

"I'll have one of my carriages take you," he said, pulling a bell rope beside the mantel.

A footman came and Cyrus ordered a carriage brought around to the front. Ever the gentleman, he gave her his arm and she rested her fingertips there, tentative and light. If she was thrown off kilter by the day, Cyrus was equally affected. He brooded beside her, large and silent, his well-shod feet leading the two of them slowly through his house to the front door.

Another footman pulled open the door, facing forward in the unseeing way footmen mastered. Outside, rain showered the earth, no longer a tempest but not yet a sprinkle. The carriage trundled over the drive, coming to a halt before the gray stone steps. Cyrus placed his hand over hers and led her down the steps. She didn't expect him to go out in the rain. She had a cloak; he didn't.

His water-splattered profile could be etched on some historic coin as a ruler of men. Strength exuded from him. Everyone looked bedraggled in the rain. Not Cyrus. The heavenly showers touched his strong cheeks with glistening drops, rolling gently away. If not for the downward curve of his mouth, she'd believe the King of Commerce unaffected by his last audience where an upstart woman refused his appeal for carnal connection.

She wanted badly to smooth away the tension around his mouth. Instead, another footman pulled open the carriage door and waited.

Time she left.

Cyrus surprised her again, dismissing the servant. He helped her up the step and helped her get settled inside, laying a wool carriage blanket over her knees with the utmost care.

"You need to keep as warm and dry as possible," he admonished above the patter of rain.

He tarried outside the open door, bracing one hand on the carriage's door frame. Cyrus looked to the ground a second and then his hand, palm up, reached for her. She scooted to the seat's edge, slipping her hand in his. Rain spotted his coat, deepening the fabric's hue. Droplets streamed down his granite-hewn face, but Cyrus held her fingers with care, the way a gentleman would a fine lady's.

"Promise me you'll stay inside your shop and not seek Nate." He spoke above the rain. "I give you my word, I'll do everything I can to find him."

Alarmed, she pushed back her hood. "I won't bring charges against him."

"I didn't expect you would." His mouth curved in a half smile, raindrops darkening his lashes.

His deep, knowing voice calmed her, but then he bowed over their joined hands and his lips opened on the tops of her fingers, stealing one more slow, salacious kiss.

How could a woman's hand become a territory of hot sensuality?

Her stays rubbed sensitive skin, her body agitated from the burden of too many clothes. Cyrus had turned what should have been a chaste good-bye into something fleshly and endearing all at once.

He stood upright, the rain darkening his brown hair. His smile quirked sideways, and he held her fingers another imprudent second. Strands of hair came loose from his tidy queue, turning Cyrus Ryland into a windswept, intrepid hero. Her hero. And her heart ached.

She wasn't sure what touched her more: his promise to find Nate or his tender farewell despite her rejection.

He released her fingers and stepped back to shut the door. He nodded for the carriage to proceed. She leaned her forehead against ice-cold glass, needing to see him. Cyrus was surety in an unsure world, standing there in a wide-legged stance, one hand behind his back. He followed the carriage's departure from the bottom step, a strong gust blowing his coattails.

Nothing could knock him to the ground.

Her palm flattened on the window. She stayed on the edge of the seat until he was no longer in sight, her soul sagging from the loss.

But Cyrus wasn't the last face she saw at Ryland House.

The carriage rolled past the study window where a man stood in full view, his sharp-eyed stare burning with malice. At her. Claire jerked back, scalded.

It was the Duke of Marlborough.

Why did he glare at her with such hate?

Eight

I know that's a secret, for it's whispered everywhere.

William Congreve, *Love for Love*

WHAT WAS AN INDEPENDENT WOMAN TO DO WHEN SHE found herself stuck? Her options were limited, looking as murky as London's fog outside her shop. The dark of night was here, and she needed a way out. Fast.

"Rent's due in two days." Annie peered into the modest till. "What are you going to do?"

"I don't know." Claire dropped meager coins into Annie's outstretched hand.

Above stairs, notes due needed tallying, but her quick math told her the news was dismal. The numbers outweighed the paltry pence in her possession.

Annie's work-worn hands tied her cloak shut. "You could go back to Greenwich. Find a nice man in your home village and get married."

Claire's mouth pursed at the standard advice. Why was a man considered the answer to a woman's problems?

Of course, Annie had her best interest at heart. Nor was she the first to render the same guidance. Mr. Cogsworth and his quick mind pieced together Nate's absence and Claire's harried demeanor. He asked a few pointed questions, and she spilled her troubles. Then the dear man issued the same gentle suggestion.

Go home. Get married.

That wasn't a palatable option right now. Was marriage the only path to security? To give up would be a white flag of surrender or worse, failure.

In the end, the choice to stay or go might not be hers, with time ticking onward and her funds dwindling.

Another day had passed, and business had been bleak today.

"I'd write to Edward—" Claire stopped her flow of words as she walked to the door with Annie. "I mean, Lord Edward, Earl of Greenwich. He's a friend from childhood. I know he'd help me, but he's in Scotland right now. There's not enough time."

Lord Edward Greenwich, Jonathan's younger brother, had sworn his steadfast friendship and help if she was ever in need. No one else had the means to help her, and she wasn't about to beg a loan from Mr. Ryland. To be in his debt would be far too precarious.

Annie looped the last tie under her chin, her freckled face a study in pained sympathy. "I can stay with you, you know. Tonight. I don't have to leave."

Claire lifted the key dangling from her wrist. Her cook had stayed late claiming the need to scour the already-sparkling kitchen.

"You've done enough already." Her voice was

small inside the quiet shop. "You're welcome to stay if you feel it's best not to be on the streets at this hour."

"Ah, Miss Mayhew, midtown's not bad." Annie's crooked smile was sweet. Compared to Stepney, this part of midtown was paradise.

Annie's room was in a women's boardinghouse an alley two thoroughfares past Cornhill. Her friends, a pair of milliner's assistants, shared a garret with her. They'd be expecting her, ready to pore over a broadsheet and share some gossip before falling asleep.

Claire slid the key home in the door's lock and opened the door wide for Annie to pass. Cold air gusted greedily. A dull ache struck her midsection, the pang blossoming beneath her breastbone. She rubbed her palm across the spot, to no avail.

The shop was too quiet behind her, the lonely kind of quiet.

Right as her cook was about to step through the door, Claire pulled Annie into a hug.

"Thank you, Annie," she whispered.

Her cook was stiff under her woolen cloak, but she softened, returning the embrace.

The best surprise from making her way in London was discovering the friendships of women. Doxies she'd come to know, coarse with her when she first ventured down to the wharfs midday, but a basket of fresh-baked biscuits warmed their hearts and soon those hardened women winked greetings to "the coffee shop girl."

And there were the Sauveterre sisters, both godsends with their wit and friendship. They moved on the same path of respectable business as her, facing similar struggles. Then there were the Annies of midtown, working women who made a silent force within London's wheels of commerce.

Men may have cobbled London together, but women formed it, careful sculptors adding the beautiful finishing touches to Town life.

If she had to leave, she'd miss these women.

Annie pulled away, her russet brows working. "Sure you don't want me to stay, Miss Mayhew? Won't bother me none."

Claire squeezed Annie's hand. "Go on. See your friends. I'll be here in the morning."

She locked the door behind her. For the first time since venturing out on her own, she was awash in cheerless silence. Adrift. There'd be no chocolate with Juliette. Her friend had stayed in to finish a rush order for a new gown complete with shot silk undergarments.

She smiled. Shot silk undergarments spelled sensuality. Somewhere in midtown, a woman of sober character was destined to wear seduction under her sedate day gown.

And then her smile faded. There'd been no sign of Cyrus Ryland, not even a note to follow up on his promise to find Nate. Or his kisses. Claire curled her fingers around the iron key and smoothed back wisps falling around her face. And why not? She'd closed that door on him.

What went between them was lust not love or affection.

But lust could certainly warm a body well.

"And come at a price, Claire Mayhew," she chided herself.

She blew out the last sconce candles hanging on the brick walls. Had she traded a chance at true love…for this? All her grand plans wrapped up in this narrow shop, and she was alone.

Claire pulled her shawl tighter about her shoulders. She moved on leaden feet upstairs, lifting the iron candle holder to light her way. Her hip knocked shut the narrow door to the outside world. Unadorned brick walls, as long as the shop below but confined by the timbered roof's imposing slant, lined the space she called home.

Why had she never taken the time to make this place a home?

Tired hands unpinned her mobcap and dropped the white linen atop the chest beside her bed. Wooden hairpins came next, clattering on the hard surface. The foot of her rope bed stretched toward the fire grate, but even her feet missed its mean warmth most nights.

The unbidden picture of large, male hands cosseting her was a luxury.

Cyrus's bed would be large and warm and made of goose down. And he'd be in it.

A naughty tremor played over her flesh.

She walked to the fire grate, running her hands through her hair. With her tresses sprung free, a pleasuring tingle swept over her scalp. The notion of falling into a soft bed with a hard man who could heat up her chilled body tempted her. She laughed sweetly at the image, adding more black lumps of coal to the puny inferno. Her hands spread over the flaring orange.

"And that's all the heat this proprietress gets tonight."

Claire set her lone candle on the table by the window. She gathered the scattered notes with their unforgiving numbers and went through each one. She wrote the amount due in a column on her freshly opened ledger. Her hand was poised to count a stingy pile of coins when a spray of pebbles hit her window. A voice yelled from the fog below.

"Miss Mayhew, are ye there?"

Not any voice. *Nate?*

She touched the glass. Gloomy air made the silhouette fuzzy, but he raised a candle lantern high, shining tepid light on his face. She grabbed her key and ran downstairs and through the shop.

Nate pressed his face close to the door's square window, hefting a rusted candle lantern for a better look inside. Under his Dutch cap, the lad's black forelock hung over sheepish eyes. He pulled back into the shadows, lowering the lamp when he saw her.

Unsteady fingers jiggled the key in the lock. She flung the door open and pulled Nate into a tight hug.

"I've been so worried about you." Her cheek smashed into his coat, the coarse fabric smelling of streets and mildew.

Her eyes watered, the wetness clinging to her lashes. The notion struck her: twice in one night, she'd wrapped her arms around people who mattered a great deal to her. With Nate at her door, at least one heavy weight lifted from her shoulders.

She stepped back, holding his shoulders at arm's length to examine him from head to toe. It was a motherly thing to do, but the lad needed someone to look after him. His clothes were begrimed, his hair unkempt, and a fist-sized, red-and-purple bruise mottled the side of his mouth. He looked too thin. Had he eaten?

"What happened to you?" She didn't wait for an answer, tugging his arm. "Come inside."

"We don't have long, miss." He stopped, resisting her pull to go in the shop.

And he said *we*.

Her shawl slid to the crook of her elbows, a blast of cold sharpening her senses. Excitement at seeing Nate alive and well wilted. She adjusted her wrap, yanking the cloth higher with this new chill stealing over her.

"What do you mean?" She crossed her arms, her gaze skimming the awful swelling of his lower lip.

Nate moved in front of the door, a subtle gentleman's move to absorb the draught for her. The candle lantern hung low from one hand. Tension vibrated off his thin frame. His eyes, bloodshot and weary, looked a decade older.

"Miss Mayhew, I need ye to get every last coin ye have and come with me. Right now." He spoke in measured tones. "I need ye to trust me."

"All my money?" she blustered. "See here, Nate Fin—"

"I'm tryin' to save yer shop." His words snapped with urgency. "I'll explain about yer necklace on the way. I've been tryin' to get it back, but we've got to go. Now. Or we'll be too late."

Too late for what? Her brow furrowed something fierce. Nate's feet shifted and he cast a harried glance out the door.

"Will ye come with me?" he pleaded. "Please."

She squinted at London's thick, unwelcome fog beyond her window. He needed her to trust him as badly as she needed money and explanations.

Why all her money now? Couldn't this errand be done in the light of day? She wanted to demand he explain himself, but trust didn't work that way. Trust grew strongest from the weakest places. The virtue wanted to wrench a body dry until all that was left was a belief in the goodness someone offered...perilous ground for a woman like her to stand on.

Only this wasn't the same as standing on something solid.

This was like hanging from a tree branch. She had to let go before finding firm ground.

Claire sucked in a deep breath and turned from the window to Nate's open face.

"I'll get my cloak and pattens. Give me a second to pin my hair up—"

"No." He eyed the cascade of hair falling about her shoulders. "Please leave it down. There's no time."

She walked briskly to the stairs, his voice calling after her, "Every last farthing, miss."

Upstairs, she whipped her cloak from its peg and donned her pattens with an eye to her humble cache of coins. At the table, her hand hovered over the bits of copper and silver, all the money she possessed.

Trust demanded her due in full tonight; she could only hope the reward would be worthwhile. In one swipe, her hand brushed every last coin into her small money pouch.

Nate tarried by the open door, looking out into the fog-filled street. He turned around when her wooden pattens clunked loudly on the floor. When she drew close, he held out his hand, eyeing her coin pouch.

"Ye'll want me to carry that."

She looked at Nate's outstretched hand. The sense of unmooring the last rope before setting sail into parts unknown struck her.

If she was to embark on this evening's journey, then she'd go all the way. She handed over the coin bag. Nate jammed the small leather bag inside his coat, where another pouch bulged from his pocket.

She locked the door behind them and tucked the key into the safest place—her cleavage. Nate stepped onto Cornhill, his lantern raised high in ghostly, swirling air.

"Stick close," he said.

They sped down Cornhill, moving east. She hoisted her skirts high, the rain-soaked road grabbing her pattens. Then they turned onto Gracechurch, which quickly narrowed into New Fish Street, where the rank odor of fish offal clogged her mouth. Her nape prickled from the pitch-dark alleys rendering strange noises of man or beast, she couldn't say.

Nate kept a rapid pace, his long legs eating up the distance, splashing through puddles ahead of her. What happened to his promise to explain himself? But something in his bearing tensed with urgency.

Whatever the plan to get her necklace back, they dare not be late.

They crossed over Thames Street, closer to the docks where fog hung the thickest. She was about to demand Nate stop and explain himself when a noise banged to her right, a persistent clunk of wood that didn't stop. She turned to look.

Her mouth flopped open. Standing still as she was, her feet sunk deeper in the mire.

A man rutted a woman from behind, her body folded face down on a barrel. With her skirts yanked up behind her, the doxy stared into the darkness, gripping the barrel's rim. The frizz-haired harlot turned her face toward the street, her head jerking in time with the barrel's thump.

The woman's flat-eyed stare brought to mind holes in moth-eaten cloth.

The urge to run made Claire speed up to Nate, her breaths a salvo in the night. Most dangerous of all, every last pence she claimed in the world trotted out of reach.

"Nate," she called. "I'm not going another step until you explain yourself."

She sought support on a brick and flint stone wall. He stopped short, his shoes squishing as he circled back.

"Shhh." Nate raised a quieting finger near his lips. "Come on, Miss Mayhew. We're close. Best to keep moving."

She shook her head, gasping at air that tasted of mildew and muck. A stitch in her side had started, jabbing worse than a broken whalebone stay.

"Not…another…step."

"At least keep yer voice down." He looked over one shoulder and then the other. "It was Sharp Eddie. He stole yer necklace. I tried to get it back. That's why ye haven't seen me. I was chasin' him down."

She searched his face but Nate was little more than a dark silhouette to her, with his lantern hanging low at his side. The lad wasn't winded at all. Did he jog through London's streets as a daily habit? The news of Eddie's thievery angered her, but the growing pain in her side needed rubbing and emotion was a luxury she couldn't afford right now.

"I don't understand." She dug her fingers into the cramp, her lungs sucking down great gulps of air. "Aren't we going to see him? Demand he give it back?"

"Ye don't demand anything 'round here, miss," he scoffed. "'Sides, Eddie sold yer baubles. Took off for the West Indies on the first tide out of here today."

She slumped against the cold brick. Why did Nate give her hope she'd get the necklace back? Her eyes squeezed shut. Her sole means for her future, truly gone. For good.

"My plan wasn't to get yer necklace back, but to save yer shop." Nate grabbed her arm, pulling her close. "C'mon. We're almost there."

Where?

They trudged through the mud, but she was too dispirited to ask what he meant, her brain clogged with too many troubles. At least there was the comforting news that Nate wasn't a thief. He had tried to help her.

"We're here," he said.

She looked up. Two ships' masts poked through layers of fog. They were in Billingsgate Wharf.

Her breath labored from their near run. "Why take me to the wharf at this late hour, Nate? I demand to know what this is all about."

Her trust had found its limit. Nate let go of her arm, but he held his lantern high to light the way.

"About Eddie...we both talked about changing, trying to be honest men." His profile pinched hard in the shadows. "But all the changing Eddie did was back to his old ways. Said honest work was too hard and paid too little."

Claire pushed back her hood for a better look at him.

He swung around to face her, the familiar scowl present. "Ye've been good to me. I needed to make things right."

"And your bruise?"

"Got it when I found him." He gingerly touched the side of his swollen mouth. "Ye could call this our way of workin' out a difference of opinion. He won, but it gave me an idea."

Nate pointed to double doors, a maw of an opening ready to swallow the heedless passerby. At this late hour on the wharves, nothing less than trouble would be found beyond those doors.

"That's where we're goin', miss."

Of course. Her eyebrows shot high at the unsavory sight.

Candle lanterns lit ramshackle edifices, taverns by the revelry and aroma of bitter ale, and dark warehouses in other places. On the other side, the Thames held court, a flat, silent lady dirtied by time and use, yet London thrived through the ages on her brined appeal. Claire had never seen this much of London at this time of night, and the spirit of daring touched her. If all was lost, then at least she'd lived as she saw fit.

"Warehouses on Dark House Landing host

bare-knuckle fights now and then," he explained. "Tonight, our plan is to bet all yer money and mine. But don't worry. We'll win it back and lots more."

"That's your plan?" she huffed. "*Gambling* on a fight?"

If he'd said this to her at the shop, she would never have set one foot outside her door. Her spirit of daring wasn't this bold.

"Nate Fincher, that's the worst idea I've ever heard. You want to wager what little money I have on a fight?" She stopped short, her arms clamped tight across her chest. "How can you be so sure we'll win on some sweaty brutes?"

He grinned. "I've an ace up my sleeve, miss. We'll win big."

"Or lose big. Besides, I can't go in there." She eyed the dark doors. "Proper women don't attend bare-knuckle fights, and they certainly don't wager on them."

Nate heaved a deep sigh; he could be a patient tutor with a rather dull student.

"Ye're right…about proper women, I mean. They don't see bare-knuckle fights, but neither do they run down New Fish Street gawkin' at strumpets plyin' their trade."

He gave her a shameless wink and smiled as big as his swollen lip allowed.

She gasped, her cheeks stinging hot. He'd seen her fascination with the doxy. Nate pushed back his coat and planted a fist at his hip, his smile fading.

"Ye know what else? Most proper women don't leave home to start an honest business all by themselves.

Neither would they give a questionable lad from St. Giles proper employment." Something bright flickered in his eyes. "But ye did. Ye're a brave one, miss, and that puts ye in a class all by yerself."

Her balance wavered under the light shining from his face. How could he say something so, so heart bursting about her? She served coffee and made pastries, yet she could have been Joan of Arc by the admiration in his eyes.

"Ye've come with me this far tonight, why not finish?" he coaxed softly.

Fog brushed Nate's shoulders, swirling around him as though he'd emerged from a magician's smoky tent. He nodded at the open doors, his mouth quirking.

"C'mon. Don't ye want to see?"

She looked again at the warehouse; a distant clamor spilled from the open doors. Yes, no proper young woman left home alone to strike out on her own and start a business. Many of her friends were married, and some still waited for the chance. None conceived of a different life for themselves.

She'd come this far. Why stop now?

"You're a good one, Nate Fincher." Claire slipped her arm through his.

But he didn't budge, instead he eyed her hair, strands of which had blown wildly about on their race to Billingsgate.

"Keep yer hair and face covered. It's part of my plan." His voice was firm and serious.

Her thick, flaxen hair was a rarity and caused her trouble from unwanted male attentions too often. She did as Nate bade her, tucking her hair behind her shoulder. Then she pulled her hood far forward, shrouding her features.

Her gait lightened at the prospect of seeing the forbidden: a bare-knuckle fight.

Once inside the warehouse, the building, dead from the outside, came alive. They walked into a wall of dank air mixed with a sweet aroma and one of fresh-cut wood. Nate guided her through a central path, past stacks of wooden crates and half-constructed barrels, closer to the light and noise. She tipped her nose high, sniffing the air.

"Ye're smellin' sugar. There's a big refinery in here." He pointed to the partially formed barrels. "An' half this warehouse is a cooperage."

Not a soul was in sight save a tabby cat curled on a high stack of crates. The resident mouser twitched his orange tail, his slanted eyes watching the latecomers. On the other end of the warehouse, the bedlam could have raised the roof. Lights shined behind a concealing wall of crates and barrels. Heads and fists bobbed above the wooden barrier's line.

So much was going on, she almost missed the old man slouching on a crate.

Nate dropped his voice. "Stay quiet. And remember, keep yer face an' hair hidden."

A small man with a peg leg scratched notes on a ledger, but he snapped the book shut and stood up to block their path when Nate approached.

"Well, if it isn't Mis-ter Fincher." He nudged his tricorne back with his thumb and glanced at Claire covered in her cloak. "And ye brought yerself a friend, I see."

"Mr. Watson." Nate reached inside his coat. "We're here to see the Swede take on the Bruiser. I want to place a bet."

"Well now, ye're fine to catch the Swede and the Bruiser, they're at it now with one round left. But ye're a wee bit late to place a bet, lad." Mr. Watson's lips pressed together, exaggerating his dismay. "The book closed when the first bout started."

"C'mon, Watson. Ye can just as easily open the book." Nate motioned to Claire. "I promised the lady fine entertainment. The thrill of a grand bet. Ye wouldn't want to disappoint her."

Watson's rheumy stare shot to Claire and back at Nate. Begrimed hands scratched whiskers peppered with black and gray.

"Well, now, if ye make it worth me while…"

From his inside pocket, Nate pulled out the two coin bags in one hand and a gold guinea in the other. He held the guinea between his middle finger and forefinger.

Claire breathed in sharply. The guinea had to be the same coin Mr. Ryland had given Nate earlier this week. He was ready to separate himself from it on this mad scheme to help her.

"Is a pretty guinea worth openin' yer book?" Nate asked, luring the old man like a street hawker.

Watson swiped his forehead, squinting hard at the coin.

"Place yer bet, Mr. Fincher. Anything ye want."

Nate set the gold piece in Mr. Watson's grimy, outstretched palm. Claire watched Nate dump his coins and all of hers on a barrel top, and the old bet taker flicked beckoning fingers at a ruffian the size of an outbuilding. The giant must've been behind some crates, but he lumbered forward and plunked a smaller chest on the same barrel. His colorless stare roved over them before he started counting the coins.

"Now about your bet." Mr. Watson opened his ledger, his lead stick tapping the page. "What'll it be, lad?"

"Ten to one the Bruiser's out fer the count. Doesn't finish the fight."

Watson choked into his balled fist.

"Ye're expectin' the Bruiser to fall?" he argued. "He's favored to win three to one. And ye're bettin' those kinds of odds?" The old man wheezed a sickly chuckle and wrote the bet down. "But as ye say, lad. As ye say. A pleasure doin' business with ye."

Mr. Watson bent over the coin-strewn barrel, poking a knobby finger through the silver. There was a lull in the noise on the other side of crates stacked high, and the bet taker cocked his ear at the stirrings.

"Last round's about to start." The old man gleefully tipped his hat at Claire. "Best get to it."

Nate grabbed her elbow, rushing her to the commotion ahead. "Looks like we don't have much time."

They went around the barrier of crates and barrels, finding rough necks and macaronies elbow to elbow around a wide makeshift ring. She couldn't see much beyond the backs of the raucous audience. There had to be at least a hundred people there. Nate pushed for a particular point in the crowd.

A man stood above the crowd, his feet braced wide

on a barrel. He waved a battered tricorne through the air.

"Last round!" he shouted and tossed the hat into the ring.

The crowd's noise swelled. Candle lanterns gave light to the dark and dingy warehouse. The stamped earth was as hard as any stone floor, with sawdust crunching underfoot. Nate gripped her arm, positioning her away from the yelling, cheering crowd. He surged partway into the mass of bodies and rose on tiptoe for a better look.

When he came back, he issued his odd requirement again. "Keep yer hood on, and at the right second, ye'll see everything."

Everyone milled close, fists pumping the air and shouting at the ring. She covered her nose, affronted by heady whiffs of men in need of soap and water. A few women were scattered in the mix, some grizzled, time worn, and toothless. A pair of young, velvet-cloaked ladies in confection-colored silks were among the revelers.

Heavy cosmetics painted their faces white with red, Cupid's bow lips. Padded coiffures pulled a foot high off their foreheads in dramatic fashion. Those towering piles of hair touched when they leaned close to gossip about the goings-on inside the ring.

Nate spoke against her hood near her ear. "Those ladies, *Incognitas*…high-priced strumpets." And then he started to pull her close into the crowd, saying above the fray, "It's time."

"Nate, I'm not sure this is to my liking." She braced a hand on a barrel.

Her head and shoulders flinched at the barrage of horrible noises, the coarse crowd and their awful odors merged wrongly on this late-night adventure.

"Ye've come this far," he coaxed. "Just a few more steps."

Her grip on the barrel eased. She'd look and then slip to the back of the crowd.

Nate pushed through a bellowing mass, one arm up high to shield her against the fists and elbows striking wildly. Bodies bumped and squished. At the rope, he eased around behind her, but she stared agog at the sneers and spittle of the scrawny man beside her.

"C'mon, Sven, give it to him good!" he yelled. "Bellows to mend, man. Bellows to mend."

The Incognitas jabbed the space in front of them, their painted mouths snarling. And then she looked into the ring where two brutish men had stripped off their shirts and now fought a primitive battle for dominance.

Sweaty brutes indeed.

Two Titans maneuvered on large bare feet, the hair on their legs springing dark from well-formed calves. One man wore buckskin-colored breeches, the pewter buttons on the side of his knees gleaming like great bolts fastening his legs together. The other man wore plain, brown homespun with no such fine buttons. Both men were equal with fists cocked high, trying to slam the other with vicious swipes.

For the second time in one night, Claire gawked. Her jaw unhinged at the play of muscles, great slabs of them, shifting under glistening skin. Raw power roused, displaying itself in human form. Both men's arms were the size of hefty iron hammers, and their limbs looked just as hard and strong as hunks of shaped metal.

She touched her skirts, needing something tactile. Her blood raced…at once repulsed and excited. Her lashes lowered; her ogling eyes needed to keep this a secret.

The men, giants come down to earth, punched and bashed. Their fists knocked air when the other jerked sideways to avoid the hit. The fighter with his back to her clubbed his foe on the chin. A spray of blood and sweat spurted off his head, but the monster of a man kept going.

She clapped a hand over her mouth. Yet she stared, finding peculiar interest in the queue of the other fighter. A black silk ribbon wrapped around the length of his hair, resting in the furrow of his spine.

A black silk brawler?

The wide V of his back was a near-perfect triangle turned upside down, an archaic display of strength. His muscles moved under skin sheening with a fine layer of sweat. Beneath her skin, embers struck, tingling everywhere. She pushed back one side of her hood, hungry for a better look.

The bare-knuckle fighter facing her wore his hair cropped short, the sweat beading all over his head. Blood trickled down his chin. His broad bull's head tipped low, ready to ram his opponent.

She craned her neck for a better view of the ancient battle for dominance, one man against another. Behind her, Nate gripped both her arms, keeping her in place.

Did he think she'd rush into the ring?

"Wait," was all he said, drawing out the word. "Wait."

Nate spoke in the same way an announcer primed runners about to start a race. For what did she need to wait?

Thundering voices outside the ring rose to a fevered pitch. Inside the ring, the Herculean pair moved in a slow dance. She recognized the profile moving toward her, the large, proud nose. Sweat dampened the sides of his face, trickling down the square jaw.

Cyrus Ryland.

The buzz in her head drowned out the crowd's rumble. His fists curled in giant knots, blocking most of his face. He wasn't breathing as hard as the other man. Primordial power shot from hard, pewter eyes. Cyrus kept moving, studying his adversary behind the screen of his own knuckles.

She recognized that look: he worked some strategy each time he balanced on the balls of his feet. He was searching for something, an opening through which to act.

The battle danced around the ring, and Cyrus faced her, his glare locked on to his rival. Even she could tell the crowd was little more than shapes on the periphery for him. Fists moved. His nostrils flared. The colossal beast was about to attack.

Then Nate planted a hand high on her back and pushed. "Now."

In seconds, everything spiraled faster than a child's spin toy—the same seconds one took to let go and fall from a tree in want of hearty ground.

Nate nudged her too hard. She lost her footing.

Her arms reached wildly for something solid but grasped air. The top half of her body leaned over the heavy rope. She planted one foot forward to stave a fall. Behind her, a hand yanked the hood off her head.

Her light blond hair swung forward, a white flag.

She grabbed the barrier rope holding her up at the waist. Painful, itchy hemp scratched her palms. Claire gaped into the ring, too shocked to move. She heard her sharp gasp of breath.

Cyrus craned his head at her, his neck tendons standing out in strained relief. His eyes went saucer wide.

"Claire!" he shouted, rock-sized fists going slack.

The storm of noise around them changed. Some yelled at her. Some yelled into the ring. The rampage didn't fully register. They all could have been wailing in some foreign tongue.

One name she heard: *Stretford Bruiser.*

Cyrus.

She blinked at him, openmouthed and enthralled.

Masculine hair smudged Cyrus's wide chest, a chest fashioned with muscles like plates of armor. Two brown, male nipples buttoned those muscles into place. She gawked worse than a wanton at what he freely displayed.

The Titan come down to Earth glared. At her. The small, slanted line between his brows was deep above his flaring nostrils. His mouth opened as though to issue a decree, but this time no sound came.

The other brawler swung wide, slamming a hard fist into Cyrus's face. His head snapped sideways, loose as a rag doll, eyes going wide, then drooping shut.

Powerful legs buckled at the knees. The black silk brawler teetered a second.

Then, Cyrus Ryland, the Stretford Bruiser, fell to the ground with a mighty thud.

Nine

Besides, you are a woman: you must never speak what you think; your words must contradict your thoughts, but your actions may contradict your words.

William Congreve, *Love for Love*

SAWDUST BIT HIS BACK, TINY STINGS TO HIS HOT SKIN the same as when he had laid down in a field as a boy and red ants nipped him. The pain was minor compared to his throbbing cheek, where a cut stung deep. Blood trickled from the spot where he'd been hit hardest, but the murky world behind his eyelids promised to spare him further agony with heavy sleep.

Because he was felled. By a woman.

His chest moved with steady breaths, a chest on which a small hand tenderly stroked the flesh over his heart.

Claire.

"Mr. Ryland. Are you awake?" her voice called to him. "It's Miss Mayhew."

Another heave of his chest brought robust, life-giving air, as sweet as the feminine thumb stroking his breastbone.

"Of course it's you." His lids opened halfway with sluggish fortitude, a lazy smile forming. "The Swede wouldn't dare caress my chest."

Her hand stiffened over his heart. "I'm *not* caressing your chest, Mr. Ryland. Someone needed to take care of you, and that oaf who hit you wouldn't do it…though he did bring a bucket of water." Amusement touched her voice. "He wanted to douse you."

"I'm sure he did." Cyrus let his lids fall shut again. "And since your hand is on my bare chest, we can dispense with proprieties. Call me Cyrus."

If he had to be flat on the ground, why not surrender to her hands on him? He could get used to her tending him. Hands and cloth moved with gentle touches, cleaning him. Near his head, water dribbled on water. A cool, damp cloth wiped the sweat from his forehead again. She leaned over him, and he smelled cinnamon on her clothes and skin, something far better than the rest of the crowd.

The crowd…

Cyrus raised his head, squinting as facts sunk in. His last fight, a lost fight. Men loitered around crates and barrels, a hum of noise on the perimeter. The ringmaster set to work coiling the ring's heavy rope with another man assisting him.

The Swede was nowhere to be seen, probably at the Fox Tail, raising a victory pint. Just as well. His opponent had seized a moment of weakness and took his shot when Cyrus let his defenses down. He would've done the same.

He shut his eyes and stole the luxury of quiet seconds, nursing his bruised pride at the loss. He was favored to win despite having more than a few years on the Swede, but once again, he'd been stunned— floored it would seem—by a particular woman, this time amidst a rough mob instead of his refined West End home.

"Do you take joy in leveling me, Miss Mayhew?"

She hadn't given him leave to call her Claire. Best he played this safe. The cool cloth brushed his forehead. Her tender care was a pleasure he would milk as long as possible, even if he had to stay flat on his back in sawdust.

"I don't know what you mean." Her hair trailed over his chest, feathery and ticklish.

"First the masked ball and now this." His voice rasped from the sharp aches claiming his limbs.

"You fell down at your sister's ball?" Concern notched her voice. "I'm sorry to hear that. Must've been awful."

Of course she didn't fully grasp her effect on him. Yet.

Her officious cloth dripped cool water high on his chest, stroking his skin. Her breath fanned the side of his face and ear as though she scrutinized him. The cloth dabbed his cheekbone where the Swede had done his best.

"Sorry to touch the wound direct. I'm cleaning up the blood. Of course, you'll heal, but you may have a scar." Another gentle tap of the cloth, and her prim voice hovered close to his ear. "Really, I fail to understand the appeal of these fights."

"A test of skills, the chance for one man to bash another." His tired hand batted the air. "All quite acceptable."

In some social circles, that is.

Sportive West End men practiced polite fisticuffs in their gentleman's clubs, mincing their way through a mockery of a fight. Real bare-knuckle bouts called for blood and sweat. A man could test his mettle, giving in to the explosive need to hit something hard.

He worked diligently to hide his youthful pastime from his Piccadilly acquaintances, trying to distance himself from his rough, Midlands roots. But the truth was he hadn't given much time to the sport for a long while. People and responsibilities pulled his attentions in too many directions.

And the one woman who didn't want his attentions knelt beside him, cleaning his bare chest.

In his warehouse, late at night.

If ever there was a perfect example of a woman in need of protection, his protection…

Head aching, he opened his eyes and hoisted himself up on one elbow.

"You shouldn't be here in the first place. Billingsgate after dark isn't safe for a woman." Cyrus scrubbed a hand over his face and scanned her glorious hair falling wildly everywhere. "How did you know about this?"

Watson never posted placards when he used Cyrus's warehouse. Everything was done by word of mouth.

Miss Mayhew's kerchief-dabbing hand dropped to

her lap. She crouched in the dirt beside him, cloak and skirts pooling around her.

"Nate brought me. To place a bet."

"Nate," he repeated, wincing as he hitched one knee up to move off the ground. "I'll have a word with Mr. Fincher. He shouldn't have brought you here." He brushed sawdust from his palms before offering her his hand.

"As to that," she said as he hoisted her upright. "You don't have any say in the matter."

Miss Mayhew shook her skirts. He frowned, taking great swipes at the mess clinging to his breeches, not liking the truth of what she said.

"Be reasonable. Even coming here in a hack"—he winced, turning his throbbing head for a view of his back—"can be a bad risk." He tried to clean the sawdust from his shoulders.

"Let me do that." Claire stepped behind him and wiped her damp kerchief in long strokes down his back. "As to taking a hack, you'll be interested to know, Nate and I walked."

She peeked up at him around his arm, her pretty face impertinent among all that untamed hair. Her tone and bearing matched the prim coffee shop proprietress, but the view was pure brazen tavern maid at the end of her day.

His arms flexed. So, the East Ender gave him up. He wanted to thrash the lad for doing something so foolhardy as bringing Claire here. Too many bad things happened to women in this ward, even those who lived here and knew their way around.

Claire placed a hand high on his arm while her

flimsy linen cleaned him. She made small, soft sweeps low, where his spine met his breeches. Her skirts brushed the backs of his exposed calves, something more intimate than their first dance. A wicked need to tease her struck, lightening his mood.

"I have a better idea for getting my back clean. It involves a copper tub, large enough for two."

The swiping slowed. Her hand on his arm lifted, and the loss left his skin cool.

Perhaps he went too far.

Then her palm rested on his ribs, settling there with discovery. The heat of each curious finger splayed provocatively on his flesh in a lover's exploratory touch. A heady rush followed, sending a pleasant burn over his already-hot torso.

"Whatever your plans in that copper tub of yours, I'm sure it's not *safe* for a woman like me," she said softly against his shoulder blade. "Though I'm sure you have some creative ideas."

Cyrus looked over his shoulder, her blond head close to his back. "Careful, Miss Mayhew, or you'll admit out loud you want more to happen between us."

"Are you flirting with me, Mr. Ryland?"

"That would be a skill I've not mastered."

If he read her right, he was closing in on the hunt for the elusive proprietress. What did he need to do to finally snare her?

She moved around to face him, her hair brushing his bicep. Her pink mouth opened as though she'd give him a retort, but her jeweled gaze dropped to his navel, dawdling a long stretch on the indent surrounded by a whorl of brown hair. When she looked up, he met her hungry, fascinated stare with a silent challenge.

Go ahead. Touch.

The light in her eyes wavered. She read his invitation, her slender nostrils flaring when she took a deeper breath of him. She fought their attraction hard, her fair face tilted up to his, fine boned and flushed.

The high tip of her nose and set of her pale pink mouth told him his shopgirl's defensive wall was well in place, but she was like a moth drawn to a candle lantern, bouncing against the glass. What was her self-imposed barrier?

The proper midtown woman stepped back, pulling her cloak about her. "You know, I've figured something else about you."

"Yet another observation?" A light chill swept his exposed torso. "Pray tell."

He grabbed his shirt off the barrel where his clothes draped. He slipped his arms inside the linen, steeling himself for the worst.

Miss Mayhew's heavy-lidded stare followed the twitch of his muscles. "You welcome a woman speaking her mind as long as she heeds your words…toes the mark you set."

"Exactly." He donned his waistcoat, securing a few buttons. "None have found fault with how I conduct matters. And for those women I've shared a"—he paused and slid an arm through his wool coat, searching for the right word—"connection with…they did not leave unsatisfied."

Her mouth pinched when he finished the arrogant

proclamation, and Miss Mayhew's jeweled gaze flickered elsewhere. Brashness worked for a freehold farmer climbing to his current place in life, but would do little to win the heart of one independent proprietress.

Her heart?

He fixed one sleeve and then the other, his brows pressing in a firm line. Was her heart what he wanted?

A high-pitched, cheery whistle cut the air. Nate Fincher ambled into the ring with two coin bags in his grasp, both bursting at the seams. The lad quit his jaunty tune and bowed with a flourish, presenting one coin pouch to a delighted Miss Mayhew.

The hunt for a certain woman would have to wait.

Nate rose to his full height and set his candle lantern on a crate, whistling a high note when he saw Cyrus.

"The Swede got ye good, didn't he?"

"I have you to thank for this, don't I?" he asked, tipping his head at Miss Mayhew.

She cupped her wilted kerchief and the winnings with both hands, her mouth dropping beguilingly open. The lad's black forelock covered part of his smirking face.

"I didn't cry rope on ye. Ye said not to *say* a word to her, but you didn't say not to *show* her." The East Ender tucked his bag inside his shabby coat, his grin cocksure. "Comin' here tonight was my idea. She didn't know about ye till she saw ye in the ring."

Cyrus slid on his shoes, not bothering with his stockings. He wouldn't split hairs with Nate, because he figured out quickly what the lad was about with the hefty winnings. Miss Mayhew needed funds badly.

The odds favored Cyrus over the Swede, and Nate must've bet against him.

The lad reckoned on surprising Cyrus with Miss Mayhew's ringside appearance. These fights had few rules. On one hand, he couldn't fault Mr. Fincher: the brazen plan worked.

"And you think it was a good idea to walk her here?"

The cocky grin slipped. "Did what I had to do. 'Sides, I figured ye'd take her home. Mr. Watson already had yer carriage fetched. It's out front."

"And do you need a ride home?"

"Naw. Need to hide my winnings." Nate tapped his chest, where his newfound wealth clinked. He slipped out the other side of the now rope-less ring, his lantern hanging from his fingertips. "Then I'm meeting the others at the Fox Tail."

Walking backward, Nate dipped a parting bow, doffing his black wool cap at them both. "A pleasure doin' business with ye."

"Wait," Claire called to his retreating form. "Will I see you tomorrow?"

The youth sidled a barrel, his feet slowing. "Ye want me back?" His voice rose in a boyish pitch.

"Oh, Nate, of course."

The lad's bruised face cracked in a wide, comical grin. "Bright and early then, miss."

Young Mr. Fincher bowed again and waved a hearty farewell before slipping from sight with a bounce in his step. He didn't have to work again for a long time, but he wanted to...at least at the New Union Coffeehouse for Miss Mayhew.

A tender expression played on her features. A light shined in her eyes, brighter than any polished shilling bagged neatly in her hands. Mr. Fincher gave Miss Mayhew something she badly needed: better footing in this world. Her winnings did as much, saving her shop and her from financial ruin.

But there was more joy in the exchange with Nate, in the lad himself, than the silver.

Truth opened Cyrus's eyes, at once revealing and trouncing him in the gut.

He had this, *her*, all wrong. Some women wanted a man to bleed money, shower her with gifts. Others needed to be worshipped, wanting lavish words and time spent on them. Some simply wanted sexual pleasure, a diversion from their bored lives. Hadn't he met all kinds of women?

Miss Mayhew sought equal footing with a man, yes, but even more she wanted, *needed*, a man to give of himself. Silver and independence were nice, but his proprietress wanted much more.

She craved a man's willingness to trust her. A man needed to expose himself to her, all his defenseless parts.

Hadn't Nate done that? Trusted her with the truth of his St. Giles thievery? His past *failings*? And in doing so, endeared himself to Miss Mayhew all the more.

Cyrus's arms hung limp at his sides. This knowledge knocked him down a peg, floored him as good as the Swede had.

❧

What was she going to do about this unrelenting attraction to Mr. Cyrus Ryland?

She was still warm from cleaning him up, touching him. Cyrus's large, masculine frame set her pulse thrumming, a fact she could not push away no matter how hard she tried.

Until tonight, a man's chest was not a thing of beauty, but seeing him stripped down and half-naked captivated her. She wished to discover each sizable curve and angle. His legs were bared below his breeches, and the bristly hairs on his large, tapered calves begged for exploration.

And he wanted her.

Claire turned around, her movements stiff and mechanical. Her body twined with unexpected tightness, a craving sensation pooling low in her abdomen. She bumped Cyrus awkwardly when she slipped her hand through the crook of his elbow. She leaned close, his strength her bellwether.

"Please, would you take me home?"

She now possessed the coinage to live well and could safely ignore the advice to get married for security's sake.

"I'd be happy to give you a safe escort home." Cyrus extended his open hand, gesturing to her flush coin bag. "Will you allow me to carry that for you?"

She set the leather pouch in his hand, the trust coming easy. They moved out of the warehouse, her limbs taut with vexing need. Her stalwart protector didn't say anything. He was solicitous of her but quiet. She glanced sideways at his taciturn profile, unmarred save the egg-sized, maroon bruise swelling on his face. The gash high on his cheekbone already clotted dark red. He looked to heal quickly from his wounds. Was he like this with other pains in life?

Her gallant hero inadvertently saved her tonight by taking an unwanted fall.

Claire kept her vision on the ground. What Nate did tonight would not be listed as a crime in Bow Street's *Gazette*, but stealing a look at the stone-cut profile beside her, a spirit of wrongness hung heavy. She was complicit in the evening's doings, however unintentional.

And the belief *no one will get hurt* turned stale among other notions wrestling inside her.

She stole something from Cyrus Ryland again, though she couldn't put a name to her transgression.

His shoulders squared in that implacable way of his, but his mouth pressed in a taut line. He stared straight ahead, fixed on some unseen point. Was this turn in him because she disrupted the fight, causing him to lose? Somehow the explanation didn't sit right.

They came to the warehouse door. Clouds swirled wraithlike everywhere. Her pattens walked on the smooth surface of Billingsgate's flat cobbles, but she couldn't see the ground below or the sky above. Across the way, the ships were gone, swallowed in a ghostly fog.

Heaven had fallen to earth.

The Ryland carriage sat directly in front of them at the ready, a great black beast on wheels. Candle lanterns hung from the carriage, their light haloing in the mist.

"Sir, fog's worse than an ol' buttermilk sky." The coachman approached, holding a lantern high over his tricorne. "I'll have the footmen lead the horses, but it'll be slow goin'."

"Do whatever is safest," Cyrus said. "We stop first by way of the New Union Coffeehouse on Cornhill to see Miss Mayhew home."

Cyrus gave her a lift up into the carriage and she settled on the seat, grateful for the luxury of a ride home. Before Cyrus found his seat, the attendant's outside light bounced off hundreds of dazzling brass tacks. The burnished points pinned the cushioned leather squab into place, a rich sight to behold. Then the door was shut, and all went dark. Claire touched the cold glass window.

"Odd night," she said, shivering.

"You'll need this." Cyrus set a woolen carriage blanket on her legs, his hand bumping her knee with impersonal delivery.

He knocked twice on the roof, and the carriage lumbered forward. She spread the heavy wool over her legs, her vision adjusting to the dark. Cyrus made a hulking shape on the opposite seat, and if she dare let her imagination run wild, she'd say he brooded.

This was an angry kind of melancholy, not the sullen variety. He was one to sit or stand square shouldered and strong, but this man facing her mulled something of considerable weight.

What was troubling him?

Cyrus pulled his coat closed, his shirt's spare bit of white showing in the dark.

"Mr. Ryland, don't you have a carriage blanket to keep you warm?"

"You've got the only one. The coachman wasn't

expecting two riders tonight." His voice was cool to her.

"I'd be pleased to share." She folded back a corner of the wool and patted the seat beside her with invitation. "It's unsafe for you to be uncovered after your evening's exertions."

And I find I want you next to me.

His shoes scraped the floor, and the well-sprung carriage bounced a little from the shift in weight. His arm brushed her, but Cyrus pulled away when she arranged the blanket over them. He sat beside her, his legs opened wide and comfortable under the blanket. Though close in body, he could've been a hundred miles away.

She stared at him under her lashes, the caution unnecessary with the dim interior. The carriage progressed with painstaking slowness over Billingsgate's cobbles, and he sat, arms folded loosely across his chest, his head tipped back against the high, flat squab behind him.

Outside, the coachman and the footmen called instructions back and forth, but inside, silence reigned. She squirmed on the leather seat, her hands fidgeting with the wool.

"Is the seat not to your liking, Miss Mayhew?"

Cyrus's stony profile was a stark line in darkness.

"The seat is fine, but I think the carriage is chillier inside than out, Mr. Ryland."

His head tilted toward her slowly. She caught a glimpse of his quicksilver eyes. The black silhouette of his head and shoulders loomed, expanding and contracting with each breath.

"I won't insult you by making flimsy excuses or denials," he replied. "But this is none of your concern."

He deserved some credit for not denying the strain that seemed to come right after Nate placed the fat purse in her hands.

In the ring, he was a force to behold, but in the dark, Cyrus made another kind of dangerous predator of which she was unsure would pounce or slumber. Either image should cause the wise woman to sit under a mantle of caution.

But what about tonight was wise or cautious?

"Pray tell why not?" Her voice dropped softly. "I make a fine ear for the man who wants to unburden his soul, you know. A certain man once asked me if listening to men was a particular talent of mine."

His teeth gleamed in the dark.

"A very perceptive man, I'm sure." The smile disappeared. "But no."

His head rested on the squab again, and she shifted nearer. Their legs touched. Cyrus allowed the contact, not moving away from her. His breath moved with steady rhythm, expanding and contracting as though he would seek sleep.

In the whole give-and-take of previous conversations, she couldn't imagine him closing down like this. Nor could she ascribe his silence entirely to exhaustion, though his body must have been wracked from his exertions. The picture of a man quietly licking unseen wounds came to mind, and something vital inside her needed to reach him.

Her fingertips grazed his sleeve. "Please."

His head rolled to face her again, an outside lantern

swayed, the light painting his enticing, granite-cut mouth in pale shades.

"Why am I not surprised you won't take no for an answer." His words were rife with intimate notes. "Or are you finding my attentions more to your liking?"

A little shiver touched her. His low, Midlander's accent played sweet music to her body's senses, even her nipples rejoiced at his sensual tone.

"I seem to be rethinking many things of late, but there is something I've wanted to say."

He didn't move.

"You gave me the best surprise with the strawberries. Thank you." She paused, searching the darkness. "For the thoughtful nature of your gift."

He relaxed under her hand.

"Despite certain of my intentions, Miss Mayhew, I do wish you well. Imagining your delight at the fruit pleased me."

"And you're not angry with me about tonight's ill-gotten gains?"

He rubbed his neck, his laugh low. "Aside from the fact that you were an unknowing participant? Don't worry, I'd be the last to find fault with your actions."

Something distant and aggrieved haunted his last words. What was this place he guarded in the shadows?

"Good, because I'd hate to be in your debt for another trespass." She tried for lightness, but he shut his eyes again, locking himself away in a private place.

Tenderness welled up, fresh as the sunrise, for this man protecting something deeply hidden. Her stalwart hero rubbed his nape, stretching his head as though the muscles bothered him there the most. Then, either despondent or tired, he let his hand drop to his lap. His heat and strength called to her as did his shirt open at the neck, the white cloth teasing her.

Cyrus needed touching.

She licked her lips and opened her mouth wider for needful air. At her age, ought she be more experienced? Sitting here, ogling a man in the dark, she felt foolish and young, not at all a woman of twenty-six. What happened to the brave woman she was at the masked ball?

The truth was she'd acted fearless that night because she'd been masked and unknown. Now, the awful specter of rejection hung over her, yet she was the one who turned away from Cyrus's advances, repeatedly rejecting him.

Did anything shake his confidence?

Juliette would know what to do.

She winced at the notion of her friend, or any other well-practiced flirt, sitting in her place. Such women would act with smooth adroitness here in the dark. She was short on experience.

And there was only one way to change that.

She reached for his coat sleeve, finding finely woven wool and a well-hewn man underneath. She slid her open hand up his forearm, his warmth and solidness unmoving. Her palm explored the hills and meadows of iron-hard muscles, lingering on one large curve high on his arm. She pressed harder on his shoulder, not wanting to miss any part of him that had been bared to her less than an hour ago.

Her breath was labored, a rhythmic strain in the silence. Her hand reached his nape as much in want of his naked skin as to give the only curative she knew for an aching neck.

Would he push her away?

Cyrus sat with eyes closed, his body rooted in place, but the air whispered of new intimacy.

Was there more pleasure in giving than receiving?

Her fingers worked their magic on his aches, loosening him. Cyrus's breath moved with the ebb and flow of a relaxed man, his resistance faltering under her care. The skin under her fingers was still fiery at his hairline from the fight. His thick, silk-wrapped queue rubbed the back of her hand, all while his head lolled against the squab.

"Did you plan to loosen my tongue under your skilled hand?"

"I want to touch you," she murmured. "Please don't tell me to stop."

His breath hitched. "I can't think of a single man who'd ask you to."

"No other man has my interest, Mr. Ryland. Only you."

His hard features softened, and her heart melted at the affection she witnessed. He smelled of wool and wood, and something else that called to her—a masculine solidity, the kind a woman could count on no matter what.

They sat in a sphere of quiet, save the sound of their breathing and the carriage's creaks and sways. Outside, the coachman yelled his encouragement to the steeds moving them forward. The whole carriage cocooned them in a peculiar world with the heaven's wool-thick mists pressing against the windows.

Her hand didn't stop rubbing his neck, but she shifted her leg, bending her knee to rest her leg on his thigh. Her patten slipped off, dropping to the floor with a thud.

Cyrus's head moved off the squab. "Are you undressing for my benefit?"

His smile's wicked curve played on her. From her stays to her drawers, everything was too tight, too much against her skin. Cyrus reached for her hand working his neck muscles. He brought it to his lips and kissed her knuckles thrice with slow adoration.

"We don't have to stop," she said, her voice breathy and quick. "I'm sure you have more aches and pains."

Mid-kiss, he smiled against the back of her hand, his warm breath brushing her skin.

"There are so many ways a man could go with that." Humor lightened his voice. "But I'm sure you mean to provide tender care to my neck only."

She grinned at her unintended innuendo. This was the experience she craved—to flirt and tease, to kiss and touch. Cyrus put his lips to her wrist, marking her with hot kisses. A spangle of pleasure shot up her arm.

"You would break down the meanest soul with your soft heart." He set her hand on the blanket's scratchy folds, his thumb caressing her wrist.

"High praise, indeed, sir."

Tinseled sparks danced across her skin, not letting her recover from those gentle touches, his lips to her arm. He stroked a lone finger on her hand that rested between them.

"And you don't care one bit that I'm the son of a Midlands swine farmer, do you?"

Cyrus asked the unexpected question, but his voice conveyed confidence in her answer. Was her chivalrous brawler showing a hidden spot? She peered at him, wanting a better view of his shadowed features. How was she to decipher this latest turn?

The carriage bumped and rocked, and the outside candle lantern swung another shaft of light inside. His quicksilver stare pinned her.

"Miss Mayhew, have you ever wondered how a freehold farmer got to be in such a fine place?"

Ten

Fear comes from uncertainty. When we are absolutely certain, whether of our worth or worthlessness, we are almost impervious to fear.

William Congreve

IF HE WAS GOING TO BLEED HIS SOUL TONIGHT, HE'D hold nothing back.

His neck and shoulders tightened with discomfort stemming from a pain far beyond the evening's bout. Not even the iciest bath could drive away this hurt. He hated the wound he was about to reopen, but he would. He needed her to know the truth.

He sought the reward of basking in Claire's genuine affections. She incited a yearning in him. He craved depth with her, a want that could shake the most stalwart of men.

The whites of Claire's eyes widened noticeably at his bold question about his place in Society.

"As a passing thought, I've wondered about your success," she admitted. "But your status in life has not been a preoccupation of mine, if that's what you're wondering."

He chuckled at her forthrightness. "One need not worry about an excess of flattery from you."

Her bright smile was his reward, a flash of white matching her white-blond hair falling wildly around her face. With her simple work woman's dress and flaxen tresses flowing to her waist, she reminded him of an engraved print in one of his sister's childhood fairy-tale books. The fair-haired maiden in the book enthralled him as a youth.

Growing up, his family possessed few books, but that translation of fairy tales had captured his sisters' interest night after night. They'd pore over the stories, discussing the merits of one character over another. One night, the treasured tome was open on the table, and he, stirring about for more food near midnight, stumbled on *her*.

The hearth's flame had lit the maiden's fine features, drawing him into her tale. The pretty woman had stolen one night in a castle, daring to dance with a prince. At midnight the maid fled, leaving behind a shoe. She returned to her old life where she labored long, living in a sparse tower. The fair-haired woman in the story became a hidden treasure in Cyrus's humble life, but her simple, gracious beauty stunned him.

The same as Claire Mayhew did now.

She inched closer to him. Under the blanket, her leg resting against his thigh was about to hook over his leg. He was certain she wanted to climb into his lap, but caution beset his pretty proprietress.

How many years had the fair Miss Mayhew been plagued with saying no to her body's wants after painful rejection from Lord Jonathan? Now, she struggled to reacquaint herself with saying yes. To him.

"You don't have to tell me if you'd rather not," she announced.

"Says the woman who offered her listening ear." His fingers stroked her hand with a featherlight touch. "Sounding a retreat?"

She said nothing, but her fingers curled into his. The sweetness of her hold could be a balm, spreading its healing powers inside his chest. Holding hands was a lost art, rarely found in the hot and sweaty grind of sex.

"You know, there's something singular about your nature. It sets you apart from other women of my acquaintance."

"Something different than my wanting to be in business as an unmarried woman?" she jested softly.

"There is that." He looked at her palms as though he could read them in the dark. "You want a man to bleed his secrets, his fears, all the things he doesn't want others to know."

Her head canted sideways upon hearing that. Had he snared her interest with his insight? He had his years as a son, a brother, and a lover to women. He was not without some knowledge of the complex, fairer sex.

His thumbs stroked the flesh of her palms, making soft circles, all while sweet Claire waited patiently.

He took a bracing breath. "I've always been big. Brawling came natural to me. My mother forbade me to fight, but I had plans to make my way as a bare-knuckle fighter."

"And your father?"

"He understood a lad needing to test his strength." His confident smile spread. "Much as we loved my mother and sisters, we both needed a rest from the swelter of female emotions at home."

"And he took you to fights?"

"No, he supported my mother and forbade me to go." His smile quirked sideways. "But he'd look the other way now and then…give me the nod if a fight came Stretford way. The bouts were small. Organizers would let local lads have some fun."

"Surely you had bruises and cuts. Wouldn't your mother know?"

"Sometimes I came away unscathed, sometimes not." He shrugged a shoulder, the wool of his coat scraping the squab. "With eight of us children at home, my mother eventually had to choose her battles. I was near full grown." His voice snagged on those last words. "But my rebellious choice caused us all no end of sorrows."

Claire's leg slid over his. His sore body tensed, preparing for the worst.

"I'd slipped away to a local fight. We'd been repairing our barn, but my father let me go, said he'd finish the job himself." An awful weight crushed his chest in the retelling. "I was gone an hour." His voice threaded unevenly. "When I came back…he was dead."

Claire gasped.

His body chilled, shuddering at the picture his mind refused to erase. Claire's hand in his was a lifeline.

He sunk lower on the seat, his words gutting him like sharp, vicious knife points. Claire's other hand reached for him. Her fingers touched his jaw—or rather, he saw them in the darkness, but he couldn't respond. He couldn't fully feel them.

"A beam fell on him." Thickness strangled his throat, holding him hostage in a dark, arid place. "If I'd been there…"

His gaze dropped to the carriage floor. Hauling eviscerating memories out for another to witness was a painful endeavor.

"I was sixteen, and I was a fool." His voice sharpened on the last syllable. "And my sainted mother never blamed me for one second."

Her hand slipped lower, finding its way inside his coat.

"Because she loved you…it wasn't your fault. It was an accident." Claire's hand rested over his heart, the fabric of his shirt a flimsy barrier between them.

The warm touch gave him connection, grounding him.

"After what happened, I'd like to say I grew up quickly, but I didn't." He stared into the gloom. "I was the head of our farm at sixteen, something I never wanted. But my mother, my sisters counted on me to take care of them. And I failed miserably."

He turned away from Claire. Had to. Acceptance softened her features; her goodness proved too much. She offered tenderness, the gentleness washing over him, clean and kind.

The woolen murk beyond his carriage window swirled as heavy as his self-loathing. His eyes shut against the pain, keeping private the humbling wetness on his lashes.

Claire scooted closer, leaning her head against him. Could she hear his heart's erratic pounding? Her hand caressed his chest over his shirt, the fabric hushing whispers with the movement.

Then she slipped her hand inside his shirt, the fleshly contact a sharp, sweet pain. He shuddered. Her touch was an undeserved gift. Claire's hand rubbed a circle over his heart, her warmth and nearness crumbling him. The tender-souled, midtown maiden lured him, pulling him back from the abyss.

His eyes opened, and he took a deep breath, shaking his head.

"I wasn't a good farmer. My family suffered under my inept care."

"You were sixteen."

She said the quiet words as though the number was sufficient explanation. Her gentle hand cupped his chest, the caress discovering the heaviest curve. He should rejoice at her blatant exploration, but he needed her to understand, to know the man he really was.

"For years we struggled, then my sister, Elspeth, married. Her husband ran the farm, but we needed more funds to rebuild the herd. We'd already lost many swine to a fever, losses caused by my mistakes." His voice was graveled and sparse. "I did the only thing I knew. I sought fights whenever possible, took on odd jobs."

"And you never got hurt? From the fighting?"

With her cheek pressed close to his coat, her voice

vibrated on his skin, as intimate as a kiss. Her tender trust softened him, making him want to be the man worthy of her.

"Knocked around some. Nothing bad," he said. "But I found a position helping one James Brindley, an engineer. He was set on a two-month survey of Midlands territory for the Duke of Bridgewater." His low laugh was a dry sound. "We'd heard of the duke's half-cocked plan to build canals, some in places where no river ran. The Duke's Cut it was called."

He closed his eyes a needful second. Her thumb rubbed his breastbone, and those feather-light touches led him like a bread-crumb trail through this dark forest to keep going. He needed to finish this…have her know the full truth.

"James and I got on well. I was quick with numbers and good for moving logs." He opened his eyes and smiled thinly.

The heel of her palm grazed his nipple, sending jagged shocks through him. His breath caught. Of course she meant to render care—his mind knew this, but his ravaged body would not discern lust from gentle ministrations.

Over his coat, he set his hand on the shape of hers hidden under his shirt and coat. "During those two months, James spoke to me of things beyond the world of Stretford. Of the duke's plans to build canals all over England, of the warehouses that needed building where good men like me could get a leg up in the world."

Claire tilted her face to him and listened attentively, their breath mingling.

"When construction began, I was twenty-six and my connection with Brindley gave me a good position overseeing other laborers. But I wanted more, could see this was going to be something big. Then the duke came one day to survey progress in Stretford."

A deep, looseness expanded his chest.

"I'd been digging and was covered in mud, but this was my chance. Brindley had spoken of me to the duke and brought me up to meet His Grace." He tipped his head back against the squab. "I surprised everyone by asking for a moment of his time. I had a business proposition."

"Then you understand bold persistence well, don't you?"

He could hear the smile in her voice.

"I understand going after what you want," he agreed. "I walked the trench line with the duke, asking how much would it take to become a stake-holder in his new scheme."

"He didn't laugh, did he?"

"The bankers with him did, but I had little to lose in the asking." His mouth curled in a smile of a different nature. "And now those men work for me."

"A bit vengeful are you?"

He snorted. "More like practical. And the duke, to his credit, listened. Too many people thought his plan for canals the mark of lunacy."

"Apparently, you and the duke were visionary."

His shoulders lifted under her praise; he was warmed that she wasn't put off by his brashness or that he was a man who once earned his way by hard labor.

"His Grace was at least, but the minimum starting

investment was a thousand pounds." His head rested again on the squab again. "The duke said he'd come Stretford way again in one month. If I had a *hundred* pounds, he'd let me in." He snorted. "For the likes of me, he could've said a million…both amounts were nigh to impossible."

"Then you brawled your way to a hundred pounds."

"If it were only that easy. I fought at every opportunity. But the month was ending and I was still seventy-five pounds short."

"But I thought you won enough money?"

He shook his head. "I went south to the Bristol Inn. Famous for bare-knuckle bouts. Men come from all over…Scotland, Ireland, the Netherlands, Germany… all to fight. Sailors, farmers, soldiers. A few knew of me as the Stretford Bruiser, but this was big, and I had this one night."

"They had me squared off against an Irish lad, younger and less experienced, but the same size as me. Everyone expected me to win."

"And that's how you won the seventy-five pounds?"

He scrubbed a hand over his face. He had to face this moment.

"No," he said, looking into the fog beyond the window. "I cheated."

Claire's body went taut against him, a tenuous change, but she didn't move. He would finish this and lay all bare before her. An inner drive made him want no secrets between them.

"I asked a friend to take all my money and bet steep odds against me. He wanted to leave for the colonies, so we worked out a plan. I took a punch from the Irish lad. Let him knock me out."

Claire's exhale stirred his open shirt. "Then, my forging your signature doesn't look quite so bad."

"More like I understand desperation and going hard after something you want. And I understand Mr. Fincher's bold move tonight." He reached for her, running a single lock of white-blond hair between his fingers. "Most of all, I hated how easy it was to be dishonest."

For a moment he was suspended, free of past failures and judgments. His evening's toils charged his joints and sinew; the price would be stiff movement tomorrow, but tonight, he sailed with newfound freedom. There was lightness in confession, an easing of the shared burden of condemning choices.

"Aside from my friend who left for the colonies, no one knows, save you." He brushed hair away from her face. "Even my family thinks I managed to scrape together enough funds from my fights."

Claire turned her head slightly and kissed the hand touching her cheek. The innocent peck was a ray of light breaking him free of this murky part of his past.

"I went home and met the duke soon after. I did what I had to do to help my mother and sisters," he said, his tone striking firm. "Over time, I was able to pay for tutors for my nephews who showed interest in advancing themselves, buy a farm for another sister, and pay for a curative tea for Lucinda's lung ailments."

His voice was resolute. There was nothing heroic in what he did, but he did it.

"And what happened?"

"My friend left for the colonies, and I went back to digging the Bridgewater Canal, taking it from Stretford to Manchester with a lot of other men. I constructed warehouses for the duke first and later was able to build mine. One by one." He grinned in the dark. "I didn't become wealthy overnight, despite the broadsheets' claims. I worked hard for years, with my bare hands by day, working my ledgers by night."

"Ah, the ledgers," she said ruefully.

He gave the blond lock he stroked a gentle tug. "Yes, the ledgers. Eventually, I bought land and built more warehouses. It was slow going, but I learned the law of percentages. Live on a small percentage and reinvest everything else. Something Brindley taught me."

"And your fighting?"

Air left his lungs in a hard rush. "A younger man's dream. That pursuit dwindled…had to because of other responsibilities."

The carriage passed buildings dotted with candle lanterns. The horses snorted at their evening's labor, and men, not so far removed from Cyrus at one time, worked to bring Miss Mayhew to her doorstep.

"I hardly fight at all…practice some at London's gentlemen's clubs, but tonight was my last bout. Bareknuckle brawling's not best for fitting in to Piccadilly. I don't speak of it to others."

He rested his cheek on top of her head, breathing in her scent. Claire's hair smelled of cinnamon, something far better than any fine perfume.

"The bruise on your cheek will give you away." Amusement threaded her voice, reaching him from the shadows.

He touched the small cut.

"Tonight was a chance for a man moving past his prime to test himself one last time."

She pinched his chest. "What I saw tonight was hardly past prime, sir."

His sore arm wrapped behind Claire, bringing her close. "The sport favors the younger man."

He took a deep breath, lighter, cleaner even from sharing his burden. He wanted fiercely for Claire to accept him as he was: a barely educated laborer who took a risk and won.

"Then, you're not…repulsed by me? What I've done? Or my size?"

Claire pulled away, the loss of her warmth against his side making him cold. Her blond hair trailed to her waist, an obscure light in the darkness. Did she need a better look at him?

His soul was hanging there by a thread. If she rejected him again…

She slid a finger over the cleft of his chin, rubbing the indent up and down with the softest touch. A hot twinge shot to his groin. His carnal mind equated the move to similar strokes he'd like to do inside Claire.

"No," she replied. "I'm not repulsed by you in any way. Quite the opposite."

He closed his eyes, aware how much he wanted her. The torment came in wanting a woman and not knowing how to express the right words in the right way. She was bent on living independently, making her own mark in the world, a woman not in need of a man.

Giving and providing was all he knew.

For him, love's lifeblood flowed when he took care of others, but to be on equal footing with a woman? And share his heart? He'd rather face a dozen brawlers than one slender midtown proprietress in the ring of words and emotions.

Claire slid forward into his lap, finding a perch there. Those perfect twin circles of her bottom burned a saucy message on his thigh.

"You plan to have me flat on my back again?" His voice was as stiff and strained as another part of him.

With her skirts bunched up behind her, only the trifling cloth of her drawers separated her bottom's cleavage from his breeches. He could *feel* the shape of her, but she squirmed against him, likely having no idea her effect on him.

His eyes shut; he was badly in need of stout-hearted restraint.

"I don't think we have the room for that sort of thing," she said, tucking her head under his chin. "But you could give me helpful insight."

Right then, the blasted carriage bounced hard. He winced. The mishap was minor; the innocent brushing of her hip against his phallus was not. The shot of pleasure was a torment.

"You'll have to enlighten me on the nature of the"—he paused, seeking control when her hand slipped inside his open shirt again—"insight you require."

Her middle finger discovered the tip of his nipple. A butterfly could be touching the nib of his flesh the way she toyed with him.

His muscles burned from brawling three rounds

with a man nearly a decade younger. Now his sinews tensed from head to toe with hot embers teasing him everywhere, and his present opponent was willow slim and winning.

"I was thinking you could provide much-needed assistance." Her voice purred a soft vibration against his neck. "With sensual flirtations. I seem to be lacking in experience."

"I'd say you're doing very well."

He had a pretty good idea what Claire wanted: to explore sensual delights, to go so far and stop. If he were a betting man, he'd wager his proprietress was finding her way and getting comfortable with saying yes to him.

Did he have the fortitude for the battle ahead?

Neck tendons strained. He worked to keep himself in check so as not to overwhelm her. And then she pulled back his coat to free the few buttons on his waistcoat that he'd fastened earlier. Determined hands pushed aside his garments with a whisper of sound.

His chin dropped to his chest, all the better to watch her. He lounged on the seat, hips slung low, his feet bracing the floor.

Outside, the candle lantern swayed, doling meager slashes of light inside. Claire stared at the dip in the middle of his chest muscles. Her intent gaze scoured him, sending waves of gooseflesh over him. Even his male nipples peaked, hungry for her to touch him again.

His breath tripped at her soft seduction. Claire had unknowingly played Eve tonight when she'd pulled back her blanket, beckoning him to sit beside her.

Now, her fingers feathered his ribs, exploring the trenches and ridges of his flesh.

"I never thought of a man's torso as beautiful." Her voice was fluttery and sweet in the darkness. "But yours is."

Weakened as he was, he warred with his intentions to be honorable, but there was only so much a body could receive before much giving ought to be done.

Her cloak fell off her shoulders, his resolve falling with it.

His hand rooted under the blanket covering their legs. Her skirt's woolen weave brushed his hand. Claire's underskirts gathered mid-thigh, but his quest-ing hand didn't have to work hard to find the thin cambric chemise. The flimsy fabric taunted him, dipping between her thighs…her warm, firm thighs.

Cyrus curled his hand over the spot above one knee, his fingertips pressing her flesh.

Her body shook with small tremors when his fingers traced the contours of her leg. Her one hand on his shoulder held on tight, digging in five points of pressure. Was this desire *and* nervousness?

The fact bolstered him. His proper midtown pro-prietress wanted him, was inviting him to touch her in this most private way. Her other hand spread across his chest as though she needed the maximum feel of him under her palm.

"I know I'm not very skilled at this." She breathed into his neck, her lips grazing his collarbone with a tender kiss.

"My hand's under your skirt," he said, stroking her thigh. "I'd say you've mastered the skill."

She tittered and squirmed before sitting up straighter in his lap. Each shift, each move threw more fuel on the fire already crackling between them. He suspected they sat at a crossroads of wants—a contrary place for a man with a hard phallus and a softening heart to be.

One could so quickly overrule the other.

And his seeking fingers slipped to her inner thigh, hunting for a hot feminine place with deliberate sluggishness. He wanted her to want him. Badly.

"There is some-*thing*"—Claire's voice pitched high when his fingers traveled up the inside seam of her drawers—"else."

Her breath huffed hard enough to stir the tendrils falling across her face. Inside his shirt, her nails dug into his chest. She held on for dear life, overwhelmed, he was sure, by the shocking feel of a slow caress. His midtown proprietress was hot and ready to explode with barely a hint of touch, and he hadn't reached the secret opening of her drawers yet.

"Shhh…" he hushed, soothing her while his fingers stalled inches from the palpable heat under her skirts. "We need to take this slower."

Claire pulled away, blinking at him like an owl. "You mean we're going too fast?" Her chest moved up and down as though she'd been running hard.

He chuckled, finding her brand of innocence and knowing a pleasure. "Exactly how did things go with your Lord Jonathan?"

As soon as the words were out, he regretted them. She teetered on his thigh, and her hand inside his shirt went slack.

"That was ungentlemanly of me," he said. "Forgive me."

At least she stayed on his thigh, but his hand retreated from the trail of her drawers' inner seam. She shook her head, more hair slipping over her shoulders.

"Don't. I want no words unsaid between us. No secrets. Even if they're unpleasant." Her hand on his shoulder rubbed back and forth. "And I rather liked what we were doing."

"I won't rush you." He rasped a chuckle. "Accosting you in my carriage wasn't something I planned." They hadn't bothered to draw the curtains, though no one roamed the fog-filled midnight streets. He couldn't recall passing a night watchman.

"Accost me at will," she murmured. "You know you haven't kissed me yet."

Her words were a gratifying entreaty, but she needed silk sheets and soft candles, not midnight groping under a carriage blanket with his coachman bellowing outside. The wilt of her lips at their lack of kisses charmed him. His arm tucked around her backside, and his other hand left the warmth of her leg, seeking the corner of her mouth.

"Claire," he chided, his finger stroking her cheek. "You need to be sure of this."

She clutched his hand touching her face and kissed the center of his palm.

"I'm sure of one thing, Cyrus. You are the best treasure I've found since coming to London." Her words curled around him with reverent confession. "I admit I don't know exactly *what* I want when it comes to you, but please tonight...*touch me*."

Her plea, a mix of yearning and confusion, grabbed him. Claire guided his hand lower, dragging it over her square neckline until the center of his palm nestled over her breast. She pushed her hair back, a leisured move, all while looking him in the eye.

Beneath his hand her heart quickened, but Claire placed both her hands slowly over his like an unspoken vow.

Midnight smoldered with enticement. Nothing was cold inside the carriage. The windows clouded, covering the glass as good as any curtain. Claire fixed her gaze on him and untied the neat, proper bow that closed the front of her bodice, slowly freeing herself one prim X of lacing at a time.

Languorous and heavy lidded, his fortitude crumbled under each loosened tie.

Claire's breath skipped and bumped its way in and out of her lungs when the top of her bodice drooped. Practical, pale-colored stays pushed her small breasts up with modest invitation. The allure was more appealing than any strumpet's overflowing corset.

His fingers flexed against the wool blanket with an itch to touch her, to free her. Soft, white half-moons waxed and waned above the fabric of her stays with each breath she took.

Nostrils flaring, his threadbare control snapped. He planted his hands on her ribs and plucked her from sitting sidesaddle on his leg to face him and straddle his legs. The move would undo them both.

She gasped at the sudden change of position. Sitting astride his lap, her body jiggled when his fingers pulled free the front lacing of her stays with more determination than seduction.

All thoughts of where they sat and his good intentions evaporated.

Claire gripped his shoulders, her bodice slackening under his firm intent. She tipped her head, watching his fingers do their best.

"Is this a talent of yours?" she asked saucily. "You unloosed my stays faster than I do on a bad day."

His gaze shot up briefly from concentrating on her bodice, but he looked down again at his labors, yanking free one more impertinent X of lacing. He didn't pounce on her almost-freed breasts. Instead, his hands surrounded her body high on her ribs as though he would memorize her shape, treasuring the feel of her.

She stared at his encircling hands, white-blond tresses slipping forward, a frothy waterfall over his hands. His hands moved with agonizing slowness up her flimsy, open bodice. Wool abraded his palms as if to give fair contrast to the pearled skin he was about to touch. His hands stopped at the bottom of her high curves.

Her stare sparkled, meeting his. A message poured from her, an entrancing thread of connection. Claire's lips parted. His jaw loosened. He wanted to tell her how beautiful she was with flour on her hands, giving him her opinions, how she was the prettiest woman he'd ever seen in her simple dresses, but words became flimsy and insufficient.

Where words failed, touch would not.

His thumbs slipped inside her bodice, the pads brushing the small tips pointing at him. Her breath hissed. Claire's fingers dug into his shoulders, clamping him as if she feared falling off his lap. He made tender rosettes over her areolas in careful adoration. He cupped her downy-soft flesh, his eyes burning to capture every detail of what she revealed to him in the dark.

The laxness of her lower lip...the slant of her eyelids...the tiny spread of her nostrils...

Claire was unhinged by the shocking touch. Her head fell back, exposing the white column of her throat.

He moved to the edge of the seat, all the better for her to sit flush against him. The action coiled another layer of tension on their oversensitized flesh. His vixen jammed her mons against him, rubbing and searching. Her knees gripped the sides of him the way riders grip a galloping horse. His breath turned ragged at the picture of her riding him thus, and clear thoughts tumbled.

He planted his mouth, hot and open, on her neck. It wasn't quite a kiss, more insatiable hunger for Claire. His body rattled hard against the squab when her rubbing turned to a desperate grind. His hips followed nature's rhythm, his aching erection rubbing against her.

If there were noises outside, if his carriage stopped, if London had been invaded, he wouldn't know for the pounding in his ears and scorching heat in his breeches.

In a flash, his hand went to his placket, loosening a button.

Claire's body quaked, tremors wracking her torso.

She rubbed against his hand slipping between them, stirring up flames with her mewling cries. He knew what she craved…and he groaned, unable to deny her. He angled his knuckles at her damp heat seeping through her drawers, glad for her most secret place to abrade the back of his hand.

"*Cy-rus…*" Her plea was soft and high.

"I know," he said, his voice ragged against her skin.

Grace of movement was lost. He fumbled with his placket, springing free one button and then another. With his other hand, he grabbed her hip, trying to stay the wild, bucking ride. Their panting, staccato breaths drummed a muffled noise.

His questing mouth kissed her collarbone on a trail to her nipple, the color of that, desired circle a pale contrast in the dark. She cried out when his lips encircled her petite nipple, and he sucked. He buried his face in her gentle cleavage, kissing and nipping heavenly flesh when his mouth banged something hard and metallic.

He jerked back. The object dropped from her bodice and clattered on the floor.

Claire clamped a hand on her gaping bodice, her breath heavy, meeting his effort for effort. His hair was hot at the back of his neck, same as during his bout.

"What was that?" he asked.

"My key."

"To your heart?" he teased, his lips brushing the underside of her breast where the metal had rested.

Her hand slipped from his shoulder, pressing his head close to her. "My shop."

Cornhill. Their destination…a place they'd be at soon.

Her breath skipped as hard as her heart. He kissed her breasts, lingering on one pale side curve. The tip of his tongue tested the smoothness of her skin there. She was perfect, and she needed calming. He needed calming to get a better grip on this rampant, unintended seduction.

He pulled away, gulping down air. They teetered on some edge—one he had to draw them both away from. His fingers stroked her hair and grazed her collarbone, wanting connection of some kind to ease them both. Claire's sensitized body shook with delicious shivers under his hands, a tantalizing excuse not to stop.

Outside, more establishments with vague dots of lights passed his window…midtown.

"We've got to be close to your shop." He brushed the back of his hand high on her chest, caressing her skin.

His hands banded her ribs, and he set her on the opposite seat. The blanket and her cloak slid to the floor. Claire covered her bodice with a limp hand. Her head and shoulders lolled against the squab, and with her hair flowing to the seat, she made a perfect picture of a temptress in a bawdy house painting.

The carriage jolted to a stop. Men called to each other outside. Slowly, his hearing became attuned to the outside world, his coachman and the attendants. The sound of slogging footsteps through mud approached. Cyrus jerked the curtain shut, light peeking through the sliver of opening at the curtain's end.

The voice outside called, "Sir, the New Union Coffeehouse."

"Wait," he called back, grabbing the door's handle from the inside just to be sure. He spoke in a hush to Claire. "Your cloak."

Cold seeped in little by little, the sudden stop dousing him. Both of them were dazed by the flare of passion that had been near out of control. Claire tugged her bodice higher, yanking her laces together to tie a makeshift bow. She fumbled on the floor for her cloak. When she sat up, her bodice gapped loose and low.

She looked nothing of the properly clothed proprietress, but she swept her cloak around her, the dark shape hiding her form. Her nimble fingers tied a quick bow under her chin, and she dropped lower, her hands patting the carriage floor.

"What are you looking for?" he asked.

"My key, my patten…"

He let go of the door to help her, and his hand brushed iron. "I found it."

He gripped the key in one hand and stuffed the blanket on the seat beside him, closing his waistcoat and placket with a few buttons. He had very nearly turned his carriage into a makeshift bed. The notion made him smile. This was no different than foolish times when, as an eager young man, he'd sought secret places to tup a willing maid.

Claire found her patten and slipped on the outer shoe after a second attempt. Her awkward, fumbling movements had to be born of frustrated flesh. His own body rioted from lack of fulfillment.

Cyrus checked her and took a deep breath. "Ready?"

"Yes." She gave a shaky nod and lifted her hood.

Her smile, likely meant to reassure him, floundered. She needed soothing. He reached across the short chasm and brushed back her hair. Her lashes fluttered low, her body drooping into his calming touch. When she looked at him again, Claire nodded.

"Open the door," he ordered.

His body strained at having to unbend from the seat and step into the cold. From sore muscles to his stiff phallus, discomfort was his. They exited the carriage, walking in a fog no less thick and gray as when they'd left Billingsgate. The heavens swirled their mysteries as stirring as what went on with Claire.

At the shop door, Cyrus winced from the erection raging in his breeches, one part of him resenting the evening's intrusive end. He was grateful the mist concealed his unruliness; the placket of his breeches bulged fiercely in want of the temptation beside him.

Claire was an enchantress within her dark hood, his fairy-tale maiden looking up at him with sparkling eyes. A white hand reached up and the backs of her fingers caressed his jaw.

"Thank you," she whispered, glancing at his cheek. "You took a blow for me tonight, even if you didn't mean to."

The swelling was high enough to push skin into the lower plane of his vision, a fact that had eluded him in the swelter of sensual groping. He grinned wide, his body sore yet invigorated to his marrow at the light shining from her eyes.

There was something good in being the man, the hero, she needed. He'd take a hundred more blows for her, but he couldn't resist the sexual thread that bound them together this night.

"There are parts of me that hurt more." He braced one hand high on the door frame of her shop and looked down at his placket. "Parts only you can soothe."

Her lips pressed together, fighting the brazen smile bursting forth. Her fingers slid to the cleft in his chin, an indent that seemed to fascinate her.

"You tempt me, Mr. Ryland. You truly do, but…" She glanced at the carriage and her lashes dropped.

Her shop was frequented by some of his servants. The midnight carriage ride was already questionable, but sending the carriage home without him in it would besmirch her in the worst way. Her reputation deserved to be honored.

He squared his shoulders and put her key into the lock. "Then, if I come again, I must arrive as an anonymous caller in a hack."

She said nothing, brushing close to his arm, smiling quiet encouragement from the edge of her hood. The metal lock sprang free, and he pushed open the door.

Claire stepped past the doorway. He pulled her heavy coin pouch from a pocket inside his coat and handed it to her. The horses snorted their impatience behind him, a good reminder all needed to be abed. Her blue-green eyes flickered with unknown emotions, as though she would say more. She searched his face, and he imagined her wanting to pull him inside and shut the door forever.

In that sweet state of confusion, he did the gallant thing and stretched out his hand.

"Your key," he said quietly.

Her fingers grazed his palm, and his hand closed in a gentle grip. He bent over her receiving hand, kissed the star-shaped scar, and let go. Before he did something regretful, he shut the New Union's door.

He stood in the cold, dampness clinging to his face. The lock slid into place and Claire barred her door. On the other side of the door's window, she hesitated, clutching the key to her chest. Her face through the wavy panes brought to mind an angel etched in stained glass.

Was there longing in her eyes? He wouldn't know, for she turned and the shop's darkness swallowed her form. Walking back to his empty carriage, his head hung heavy. He would find his way back to Piccadilly and soak his pained parts in the finest copper tub in his well-appointed room. His hand covered his heart— this part of him hurt worse.

The woman he wanted slept alone by choice in a sparse garret meanly furnished above a coffee shop, a woman content with her life as is…a woman not on the hunt for wealth or position.

He climbed back into his carriage. The attendant shut the door, but Cyrus couldn't bring himself to knock on the ceiling, signaling time to leave. He waited, keeping a careful eye on the window above the shop until scant light flickered on the other side of the glass. Then he knocked twice on the carriage roof.

Sitting in the dark, he was cold. No fire, no blanket could warm him. A scrap of white pooled on the floor. He picked it up. Claire's neckerchief, the same one she used for her tender ministrations.

His hand slipped inside his coat, the neckerchief in his grip. The ache in his chest raged. Claire had full grasp of her desired independence. She didn't need him at all.

Eleven

Wit be my faculty, and pleasure my occupation…

William Congreve, *The Way of the World*

TEMPTATION WAS A RED DAMASK DAY GOWN, STRAW-*berry red* to be exact.

There'd be no mistaking the luscious shade or the intent of the gown's purchaser.

Claire clutched a bowl under one arm, voices and the clink of stoneware buzzing beyond her kitchen. Nate had the shop well in hand, leaving her to the sanctity of her kitchen and the blessed relief of baking. Doughy ingredients folded into chaste submission under a wooden spoon, her instrument of choice.

Above stairs the siren's silk spread across her bed, lace-trimmed elbows and lush skirts daring her to don the decadent fashion.

And then there were *those* undergarments.

Shot silk drawers shimmered with sensual promise— demure white, no less.

"Humph." The sound burst through the kitchen's warmth while her footsteps trod a well-worn path.

"What's that, miss?" Annie skimmed a paring knife over an apple, her blue eyes cautious from under her mobcap.

Claire stopped her pacing. "Did I say something?"

A long, green curl of apple skin dropped into a bucket.

"You didn't exactly say anything, but you've been beatin' that dough like it's your worst enemy." The freckles around her mouth twitched. "Are you angry?"

Claire set the bowl on the table and sank into a chair. "I'm not angry. It's…it's today. I don't have time for the luncheon."

She had no predilection for frivolous lady's luncheons or meetings meant to convince pampered women that trouble existed for others of their sex. But did she have time for Cyrus? Time to fritter away the afternoon in search of melting kisses? Since the carriage ride two nights past, a particular shirtless, bare-knuckle brawler invaded her mind.

Annie denuded another apple, the skin coiling like a thin, green snake.

"Then something's got you afraid." Annie said the words as though matters boiled down to a few simple emotions. "But I can't picture that bein' you."

Claire's hand froze on its journey to the sugar bowl. "Afraid? I'm not *afraid* of this luncheon. It's as simple as eating food with other women. What I lack is time."

"Ahh, then if it's as simple as you say"—Annie nodded sagely, dropping another naked apple into her bowl—"you won't be afraid to go upstairs and put on that pretty gown a certain man bought for you, a man who wants you to be comfortable dining with other fine ladies. No one has to know how you got the gown."

Annie made a "certain man's" purchase of clothes for Claire sound like a reasonable thing. But the gown above stairs was not the same as a gift of lush strawberries.

Claire's fingers dipped in the sugar bowl, the fine grain rubbing her skin. She sprinkled the sugar into the glaze meant for the apple turnovers fresh from the oven. Cyrus was meant to have one of these desserts at the luncheon.

"Or is it the man himself that's got you flustered?" Annie eyed the doughy mass. "'Cause I've never seen you give dough such a thrashing."

She was about to chime in something about the shop being so busy, but a rattle of footsteps shook the stairs and Juliette's embroidered hems flounced into view.

"Claire," she called into the kitchen. "You must come up *now*."

Juliette bent over the rail, her volume rising on the last word. One hand clutched the rail with the other fanning a dozen hairpins.

"A few more minutes. The tarts aren't wrapped. The turnovers need sugar—"

"I'll do it," Annie said. "Go on and have your bath, miss. I can sprinkle sugar just as good as you and wrap the pastries when their ready." Her russet head tipped toward the shop. "And don't worry about the shop. Nate and me have a good hand on things."

Juliette muttered rapid French under her breath as she stormed up the steps, flashing saffron underskirts in her charge. Claire tugged off her mobcap, eyeing the plump, golden turnovers lined up for the luncheon. This would be good for business, but business wasn't what drove her today.

Cyrus Ryland did. The image of his carved stomach muscles was forever branded in her memory. Her fingers would suddenly touch things, needing something tactile when the fascinating circle of hair around his navel came to mind.

She lived with a curious push-pull over her rough-edged landlord. He fought life hard, not giving up, and he carried familial responsibility on his substantial shoulders, thinking of others over his own wants.

It was his want of her, that was nothing less than dangerous.

She squeezed Annie's arm. "Thanks."

"You havin' a good time's the best thanks I need. Besides," the cook said, winking, "I want all the news of what's what with your Mr. Ryland come Monday."

She sped upstairs, one corner of her mouth curling in a conspirator's smile. "He's not *my* Mr. Ryland."

In her room, the tub sat near her fire grate. Stockings, underskirts, and patched drawers hung on clotheslines strung across the room, the common woman's laundry.

"We must get you out of those clothes and cleaned up." Juliette's nose wrinkled prettily. "I cannot have one of my creations smelling of coffee and sugar."

Her friend played lady's maid, making quick work of helping her into the bath. She piled Claire's hair high on her head, speaking under her breath about no time to wash the tresses, tresses Claire was sure smelled of flour and sugar.

"The bath is tepid," Claire said, hugging herself in cooling water.

Juliette handed over soap and a cloth. "Hot water is for the timely bather."

"I'm duly chastised." She splashed and scrubbed and surrendered herself to drying and dressing.

The transformation would have to be a quick one. Fine silk drawers and a chemise came first, followed by a corset strong enough to stand on its own. Claire held fast to the bedpost while the Frenchwoman tugged the silk corset from behind with the insistence of a sergeant-at-arms corralling a new recruit.

"I'm sure you don't have to cinch me"—Claire's voice wheezed from another heave from behind—"that tightly."

"I'm sure I do."

The red gown spread across the white coverlet, a brazen slash of color in her sober garret. The daring neckline was pure Juliette in design; the sedate damask's pattern of red on red posies and a small trail of white lace rimming the neckline saved the fashion piece from pure licentiousness.

Juliette spun Claire around, her brows snapping together while she assessed the shape she wished to form. For the Frenchwoman, fashion was built from the first layers, artistry to be taken seriously.

Claire touched the decadent white silk drawers. "Rather audacious for a man to order undergarments for a woman, don't you think? For that matter, ordering garments for me at all is highly inappropriate."

"He wishes only for you to be comfortable and dressed well for the event." Black brows winged high.

"I do not understand this need of yours to argue about a man's gifts. There is no such thing as appropriate or *in*appropriate. You are a grown woman. There is only what you want or do not want from a man."

A Gallic shrug followed her friend's reasoning. Passion and beauty trumped propriety in Miss Sauveterre's mind. Claire laughed, a jittery sound.

"But, Juliette, *undergarments?*"

Lush lips turned a familiar moue. "Do you like wearing them?"

Her hesitation added fuel to Juliette's argument, those dark eyes flaring wide at Claire.

"You see? That is what this is about. Besides, your Mr. Ryland and I were of the same mind when it came to the ensemble. My finer creations begin with what's underneath."

She would argue that he wasn't *her* Mr. Ryland, but everything was blurring in a sea of wants. One thing was certain: boundaries of friendship and loyalty and confidences had shifted these past few weeks.

"And you never breathed a word to me. You and Elise, sewing clothes for me."

"You would too if he offered you the same outrageous sum. He bought my talent *and* my silence."

Was all of midtown up for sale? Mr. Ryland tried to buy Nate's silence with a gold guinea, and now her friends. She studied the salacious red cloth.

Juliette's gaze slid to the gown. "It is not such a bad thing to be wooed thus by a man. He was most emphatic about the gown's color."

The *strawberry*-red color. Her friend smirked at her.

"Step into this." Juliette held out a white shot silk

underskirt, the iridescent fabric shimmering with the palest shades.

Claire had seen the fine, woven silk on ladies of the highest water. Her fingernails scraped the cloth, playing a whispered tune as Juliette secured the tapes.

"Did he specially request the shot silk?"

"*Non*, but he paid for it." Juliette peered around Claire's shoulder, her mouth curving in a wicked smile. "The man could not possibly know the undergarments he sought. So I helped him. All in the name of seduction."

Seduction, indeed.

The red damask gown came next, beautiful enough to lure any woman into sensual territory. It was seduction masquerading as a proper day gown: practical in length, for showing pretty ankles, and a bodice trimmed with a dainty line of white lace. There'd be no modest disguising of her bust today. Three flounces decorated the back of the skirt, a visual diversion for a gown lacking substantial false hips.

They had to move to the center of the room with the laundry lines crowding them.

"Raise your arms," Juliette ordered.

A red cloud descended over Claire's head, and another layer of silk slipped provocative softness over her body.

"Today is not about seduction." Claire's fingers skimmed the low, scooped line. "Though there seems to be a dearth of fabric here…"

Juliette fussed with the fitting before lacing Claire from the back.

"Trust me, if a man requests a woman wear a red dress, he has only sensual pursuits on his mind. And there will be *non* neckerchief to ruin the lines of this bodice." She worked efficiently at tying Claire into the dress. "Now for finishing touches. Hair and cosmetics."

"I don't need cosmetics."

The Incognitas sprang to mind, with their towering hair and tiny, red bow lips. High-priced strumpets, Nate had called them. She opened her mouth to say as much, but arguments stalled under Juliette's sharp glare.

"Of course," she conceded. "Where do you want me to sit?"

Juliette pointed to the table laden with pins, tiny ceramic pots, and a brush and hair pads of varying sizes. Dutifully, she perched on the chair and let her friend brush her hair from scalp to waist. Though this was a simple daytime luncheon, she couldn't help but feel she was being armed for a battle of a different sort.

Juliette's snappishness was edgier than usual. The mantua-maker cum lady's maid, stepped back, assessing the architecture of what she would create.

"We will have to go with a simpler style, *non*?"

A smaller, cushioned piece crowned the middle of Claire's head, but this modest pad gave her hair tasteful inches of elevation. Juliette coiled locks in a modest pile, covering the accessory. Pins scraped Claire's scalp. Juliette stepped back again to assess her work, dark brows slashing downward. Her lips pursed before fingers tugged loose wisps here and there. Small scissors snipped, creating dainty strands of hair.

"A little white powder for your skin, some kohl, a touch of rouge for your lips and cheeks would do you good, *non*? *Très à la mode*."

Claire tipped her chin high, grinning. "I thought you wanted a man to put color in my cheeks?"

Juliette didn't rise to the bait. She sat in the chair facing Claire, brushing a white powder of smashed vanilla, cacao, and almonds onto her palette. The powder's aroma at least was pleasant. Claire closed her eyes, surrendering to the artistry. The gentle smells and the soft brushing on her skin calmed her.

Outside, Cornhill burst with carts and carriages, a colorful buzz beyond her small window. Inside her garret, the soft clink of small ceramic pots sounded as Juliette worked. A brush tapped a jar, the music of a different kind of artist. A scrap of clean wool dipped in a tiny pot of carmine, and the Frenchwoman rouged cheeks and lips. Kohl rimmed the edges of Claire's eyelids, giving the final touch.

"Today is not simply about the art of fashion. I prepare you also for battle," Juliette said, her voice hitting melancholy notes.

Claire's spine stiffened, already properly rigid from the whalebone corset. She opened her eyes, surprised at the faint lines etched around her friend's mouth and eyes.

"Juliette?"

The Frenchwoman set down the slender kohl brush with deliberate care.

"You, my friend, will lunch with some of London's finest ladies today. They will not take kindly to one such as you walking in their midst." A furrow slashed her forehead. "Especially because you've caught the eye of a man they covet for themselves or their daughters."

"It won't be all that bad."

"You don't understand." Juliette sighed. "You are beautiful and you don't *need* them. You don't obey the rules of their world." She patted Claire's hand. "These things make you a dangerous woman. The power you have, and you aren't even aware."

Covered in decadent silks and arrayed as a woman of fashion and leisure wasn't her natural state. This was stiff and new, the same as her mind thinking constantly about a certain man was new.

But powerful?

The corners of her mouth curled in a private smile. Better to say she was a woman falling weightless into a gray sea, unsure where this way led.

"And you have *his* attention." Juliette's dark eyes sparkled at Claire before she rummaged around her basket and found a thin strip of black velvet. "This works since I have no jewelry to offer."

The slender adornment went around her neck, the velvet bow tickling her nape. Silks, velvet, and Cyrus: she was awash in sensual stimulation and she wasn't in his presence yet.

The silk drawers brushed her legs, the intimate scrape as enticing as his fingers exploring her drawers' inseam in his carriage two nights ago. What would've happened if he had touched her there? Her thighs shifted within the brazen red skirt, the chair creaking beneath her.

If her friend only knew how close she was to yielding all to Mr. Ryland after all...

"And I thought you were going to give me advice

on how to have a proper dalliance," she said, trying for humor. Claire got up and walked to the spot where she'd discarded her brown shoes before the bath.

Juliette planted a hand on her hip. "You mean with the man you keep telling me you have no feelings for at all?"

She hid her smile while slipping one foot into the worn leather. There was nothing like low-heeled footwear to proffer gentle reminders of where she came from and to where she'd return. In the act of sliding on the other shoe, Annie poked her head around the doorway.

"Miss Mayhew, Mr. Ryland's carriage awaits." She stepped into the room and ducked past lines of hanging laundry with a box in her hands. "And this came for you too. A footman brought it to me when I gave him the pastries for today."

She waved the cook in. "Put it on the bed, please." More strawberries?

There'd be no privacy for this opening. Two inquisitive females hovered close, staring at the unadorned box. Claire lifted the lid and there, amongst a soft sea of white linen, sat a pair of red silk shoes, the same damask silk as her day gown. Elegant, curved-heel court shoes, but these tied with a black silk bow.

Her lips parted on the beautiful sight. With care, she lifted one shoe, a work of art in her hands. Inside, her fingers rubbed buttery smooth leather dyed to match the red of her gown. The Waverly & Sons imprint pressed the inside heel, a circle embossed in gold…the finest cobbler in London, known for crafting footwear for Queen Charlotte and the young princess.

"There's a letter," Annie said, pointing to folded foolscap half-buried under the linen.

Claire looked to both women, whose heads bent close. Both inched discreetly back, Annie with her eyes wide and light as pale blue glass and Juliette, another smirk on her lips. The *I told you so* knowing on her friend's face couldn't dampen the heavenly lightness enveloping Claire.

"Did you know about the shoes, Juliette?"

"*Non*, but I am not surprised."

Claire set the shoe back in the box and opened the note. What she found inside was concise and to the point, rather like the man who wrote the message.

> *No need to return the shoes to me at midnight or any other time. I'd have difficulty wearing them.*

She laughed, pressing the note to her chest. His brand of humor was a nice surprise. She lowered the missive, the paper crinkling in her hands.

> *Since you have trouble keeping your shoes on in my presence, bows will save you the problem of broken buckles.*
> > *With hopes for more midnight meetings—*
> *Cyrus*

Naughty images of her patten slipping off her foot on their midnight carriage ride came to mind as did black silk bows—the same as a certain queue she wanted very much to unravel.

※

A pair of fine doors parted, their intricate gold-leaf etchings drifting into her periphery. Belker announced her name to the drawing room, but her mind was in a daze. She wanted to see Cyrus and, tasting the carmine on her lips, decided she would kiss him too.

How to fit a romantic interlude into a staid luncheon created a new and interesting dilemma.

Her feet moved into the vast space, but all she could see was Cyrus. He strode through the room the way a ship captain commands the deck of his ship.

Was it possible his maroon bruise made him more dashing?

He was a fine sight in a black broadcloth coat. Her salacious gaze dropped to a brass button lower on his waistcoat. The metal glimmered, winking at her with flirtatious intent very near the tuft of hair she remembered so well at his navel.

The corner of Cyrus's mouth crooked. If she looked ready to devour him, he read the message on her face, no words required.

"Claire."

He said her name like a treasured sound. Then, her landlord bent low over her hand, kissing her knuckles and keeping her fingers in a tender hold.

Her flesh sung a merry tune recalling how she'd gripped those broad shoulders of his in a fit of passion. Was that only two nights ago? Her cheeks turned hot at the memory.

Cyrus rose to his full height, holding her hand. He planted a tender kiss on her forehead.

"Mmmm…" he hummed approvingly. "You smell of almonds." His lips lingered on her hairline, giving her another soft kiss. "And vanilla, I think. Something you cooked?"

He breathed in her scent, standing close yet not intimidating in the least. His own smell was clean and starched with a hint of coffee. She reached high, touching his face like a woman with every right to partake of the feast he offered.

"It's face powder." One finger stroked the smooth square of his jaw, her voice curving with amusement. "Today I join the ranks of ladies who meet for luncheon, and I can't be sure if I've been lured here or goaded by one very challenging man put on earth to harass my senses."

She caressed his jaw, the grain of his skin smooth to the touch. He must've shaved in the last hour. His mouth quirked sideways, pressing the maroon bruise higher up his cheek.

"Something tells me you're the perfect woman to soothe such a man or put him in his place." His pewter stare flicked over her exposed skin, settling on her cleavage. "As to your senses, I shall treat them with the utmost care."

She laughed soft and low. Her heart swelled again, the floor turning ephemeral beneath her. Lustrous undergarments rubbed her skin, a tactile reminder that her feet were grounded next to an exhilarating man.

One feminine brow shot high. "I can't say that I approve of your purchase of scandalous undergarments," she scolded, suddenly aware she hadn't checked if there were others in the room.

Her hand dropped to her side, and she peeked around his shoulder. Mirrored sconces lit the midday room to a brilliant glow. Her gaze bounced around the vast chamber treated with vibrant shades of blue and red. She paused on three stunning tapestries hanging on one wall. The large middle piece featured a well-muscled hero slaying a lion.

"We're alone. I wanted some time with you first." He stood in that square-shouldered way of his with one hand behind his back. "And I want you to be comfortable in my home."

She touched her bodice, the grandeur of Ryland House pummeling her. He wanted her comfortable in his home; she wanted to be comfortable in his home, but she wasn't.

Four polished silver tea urns lined an elegant satinwood table, ready to serve at the pleasure of a Ryland House guest.

"You look like you could use a coffee. It may not be as good—"

"No. No thank you. Though I'm sure your cook only serves the best."

His brows snapped together. She was a little twitchy, interrupting him. If she could read his mind, Claire was certain she'd find a bolstering, *You've come this far. Don't fail me now.*

Was this in some way about him needing her here?

"A house like this makes me feel like I ought to have a rag on hand to clean something. Nothing can be out of place." She took a bracing breath, looking to the back courtyard. "Why don't you show me your gardens?"

"When a woman asks a man for a walk in the garden, it means she's seeking kisses or escape."

She craned her neck, viewing the ceiling's gold-leafed boiseries overhead. The elegant design curved in an elliptical pattern.

"A walk in the garden would be nice. I admit, I feel...overwhelmed in here."

"Escape it is." He chuckled. "I won't let your reason for a garden stroll dent my pride."

Cyrus led her out to the courtyard. She welcomed the cool air and the relief found in this small slice of nature. The sedate garden, stretched half-undressed from fall's foliage. She couldn't help but wonder what her father would think of the Ryland House garden, smaller than Greenwich Park's but substantial for Town.

"Now, where were we?" he asked.

She adjusted her shawl and slid her hand over his sleeve, needing more of him. "You were going to show me your garden."

"No, you were on the verge of taking me to task for purchasing your undergarments." He steered their first steps, glancing at her hem. "And the shoes? Am I to receive a tongue lashing for those as well?"

Her free hand tugged her skirt higher, revealing the pretty footwear and a hint of her silk-covered ankle.

"For shoes this lovely, I can forgive you anything."

"I'll have to remember that. Something tells me you may require my assistance to keep you supplied in shoes and gowns." Cyrus wrapped his hand over hers resting on his arm. "The way you're leaving clothes behind, you'll soon be known as the *naked proprietress*."

"Naked?" She laughed. "Whatever do you mean?"

Their ramble took them off the pristine courtyard and onto a wide, crushed-stone path.

"You've taken on an unusual habit with me. At least I hope I'm the only man?" One brow arched high.

His bold smile told her he was already confident of the answer. If she had a fan, she'd have whisked the thing furiously to cool her cheeks despite the crisp air.

"What habit is that, pray tell?"

They meandered around a circular hedgerow trimmed waist high, the gravel crunching underfoot. Their arms rubbed intimately, and she was drawn to him in the curious way a magnet sucked metal into its orbit. Cyrus was right: a walk in the garden was little more than a euphemism for a new level of flirtation, one she welcomed.

"Let's see. You've left your shoe on my doorstep, your mobcap in my study, and two nights ago a neckerchief in my carriage."

Speechless, she blinked at his granite features. Her brain tried to recall those forgotten items. Images came to her piecemeal: the shoe with the broken buckle on the first night they met…the mussed mobcap she pulled off when she stormed into his home about the necklace…the neckerchief that washed grime from his face and chest after his bare-knuckle bout.

Those things had all been left with Cyrus.

A coquette's smile touched her lips. Their garden stroll stalled from the slow burn building between them on this chilly day.

His mouth turned in a wicked smile. "Your clothes are like a trail of clues I need to follow. A man can only wonder what you might leave next." His voice lowered with trifling softness. "Or do you have a secret wish to undress for me altogether?"

His gaze dropped to her lips while a breeze played with the black silk bow at his nape. She wanted very much to unloose his queue and explore his hair.

"For a man who once claimed he's not a flirt, you have mastered the skill remarkably well, Mr. Ryland."

He tipped his head to her, murmuring, "All from your gentle influence."

They moved along the path, their gaits in unison. She talked for a time about gardens and her love of Greenwich Park's open spaces. He shared farming tales from his youth and tales of times with his father. They wandered through his gardens, slowing when they circled around near the courtyard again.

A trio of birds chirped in a tree denuded of leaves yet beautiful in its starkness. The lowest branch was eight feet off the ground, but the structure invited the daring climber to a new adventure.

Cyrus gestured to a curved stone bench beneath the tree. "Would you like a seat?"

They shared the bench, sitting close, yet her layers of skirts couldn't spare her bottom from the shock of cold, hard stone. The bench cooled her body from hurtling quickly into hotter climes.

The way Cyrus's pupils darkened, she was in peril of passionate kisses in broad daylight. Was that what happened when hot flirtation turned to sharing stories of one's childhood? Sitting thus, she noticed the black ring that rimmed the pewter of Cyrus's eyes and the white flecks that lightened the irises she had thought were solid gray. How had she missed those details before?

The warmth of his thigh limned hers, firm and strong. His hard body might have been hewn from rock, but his hand moving over her leg was every bit welcoming flesh. He traced a pattern on her thigh, following the red on red posies woven into her gown's fabric.

The touch stole her breath, her thighs tensing under the attention.

"Cyrus," she said, glancing at the drawing room's back doors. "It's the middle of the day…your guests—"

"Are not here yet, but when they are, will see nothing improper. We're two people sitting on a garden bench in broad daylight. But mark me, Claire, I've nothing against touching you be it day or night." His voice, like his exploring fingers, wooed her.

Beneath her skirts, the silk drawers stroked her skin from her knees to her bottom, driving her mad. Her legs prickled with awareness, battling the need to spread wide for him.

Truth was she wanted him to explore higher and finish what was started on their innervating carriage ride.

Her hands folded into her shawl's ends, and she fought a naughty smile. She grasped what Cyrus was up to directing her to this particular bench. The hedgerow obscured them from the waist down.

"Do you have this spot saved especially for garden interludes?" Her lips parted for a sharp, needful breath of new air.

His finger found a new outline of flowers on her skirt, higher up her thigh.

"You would be the first and only woman to sit here with me."

His simple confession shot a new thrill, a tingle on her skin from her cleavage to her corset's silk bottom.

She was the only one.

He made her bid for propriety nigh too difficult. She eyed the back doors of the drawing room again, the highly visible glass doors. To a casual witness, they probably looked like a pair enjoying a fine late-season garden. The two of them couldn't look more proper, save the improper heat crackling around them and the indiscreet movement of one masculine hand on her skirt.

Dangerous daylight flirtation was…fun.

Her gaze shot from a vigilant watch of those doors back to Cyrus. His fingertip traced a new spray of flowers, the pressure of it seeking her inner thigh. Her fingers dug into her shawl. Bursts of pleasure tickled high on her legs.

"We could talk business if you like," he drawled.

"Oh, now you're really flirting with me."

He laughed, a rich deep sound. "And you please me, Claire Mayhew."

Her body tilted toward him, her lashes shuttering. Cyrus whispered words to her, sweet nothings about her hair, her face. She was lost in him, and the garden's cool, peacefulness. Being with Cyrus swept her into new places, removing awareness of time. How long had their carriage ride been the other night?

Yet this wasn't the same as being hidden away in his carriage or closeted in his study.

This was a public declaration of affections.

And here, on his garden bench, they could flirt,

they could tease, but they could not touch—at least nothing beyond his covert, posy-tracing finger on her thigh.

"Being with you has turned out to be the best gift," she said, forcing herself out of the Cyrus-induced trance. "But how far can this go?"

"As far as we want."

His firm, cryptic words weren't quite the answer she wanted, but neither were they unwelcome. Cyrus stopped exploring her skirt and reach for her hand gripping the shawl.

She looked down at where their fingers joined, liking the way he wanted to hold hands in the way of enamored lovers.

"Some women can give their bodies and not their hearts." Keeping an eye to their linked hands, her breath moved with a heavy ebb and flow. "I'm certain I'm not cut from that mold."

"Not very independent minded of you," he mocked.

She flinched at the unexpected cut and followed a diminutive winter bird scratching the dirt. When she looked up, Cyrus's pewter stare honed on her.

"Would it help if I confessed to thinking of you day and night?" His finger stroked the pink scar that seemed to fascinate him.

Just as I do with you.

In the haze of their garden seduction, heels clicked sharp sounds on stone, snapping their attention to the house. *The luncheon.* Lucinda stood on the elevated courtyard behind the drawing room, her hands clasped at her waist.

"Cyrus, Miss Mayhew," she called out to them. "Our guests have arrived for luncheon. Will you join us?"

"Of course." Cyrus rose from the bench in one fluid movement.

How could he acclimate so quickly? Claire's mind and body drifted, in a muddled state from nerve-melting heat. Her legs needed a minute before they'd work right, she was sure.

Cyrus offered his hand as though he understood she needed steadying.

"You can do this."

Standing upright, she smoothed her skirts, grateful for a few seconds to collect herself. Several pairs of female eyes peered at them from the expanse of glass doors. Poised as the two of them were, they could be a curiosity on display.

But her courage faltered. "I'm not sure I can begin this, Cyrus."

A low laugh rumbled from his chest, sounding more predatory than humored.

There, under the garden tree for all to witness, he lifted her hand to his lips and kissed her, his mouth lingering on her skin. He'd as good as marked her as his with the romantic gesture, as enchanting as it was goading. His gray stare met hers over the small scar on her hand, and he planted a kiss there.

"Can't begin this?" His deep voice was firm. "We already have."

She opened her mouth, but no retort came. Her skin flushed, and she didn't miss the challenge in his eyes.

"I'm not a man for games, but what goes between us is like chess. The next move is yours."

Twelve

They come together like the Coroner's Inquest, to sit upon the murdered reputations of the week.

William Congreve, *The Way of the World*

CLAIRE CHASED A PIECE OF ARTICHOKE HEART AROUND her plate with her fork. Failing in the hunt for the errant vegetable, her gaze flitted around the table, finding the women not so different from herself. Mount Olympus wasn't insurmountable after all. Her wandering gaze collided with the Duchess of Marlborough's.

Well, perhaps not entirely scalable.

The beldam frowned often, bringing to mind a sharp-featured bird ready to devour unsuspecting prey. Her Grace's pale brown eyes narrowed, hovering on Claire's décolletage. The show of skin seemed to cause thin, ginger brows to snap together.

The luncheon, however, flowed beautifully with conversation interspersed over cream soup, ham, and a delightful variety of vegetables. Spearing the artichoke tidbit, one goal was clear: she would sail through the rest of the event with flying colors.

Nor was the day without its benefits. Tension was building for her other secret plan: another interlude with Cyrus.

Seated to the right of him, the position afforded his surreptitious caresses to her knee under the table. His foot nudged her calf with a gentle stroke all while he listened with rapt politeness to Lady Millicent Seabright, a cheerful woman as round as she was sweet natured.

Forks scraped plates and conversation floated with the aromas of delicious fare when Lady Seabright squinted at Cyrus from her spot three seats away.

"I say, Mr. Ryland. Did you know you have a large bruise on your cheek?"

Cyrus's fork paused midair, his mouth turning in a polite, repressed line.

"Thank you, Lady Seabright. I am aware of it." His fork resumed its travels, delivering pieces of haricot vert.

Silks and taffetas once stirring in seats paused at the mention of the wound. Surreptitious glances drifted his way, among them the self-assured Lady Isabella Foster. Claire recognized Lady Foster from the day she had stormed, dripping wet, into another Ryland House function.

Perusing the table, Claire was certain more than a few of the dozen ladies in attendance wanted to know the origins of the bruise, but social niceties gripped them in silence on the topic. No one would be so forward as to ask what had happened to his face.

Not so the persistent Lady Seabright, her roundish head angling for a better view of the maroon mark.

"How ever did you come by it?"

Cyrus smiled, the patient kind of smile one saves for a meddlesome aunt, and he speared a piece of meat. "My hard head met an equally hard force, my lady."

Lady Seabright blinked owlishly. "Oh dear, I do hope you'll avoid meeting with any more hard forces."

He acknowledged her concern with a slow nod. "I promise I'll do my best to avoid them."

Claire dabbed her serviette to quivering lips. Glancing at Cyrus, she was certain banked amusement sparked in his eyes. How could he maintain such stoic composure?

"One can never be too careful," the Duchess of Marlborough said, her tone oblique.

The foot under the table wandered a little higher up Claire's hem, sending a sweet shock up her leg.

"True." Cyrus gave a serene smile to the table of women. "But I've found softer forces can be more leveling to a man."

Claire kept her serviette over her mouth, politely dipping her head. The bold scoundrel sent her a message while flirting outrageously with her leg. She tried not to squirm but she nearly burst.

Lady Seabright touched her cheek, mirroring the spot where Cyrus's small gash marred his cheek. She opened her mouth as though she would pursue the topic, but Lucinda stood up at the other end of the table.

"Ladies, Your Grace," she said, with a nod to the duchess. "Let's adjourn to the drawing room, where we can enjoy a respite before we delve into the day's meeting."

The flock of women found their way to the elegant red-and-blue drawing room, and friends grouped together in conversation. Two footmen carried in fresh urns of coffee and another pair bore wide salvers laden with the New Union's pastries.

The spurt of pride at seeing her baked goods served here was met with an off-balance sensation. With each step inside the grand room, her court heels sunk into plush carpeting, an oddity for someone who spent her days in practical low footwear on practical plank floors.

Cyrus excused himself to fetch a coffee. Standing by the polished urns, he was immediately surrounded by young, fluttering females—the eligible daughters of the matrons present at the luncheon. The way the young ladies postured brought to mind preening birds, their titters high-pitched chirps at everything he said.

Cyrus was the tasty morsel each wanted to devour.

He glanced across the room at her. Their eyes met, and his message—*I'm coming*—floated over the distance to her. She smiled, her hands resting at her sides. She was glad to be here to witness him with others. Cyrus listened with a genuine patience to the young women. And another notion hit her.

He's truly a good man.

Claire found a quiet spot by the fine tapestry draping the wall. The large, mythological battle of man and beast called to her. A well-muscled man in a loin cloth fought a lion in what must be a cave. She moved closer to the weave when the air scented with a new perfume.

"Rather like Cyrus, don't you think? All that brawn."

She turned. Lady Isabella Foster. The woman's bold perfume teased Claire with a memory she couldn't quite place.

Her feet shifted, issuing a subtle invitation for Lady Foster to join her.

"I wouldn't know." Her neck stretched for a full view of the tapestry. "I've never seen Mr. Ryland in a loin cloth."

Her ladyship's fan unfurled, a delicate half circle of blue silk and cherry wood.

"Oh, very well then, a *shirtless* Mr. Ryland. I'm certain you've seen him in some state of undress. I see it in the way you look at him."

Claire's heels sunk in the rich pile. Was her lust that transparent? Her balance tipped wrongly as much from the carpet as the lady's mocking words.

"No need to be coy with me, Miss Mayhew. I make a fine ally." Lady Foster motioned to the women clustered around the room. "And I think you'll need one."

The vibrant blue fan matched the lady's gown, fluttering like a lovely butterfly. Lady Foster wasn't precisely beautiful as much as she was eye-catching, dark haired, and strong featured. Was she part Italian?

Claire's feet moved into a wider stance; she could have been a sailor on a listing deck. "Very well, I'll agree, there is something of a resemblance."

"That's more like it." Violet eyes flashed with womanly knowing. "A bit like him too, I think, rescuing damsels in distress."

She searched the giant piece. "I don't see a woman."

The fan snapped shut and pointed high. "Look there, the figure in the distance."

Claire spied the female higher up the tapestry. "So there is."

And the scented notes hit her. Lady Foster's perfume on Cyrus.

If she had had a fan, this would have been the moment to snap the thing open and watch warily from behind the half circle of silk. What was the lady about?

She fixed her stare on the woven artwork, unsure of the lady's motives. The perfume plastered on his clothes the night of the masked ball—the woman whose attentions he didn't want. One of those former connections of his?

Lady Foster's fan flitted in the temperate room. Claire clasped her hands at her waist for want of something better to do. Idle conversation made for the smoothest sailing at these events. Isn't that what these women did with their lives?

"I don't know much about Greek mythology, but I've always liked Hercules."

"You mean Heracles." The blue fan slowed. "Hercules is Roman mythology. Heracles is Greek."

"Oh." Her chin dipped in the way of a child admonished for messing up her sums.

"Don't let something like that cow you. You've got to be made of sterner stuff, proprietress of your own shop and all." Diamond earbobs twinkled merrily, matching the mischief in Lady Foster's eyes. "Of course, something happens when you cross over to the

West End. Suddenly the women become too delicate for arduous labor."

She smiled, liking how Lady Foster poked fun at her own kind. "I should be laboring at my coffee shop now. I'm only here for Lucinda's meeting…and for Cyrus."

The fan worked faster. "If it weren't for Cyrus, most of the women wouldn't be here. Most of them don't care one fig for less fortunate women."

Claire scanned the room, her brows pressing together. It was clear most sought some kind of connection to Cyrus. Even the matrons stalled his slow travel back to her side. Lady Foster peered at Claire.

"Oh, dear. You're not on the hunt for this at all, are you?" she asked, one elegant hand gesturing to the grand room. "You're one of those hopeless cases of pure infatuation. This is amusing. A shopgirl and the rich man…only you want the man, *not* his money."

Something in her gentler nature snapped. She was not some novelty trotted out for entertainment purposes, nor did she care for the woman's tone regarding Cyrus. They spoke of a person, not a bank account.

"And what, pray tell, do you want?"

"Very good." Lady Foster's eyes flared wider. "You'll need that kind of backbone if you're to survive in this rarefied air." She glanced at the tapestry. "As for me, I wanted the man *and* his money. But it wasn't meant to be."

"You and Cyrus."

"Don't be dull. You had some idea about me." She sighed. "I certainly knew the day you barged in here wet as a stray cat. But Cyrus and I had been over for some time. Let's just say I keep my eyes open to all prospects."

"But you're a widow, aren't you? I would think your independence is something to enjoy."

An unseen mask could've slipped from Lady Foster's cool, collected face right then.

"Or it can be a lonely prospect, Miss Mayhew, believe me. Independence has two sides and one of them is an empty bed most nights, something I don't savor."

Independence. More like isolation of late. Loneliness wrapped a cold blanket around Claire, the same as the night when she stood in her dark and vacant shop, an unmarried woman with an uncertain future. Did Lady Foster feel the same?

Then she did the unthinkable. She touched the bright blue sleeve beside her, images of her own empty room coming to mind.

"You sound very much like a woman of some experience," Claire guessed.

"Too many experiences." The violet gaze rose to the tapestry, fixing on the battle of man and beast. "At this point, I wouldn't mind some rescuing. After all, who wants to be the unmarried aunt everyone feels sorry for or the embarrassing widow chasing younger men?" Her nose wrinkled in distaste. "I'll take a good man over *independence*, thank you very much."

Claire folded a protective arm across her midsection and lost herself in the tapestry. She needed a few seconds to restore her carefully assembled courage. Lady Foster's wish for a good man echoed in her mind, a want that grew inside her with each passing day.

Behind them, footsteps approached and the small, soft hairs at Claire's nape tickled from the welcome presence nearing her back. Both women turned around.

Cyrus.

His slow smile spread for her alone. He reached for her, giving a fleeting touch that slid along her lace draped elbow. Those seconds of brief contact were enough to warm her down to the toes of her red silk shoes.

"Enjoying the battle?" he asked.

"The one here on the tapestry? Or the skirmish for your attentions by the coffee?" Lady Foster's eyebrows notched higher. "Lady Sheffield's daughter looked ready to trip poor Miss Alcott when she dared converse with you."

"Colorful observations as always, Lady Foster." Cyrus tucked one hand behind his back.

The blue fan worked faster. "Only calling matters as I see them."

He faced Claire, tense lines bracketing his mouth. There were faint, dark circles underneath his eyes, a detail she had missed on their garden walk. Was that because she selfishly attended her hunger for him rather than thinking of him?

"I have to step out for a meeting," he said. "There's been some trouble at one of the warehouses, but I hope you'll stay awhile."

"What kind of trouble?"

"Thefts at Dark House Lane, some damage. I'm about to get the full report from Mr. Pentree and a man from Bow Street."

A twinge stung Claire at the mention of the thief

takers. Not long ago, she was the subject of their search. How many people tried to take some part of Cyrus in one fashion or another? Many more than she had realized…and she had to count herself among them.

"I've no doubt Lady Foster will turn your head with fine tales about me," he began. "And she might even spin some mythological stories for you as well."

"*Humph.*" The disgruntled noise came from behind the fan. "Your male pride knows no bounds. You'd like to believe we'll talk about you."

"That's because we already have," Claire admitted, grinning blithely.

She didn't mind confessing the truth, his warm attention her reward. The expression wiped some tiredness from his features, and the notion of wanting to take care of him poured over her. This foreign wish blended well with familiar, titillating thoughts.

Her gaze dropped a long second to his strong hands, hands good at tracing things and stirring hot fires in unexpected ways. His blunt lashes dropped half over his eyes as though he read her mind.

But Belker's discreet cough in their vicinity cut those interesting threads, and Cyrus bowed his exit. Departing the room, she noticed the relaxed set his shoulders had morphed into a tense squaring of his frame. The transformation was subtle, and her heart ached, wanting to ease his burdens.

And the diverting black silk-wrapped queue settled down the middle of his back, a thick coil she wanted to unravel. Beside her, blue silk rustled, the fan moving languidly.

"You know you ought to consider playing a little hard to get." Lady Foster's voice hit droll notes.

Claire's cheeks flushed with warmth. She brushed her palms across her frothy red skirt and gave her attention to the tapestry, stifling a wicked smile. If the lady only knew...

Lucinda raised her voice enough to be heard around the room. "Ladies, we shall convene our meeting in a few moments."

The women gathered in the circular array of chairs and settees while footmen began to place pastries on dishes. Silver forks glinted on fine china plates, and conversation sprinkled the room, part of the meeting's preamble.

Lady Foster took the seat beside Claire, whispering behind her fan. "Prepare yourself."

The frowning Duchess of Marlborough claimed the red settee angled close by, arranging dove-gray-and-yellow skirts with a harsh eye on Claire. Her Grace's hip roll allowed only her plumpish friend, Lady Sheffield, to share the settee.

Bad winds were stirring, turning the afternoon's smooth sailing stormy.

Claire tried to remember the proper comportment for drawing rooms, crossing her feet at the ankles, sitting tall, and linking her fingers in her lap. Lady Foster gave the barest nod of approval before shutting her fan to accept a coffee.

"Miss Mayhew, how delightful to have you in our midst." Pearl hairpins glowed like tiny moons in Her Grace's graying ginger hair. "What you shared earlier about unfortunate women in need was most informative. Yet I can't help but wonder about you."

"*Me*, Your Grace?"

"Yes. In particular, why a woman would pursue the life of a shop proprietress over marriage. I daresay an appropriate marriage."

Did her marital status fall under the purview of the duchess?

Claire waved off a footman's offer of coffee, and said, "I may marry someday, Your Grace, but for now I like living by the labor of my hands. I always have. There's satisfaction in it."

"You *en-joy* making coffee?" Lady Sheffield gasped.

"Not only do I enjoy making it, but I *enjoy* making pastries and jams and jellies."

Did Lady Foster smirk in her cup when Claire emphasized enjoy?

"Miss Mayhew was gracious to bring the pastries we're about to enjoy," Lucinda said, balancing her cup. "My brother has taken me to her wonderful coffee shop in Cornhill."

Lady Sheffield's subtle hiss of censure couldn't match the duchess's silent condemnation.

"Someone should counsel your brother about that," Lady Sheffield advised. "But without a motherly influence, one can only guess what social misfortunes a young woman might fall into."

The sweetly daft Lady Millicent Seabright took the chair beside Lucinda, nodding her agreement. "A young, unmarried woman roaming London…it simply isn't done, my dear."

At the mention of young ladies, Claire looked to

Her Grace's daughter, Lady Elizabeth Churchill, still chatting on the other end of the drawing room. She felt sorry for the cloud of rules and disapproval the young woman must live under.

Lady Seabright peered at Claire over her coffee cup. "Did you say you make pastries *and* jams and jellies?"

"Yes, my lady, I hope to sell my rose petal jellies to Fortnum and Mason's grocery here in Piccadilly."

"Oh, I do love a good rose petal jelly." Lady Seabright inched forward. "It is so hard to find a cook capable of mastering the delicate flavors."

"If you send a footman by my shop, I'll be glad to return him to you with a small jar free of charge."

"Thank you, Miss Mayhew, I shall indeed."

"Millicent," the duchess scolded. "You are ruled far too much by your appetites."

With that, the other ladies ducked into their coffee, if only to avoid Her Grace's censure.

The footmen began serving the plated pastries. Claire rubbed one of the flowered patterns on her skirt, a satisfied smile forming. Fine food ought to keep the waspish duchess silent; if not, glowing compliments from the other ladies would drown her out.

The duchess opened her fan. "And where, pray tell, did you develop your jelly-making skills?"

"I come from Greenwich, Your Grace."

"A Mayhew from Greenwich?" The yellow fan rested near thin lips. "I've heard tell of a certain Mayhew of Greenwich, an adventuress of sorts. A crass social climber who seduced the now-departed Lord Jonathan, heir to the earldom. Would you know of her?"

A chill touched Claire's scalp. Her Grace unloosed cannon shots with her words, and Claire was the target.

"I don't, Your Grace." Her mouth turned dry on the half-truth.

"I thought you might know her since you strike me as a woman of…relaxed morals."

Collective gasps filled their small circle. Her Grace sat at the pinnacle of Society, with undisputed power. Who would cross her in defense of a coffee shop proprietress? The duchess's eyes narrowed on Claire, pale brown bayonets ready to eviscerate her from head to toe.

Across the room, disaster of another kind landed.

Dishes smashed to the floor. Four ladies gagged and choked. Finely coiffed heads bent low, bobbing and straining in an effort to expel something. Lucinda jumped out of her seat, spilling coffee.

"Get buckets and linens quickly," she ordered the footmen.

The gentle luncheon took a sudden, violent turn. Remnants of dishes and mashed pastries littered the floor. Miss Alcott heaved, her hands at her throat. Another lady retched into her serviette.

The pastries served for dessert…

"Please!" someone cried. "Some water."

Claire and Lady Foster rushed to the aid of the women. Tepid tea was brought in from the kitchens. The women downed the tea like thirsty sailors, splattering their fine gowns. Footmen and a maid strove to clean around the stirring assembly. Shrill demands were made for carriages to be brought to the front.

The Ryland House drawing room was pure mayhem.

One woman wiped her mouth with a handkerchief. "The pastries," she moaned, her mouth working as though she swallowed brine. "They're horribly, *horribly* salted…not fit for man nor beast."

Lady Atherton gagged behind her serviette, grabbing another serviette a maid passed to her. She grimaced at Claire, her voice shaking. "Why ever would you serve these to us?"

Claire passed a fresh cup of tea to Miss Alcott, the room a jumble of people, but the chaos slowed.

One by one, heads turned her way—a maid wiping the floor, the footmen with fresh cloths, the ladies in attendance. Some eyes were curious, some rounded from shock, but several skewered her with accusation.

Numb from head to toe, Claire couldn't feel the floor. Her mouth opened, but no words came out.

Thirteen

A little scorn is alluring…

William Congreve, *The Way of the World*

JACK EMERSON'S SCARRED CHEEK CREASED, BUT CYRUS couldn't be sure if the runner smiled or smirked. The tall thief taker had already folded himself into a chair and crossed one dusty boot over his opposite knee.

"I heard you found your flaxen-haired housebreaker."

Cyrus stood behind his desk, one hand on the back of his chair. At the mention of Claire, he softened, his gaze flicking to the closed study door. He wanted to be with her. Truth be told, he didn't want to attend details of a petty theft at one of his warehouses; they were a fact of business, something attended by others. Pentree's message, however, made the matter sound dire.

"If you're concerned about not getting the reward," he said, "I'll leave a portion with Sir John…compensation for your efforts."

"Keep your gold, Ryland. I didn't solve anything," Emerson said, a faint brogue in his words. "You're not the first nob to show up at Bow Street asking us to hunt down a woman."

"It's not what you think."

Emerson's smirk spread. "I'm sure it isn't."

Mr. Pentree hugged his folio to his chest, sitting in the chair beside the thief taker. His stare scuttled from Cyrus to Emerson. Cyrus could only guess his employee was trying to decipher what went on here.

Bow Street's best slouched in the chair. Emerson's manner reduced everyone to level standing, Cyrus could see it in his assessing eyes. But he had to acknowledge his burgeoning respect for a man who refused to be paid for a job he didn't finish.

He gave Emerson a subtle nod. "Then may the recent events at Dark House Lane provide ample reward instead." Cyrus took his seat, ready to listen. "What did you find?"

Mr. Pentree dug into his folio. "While Mr. Emerson inspected the warehouse, I compiled a list of the stolen items, their value and origin, as well as replacement costs."

The agent passed a sheet of paper to Cyrus.

The document listed neat columns of words and numbers, but a flurry of carriages clattering through his driveway drew his attention outside. The wind of fast-moving vehicles blasted the footmen hanging on to the back. The luncheon was already over? Good.

Pentree cleared his throat. "Most of what was taken was minor and of little value. In fact, some of the crates taken were empty. Quite baffling."

Cyrus glanced from the page to his agent. "And you did a thorough inventory?"

"Yes, sir. I combed the warehouse with Mr. Talbot, the Dark House Lane supervisor. What you see there is the extent of the thievery."

Emerson withdrew paper and a lead stick from inside his coat. "I'd like a copy of that list."

"I made one for you." Pentree pushed up his spectacles and dug another paper from his folio.

When Emerson reached for the sheet, something metallic glinted from his wrist. He read the paper and put it on his lap, another quick flash of metal visible on his forearm. Was the thief taker carrying knives in his sleeves?

"The destruction to your sugar vats. There's your trouble." Emerson tapped the paper. "This isn't about thievery. A business rival perhaps? Someone wants to get an edge on you." His brows pressed together. "But there is another possibility…"

But the thief taker let his thought trail into silence, all while squinting at the paper as though he could dig more information from a list of words and numbers.

Cyrus looked over the list in front of him, finding nothing worthy of alarm. "What do you mean?"

"If this isn't the work of a business rival, then I'd say there's a distinct possibility someone's giving you a warning."

"A warning?" Pentree riffled through more papers.

"Someone wants your attention." The thief taker scanned the list again, his finger tapping one spot. "Taking low-value items, that's nothing. But damaging your vats dents your business."

Pentree's eyes rounded behind his spectacles. "Sir, the iron vats are completely ruined. They'll have to be replaced. But I've no idea how long that'll be. They're forged in Brussels."

"This isn't simply about the end result. There's *how* they went about damaging your vats. Acid was poured all over them. Something called *spirits of salt*," Emerson explained. "Then whoever did this tossed salt everywhere. You won't make or sell sugar for a long time."

"Months," Pentree added. "Many months, in fact, before the refinery is fully functioning again."

"Less sugar for Londoners." Emerson's half smile returned. "There's the slim chance this could be random destruction…angry foreign sailors leaving the Fox Tail…did their damage and left on the morning tides." He shrugged then added, "Maybe East End lads out for a bit of fun."

Cyrus dropped his list on the desk. "But that's not what you think."

"No. This has the feel of a calculated move."

"There's something else," Pentree said. "The night watchman was found bludgeoned on the wharf. He survived, sir, but remains unconscious."

Emerson's eyes glittered like hard pieces of glass. "Given the ward he patrols, the attack might be related or might not. But he was found at the end of Dark House Lane."

Pentree adjusted his spectacles, scooting forward in his seat. "Now you see why I'm not treating this as minor thievery."

The thief taker began to fold his copy of the list. "I'd like to go back to the warehouse and—"

The study door burst open.

"Cyrus!"

He stood up, as did Emerson and Pentree, the reflexive nature of well-mannered men, when Lucinda rushed into the room. Her face was pale.

"Lucinda?" Cyrus hurried around his desk in time for her to collapse against him.

"I know you're in a meeting," she cried, her voice muffled against his sleeve. "But I must talk to you."

He wrapped an arm over her shoulders and looked to Emerson and Pentree. "Gentlemen…"

Cyrus didn't have to finish his words. The men nodded silently.

Pentree tucked his folio under his arm, speaking in hushed tones. "Sir, Mr. Emerson wants to visit the warehouse again. I'll take him there now."

"Thank you. Please alert me as soon as you find out anything, anything at all."

The men took their leave and Cyrus withdrew his handkerchief for Lucinda. He settled her in the chair Pentree vacated and planted himself on the edge of his desk in front of her. He folded his arms loosely across his chest and waited. Lucinda wiped her eyes, her sniffles decreasing.

"Doing better?" he asked, gentling his voice.

She nodded, watery, woeful eyes searching him. "Something awful happened, Cyrus."

Lucinda dabbed her reddened nose with the crumpled handkerchief. After living with seven sisters, he understood a good listening ear and patience with feminine tears was the best course of action.

"I'm not even sure…" Her voice trailed off, and

she looked into the distance. "Everything was going so nicely; then some of the ladies started retching…right there on our floor."

"*Retching?*"

"Yes. Something was terribly wrong with the pastries. It affected only a few ladies…not everyone had eaten them yet, but Lady Atherton and Miss Alcott claimed they were terribly salted."

His body went still.

"You speak of Claire's baked goods. Salted?" He couldn't ignore the ugly chill from the news.

"Yes." She blinked at him. "Though I don't believe it was intentional, as some said. Miss Mayhew was terribly distressed."

"Tell me everything. Start with what happened after I left."

His sister relayed minor details mixed with salient facts. She started and stopped, looking to him when she stalled or forgot something. He nodded his encouragement, and Lucinda finished with the ladies demanding their carriages.

"And what of Claire?" he asked, not bothering with the social niceties of proper address. "What did she do?"

"After Lady Atherton accused her of salting the pastries on purpose, Belker and Lady Foster went with her…to the library, I think." Lucinda's hands twisted the handkerchief. "But I was tending the other guests."

One hand fisted on his thigh. "And is Claire still here?"

"No. Belker arranged one of our carriages to take

her home. She left from the mews. Then he went back to the kitchens to investigate—"

He moved off the desk and paced the room. The vats. The watchman. Claire…alone above her shop.

Lucinda sighed, slumping lower in her chair. "You ought to know the Duchess of Marlborough said some spiteful things to Miss Mayhew."

"Such as?" He stopped at the settee and turned to face Lucinda.

"Something about a Lord Jonathan and an adventuress from Greenwich reaching above her station. She made similar unkind remarks when I was calling for the carriages, and that's when Lady Foster took Miss Mayhew to another room." Lucinda's face crumpled. "What Her Grace said could easily apply to me… to us."

"Luce," he chided, but a mild sting touched him. The same high reach applied to him.

His lips firmed. He needed to extract himself carefully from Their Graces, though a great deal rode on the tentative connection. They assumed much between him and Lady Elizabeth.

"It's true. I see how some ladies regard me when they don't think I'm looking. Sometimes all I want to do is go back to Stretford." She sighed wistfully. "Miss Mayhew is very brave."

Miss Mayhew. Claire. His hand rested on the same back cushion where he'd first seen her and where she'd announced she was no lady. He couldn't help but smile.

"It's rather obvious, Cyrus. You're in love." Lucinda's startling words broke the silence.

He looked at his sister, another daze setting in on an already baffling day.

Love?

Lust most definitely. Attraction and enjoyment, no argument there. But *love*? Dangerous, foreign territory.

"It's written all over your face…the way you watch over her." She smiled enough to show her dimple. "And I've never seen you fret over a gift before."

He jammed his hands in his pockets. "I don't fret."

Lucinda chuckled sweetly over that, her dark brown curls bouncing on her shoulder. Then one hand slipped inside his coat, finding the spot over his heart where she'd caressed him a few nights ago.

Love?

The floor blurred. Yes, love.

He was a fool for not seeing, not knowing, and having his imp of a sister inform him of his state of being.

But then, he'd never been in love.

He moved off the settee and strode to his desk.

The salt.

The truth of something afoot demanded he act. First, the goings-on at Dark House Lane and now what happened in his own home. This couldn't be a coincidence. He dragged hard on the bell rope near his desk.

"Cyrus, what are you doing?"

"I'll be out tonight…all night." He glanced at the clock on his desk. "Simon and Zach will be here within an hour. Peter should be along too. You'll stay in with them. Understood?"

She nodded, her eyes rounding. Then he yanked

open a drawer, revealing a row of iron keys. He knew which one to pocket.

Emerson's words rang in his head: *Someone wants your attention.*

Fourteen

Beauty is the lover's gift...

William Congreve, *The Way of the World*

HOW DID A MAN GO ABOUT WINNING A WOMAN WHO didn't want to be won? Especially one who needed him to look after her? His fist rose to shoulder level, rapping hard on solid English oak. Chill winds swirled against his back, goading him.

Use the key. Go inside.

The shop was closed for the day; not a soul stirred inside. He checked the darkness beyond the door's window again. These two salting incidents couldn't be a coincidence. Lucinda would be safe with his nephews returning tonight, but Claire?

She needed his protection; she'd have it. Tonight.

One hand slipped inside his coat pocket, his fingers curling around the iron key, a replica of Miss Mayhew's. He'd pound on the New Union's door once more, and if she didn't show, he'd take matters into his own hands.

Cyrus had raised his fist again when he spied her through the shop door window. She walked through the shop, cupping a lone taper. Claire unlocked the door, her jeweled eyes peering from the crack.

"Cyrus. What are you doing here?"

"Making sure you're safe." He flipped his collar high against a cool gust. "Let me in?"

Another draft blew his coattails, the noise of late-day commerce at his back. Outside was a cold place since he had failed to don a cloak and gloves in his hasty exit.

The door creaked in a wide, slow arc. He stepped inside, rubbing icy hands; an open conveyance with brisk winds blasting didn't make for a pleasant cross-town ride.

"Of course, I'm safe," she said, poking her head beyond the door. "Where's your carriage?"

"I came in a hack."

Red-stained lips formed an O. Did she remember what he'd said about arriving as a gentleman caller in a hack? He eyed her tempting mouth, finding a damp spot. He reached for her, his thumb brushing the plum-red mark at the corner of her mouth.

A reddish smear covered the pad of his thumb. "Have you been drinking wine?"

Claire fussed with her shawl. She looked a little… off. Her bodice slacked. One long, messy braid trailed down her back, her hair free of any mobcap. A new gust blew past the half-open door, swishing her hem. He glimpsed slender shoeless feet encased in white silk, the outline of her toes obvious.

A hot, shaky tremor rocked him.

Cyrus shut the door, keeping his hand on the knob. "Are you alone?"

"You ask strange questions, Cyrus." She huffed. "Am I safe? And now you wonder if I'm alone? Of course I'm safe and alone, and, yes, I've had some wine. I'm a grown woman." She spoke in a rush, pushing stray tendrils off her forehead. "This hasn't been the best of days."

He let go of the knob, grinning. "I'm aware you're a woman full grown."

He eyed her gaping bodice, and Claire folded one shawl-clad arm over the other. "And I'm sure you're not here to discuss my maturity."

"You're a prickly one," he chided, his chuckle a soft sound. "And that's good. About you being alone." He locked the door and put the bar in place. "Because I'm staying the night."

Her eyes followed the key back to his pocket, one brow arching. "Rather presumptuous of you. Landlord or not."

Use of his key? Or staying the night? Didn't matter. She was right on both counts, but that wouldn't deter him. And he liked that she didn't protest much.

He lifted the taper's iron holder and grasped her elbow, steering Claire toward the back of the shop. He nodded at the shop's black lacquer benches. "I can bed down there."

"Why do you wish to sleep on my shop's bench?"

"Because you haven't offered me a place in your bed."

Her wine-lax body jerked to a stop near the stairs.

She gaped at him, and he nudged her onward, pleased at having shocked her.

Claire's silk-covered feet moved with sluggish intent, the steps creaking beneath her. "Just because we kissed—"

"I'm here to make sure you're safe." He raised the candle, the light jabbing at shadows. "Someone destroyed my sugar refinery at Dark House Lane last night, dumping acid and salt on the vats." His voice firmed. "Do you understand? They used *salt*."

She gathered her skirts in one hand and set the other on the banister, looking over her shoulder as they climbed. "And you think my mistake with the pastries, using salt instead of sugar in the glaze, somehow connects with that?"

They moved through her slender doorway and the door clicked shut behind him. If he could lock and bar it, he would, but the portal offered no such barrier to the outside world.

"Yes. It's too much of a coincidence."

She planted a hand on her hip. "Really, Cyrus, my salted pastries?"

One of the Sauveterre sisters must've supplied her with a hearty vintage to get his proper proprietress this uncoiled. She didn't slur her words, but their prim edge was gone.

What would she look like unwound all the way... by him?

He took a deep breath, carnal wants warring with the reasonable need to assure her safety. He lost himself on those wine-stained lips...moving lips, lips saying words to him.

"…sure the salt was my error with the glaze, or it could've been Annie"—her eyes slanted away from him—"I was…distracted this morning by the thought of seeing you."

The simple admission touched him, his chest swelling at her words. What moved between them often went from soft simmer to crackling heat in seconds. And then there was how he felt about her—completely unknown territory, as hot and mysterious as trying to grab a flame.

He'd never uttered the words *I love you* to a woman.

How was he supposed to do that?

Claire stood before him, her eyebrows puckering over the day's drama. The salted pastries tainted her good name, something from which she'd eventually recover. But right now she stood mired in the crisis, needing cosseting. She poured out words, talking in a muddled rush.

"…won't matter to Miss Alcott or Lady Atherton who had the unfortunate experience of gagging on something *I* made." Her hands fretted with the seam of her shawl. "In the end, I'm sure those awful pastries have no connection to what happened at your warehouse."

Cyrus stepped closer, his fingers brushing away fine hairs curling around her face.

"That may be, but I'll take no chances with you. I mean it. I'll sleep below if it makes you feel better, but I'm not leaving."

"Cyrus," she whispered, drawing out his name. Her lashes fluttered low, her body leaning closer with each luring stroke.

"For tonight at least. Until the runner has some news." His fingers slipped into her hair, all the better to coax her to his will.

"You are gallant to be so concerned, but I'm sure it's nothing." Her hand covered his, cupping the side of her face, the shawl slipping off her shoulders. "And what will you do here?"

"Whatever you were doing when I showed up at your door."

Her body shook with gentle laughter. "Isn't it obvious? I had wine while finishing my laundry." She motioned to the room behind her. "Or didn't you notice?"

He scanned the room, seeing the place for the first time. Two ropes strung diagonally from one corner of the garret to the other. Underskirts, stockings, and aprons floated from those lines, feminine garments in practical shades of black, white, blue, and gray.

A half-filled basket squatted in the center of the floor. He shouldn't have been surprised he missed the obvious. Once Claire Mayhew, his fairy-tale temptress, moved into his sphere, she consumed him.

❧

Cyrus set the candle on a small table near the door and shrugged out of his coat.

"Why are you taking off your coat?" Her shawl slumped to her hips. Wine and tender touches had relaxed clear thinking right out of her.

He hung the coat on a hook and rolled up a sleeve, smiling wide enough to crinkle the corners of his eyes. "All the better to do laundry. Been a while, but if you promise to go gently with me, I may prove an apt apprentice."

"*You're* going to do laundry"—Claire pointed at him, then tapped her chest—"with me."

"You can give me lessons," he suggested, ambling over to the first line. "Ironing, mending, and the like."

"Lessons in laundry."

The idea amused her, but the sight of his tightly muscled bottom going straight to her laundry line made her heart skip.

He gave her a mischievous smile while slinging white petticoats over his shoulder. "Unless you have something else we can do?"

Her mouth curved as she witnessed her brawny landlord work his way down the line with quick efficiency. The feminine clothes went along for the ride, yielding to his capable hands.

Isn't that what she wanted to do?

With seven sisters, he had surely seen an underskirt, but this was different. Those were her underskirts tossed over his shoulder. Yards of practical cambric and linen could have been winking at her like a tawdry tavern maid about to tumble in the hay. The notion teased her, messing with secret places covered by decadent, shot silk drawers.

Let him take them off.

Distinctly warmer, she shook her head and hung her shawl on a hook beside his coat. Her palms rubbed the wool in a downward slide. Her clothes beside his made a strangely intimate picture. She touched his coat, burying her nose for a second in his smell— warmth and stone.

And in the middle of her small abode, the man was busy with her laundry. For a man who liked to tell women what to do, he was thoughtful. Her unshod feet journeyed over the plank floor. She ducked under the rope to face Cyrus.

"If you wouldn't mind putting those in my ironing basket." She motioned to the froth of petticoats and aprons tumbling over his shoulder.

She flushed at having her garments brushing his neck and jaw. Her skin within her corset and drawers kindled at having him close, helping her with the mundane task.

Who knew a man doing laundry could be so seductive?

Cyrus obliged her and dumped his burden into the basket. His hands made fast business of the first row. She worked near him, her mind connecting the places his hands touched on those lifeless garments to places on her body.

She followed his progress under her lashes. A loose tape trailing over his fingers was akin to his touching her waist. His hand straightening a hem was a skimming caress to her ankles. Her tongue slid over her lips. Between enticing male and rich wine, warmth rolled over primed and ready flesh.

And then he started plucking garments off the second line, which held more intimate items.

"An interesting stitch you have here." Cyrus held up white linen drawers, tapping black thread. Those stitches mended a small tear on cloth meant to cover the landscape of her bottom.

A man was never supposed to see the hideous stitch work.

She snatched the drawers from him. "I'll take those, and thank you to take a seat, sir. I can finish this row."

"Dismissed from my labors already?"

Black wool stockings punctuated the second line between the white drawers. She did her best to tame the riot of images in her head while her hands folded the undergarment into a rough square. She nodded at the sole cabinet in the room, anything to get his attention off the drawers in her hands.

"There's some wine on the table, a gift from Juliette." Her foot scooted the basket along. "I can't offer the vintage in an air twist glass the likes of which grace your table, but if you look in my cabinet, you'll find a New Union mug."

Cyrus ducked under the rope and poured the wine at her table. He sipped from plain stoneware, staring out her humble window. About this time of day, Cornhill's carters and drays finished their labors, yielding the road to finer carriages, men and women in pursuit of evening entertainments.

But the hum beyond her window couldn't compare to the hum inside her.

She rolled the last pair of black stockings, rotating the wool hand over hand in lethargic fashion. Having Cyrus here changed the air, lifting her spirits better than the wine had and at the same time tempting her to take a leap. With him.

He'd brought up Bow Street and the damaged vats at Dark House Lane downstairs. Yet they weren't long in her garret, attending the laundry, and the troubles at his sugar refinery and the luncheon's awful ending faded.

They were two souls craving a rest from all that went on beyond her door.

She dropped the stockings into the basket, her other hand trifling with her loose bodice. No modest neckerchief covered her, and she was part undone, saucy as any tavern maid. Earlier, she'd pulled pins and padding from her hair and, with Annie's help, changed out of the red gown. Thinking she'd be alone, she hadn't fully laced herself up in the dark blue dress she wore now.

But she wasn't alone.

And there was that black silk ribbon wrapped around his long queue—black silk in need of unraveling.

Is this the wine talking? Or time I discovered what happens when I untie his queue?

Cyrus drank his wine, engrossed in Cornhill's bustle. She moved nearer to his wide shoulders on silent feet. Her hand reached for the silk-wrapped coil resting in the furrow of his spine. She stroked its thickness up and down with unhurried exploration.

He set his mug down with care, keeping his face to the window. "Finding something more to your liking than laundry?"

His voice was level, a calming tone, as though he didn't want to frighten the skittish vixen. Little did he know how often she lay in her cold bed wondering about his warm body.

The flat of her scarred hand slid high up his back and pulled on the black tie. "There's a strip of silk that requires my attention."

The onyx ribbon ceded defeat, abdicating its position high on his nape.

Cyrus's chin tipped close to his shoulder. "Would this be part of my lessons in laundry?"

His deep voice melted over her hidden parts.

"This is a domestic requirement only you can fulfill."

The glass reflected the smile playing on the corner of his mouth. "I'm of the belief a man should always be ready to fill any household needs."

She dipped her head, biting back laughter, and inched closer. The tips of her toes nudged his fine leather shoes. One hand sought his rock-hewn bicep while her other hand unwound the ribbon of his queue. Black silk uncoiled, freeing thick brown hair sprinkled with silver threads. Her fingers trailed the length.

"How could a man have such beautiful hair?" she murmured, looking to his reflection in the window. "So many women would be envious."

Glass panes muted his masculine angles and strong nose, but neither late daylight nor dim candles could dull the quicksilver eyes flashing back at her. A shiver danced over her skin—the same skin covered by her slackened corset, a garment she was certain would be removed by his skilled hands.

She breathed in his male scent, his skin smelling of depth and strength. Cyrus turned to face her, his hand knocking clutter off the table. Wooden hairpins clattered to the floor, the fashionable hair pad tumbled as did a piece of paper. She was too muddled to care, but Cyrus crouched near her hem to retrieve the fallen items.

With one hand, he dropped pins and the pad onto

the table, but when he stood up, the paper stayed in his grasp. His brows slashed a hard line above his nose as he scanned it.

The letter.

She squeezed her eyes shut, paper crinkling in the silence. The sound alone was accusing.

"I can explain," she offered, opening her eyes.

The pewter stare pinning her would give no quarter. "Yes. I'd like to know why Jonas Bacon thinks he's going to the colonies with you."

They stood nearly toe-to-toe, her skirts brushing his legs. She took the letter from Cyrus and set it on the table. The letter was short and life changing, same as the two notes Cyrus had sent her.

What is it with men and their brief messages?

Cyrus moved away, crossing his arms. She didn't like that there was too much air between them, but her life was hers and hers alone to navigate. Who was he to insinuate himself in matters?

Her nose tipped higher. "I'd be fully in my rights to tell you that my affairs are none of your concern."

An unpleasant sting followed those tart words. At some point, the two of them had crossed a threshold. Was it the day he stood like a steadfast hero of old, promising to help her find Nate despite her silly rejection in his study? Or the moment he awoke from a flattening blow, a blow benefiting her?

"A sentiment I understand." He nodded, his mouth flattening. "And acknowledge."

His bruised cheek twitched. She balked at the sight of it. The wound could be accusing her of being a fickle maid.

She didn't want him closed and distant. She preferred the picture of them entwined, body and soul, and such a want meant prying open shut places.

She cleared her throat. "My secondary plan, if I was unable to obtain a shop here in London, was to journey to the colonies. New York, to be exact."

She clasped her hands waist high, waiting.

Hard, truth-seeking eyes examined her. "And do you want to go? With your Jonas?"

"No. I want to stay."

With you.

His eyes widened a fraction. Did he see those words in her eyes?

"And he's not my Jonas. Never has been. I know him from my days in service at Greenwich Park. He was the earl's man of business," she explained. "Jonas lived once in the colonies and offered to go with me for safe passage. Nothing more."

Heart pounding, she stepped closer, setting a tentative hand on his forearm. Roped muscles jumped under her hand where his rolled-up sleeve exposed his arm. Was he restraining himself from touching her back?

"But he's not aware of your decision to stay."

"Because I haven't had the chance to write him," she said softly. "My mind has been otherwise occupied."

His nostrils flared, bringing to mind a predator watching over prime territory. "Are there any more men waiting? Men wishing to see to your safety?"

"You'd be the only one." She fought back a smile. "Seeing to my safety, that is. As to waiting, I can't imagine you doing that for any woman."

"I've been waiting for you." Cyrus's pupils expanded, black as midnight.

His simple words disarmed her, words delivered with banked fire in his eyes. With his hair unleashed, square jaw, and bruised cheek, the upright hero of the colorful tapestry was gone, replaced by the hard rustic from Stretford.

"It's not been that long between us."

"You don't understand. Years I've waited. For you. Not just a woman like you." His arms dropped to his sides. "*You*, Claire Mayhew."

His admission, deep voiced and raw, poured over her. Emotion and want spilled from Cyrus, but he didn't move. He waited, his naked honesty drawing tightness around his eyes.

A man like that needed touching.

Slowly, she reached for his cravat, and with one gentle tug, starched cloth rustled free. His lashes dipped lower, his eyes dark and steady on her. Outside, voices rose above the wind, calling to each other on Cornhill, but inside stayed quiet. Cyrus didn't move.

Her stare dropped to his chest, her trussed breasts brushing him. "Something tells me you'll not sleep on a hard bench tonight."

Brawny arms clenched under white fabric.

Cloth whispered against skin as her hands went to work, freeing the buttons on his waistcoat. Images of Cyrus sweating bare chested in the ring at Dark House Lane flashed before her. She wanted him bared to her again.

At the first peek of skin, she touched him like a

curious maid who stole away to explore a sculpted stone statue. The top of his shirt and waistcoat parted, and her hands sought the large plates of his chest muscles. His breaths were a hint of sound above her head.

Cyrus was warm and glorious, his sprinkles of dark chest hair tickling her palms.

She unseated more buttons, stopping to graze her fingernails along his ribs. Waves of gooseflesh followed her hand. The sight gratified her, a chance to be in control of Cyrus. His catch of breath, a small moan of pleasure, his body twitching…all offered unspoken permission to keep going.

Her hands worked the last few buttons. The bottom of his waistcoat and shirt parted, the cloth crinkling softly. A strip of male flesh and a small patch of masculine hair peeked out from the folds.

Claire's gaze drifted up to meet his. Dark gray eyes smoldered. Her hands spread apart Cyrus's shirt and waistcoat, the effect on her headier than the sweetest brandy.

"You say my forbidden fruit interests you the most," she said, her finger tracing a single rib. "This part of you interests me."

Muscles flexed under her playful inspection. She slipped the shirt and waistcoat halfway off, pinning his arms to his sides, control over this powerful man an alluring, potent thing. His dark stare locked on her, daring her to continue.

"Or I could say these parts," she whispered.

Her hands breezed over button-like male nipples, and Cyrus's breath hissed from the contact, his eyes glittering under sluggish lids. She pushed the shirt and waistcoat to the floor, her lips parting. She needed more air.

She took a step back, consuming him with her eyes. Iron-hard shoulders curved into rounded epaulets of muscle—the kind of shoulders a woman could rest her head against and know she was safe. Her body quivered and she was cool and hot all at once.

And there was the light whorl of brown hair surrounding his navel.

"But this one fascinates me very much." One finger skimmed the spot, her voice coming breathy and light.

His muscles clenched under her hand. She made small circles, reveling in the contrast of smooth skin and wiry strands of hair. In her exploration, the heel of her hand bumped the placket of his breeches.

Cyrus stopped her hand mid-circle. "Claire…" he rasped. "Am I the only one?"

She blinked at him. "The only one?"

He steered her hand away from his body, keeping his grip firm. "The letter? Any more secrets or secret plans?"

"Secrets?" she repeated, her lips parting for much-needed air. His warmth and the smell of his skin blurred clear thinking.

The hazy remembrance of dancing with him at the masked ball, his fleeting moment of jealousy came to mind. Was this another chink in her hero's armor? She didn't care if he showed a hundred flaws tonight. She'd welcome them all and keep touching him; this was what she wanted. He was what she wanted.

"Cyrus, until our first midnight meeting, I hardly

gave any man a moment's thought. Now there's you. Only you."

His jaw's tightness eased, but he stayed quiet.

"Tell me you're not the terribly jealous sort."

He looked at his grip on her wrist and let go. His heavy brows slammed together, the line above his nose pronounced. "I want no secrets between us."

"There will be none." She planted her bottom on the table's edge, her arms braced beside her hips. "Between us, we have a few, don't we?"

She meant the words as a gentle reminder, not to prod old wounds. Tension melted from his face.

"You have me there," he murmured.

"More like I prefer you here, close to me."

Cyrus reached for her, and one large hand stroked her hair down to the tip of her braid. He kissed her forehead, her hairline, her temple with little, feathering kisses, the slow, tender kind, seeking restitution.

He pulled back and looked her in the eyes, his thumb stroking her jaw. Cyrus opened his mouth, as if he was about to say something, but didn't. Instead, his mouth sought hers, hot and urgent.

He lavished attention on the wine-stained spot at the corner of her mouth, the ticklish kiss making her squirm. She kissed him back with equal fervor, her tongue rubbing his. Her legs fell open, an urgency growing inside her. His body pressed against her thigh, and Cyrus stepped slowly into the V of her legs. Skirts hampered his progress, but he was cradled close to her.

Her lungs worked hard. "Why is it when I'm near you, there's not enough air to breathe?"

His low, masculine laugh stirred her. Both of his

hands trailed her spine, his fingertips rubbing up and down. She touched the flat, smaller muscles at the demarcation of skin and breeches.

This was a hot, slow consuming of each other with still too many clothes on. Her inquisitive hand slid inside his waistline, kneading smooth skin.

Cyrus sowed seeds of affection with close-mouthed pecks along her cheeks and nose, traveling to her mouth. His lips burned her with searing kisses that swung between a connection and a claim. Her mouth moved under his, glorying in his skin smooth from his late-day shave.

Then, cool air touched her shoulders.

"My bodice." She pulled away, breathing the words more than saying them.

She looked down. Her dark blue dress drooped on her frame. The pale corset smashed her breasts high, crescents of white pulsing up and down.

"You've unlaced the front of my dress," she said, her jaw dropping.

Cyrus's triumphant smile was dark and very male. His fingers finished off the already loose ties.

"And you're quite pleased to have accomplished that unbeknownst to me."

He leaned down and kissed plump flesh rising from her corset. He lingered there, speaking words on her skin. "A man takes his accomplishments where he can."

Heat stewed between her legs with their affectionate touches turning carnal. His hands splayed the sides of her corset-covered ribs, and Cyrus planted hot kisses on her high curves. Her nipples were so achingly close to his attentive mouth. She arched into him, hoping he'd find at least one, but there were too many clothes that needed to come off.

Her body, fluid from wine and sensuality, wiggled with the work of his hands. Off went the dark blue dress, along with miles of silk underskirts. He knelt before her, his gray eyes simmering with heat. His gaze locked on hers, and Cyrus hooked one finger in her garter and tugged.

Silk slid down her calf, the white stocking languid in its trail.

She watched, fascinated by the act of Cyrus undressing her. This was trust and tender care, a slow appreciation of hidden places. He cupped her drawer-covered bottom with one hand and gave one bottom cheek a gentle squeeze.

Then his dark head bent close, and Cyrus kissed her inner thigh.

She sucked in a sharp breath. His bold kiss lit a wick of heat that shot up her leg and burst hot wetness between her thighs. He did the same with her other leg, his mouth quirking when he glanced up at her.

Cyrus rose to his feet. Control was his, and she was glad of it.

She stood before him in her new corset, chemise, and silken drawers, the table's edge pushing into her backside. The wood was solid, but the world was out of kilter. This was her home, yet colors burst differently.

Those white silk underskirts puffed pretty as clouds on her plain floor. Cyrus flipped her dark blue worker woman's dress over a barren laundry line. On the wall, her strawberry-red gown hung from a peg, a glimmering splash of decadence. Underneath the limp skirt, her new red court shoes sat primly beside her brown leather footwear. She smiled at the unlikely pairing.

The loss of her shoe was why she now stood nearly naked.

Quicksilver eyes perused her body in leisurely fashion, lingering on the crux of her thighs as though he was determining where and how he'd touch her. The idea sent more dampness to her drawers' convenient opening between her legs, where cool air brushed bothered flesh. Her legs pressed close together, a blush of modesty dusting her skin.

"No." The word cut the silence. "Don't close your legs to me." A faint smile creased his face. "I know what I'm going to do to you."

Her limbs turned heavy with those words—good thing the table supported her. Cyrus stood watching her, shirtless, with black breeches on and little else, just as he had in the fighting ring. But tonight was a battle of a different nature.

He set his hands at his hips, his broad chest expanding with each inhale. The view of him—hair untied and cut cheek—was how he'd have been if fate hadn't changed his life from bare-knuckle brawler to man of commerce. His watching her sent little quivers across vexed skin.

Of course, she had an idea what they'd do; she'd done this before and was no novice. Or was she?

"What do you mean?" She blinked when Cyrus angled his body beside hers. He stood so close, his hair spilled over her shoulder.

"I know how I want to touch you." His big hand tugged loose the corset's ties.

His lips caressed her shoulder, her neck. Cyrus teased her, his tongue grazing her flesh while he worked the last lacing free. Between his nearness and the sensual kisses, her brain worked piecemeal on what he said. Words connected in listless fashion, taking their time to form...even longer to reach her tongue.

She leaned against the table, and he dropped the silk and whalebone corset beside the jumble of his shirt and waistcoat on the floor. Her chemise hung loose, slippery silk and hot man invading her senses.

Cyrus kissed her deeply on the mouth. His hands slinked over her hips, and he nudged her closer to him. He gathered the bottom of her chemise little by little, his mouth never losing enticing contact with hers. He whisked the chemise high and broke their kiss when the flimsy garment touched her chin.

She shivered. Cold air grazed her back and her breasts, a shock to her system. Her forearm made a protective line across her chest, a last reserve against the sensual tide of Cyrus Ryland washing over her. This was like falling into a wide swath of black velvet. And she remembered his words: *I know how I want to touch you.*

"Do you want me to lie down? On the bed?" she asked between kisses. "Then my body receives you?"

Cyrus's sweet, rough laughter vibrated on her lips. "Is that what you want me to do?"

He pulled away from her mouth, his breath laboring against her neck between small pecks and big kisses. She arched her neck and swallowed hard. Heat and craving crackled inside her. The room's timbered ceiling was hazy in her vision.

Cyrus asked his question as though she had some say in what they'd do, but his distracting hand wandered over her body, his palm rubbing her ribs. The air was cool; his hands were hot.

She squirmed under his slow, claiming hand, her thighs scuffing silk together. He inched an agonizing trail down her torso, toward the only cloth covering her.

He filled the space beside her, around her, letting her slump into him. Her arm became too heavy to shield her breasts. Cyrus pulled her arm away, exposing her. She liked the chill air touching there; her nipples, tight pinched points, begged to be touched. She liked being bared to him.

Her back arched with invitation. The wanton ploy wasn't planned; she simply moved. No thought— only feeling.

She looked up, giving wordless appeal. Their gazes locked with a mysterious, powerful connection. His hand splayed on her torso, inching higher. She shivered from the slow caress maneuvering toward her breasts, and closed her eyes.

"You didn't answer me, Claire." He spoke muffled words into her hair. "Do you *know* what you want me to do?"

"Please…touch me…"

The pad of his thumb touched the tip of her nipple, whisper soft. He made slow circles on the tender flesh before stroking the side of her breast. She moaned from the sweet ache he stirred. And then he did the same to the other nipple, driving her mad with his faint, teasing pressure.

Cyrus stopped those aching circles to stroke the valley of skin between her breasts. He turned his hand around and brushed his knuckles along the center line of her body, going lower and lower and lower.

She opened her eyes when he untied one tape securing her drawers. His other hand splayed across her back.

"What else do you want me to do?" he asked, his voice a murmur overhead.

Her lips found the crook between his chest and shoulder, kissing where those places fashioned him together.

"I..." Words stalled the more she buried herself against him, tasting his skin.

She didn't care. Right here with him was what she wanted.

Cyrus stroked the lower part of her abdomen, rousing heat everywhere. He pulled gently on her braid, tipping her head back, kissing her full on the mouth. He kissed the corner of her mouth, his tongue seeking hers. She liked this, would do this—

Distracting male fingers caressed the tuft of hair on her mons.

Her limbs bolted, stiff and shaky. She blinked, a strange haze clouding her vision. Delicious fever spread, singeing flesh not yet touched. The drawer's thin silk barrier was the only thing between his skin and hers. Against her will, her hips pumped his caressing hand.

A long, wanting moan escaped her lips. "Uhhhhhh..."

Cyrus slid one finger into the top of her cleft, pushing the silk into her wetness.

Her hips jerked off the table. His finger stirred an ember of heat, biting and enticing all at once. Her mouth dropped open, sucking air. Fireworks wouldn't shoot off so hot and hard.

"Is this what you want?" Cyrus kept his vigil on the nub of her flesh veiled by shot silk.

She tried to talk but couldn't from the engulfing, spangled fog. His breath came hard too.

"Do you know what this spot's called?" he asked close to her ear.

She looked down, entranced at the sight of his strong hand doing nimble things between her legs.

One finger circled her scorching, little nub with agonizing slowness. "This spot is the key"—then his finger slipped lower inside her most private flesh with the barest touch—"to open this door."

She was enthralled by his big hand stroking her. Burning pressure built, shooting cinders across her skin. Every muscle wanted to tense and be loose all at once. She squirmed against Cyrus and the table, this mad craving increasing inside her. Her lids drooped. With one hand, she gripped the table's edge; the other wrapped around his shoulder.

"Gahhh." The noise burst from her lips, followed by a keening inhale.

Searing coolness spread across her bottom smashed into the table. That hot-cool sensation blossomed, sweeping outward from wherever Cyrus's talented hand touched. Her mouth worked, unable to form coherent words.

"No secrets between us, Claire," he uttered the words, his hand swirling faster.

Another swell of searing bliss swallowed her, the force pushing, threatening to take all of her. This time, the grip on the table wasn't enough.

She needed something more solid; she needed Cyrus. Her hand shot up, grabbing him. She needed to hold on to him with both hands, lest she float away in pieces.

"Promise me," he whispered.

Claire's legs jerked. Every muscle tensed again with excruciating tightness. Her bottom jammed hard into the table, her feet lifting off the floor. An explosion crashed through her the same as the thunderstorms she loved. Her body bucked and another shock wave took over.

"Yes!" she cried, quivering against Cyrus.

He swept her into his arms, his mouth consuming the rest of her cries. Throbs of pleasure twitched on highly sensitized flesh. She gulped air, one side of her body pressed into him, a warm sheen and masculine hairs rubbing skin acute with awareness.

Cyrus laid her on the thick, white counterpane stretched across her bed. Rough cotton teased her bothered skin. Her heart banged behind her breastbone, and she lifted one lazy hand to scrape back tendrils stuck to her cheek.

Thought and movement came back to her little by little. She weakly hitched up on one elbow, spying a wet circle on the front of her drawers.

Time the silk came off.

Cyrus towered over her at the side of the bed,

undoing the buttons on his placket. The way his gray stare ravaged her, she could have been the damsel Hercules saved. Now, the hero would claim his reward.

Muscles flexed under masculine skin that rarely saw the light of day, and pitch-dark eyes narrowing on her spoke louder than words. Claire sat up, mindful of her life changing today as sure as it had one midnight dance not long ago.

Her legs, languid with pleasure, swung over the bed, the soles of her feet finding wooden planks. The brute's hands slowed on freeing the last button, his brows arching at her movement.

She stood up to face him, swallowing hard, but couldn't look him in the eyes. No, if she did, she'd spill emotions tethered by a thread, emotions she didn't fully grasp. This was dangerous ground with a man she wanted to give heart, soul, and body to, and yet...

"You said no secrets."

Fifteen

But say what you will, 'tis better to be left than never to have been loved.

William Congreve, *The Way of the World*

SECRETS REVEALED? OR PLEASURE EXPLORED?

Want swept a pendulum between two demands. Claire stood before him, her alabaster skin begging to be touched. His breech's half-open placket almost freed gleeful male parts ready to act. He was sorely tempted to ignore his better judgment and not probe what she meant.

And then she stepped close, one nipple poking his ribs. His tender temptress mesmerized him, slipping an exploring hand inside the V of his placket. His breath hissed at the invasion.

Her fingers cupped his bollocks, playing with him. He reveled in her touch, the sensation like standing in the sun, the warmth spraying his skin. Being with Claire awakened parts of him that went beyond his understanding. The want to take care of her, to love her, to protect her was a drum beat inside, but their sensual connection scorched him. And he wasn't inside her yet.

Then, his chin dropped to his chest. Her arm moved inside his breeches.

The view alone would have undone any man.

"Claire," he groaned.

Secrets could wait.

Her exploration inched his breeches lower. She rubbed the narrow strip of flesh between his bollocks and backside. Inexpert fingers, fumbling and sweet, gently stroked skin rarely touched. Her inquisitive hand sent an elixir to his limbs.

Feminine legs rubbed his with featherlight torment. Plum-red lips sought the hills and valleys of his arm muscles, her mouth planting sultry kisses on his skin. Claire glanced at him, dark pupils filling eyes glossy with carnal need.

"Cyrus," she said, her lashes dropping. "I know how I want you to take me."

Was that it?

He caressed her shoulders, his head dipping lower, all the better to kiss her. A woman saying things like that needed kissing. Lots of kissing.

His mouth tugged on her lower lip. He'd planned to lay her across the bed and whisper words of affection and, if he dare, love, before seeking tender consummation. He was ready to tell her. But the way her innocent hands moved in not-so-innocent ways, the battle to express himself slipped into clouded climes.

Plunge into numbing bliss and save deeper emotions for another time? Or declare himself now?

Her nails grazed his bollocks with light, teasing

scratches. He sucked in a quick breath, the pleasure excruciating. Claire broke their kiss, but their bodies pressed close.

His thighs clenched hard within breeches slipping to his hips. Muscles around his navel knotted when his phallus sprang free, the tip of his erection bouncing on Claire's skin. She bent lower. Her fingernails raked his backside, moving down his thighs, pushing his smalls and breeches to the floor.

Feminine eyes glittered at him a second before looking away. *A tentative seductress.* She stepped back, her hands hesitating at her waist. Claire's rib cage expanded and contracted with an unsteady cadence, her breaths shallow and quick. She untied the last tape securing her drawers, and the flimsy fabric dropped.

He licked his lips, tasting her kisses. Claire dipped her chin, not giving eye contact. Neither had on a stitch of clothes, yet something honest and deep grew between them.

His lids drooped over his eyes. He was lost to her soft skin and the pale gold curls between her legs. Then Claire did a curious, mind-jarring thing.

Her knees went down on the floor, and she rested her head and chest on the bed. "I want you to take me like this."

His head snapped back at the sight. The counterpane muffled her voice, but her body's position expressed intent. A tavern wench or practiced widow would seek pleasure this way, but his proper proprietress?

This was her secret?

His eyes refused to blink, choosing not to cooperate with the better side of him that was ready to declare brave emotions. Instead, his greedy eyes ogled her bottom's soft, white globes curving off the bed. A flaxen braid snaked the length of her back, the feathery end touching her bottom's soft crease.

Aching demand for release rushed him. For all his steadfast strength, he stood weak as an untried lad.

His prim, sweet shopgirl wanted hot, sweaty sex.

Scalding want blasted him. Holding her in his arms and tender whispers of love and affection would have to wait for a better time.

He went down on his knees behind Claire with the knowledge she had leveled him. Again. His mouth sought the skin near the end of her braid, and he kissed her. Her skin smelled of simple cleanliness, like the laundry he'd touched, something tantalizing and pure.

If softness had a scent, it was Claire.

He swept light, fevered kisses up her spine. Claire's alabaster skin shivered beneath his lips. He dug into the counterpane with both hands, her slippery wetness still coating his fingers that touched her intimately on the table.

She was prepared for him, but was he ready for her?

His erection bobbed, hard and happy, into the welcome space between her thighs. But this would unravel him. She would unravel him. He'd lose control and knew it.

"Claire," his voice labored. "Are you sure?"

Her legs spread wider.

"I want this, Cyrus." She turned a cheek against the counterpane, her eyes shut. "I want you."

Her three words bound them like a cord and were as real as what he longed to say to her.

Wine-stained lips marked vivid color on her delicate profile against the sea of white. His hands palmed
her bottom, resting on her sweet roundness. Then,
ever so gently, he slipped the tips of his thumbs inside
her bottom's cleft. Claire whimpered.

"Shhhh…" he whispered, wanting to calm her.

Claire's hand moved over the bed toward him. But
the smooth, round flesh brushing his palms entranced
him. Tiny pleasure bumps rippled everywhere on her
quivering skin.

He sat back on his heels, sweat pricking his hairline. He didn't want to scare her or hurt her. With the
utmost care, his thumbs dipped lower until damp curls
brushed them. Gently, he spread her pink quim open.

Hot sensation wracked his body. The view would
weaken the strongest man.

Everything in him wanted to tup Claire senseless.
The need stole coherent thought, kept him speechless
even though he wanted to whisper tender words.

He rose up on his knees again. The tip of his phallus
slipped into her welcoming wet folds. She moaned
beneath him, squirming.

Muscle and sinew jerked at her unintended tease,
but he held himself in check. Barely. With one hand,
he found Claire's opening, stroking as though he'd
calm her. She hissed at his invading fingers, her hips
bucking into him.

"Patience," he rasped, needing the advice himself.
His thighs tensed so hard, they shook.

With his other hand, he grabbed himself and
rubbed her slickness. He grimaced, the slippery feel
driving him mad. He needed to be inside her. Now.

Another spasm seized his body. His vision turned murky. The tip of him lingered an inch inside Claire. Caution reminded him it had been a long time for her. She was tight.

"Cyrus...more," she moaned, her slender bottom nudging him.

Burning need won.

He grabbed her hips and pushed. She cried out, her head lifting off the bed.

Pleasure? Or pain?

"Claire." Her name was a scrape of sound.

She flexed and arched, pushing against him. "Don't...stop."

His hands clutched frantic feminine hips. The bed's supportive ropes creaked as he began a pulsing grind. Sweat prickled his chest, his forehead. He was out of his mind feeling this good, pumping against her.

He wanted to go slow, to let her adjust, but raging need seized him.

Slick sounds played where they joined. He looked down. Hot and fast, he slid in and out of her. Claire's white curves slammed back into him, wild with need. Flesh slapped flesh. Their bodies strained with urgent strokes. Her moans came louder by the second.

And Claire's hand sought the bed's corner.

The pink scar.

Cyrus covered her splayed hand, his fingers slipping between hers. That thoughtful lover's move was the sole tender act.

The bed rammed the brick wall. The wooden frame creaked. They were lost, thrusting faster in frenzied, primal rhythm. Claire's cries grew louder, matching his hoarse pants for breath.

Near blinded and lost as he was, he couldn't help her find her pleasure; he was too far gone to his. His peak ripped a coarse bellow from his throat, the dim haze around his vision consuming him. Eyes shut tight, he fell forward on her hot back and spent himself inside her, Claire's little tremors milking him.

He had meant to spill his seed against her thigh but was weak as a lamb, helpless to pull away from this woman he loved. That was the last thing he wanted.

And when his eyes opened, her fingers were twined with his.

Carefully, he pulled free and found a cloth to wipe them both. He was drained. Of thought. Of feeling. Of strength. Claire crawled into the small bed, hugging the white linens around her.

He smiled, aware someone needed to snuff the candles and tend the fire. This was in one small way proof that he would take care of her. On quiet feet, he blew out the few candles lighting the garret and knelt before the humble fire grate. He fed coals to the box and looked to the bed.

Claire watched him, her head propped up on her pillow. Now would be the time to declare himself, but when he stood up, her eyes turned wary. He walked to the bed, comfortable without a stitch of clothing.

"Would you like me to get a chemise for you? A night rail perhaps?"

She shook her head and pulled the bed covers away from her mouth. "What about you?"

"No barriers. I want to be as close to you as possible."

Claire lifted the fluffy counterpane, and he slipped inside the bed with her. The linens were cool, but her body was still very warm to his touch. She smelled of sex and him. She lay on her side, facing him, her expression curiously hesitant. He stroked her hip, aware the day had taken them both from one extreme to another. Or was this the aftermath of exploring her sensuality?

She needed soothing, not an onslaught of emotions.

He yawned, the best kind of exhaustion seeping into his limbs. His lids drooped, but beneath his lashes, he watched her. He was having a hard time fighting sleepiness.

Tucked close together in the smallish bed, Claire stroked his jaw. "Good night, Cyrus."

His face mashed against the pillow, he mumbled, "G'night."

This was the best he'd felt in a very long time.

Door banging woke him. Cyrus jerked his head off the pillow he shared with Claire. The knocking increased, coming from below stairs. What time was it? He checked Claire. She slumbered, lost in deep sleep.

He slipped out from the counterpane and dragged on his smalls and breeches. By the table, he braced a hand on the wall, squinting out the window at Cornhill, near empty and gray with light fog. He was about to go back to bed when movement caught his eyes.

Emerson.

How did the runner know he was here?

The tall thief taker walked backward onto the street, neck craning as he stared at the garret window. When he spied Cyrus, the runner shook his head, his smirk increasing beneath the rim of his hat. Thankfully, he grasped discretion, pointing silently at the New Union's door from the street.

Cyrus slipped on the rest of his clothes. For Emerson to come calling this early…had to be important. He went quickly down the stairs and through the dark shop. Beyond the window, the tall thief taker stroked the neck of a giant roan tethered to a post.

Cyrus unlocked the door with his key and let the runner inside.

Emerson looked him up and down, lowering the collar he'd flipped high. "Well, well, Mr. Ryland, what a surprise to find you slumbering in midtown."

"I'm sure you're not here to discuss the whereabouts of my sleep."

"'Course not." Emerson slid onto a bench by the front window, crossing worn boots at the ankle. He dropped his hat beside him and looked across the silent shop. "Don't suppose you have coffee to offer me? Been a long night."

"None made." Cyrus crossed his arms, taking measure of Emerson.

The runner's queue was a windblown mess and the skin under his eyes was dark and pinched. Had he been up all night?

Emerson shrugged out of a heavy black cloak and reached inside his coat pocket, metal glinting from his sleeves. Cyrus took the facing chair, noting leather peeking from the black coat sleeve as well.

He let curiosity get the best of him and tipped his chin at the runner's wrists. "Leather arm braces? Pretty medieval of you."

Long fingers dusted with freckles pulled back the black wool sleeve. Scarred brown leather wrapped around the runner's forearm, and a pair of knives were strapped into the arm braces.

"I prefer knives to pistols. Gets the job done quiet and clean like. No messy ball and powder." Emerson eyed the swelling on Cyrus's cheek. "Not any more medieval than bare knuckling. What you do for sport, I do to survive."

Cyrus folded his arms across his chest. He shouldn't have been surprised Emerson knew about the bare-knuckle bouts. The runner unfolded the paper, studying words scratched across the page.

"You found something," he prompted Emerson.

"Just doing my best to earn the fat reward Mr. Pentree assures me you'll pay."

The words came as though they were meant to be a jibe, but the glint in Emerson's eyes told Cyrus something different. The man was like a hound on a scent. He liked the hunt.

Why else stay up all night, searching for clues to damaged sugar vats?

"Whatever you earn will be money well spent." Cyrus relaxed his arms, linking his hands in his lap. "I can't imagine the other Bow Street men hunting down information in the dead of night. They'd sleep first, investigate later."

The runner's eyes flared at the compliment. "They're all good men at Bow Street. And I stayed up since most who'd know anything move in the dark. Best to meet them in their natural state." The smirk was back but friendlier.

Cyrus eyed the messy paper. "And what have you found?"

"Not many places in London sell spirits of salt, especially in quantities to destroy your refinery business. Chemicals speak their own language, spilling truth better than most women."

Cyrus would never have connected chemistry and Emerson, but the runner's tired eyes sparked alive and awake when he mentioned the topic.

"I started there and found interesting information."

"Such as?"

"Done much to anger any dukes, Mr. Ryland?"

"I know two and am in good stead with both," he said carefully. "Marlborough and Bridgewater."

"Bridgewater, Bridgewater," Emerson repeated the name, his fingers drumming the table "He's your partner on the canals."

"More like His Grace owns the lion's share of his namesake, *Bridgewater* Canals."

The runner folded the paper in half, revealing more scratches one could take for letters and numbers. "But if something happened to you, who'd benefit?"

Cyrus sat up taller, not liking the tenor of the conversation. "My family. An even distribution."

Emerson tapped the paper, his brows knitting together. "Kills that theory."

"Why the fascination with dukes?"

"Bear with me." The thief taker examined his notes again, one finger rubbing his nasty scar. "What about Marlborough? Any business connection with him?"

"None whatsoever. In fact, he's doing much to benefit me, helping my nephews land in some fine places. His Grace gets nothing in return for his generosity."

The runner tipped his head back. "It's a rare day when someone acts without expecting something in return," he scoffed. "And you've no other connection with Marlborough?"

"There's been encouragement to court His Grace's daughter, the Lady Elizabeth Churchill." Cyrus paused, the chair creaking beneath him. "As lovely as she is, I've no interest."

"And Marlborough knows this? You're not stringing the young lady along, are you? Giving her a merry ride?"

Cyrus exhaled long and patient. "I don't string women along, Mr. Emerson."

Emerson frowned, his lids dropping to half-mast. "Hmmm…" he hummed a thoughtful sound and folded his wrinkled paper again.

"Care to explain?"

"I have two things," the thief taker said, holding up two fingers. "One, a friend of mine received an order to deliver spirits of salt to a wharf near Billingsgate. Two, he was paid by a duke."

"You're sure of this?"

"The first, yes, a hard fact. The second…call it soft information." The thief taker tucked away the messy note in his inside pocket. "My man never saw the nob who placed the order. One of his attendants did, and he wore plain clothes. He rode in an unmarked carriage with another person. My man overheard someone say 'Your Grace' from inside the carriage."

"But I have no problems with Bridgewater or Marlborough…any duke for that matter."

"I'd say you do now. Big problems. A duke is nigh to impossible for the likes of us to reach."

He knew the runner meant impossible for commoners to take to justice, even a commoner such as Cyrus. Money was its own kind of fortress, but lofty standing in Society made the best security of all.

Isn't that why he craved marrying into nobility someday?

Not anymore. He glanced to the stairs. Not as long as Claire Mayhew walked the earth.

"A duke'd have to murder someone at noon in Piccadilly with a dozen witnesses before the Crown'd do anything." Emerson unfolded his body from the seat, his limp coat flopping open. "They're almost untouchable."

Cyrus stood up with Emerson, waiting while his morning caller slipped back into his cloak. He appreciated the man delivering this news, but he itched to be upstairs with Claire. All day. This was the one day the New Union was closed, and he had plans for more enticing laundry lessons.

"Thank you for what you've reported. Keep digging."

"I will." Emerson paused in front of the door, gray light shadowing his features. "And what'll you do in the meantime?"

"Do some digging of my own."

The light patter of footsteps sounded overhead.

Claire had to be up. Emerson put his hand on the knob, hesitating.

"May I give you some advice?"

Cyrus wrapped his fingers around the shop's key in his coat pocket. He yearned to lock out the outside world.

"Go on."

"Consider staying away from your *sleeping* companion for a while. Whoever wants your attention may go for a bigger prize than your sugar refinery." The runner's stare drifted a lazy trail to the back stairs. "The likes of her could get crushed. Remember what happened to the Billingsgate watchman."

"What makes you so sure whoever's behind this would harm Miss Mayhew?" The key's sharp bits dug into his thumb. "A shopgirl?"

"I'm not. But do you want to risk it?" Emerson set his tricorne on his head, his voice somber. "Any man can see she's more than a lightskirt to you. You're in deep, Ryland."

In deep. The words bounced around his head right as his gut turned to lead at the thought of Claire being harmed. He needed to protect her.

"Make the nob think she's not of value to you. That's my advice. You can always pick up with her again when this blows over." The runner delivered the words with a shrug.

Then he opened the door and stepped outside, his cloak stirring around worn boots.

"Wait." Cyrus moved beyond the door, flipping his collar high. "How can I see to her safety if I'm not with her every minute?"

Emerson swung into his saddle. "You'll do more to protect her by making it look like you lost interest." He tugged up his collar. "But if you like, I can set a man to watch over her."

Fog remnants stretched across Cornhill like thin bits of wool. Cyrus stared at the Exchange's arcade, the space behind the arches a dark shadow. Anyone could lurk here. Claire was wide open to harm with nothing but a flimsy lock for protection.

She won't leave her shop.

The New Union Coffeehouse meant everything to her.

His stare shot back to the runner. "Send only the best."

"I'll send Tremaine. He favors red waistcoats. Despite that, you'll never know he's around." Emerson wheeled the roan around, chuckling. "Like a ghost that one."

Cyrus pointed at the empty arches across the way. "Tell him to be there at noon. But if I don't see him, I'm not leaving her side."

Emerson tipped his hat and nudged his giant horse eastward. Cyrus stood in the cold, watching horse and rider gallop into the last threads of fog.

Behind him, light stretched into the chill. The sun was rising, but he was colder for it. His hand dug in his pocket, fingers pinching the key's shank. He wanted sorely to lock and bar the New Union door and never let another soul enter.

For years, he'd labored hard, scratching his way from insignificant farmer to the grand place he inhabited now. Yet, after last night, he'd trade it all to stay here. With Claire. When he was with her, there was no place he'd rather be.

And now?

Time raced against him. He had until noon.

❧

Her footsteps banged the wooden stairs behind him. He heated water—or tried to. She walked closer, tugging her shawl around her shoulders.

"You astound me, Cyrus Ryland. First your skills with laundry"—she peered into the pot, her voice light—"and now with water. You're quite the domestic, aren't you?"

He tucked one hand behind his back. "I'm not sure what all a domestic does, but if it includes working with tepid water that refuses to heat, then I'm your man."

"It's my stove," she said, laughing. "You don't know how to work it."

Claire repositioned the pot over a perforated iron plate.

She pulled his black silk ribbon from her pocket and motioned to a chair. "Please sit there and I'll tie you up. After we get you properly done, there's something I want to show you."

He took a seat at the table, yielding to her ministration. "Want to tie me up? You're full of surprises this morning."

Her fingers combed his hair, his scalp tingling from her attention. His eyes shuttered at the shiver snaking his spine, waking more skin in want of her touch. Claire inflamed him with the slightest provocation. They needed to get above stairs soon.

"Your queue won't be its usual perfection," she said, the silk skimming his nape from her officious effort.

His mouth curled with a private smile. She missed entirely his reference to being tied up and that pleased him. He'd be the one to introduce her to those sensual pleasures.

And she didn't ask about his morning visitor. Did she miss Emerson's visit?

He cleared his throat and chose a more innocent topic. "My mother and sisters cooked with an open hearth. Stoves, I thought, were for heating purposes."

"They are," she said, finishing the loop behind him. "But you need to see this."

She strode to the square stove set in the fireplace and knelt before the iron box. Wheat bundle designs cast in relief embellished every panel. Claire opened the metal door, her bright gaze fixed on the iron box. She scooped new coals on top of ashy embers, spreading the lumps strategically in the middle.

"Look at this," she marveled.

He crouched low and peered inside the iron box. Someone had fashioned a shelf inside, a shelf high above the newly smoldering coals.

"This is why I *had* to have this shop. Your Castrol stove. Straight from Belgium." Her fingertips grazed a unique metal rack inside the box. "Someone—Mr. Tottenham, perhaps?—had the idea to fashion a shelf here for cooking *inside* the stove instead of on top. I've never seen anything like this."

They hunkered close together in front of the iron, the walls inside sooty from use. Twin smoke ribbons curled from the coal-catching fire. Once a little flame sprung from the pile she had erected, Claire shut the door.

"This small transformation makes cooking much easier than using an open hearth or faggot oven."

She folded her coal-smudged hand inside her apron, her jeweled gaze meeting his as though she'd just bared her soul. Strands of hair fell about her cheeks. Claire had dressed hastily, and her hair was pinned loosely at her nape.

A pink crease still marked her cheek from her pillow, and he was struck by how small things could mean so much to her. His heart swelled inside his chest at her simple admission.

He rested an arm over his knee, grinning. "I've been waiting a long time for a woman to appreciate me for my stove."

"I think you have many parts women can appreciate." Her tender lips parted, flirtatious and kissable.

"But there's only one woman who interests me, a certain woman who left her shoe on my doorstep."

She hugged her skirt-covered knees. They crouched close on the kitchen floor, a place as intimate as it was humble. He lived in one of London's grandest homes, yet there was no place he'd rather be than in this modest kitchen with Claire.

His pretty shopgirl reached for him. "You scare me, Cyrus Ryland." She stroked his morning whiskers, the bristles scraping in the quiet. "I could get lost in you."

"Enough to come with me and leave your shop?"

Her fingers touching his face slowed. "Are you jealous of my coffee shop?"

Her lips quirked in a smile. Claire tolerated him, he

could see as much by the breezy light in her eyes when she called him, correctly, on his motive. But she didn't have the complete picture.

Of course she didn't. He hadn't told her everything.

He bowed his head. "Guilty as charged."

"Besides, we both live in London. Where do you imagine we would go?"

More daylight crept into the kitchen. Noon and the watchful runner would be here all too soon.

"I'd rather we explore other topics, such as your special request last night."

Laughter bubbled up from her. "Why is it I'm not afraid to ask for what I want when I'm with you?" Her voice poured a liquid smooth balm on him. "Something about you, Cyrus Ryland, emboldens me, makes me feel safe and free."

His fist pressed into his knee. Now would be a good time to tell her the truth, reveal Emerson's findings in the night, and the suggestion that he stay away from her. His mouth opened, well intended words formed, but nothing came.

More soft, white tendrils fell loose about her face, and she was the tender maid in the fairy-tale book all over again. Crouched in her kitchen in worker-woman garb, a glow of affection painted Claire's features.

"We have all day," she pointed out.

He was her protector, the fierceness of that truth ingrained in him. Emerson would go about his hunt; Cyrus had plans for his. He captured Claire's hand and kissed her palm.

How could he burden her with troubles he was meant to solve?

With the clock ticking toward noon, explanations drifted away like smoke.

Sixteen

A hungry wolf at all the herd will run,
In hopes, through many, to make sure of one.

Ovid, *The Art of Love*, translated by William Congreve

THE ROYAL EXCHANGE CROWNED THE MAN WILLING to play the odds wisely. But few ever did. Cyrus had always thought wealth and position were the greatest rewards. Yet tucked away on the other side of Cornhill's busy thoroughfare in a modest, narrow shop was the greatest prize.

Claire Mayhew.

Cyrus's lips curved. She'd chafe at being thought a prize, but the truth was men *won* the hand of their lady fair. Some rhythms never changed.

Around him, early evening stretched its cloak. A few souls exited establishments to hang radiant lamps outside their doors. Candlelight shined through the New Union's mullioned front window, gleaming prettier than diamonds on a woman's neck. Or was this his bad need to be with Claire?

Figures moved inside the near-empty shop. Claire's crown of flaxen hair was visible beyond the wavy panes. She'd taken her mobcap off. She'd expect him soon.

His smile faded.

Cyrus pressed the heel of his hand on his breastbone. The ache wouldn't leave him alone.

His polished shoes stood on midtown soil, but the ground was not so solid underfoot anymore. A few things he'd long believed as truths were falsehoods: men didn't control their worlds, and chaos came in many forms.

The Duke of Marlborough had come to the Exchange today, looking for Cyrus.

His Grace had never darkened the doors of commerce before. Now, footsteps struck stone behind Cyrus, slow in their gait but all the more powerful.

The duke stopped beside Cyrus and surveyed Cornhill's bustle, his silver-topped cane held as a king might grip a scepter. The elegant walking stick made an ornament of authority for a man who didn't need it. The old man's eyes shut and ducal nostrils flared, breathing deeply of the midtown air.

"Do you smell that, Ryland?"

"Smell what, Your Grace?"

A tang of brackish Thames air mixed with earth and man. Drays and carriages, carters and pedestrians stamped the earthen road, bringing goods from land and sea.

"Change." The duke's rheumy eyes opened. "The aroma of prosperous merchants. A frightening thing for people of my class, you know—especially prosperous upstarts like you."

Cyrus hid one clenched hand behind his back, following the hum of activity before him.

"Your class has been around for centuries, will be for centuries more," he asserted, his legs shifting to a wide stance. "Other men need only use the talents God gave them…grab a chance when it's given."

"Ah, therein lays the rub."

Cyrus peered at the duke. He wasn't strong on reading people, but balance sheets spoke volumes to a man's character and priorities. Much could be found in them about Marlborough and what he loved most: not family but his home, the infamous Blenheim Palace. Cyrus didn't want to dither with the duke over merchants and status of class; he preferred the company of the fair woman who aroused him like no other.

He regretted leaving at noon yesterday, was wavering even now on following Emerson's advice.

"If you will speak plainly, Your Grace."

The old man shook his head, a dry, dusty croak springing from his throat. Laughter was all wrong coming from Marlborough.

"There are few subtleties with you, Ryland. Very well." Watery eyes stared out beneath a loose tie wig. "Blenheim Palace was my father's reward for valor in battle. Lost it once over poor political choices. To his credit, he regained it. Now my beautiful Blenheim faces more threats." His lips thinned. "I'll not be the one to lose so fine a place in this world."

Cyrus stared blankly at the road. "You want a loan."

"I won't take a loan," His Grace sputtered. "To what end?"

He itched to say His Grace couldn't afford a loan, but that would rub salt in festering wounds.

"Why should I put myself further in debt?" the old man railed. "I'll *not* do it. I leveraged everything, *everything* on building warehouses in Runcorn. Now, Sir Richard Falsom contests the canal progress there. Before Parliament, no less."

Cyrus knew of the costly warehouses sitting empty in Runcorn. Bridgewater had come to Cyrus's bank for a loan to pay the laborers when his canal business stalled. Bridgewater had offered substantial collateral. Marlborough, by contrast, had offered none. He'd sought a loan, deeming position alone as worthy of the transaction.

"You want me to just *give* you money?" He shook his head. "Won't happen."

"But that's precisely what you'll do." The duke's eyes became hard pebbles. "Remember your sugar refinery?"

He faced Marlborough, eyes narrowing. Emerson was right.

"The night watchman was badly injured."

A thin hand waved that off. "The men got carried away."

The night breeze shifted, and Cyrus unwisely faced the New Union. Claire was about the business of extinguishing the lights, but looking at her was dangerous. Marlborough followed his gaze.

"You said a man should grab a chance when it's given. I'm grabbing mine, Ryland. There's a petition in the House of Lords to widen a section of Cornhill Road, authored by me. I shall paint myself the champion of midtown."

Cyrus scowled, his fisted grip clenching harder at the small of his back. The duke's eyes gleamed with malicious light. The silver-and-black cane swung an arc over the stretch of road before them.

"This section in particular works well, don't you think?" He waved a gloved hand at the arches behind them. "What better place than the road in front of the Exchange?"

"Get to the point."

"Very well. A row of buildings on the other side must be leveled…a blow to you since you own much of this section of Town, but a man of your wealth? You'll recover." Pallid lips turned with a cruel smile, and the duke's gaze fastened on Claire's shop. "However, certain proprietors in the area could face hardships."

"You would do that over money?"

"Same as you'd toss opportunity over a bit of muslin." The old man's voice quavered. "And your nephews? I'll make sure doors are closed to them. The only work they'd find is in some backward Irish village."

Cyrus bit back a retort, forcing himself not to look across the road. Restraint served best when facing an opponent.

"Oh, I know about your coffee-shop girl."

Cyrus jammed a hand in his pocket. "She was a passing flirtation, nothing more."

The duke shrugged a gaunt shoulder, his visage bland and disbelieving. "Marriage to my daughter works in everyone's best interest."

Everyone but mine.

His Grace's mouth twisted. "Keep her on the side if it pleases you."

Claire.

He wanted to rub his chest. A vise could have been clamping its jaws on him. Instead, his fingers wrapped around the New Union master key buried in his coat pocket.

Everyone would be in a good place. Marlborough would save his home and save himself from financial peril. Zachariah, Simon, and Peter would have only the best doors opened to them. Merchants and their families would thrive, living as they had, undisturbed. None would have to face upheaval of home and business.

The duke's plan worked neatly for others, and none would be the wiser.

Cyrus scanned the row of tidy, prosperous businesses lining the street. Claire stood outside the New Union's door in pale blue, her head angling as though she spied him in the distance.

She will keep her shop.

A well-sprung carriage rolled up to the Royal Exchange arcade, blocking his view. The carriage bore the Marlborough family crest: a white lion rampant on a black canton. The duke poked his cane at the emblazoned door like an exacting headmaster.

"See that? You're right about one thing: my class has survived the centuries." His narrow chin shot up. "I sit in the House of Lords. Because of that, we will survive many more."

Cyrus faced an ugly picture, but the shocking image wasn't the duke: it was him.

His brows pinched something fierce. Was this

old man a portrait of what could happen to him in a decade or two? A man bent under the sway of his own power?

Hungry for security at all costs?

A pair of footmen hopped from the back of the conveyance, quick to snap open the door and pretend invisibility while they stood and waited.

Marlborough leaned heavily on his cane. "I give you a week, or I move the petition forward with the full force of my name behind it."

Claire. She needed his protection at all costs.

"How much?" he asked, the words dry in his throat.

His Grace smiled, the tips of his teeth showing. "The marriage contract for Elizabeth was delivered to your home today."

The New Union's key slipped from his hand, dropping to the bottom of his pocket.

The old man stepped up to the waiting carriage. "I look forward to your decision."

❧

Earlier that hour…

"One *le petite mort* and you're ready to give him all your attention." Juliette dabbed a serviette to her lips. "What about exploring other men? Have you learned nothing from me?"

Claire's knife hovered over pieces of apple. "Oh, I had many more than one," she corrected, almost laughing.

Smiling was something she hadn't been able to stop doing since yesterday. All day, she had moved with loose-limbed, agile steps, Cyrus constantly on her mind. He would be there tonight.

"*Humph.*" Juliette's eyes rolled. "Don't let so much sex go to your head."

"Not so loud," she chided, her voice dropping lower. "Nate's mopping the floors. Besides, you're the one always telling me to let a man put color on my cheeks."

Juliette's fork circled the air. "Of course, let him woo you, bring you wonderful gifts before you are chained to one man. Some men, you know, get what they want from a woman and then they are done. Everything is about the conquest."

"It's not like that with Cyrus." She sliced the last apple chunks. "Not at all."

Annie's mouth quirked as she finished drying a dish, plain stoneware stacked in front of her. "Speaking of Mr. Ryland, miss, I saw my sister, Abigail, yesterday." She picked a new plate and ran her drying cloth over it. "She told me about the pastries and some of the ladies casting their accounts all over the drawing room floor."

Claire winced and set down the knife. "It wasn't that bad...only a few spit out the bites they had taken."

"What happened?" Juliette asked from her side of the table. "Those ladies didn't like your pastries?"

"I must've salted the pastries for Miss Ryland's luncheon...mistaken salt for sugar when making the glaze. It was a busy morning Saturday." Claire scooped up the apple pieces and dropped them in a bowl. "It's nothing."

"It's not nothing, miss." Annie's voice went higher.

"Something bad happened there and Ryland House is all abuzz."

Claire folded her hands into her apron, wanting to wipe clean the disastrous social event.

Juliette set down her fork, wiping her mouth free of crumbs. "What do you mean, Annie?"

"Abigail says a thief taker came to the house…some problems with salt and destroying property at one of Mr. Ryland's warehouses."

"I know about it," Claire admitted. "Cyrus told me. But I'm not convinced there's a connection." She grabbed another green apple and polished it on her apron. "My baked goods are of no consequence. It was just a simple cooking error."

"But it wasn't, miss," Annie insisted. "Abigail says a whole crock of salt was empty. And there was a new maid, a young woman there for a few days, but after the salting, she disappeared, left the house without collecting her wages."

Claire dropped into a chair, her head tilting toward Annie. "But why would a woman go out of her way to destroy *my* pastries?"

"I don't know," she mumbled, hefting the stack of plates in front of her. "Best I take these dishes and put them away, miss." She walked to the archway and gave Claire an impish grin. "I do know one thing: that Mr. Ryland has put some color in your cheeks."

Annie winked at Claire and disappeared into the shop, humming a jaunty tune. Claire picked up a paring knife and began peeling the apple. The apple's juice was sticky on her fingers.

"Why didn't you tell me about the salted baked

goods?" Juliette asked. "That must have been too horrible for you."

Claire smiled, slowing her progress on the apple. "Because you were in a hurry and you were more concerned with the carnal nature of my visitor than other such details."

"*Humph.* And you need to be harder to get. Men like a chase."

"Funny that you say that. Lady Foster gave similar advice."

And she's miserable, alone as she is.

"You see? It is as I said." Juliette speared a bite. "You are being too easy."

The Frenchwoman sat tall in a pretty, forest-colored dress, the deep shade complementing her features. Her friend meant well, but she turned what went on between men and women into something akin to a battle.

Claire reached for the sugar, testing the light grains on her tongue. Satisfied she had the right ingredient, she dumped the sweetener into the mix. In her grip, the wooden spoon swirled around the heavy, earthen bowl, the parts blending into what would become a luscious dessert.

Across the table, Juliette picked at her pastry. Claire pinched nutmeg into the bowl, the brown-black flecks falling lightly on sugarcoated apple pieces. Let the Juliette Sauveterres and Lady Fosters of the world have their way. She had hers, and the deep glow she felt was honest and true.

Her lips curled in a secret smile. There was hot sensuality with Cyrus, his nimble fingers and talented mouth having worked magic on her. But there was kinship, affinity, and humor. She would easily call him a friend and a partner, a man to walk proudly alongside.

"I'm going to tell Cyrus I love him. Tonight."

Juliette stopped messing with her food, her dark eyes shrewd on Claire. "Why? Has he said as much to you?"

Claire draped cheesecloth over the bowl. "No."

"Let the man be the first to make declarations of love. Then, you will be in a position of power."

She reached behind to untie her apron. "This is not about wielding power. I want Cyrus, to laugh with and talk to. He values me. I want to be the same for him."

Claire folded her apron twice and dropped it on the table. She washed her hands, smiling at her lofty ideas of what it meant to be with a man…with Cyrus—but carnal concerns overruled.

Languid hands and arms unpinned her mobcap. Next came the neckerchief, her mind drifting again to the man who'd find his way to her door, his strong shoulders offering a place upon which a woman could rest her head and hide away for a night.

A chair scraped across the floor. Juliette was up, retrieving her cloak and pattens.

"I worry you go too fast, my friend."

They walked slowly into the shop, where Nate and Annie prepared to leave for the day.

Claire lifted a sconce from the wall and blew out the candle. "And I was beginning to think I wasn't going fast enough."

With a flourish, Juliette swept on her cloak, her dark eyes softening. "I do not want you hurt."

"I won't be." She reached for another sconce.

There was certainty in her step and an unconfined feeling to her hips.

Was that what a night with Cyrus Ryland did for a woman? No wonder Lady Foster was slow to disentangle herself from him.

"'Night, Miss Mayhew." Nate called his farewell, slipping from the door followed by Annie. The cook gave a silent wave, her eyes alight with mischief.

Outside, the two bent their heads in conversation. Claire went from one sconce to the next, blowing out candles. Her task cast the shop in velvet half-light. With another candle in hand, she blew on the taper, but beyond the smoky spiral, her friend fussed with the tie under her chin.

Juliette never fussed.

"Is something wrong?"

Ebony eyes clouded, and the usually confident shoulders slumped.

"Elise will leave me soon."

She set down the sconce and rushed to her friend in time to witness a fat tear drop to the floor.

"I'm so sorry." Claire set a gentle hand on Juliette's shoulder. "The two of you are always together. I never thought Elise would leave. Not without you."

"Lord Marcus persuaded her to become companion to his mother for a time. The lady recovers from a terrible fall."

The emphatic Miss Sauveterre dabbed another tear and examined her damp handkerchief. Her lips puckered with disapproval at the wetness.

"*Non*, this is good for her. She will be paid much more than the meager earnings we share." Juliette sniffled, her lips quivering into a smile. "It is a great falsehood that I am the adventurous one."

"Do you want to go back to the kitchen?"

"*Non*, I must go." The Frenchwoman slipped on her pattens and opened the shop's door.

Claire followed, crossing her arms against the chill. She couldn't let her friend leave so abruptly after sharing painful news.

"I didn't realize Lord Marcus's mother was hurt."

Juliette lifted her hood. "She took a fall from a horse and failed to inform her sons."

"A fall from a horse?"

"According to Lord Marcus, she is headstrong." A manicured hand waved off the explanation. "Elise journeys to Northampton this week, though she hasn't met the older brother, the marquis."

"I've met him."

Claire brushed her hands up and down her arms, the friction heating her. She loitered under the New Union sign, her feet stamping the ground. Garbed in her heaviest blue wool dress, she'd wait a moment to make sure Juliette fared better before going inside.

Twilight painted midtown skies gray. Ribbons of lavender separated the clouds while, on the ground, carriages moved like black silhouettes. On the other side of Cornhill, one hulking conveyance shined with burnished brass fittings in line behind another ornate carriage.

Cyrus.

"Is that not your Mr. Ryland over there?" Juliette asked, tucking away her handkerchief.

He stood stiffly in front of the Exchange beside an older man.

"Yes. Yes it is." Claire almost sang the words.

Did he see her? Cyrus faced the New Union Coffeehouse, his pewter stare remote beneath his black tricorne. She blinked, taken aback. Had she imagined his coolness? She stretched her neck, needing a better view, but a carriage rolled forward, blocking both men.

"You need to get your cloak," Juliette cautioned her.

"Not yet." Her focus stayed on the other side of the road.

She gathered handfuls of her skirts and stepped forward, moving closer to a carter passing by. Oddness settled in her midsection, though a visit to the Exchange was quite normal. Her feet moved a half step, ready to charge the road, but the bothersome carriage trundled forward.

Cyrus was still there.

A breeze twisted fallen strands of hair over her face. Larger carriages passed and she moved farther into the road.

She waved to him, her smile wide. "Cyrus?"

Stony hardness marked his features.

Needle-sharp cold pricked her skin. Such foolishness calling to him. Her voice was lost from this distance. Her arm dropped to her side.

Cyrus motioned to his carriage, not her.

The cumbersome silhouette rolled forward, blocking her view of him. She stepped into a shallow puddle, the earth squishing underfoot. The ground lacked a solid surface, throwing her off balance.

"What's he doing?"

"Perhaps he sends his men home?" Juliette was beside her.

The Ryland carriage windows offered an unfettered view of the well-lit inside. The conveyance dipped slightly from the weight of someone climbing inside. Square windows framed a dark profile, unyielding as granite.

Cyrus didn't look her way. His fist banged the carriage ceiling, giving the order to drive the black beast onward. He was leaving.

She could be a nameless midtown woman he passed by.

Claire wandered farther onto the road, her lips parting, but not a word came. She wanted to crumple. Her body moved, though she couldn't feel her legs from the numbness creeping everywhere.

"You there," a carter yelled, his whip cracking.

"Claire!"

Juliette's cry was the last she heard.

Seventeen

Come, come, leave business to idlers and wisdom to fools...

William Congreve, *The Way of the World*

"YOU CAN'T SAVE EVERYONE."

Cyrus held his quill aloft, the nib hovering over the ink well. He stared hard at the paper in front of him before setting down the implement.

Across from him sat Simon: intelligent, thoughtful, and one born with a keen eye and kinder nature. The blond lad was fresh from his university days. If Cyrus was ever blessed to have a son, he hoped his offspring would favor Simon's qualities. The world had too many brutes and ruffians—he counted himself among them.

Cyrus linked his hands on a stack of papers. "Care to explain?"

Simon waved a hand over the scattered notes, the ledgers scratched with columns of numbers. His hazel eyes lit on the most damning papers of all—the marriage contract.

"You've been like a man possessed since that

arrived." He glanced at the settee, where a rumpled blanket covered the furniture. "Keeping long hours. Zach's chasing down strange errands for you," he said, his calm smile growing. "Even sending me to deliver a package to that coffee shop."

Cyrus shifted on his seat at the mention of the coffee shop. Try as he might, he couldn't control all his reflexes when it came to Claire Mayhew. To all and sundry, he spoke little of her or not at all.

When he did, she was mentioned as a passing flirtation. Nothing more. The same words he'd said to the duke. If Marlborough had planted any more spies in Ryland House, they'd report that Cyrus washed his hands of the midtown proprietress—all the better to face his new future.

Monday, he'd driven away from Cornhill and hadn't gone back.

He rubbed his neck where a dull ache persisted. "Excellent skills of observation, Simon. But what does my work have to do with saving people?"

Long fingers tapped pristine sheaves. "This does. Though I daresay marriage doesn't count as day labor. Lucinda told me." Simon grinned, his face pure Ryland, though nature favored him with a better nose.

"Lucinda?" His hand on his nape slowed.

"She told me about your *encouragement* that she marry the Marquis of Northampton." He eyed the papers set to bind Cyrus and Lady Elizabeth forever. "Now she fears you're tossing over your happiness all in the name of family security."

"I won't ask how Lucinda came to know about that document."

"She has a point. For some reason, you're not at your best. For one thing, you're abrupt with everyone."

His best? He chuckled, a low, hard sound void of humor. Sleep eluded him. Sustenance came sparing by choice. And his manner? He scrubbed his face, bumping his bruised cheek—the constant reminder from his time with Claire.

"There's too much work to be done and little time to accomplish it."

The duke had given him a week. Now he had three days left.

Simon folded his arms across his chest. "Collecting promissory notes? Since when are you in the business of buying debts?"

Cyrus picked up the quill, his mouth pulling in a tight line. "Since I have a long habit of choosing my path rather than letting others choose for me."

Simon's brows furrowed upon hearing that explanation. Cyrus squinted at the ledger before him, columns of numbers a blur to his tired eyes. His scowl likely preempted further conversation, as evidenced by Simon gripping the chair's arms.

"Then I'll not bother you anymore."

"You can give me a report on what happened when you made the delivery to the coffee shop." He was careful to keep his eyes on the ledger.

Perhaps he wasn't fully ready to end this conversation.

The void in his chest had worsened since Monday. He pressed the heel of his hand where the ache was the worst; the vacant heaviness never left him. In private moments, his palm rubbed the spot over his heart, the same place Claire had covered him with her hand.

"I delivered your package to the New Union Coffeehouse on Wednesday as requested. But the proprietress in question, Miss Mayhew, was not available to accept the delivery personally."

"No?" His gaze darted up. "You didn't mention this before."

"I didn't think it was important. I gave the package to the dark-haired lad behind the counter. He said he'd make sure she received it."

Nate accepted the package. That was Wednesday. Today was Friday. Had she opened it?

"And he said nothing else?" he asked, scowling again. "Gave no information on her whereabouts?"

"He gave nothing." Simon's head bent with a curious tilt. "Is this woman the same—"

Zachary pushed his way into the room, eschewing the good manners that required him to knock. Under his arm was a leather folio, similar to other harmless booklets shelved in the study. Zach's cocky smile matched his brash walk.

With a flick of his wrist, his hat sailed onto the small table. His once-polished boots bore signs of a well-traveled day. He tossed the folio onto Cyrus's desk before dropping into the other chair facing the desk.

"Today was fruitful, sir."

Dimples gave boyish appeal to the less cultivated Zach. Quick with wit and charm, Zach ferreted information without a body ever knowing they gave up a secret. His frame matched Cyrus's, from his brown hair to his square jaw and strong nose; only his light brown eyes set him apart.

He stretched out his legs and crossed them at the ankle. "What next?"

"Next, our uncle will seek proper rest in a proper bed," Simon said, sounding very much like a physician.

"He just looks like he had a bad bout and needs to sleep it off."

A knock at the door announced Belker's presence. The butler stood in the half-open doorway, bowing from the waist.

"Beg pardon, Mr. Ryland. You have a visitor." The butler looked at the trio of men in the study. "It is your friend, the Marquis of Northampton, sir."

"Send him in."

Simon and Zachary rose from their chairs, discussing what next to raid from the kitchen. North would be a welcome surprise from the tedium of his week. He rose from his chair when Belker announced his friend.

"The Most Honorable Marquis of Northampton."

North walked a few steps into the small study, his cloak draping an arm and hat in hand. Cyrus nodded at the outerwear usually collected by his butler.

"Belker's standards must be slipping." He pushed back his chair and made to move away from behind his desk. "You can put them on that table if you like."

"No." North held up a hand. "In fact, I'd prefer you stay on that side of the desk."

Cyrus froze. Sunlight filtered through sheer drapes, illuminating North's drawn features. Though Cyrus had not availed himself of a mirror, he'd have still guessed his friend looked worse than he did.

"As you wish." He pushed back his coat and set his hands on his hips. "Something wrong?"

Thin lines creased the skin under North's eyes. A small stain marked his drooping cravat.

"This is one of those times I wish you imbibed in strong drink, Cyrus."

"I take it you're in need of something stronger than tea."

Cyrus walked to a set of paneled doors near his desk. He opened one and pulled out a decanter. Brown liquid sloshed inside the fine-cut glass. He set the decanter and two glasses on his desk, finding an open space.

"Never said I *never* drink."

He removed the glass stopper and poured whiskey for them both. Light touched the stream, showing off the rich caramel and gold colors.

Cyrus stretched his arm across the desk, offering the half-filled glass. "Since you want me to stay on this side."

The words were delivered with humor, but North accepted his drink and stepped back. He put the glass to his mouth and swallowed deeply—one gulp, then another, and one more. Cyrus drank too, letting the liquid scorch his already parched throat.

He licked the flavors from his lips—wood and vanilla. One corner of his mouth curled at the thought of Claire. She unknowingly changed his thinking to want to savor tastes and smells.

He held the glass up to the sunlight, catching liquid gold. "What ails you?"

The marquis set his empty glass on the table next to Zach's tricorne. Agitated fingers bounced his hat, his gaze not meeting Cyrus's.

"I'm leaving London. For good. Leasing my house."
He winced with each pronouncement. "Taking care
of my affairs, among them looking after my mother
and finally settling on a wife."

"Noteworthy changes," he said, keeping his tone
neutral.

North took a deep breath. "I…I made a mistake."
The hat bouncing stopped. "You've called me friend
and I betrayed you."

Cyrus went still.

A hiccup of sound, guilty laughter really, erupted
from North. "I liked you when you came to Town. I
didn't expect to, nor did I expect things to go as badly
as they have…" His words trailed off.

North adjusted the cloak on his arm, failing to give
eye contact to Cyrus. Neither man moved, but the
clock ticked its persistent forward press. Time was
becoming a precious commodity for Cyrus.

Finally, North looked up.

"Three months ago, Marlborough approached me
with a plan."

"What kind of plan?"

Cyrus took a heavy draught of the whiskey, his
pulse quickening with new pressure.

"I was to help the Duke of Marlborough. Give him
information about you. And he, in turn, would help
me regain a small piece of land that belonged to my
mother, a simple cottage near the border not part of
the Northampton entail."

"Information about me?" Cyrus set down the glass.

"Yes. Things you like to do, your family, your business, who you spend your time with…everything. At

first, I believed all worked for the best. Marlborough went out of his way to make inquiries for your nephews once I told him about them. I obliged His Grace because I thought it was harmless."

"Until it wasn't," he said, his tone razor sharp.

North met Cyrus's stare. "Yes, until it wasn't," he agreed quietly. "A fortnight ago, we met, and he was different...desperate, I'd say. I tried to convince him not to damage your warehouse." North paused, his features tightening. "Then I heard of the night watchman."

Cyrus leaned forward, bracing his knuckles on the desktop. "And Miss Mayhew? You fed him information about her?" He closed his eyes, shaking his head. "Don't bother answering. I know you did," he scoffed. "And to think, you tried to convince me not to find her."

Her face danced before him...masked and flirting... untying his cravat and speaking her mind...standing up to him in the shop...him touching her and kissing her here in his study when she stormed into his home.

He would count his life fortunate if she let him touch her ever again.

His fists squeezed tighter.

"And one of the interesting facts in all of this, His Grace holds the deed on the cottage I've tried to get back." North sighed, an exhausted sound. "It's not worth much, a ramshackle place from what I hear... but he had the title all along."

Cyrus opened his eyes and sucked in a deep breath, preparing himself for another blow. "Is there anything else?"

"Yes, I also came to say farewell. I wash my hands of this and hope you'll forgive me someday."

Forgive? A twinge pinched his conscience.

He didn't move. "Then I bid you farewell."

London was not a place he liked. He wouldn't even try anymore. To most, he would always be the rustic, the outsider. He'd always be the man with canal grit on his hands.

North walked to the door and the Most Honorable Marquis looked anything but an honorable peer of the realm. He tarried in the doorway, facing Cyrus.

"Are you going to marry Lady Elizabeth?" He set his hat on his head. "She'd be a genuine prize in all this mess."

A prize? Cyrus flinched at the word.

"You lost the chance to hear my answer."

Eighteen

If there's delight in love, 'tis when I see
That heart, which others bleed for, bleed for me.

William Congreve, *The Way of the World*

THE GENTLEMAN'S CLUB WAS OF LESSER QUALITY, A place Cyrus chose just for that distinction. He read a broadsheet in an upholstered chair smelling of old smoke. Across from him, the empty chair boasted a thin cushion, sparse enough to feel the furniture's wooden frame when one sat down.

He saved that chair for the Duke of Marlborough.

Cyrus folded the paper in half in time to see the duke's approach. He didn't rise to welcome His Grace.

"Your Grace," he said, motioning to the old chair.

The duke examined the seat and removed his hand-kerchief. He held the white cloth to his nose.

"It's free of vermin, Your Grace," Cyrus assured him.

The duke sat down and stretched a leg like any country squire at rest. "Not sure the purpose of asking that we meet here. But I can humor you." The duke leaned his walking stick beside the chair.

"There seems to be ample doses of humor running rampant around Town." Cyrus tapped the broadsheet he'd folded in half. "Imagine my surprise at this gossip that I've been secretly engaged to Lady Elizabeth Churchill."

"My duchess is anxious to set plans in motion." He looked at the thin folio on the table in between them. His gloved hand picked it up. "The marriage contract, I presume?"

"It is." Cyrus nodded. "You'll find everything you need in there."

The duke's pallid eyes lit up. He flipped open the slender leather folio and perused the first few sheets.

Cyrus took joy in waiting, like a hunter watching over his trap. He waited and watched. A few younger men entered the salon, pouring their own drinks. Their jocular voices overlapped, regaling each other with their exploits in one of the local taverns. But Cyrus waited. And he knew the exact moment when his denial hit the duke.

Marlborough's thin brows pressed in a narrow line a split second before he glared at Cyrus.

"It's not signed."

"Nor will it ever be. I will not marry your daughter."

His Grace snapped the folio shut. "Then prepare yourself, Mr. Ryland, because I will do everything I said I'd do and much more." The duke's voice shook. "Much, much more."

Cyrus nodded at the documents half spilling from

the folder. "Before you make any plans, you might want to take a look at some of the other fine reading material I've organized for you."

The folio opened and the Duke of Marlborough riffled through the papers. He scanned one, then another, his lips moving though no sound came.

"What is this, Ryland?" He dropped the messy folio on the table, papers scattering. "All I see is the unsigned marriage contract and ledgers with columns of numbers."

"I gave you those numbers because I'm of the firm belief numbers say a lot about a man…who he is and what he values."

"I don't need a lesson in simple sums."

"But I think you do." Cyrus leaned forward and his fingertips pushed a page across the table. "These numbers represent your debts, Your Grace…debts that I now hold."

The duke jerked in his seat, his face going pale.

"You hold my notes," he echoed, his breath coming in labored huffs. "And what do you plan to do with them?"

"Nothing." Cyrus grabbed his hat and stood up. "Provided you leave me and my family alone. You will burn your petition and leave the good merchants of Cornhill alone."

"Is that all you want?" His Grace's laugh was weak, but the corners of his mouth drooped. He was a defeated man and he knew it.

"There is one more thing. Feel free to turn the other way should our paths ever cross again, Your Grace." Cyrus set his hat on his head and bowed his leave.

The old man leaned hard on his stick. He cast an eye to the mess of papers. "A bit hard since we both live in Town."

"Not for me. I plan to quit Piccadilly soon."

❧

"Aren't you going to open it?" Annie grabbed a pair of mugs from the shelf behind the counter.

It was a modest leather folio wrapped with twine. Nothing eye-catching about this package. Claire glanced at the brown rectangle, a bothersome thing she had been tempted more than once to feed to the coals. She was quite done with gifts from Mr. Ryland.

Her cleaning cloth made rapid circles on the slate. "No."

The plan today and every day was to forget Cyrus Ryland, not resurrect him.

She went back to swiping the message board free of every inch of chalk dust. The cold, hard pursuit of perfection was a good way to ignore pain. Keep busy doing a job over and over again. But heart-wrenching thoughts intruded:

For some men…everything is about the conquest.

I find your forbidden fruit most desirable of all.

And her mind-rattling, cheek-burning favorite…

I know how I want to touch you.

Her hand paused mid-swirl. Parts of her fluttered mutinously on that last echo of Cyrus in her head. The man wouldn't leave her in peace.

Annie cradled her coffee pitcher, having filled mugs around the shop. Claire rubbed a stubborn corner of the slate, aware of the weight of Annie's stare on her.

She turned around.

"Is something wrong?" Claire asked.

The cook set her pitcher on an empty table and wiped her hands on her apron. "Miss Mayhew, have you given any thought that there may be more going on? With Mr. Ryland, I mean."

"No."

She wanted to stay busy and stay numb. Being numb didn't hurt. The sensation wrapped her in a blanket of blessed emptiness where no man could invade.

She removed the new cargo list from her apron and proceeded to write: Corn. Saltpeter. Lumber, Swedish Spruce variety. Rum...

The chalk clacked letters on the board, the sound as reassuring as the voices of her regular patrons.

"I saw my sister, Abigail, again last night." Annie wedged herself into Claire's side vision.

With chalk in hand, she kept up a rapid succession of words...an Irish schooner, *The Selkie*, docked on Billingsgate Wharf.

"Remember that maid who'd been at Ryland House around the time of your lunch meeting?" A white mobcap and carrot-red hair pressed against the chalkboard. "One of the men from Bow Street found her yesterday. Abigail says that was all the news around Ryland House. That and whispers about the Duke of Marlborough being behind the troubles."

The chalk slowed over that piece of news.

Annie must've been heartened to go on. "And you know what else? Mr. Ryland told the man to let her go."

Claire's shoes scraped the floor when she moved

away from the board. "That might absolve me of oversalting the pastries, but it does nothing to explain why Mr. Ryland drove off the way he did…like I was some—"

Laughter burst from a pair of tables pushed together. She clamped her lips together but opened them again.

"If not for that man in the red waistcoat coming to my rescue, I might've been crushed."

"Because you were distracted," Annie said. "Upset and you didn't think right from the shock."

"Exactly."

"Abigail says the same thing of Mr. Ryland. She says he sleeps in his study and has messages and such comin' and goin' at all hours of the day and night."

"I don't know how that matters to me." She swallowed the lump in her throat, her voice shaky and bitter. "I don't know about Mr. Ryland's poor sleep, but I do know he got what he wanted from me."

"Are you sure of that?" Annie smiled, wisdom beyond her years glimmering from patient eyes. "Could be he misses you the way you miss him."

She stared out the shop's window, lost in thought. Did he miss her?

"And there's one more thing, miss. Abigail says they're closing down Ryland House for good."

She flinched, that piece of news like an ice-cold dousing.

Cyrus leaving…

That hurt most of all.

But why another package?

"Very well, Annie. You win. Please get the package and I'll open it."

Claire took a seat at the empty table closest to the counter. Annie set the plain leather before Claire, and folded herself into the opposite chair.

"I know this isn't my concern, Miss Mayhew, but I'd like to see." The young cook folded her arms on the tabletop. "The shoes and all were so pretty."

"This is too flat to be anything like a shoe." Claire's shoulders moved, listless and sore. "But, stay. If it weren't for you, I'd feed this to my stove."

A flap folded over the open end of the folio, the weight light in her hands. She turned the folio upside down, shaking free a piece of paper and a key tied with red silk ribbon. Claire pulled her key from her pocket to compare the two.

"This is a deed to the shop," Annie cried. "The New Union Coffeehouse belongs to you."

"Let me see that." Claire read the deed, a simple contract giving the shop over to her, sealed by a signature she remembered well.

Her jaw dropped. She read and reread the words *Quit Claim Deed* boldly scrawled on top. The contract's date was Monday, the day Cyrus gave her the cut.

Why would he pass this property to her free and clear?

"But I didn't earn this," she murmured.

And there was no note to explain the sudden generosity.

"Well, you did something." Annie grinned from ear to ear.

Did something? Her mind came up with some painful ideas as to what that meant. She read and read the documents, trying to decipher meaning but finding none.

"Imagine not having to pay rent, miss. You'll be a rich woman before you know it."

Lady Foster came to mind, with her fine gown and fine words about independence and sleeping alone. Claire shook her head. She pushed back her mobcap, and a pin sprang free, dropping to her lap.

Annie stood up. "I've got to tell Nate. He'll be so happy for you."

She picked up the key, letting the iron roll across her palm. The last person to use the key was Cyrus.

This key. Hot sparks tingled over her skin. Her eyes closed, and she rested her head on the bench behind her. With the key in hand, Cyrus's whispered words about a key unlocking a woman's door flooded her mind. She squirmed on her seat, plain cambric drawers reminding where silk once was.

And there was laughter too. His hands folding her laundry, kneeling with her on the kitchen floor to look inside her stove, and all that morning talking and kissing. Why would he play the romantic and then…nothing?

Beside her, men jested, talking about the broadsheet's gossip pages—Mr. Cogsworth and another trader, Mr. Branham, and the merchant, Mr. Bolks.

"Wouldn't've thought he'd be leg shackled," said Mr. Branham.

"Ah, most men want a steady hand at home. Mrs. Cogsworth needed some convincing…"

She opened her eyes, the key still in her grip and the deed on the table. Best she put this document in a safe place.

"But Cyrus Ryland?" Mr. Bolks asked.

What was that about Cyrus? She stalled in her seat, her lashes dropping low.

"To the Duke of Marlborough's daughter." Mr. Cogsworth laid the broadsheet over the table, pointing to a section. "Says '…talk in Piccadilly is the joining of one Mr. Cyrus Ryland with Lady Elizabeth Churchill' and then it says here 'Their Graces expect the banns to be read soon.'"

She shot to her feet. The key banged the tabletop. Claire set a protective hand over her heart, the organ beating twice as fast. This had to be a mistake. Had she heard the names wrong?

"Mr. Cogsworth, would you be so kind as to read again the last announcement?" she asked.

He was going to leave Town and marry a woman of fine position. The flat of her other hand rested on the tabletop, holding her up.

"Certainly," Mr. Cogsworth said, offering quick, emphatic agreement. His finger pointed to the section. "Says here 'The talk in Piccadilly is the joining of one Mr. Cyrus Ryland and Lady Elizabeth Churchill. No official announcement has been made, nor has a date been set, but Their Graces expect the banns to be read soon.'"

She looked away, a dizzy spell threatening. She hadn't eaten much lately. The key. The deed. Like a mosaic, the parts alone made no sense, but together they formed a fair image.

Her shoulders drooped. This was worse than having her name dragged through the mud in her home village. Everyone gossiped about what happened in Greenwich

Village, but in midtown, few knew about her foolish choices. The shame of feeling used was no less stinging.

"Thank you, Mr. Cogsworth." She smiled sweetly and the trader's ears turned red.

Claire collected the key and the deed. She knew exactly what she'd do with them.

⁓

The butler swung the indigo door wide open. "Miss Mayhew, you're here."

"Belker?"

"We've been expecting you."

"*We?*" she repeated, not moving from the stone step.

"The upper staff and I to be precise." He motioned to her cloak. "May I?"

Her free hand clamped the open folds of her cloak. "No, I won't be long."

Belker clasped his hands behind his back, his posture erect. "Of course, miss. That seems to be the mode of the day."

She shifted the folio, clutching it like a shield to her chest under her cloak. "You're inviting me in?"

He bowed, extending a hand in the general direction of the study. "I'm confident you know where to find him, Miss Mayhew."

"Of course," she said, gripping her folio closer.

Had Ryland House gone mad? The entire house was off.

Her heels clicked on polished stone. She turned down the familiar hallway, taking in the splendid murals overhead. The study's carved alcove looked dim, the study dimmer.

The door was open. No one was inside.

"Here's to traveling crosstown to give the King of Commerce his comeuppance," she uttered. "Only to find he's not here."

She shut the door behind her.

This time, however, messy piles of papers covered the desk. His chair would make a fine depository for the key and the document of ownership she wasn't going to keep. Standing by the windows, she yanked open the curtains.

"That's better."

"Claire?"

"Cyrus?" She whipped around in time to see him rise from the settee.

Shirt open at the neck and waistcoat gapping, Cyrus Ryland was a mess. The pristine queue, his standard, was in disarray. Hair stuck out everywhere, but his face, strong and familiar, was…endearing.

Heaven help her, but she wanted to cosset him.

He smiled in the shadows. "You came."

"I did. To return this." She held up the folio and peered at the settee, a once-elegant piece, now lumpy and awkward. "What are you doing?"

"Waiting for you."

Her knees wobbled on his unexpected words. The way his gaze drank her in, he could be a man adrift on the sea. Now it was agony not to touch him.

"You can't do that."

He ran a hand through unruly hair. "Do what?"

"Say something like that…that you're waiting for me." She rubbed the folio's leather—she needed to or else she would rub Cyrus.

"Why not? It's true."

Her heart lurched—then painful reminders of the broadsheet's announcement and news of him leaving. She clamped her arms across her chest, hugging the folio.

"That could be a little difficult if you're not here anymore...especially with your new wife."

He grimaced, holding a hand out to her. "I can explain."

"Truly?" She swallowed hard, holding the folio tighter. "You can explain how you've wanted me with you despite your driving away from the Exchange, leaving me like a fool in the middle of the road?" Emotion warped her voice. The corners of her eyes stung. Tears wanted shedding, the first one trickling out.

Cyrus rushed to her side, his arms wrapping around her. Warmth and hardness enveloped her, the smell of skin like sun on stone. He plucked the folio from her and dropped it onto his desk. Then he swept her into his arms and made his way to the settee. They reclined there, entwined in silence. His strong heartbeat was the only thing she wanted to hear until...

"I'm sorry, Claire," he murmured while kissing her hair. "I should've told you everything."

She nodded, intent on pushing open the rest of his shirt. "The Duke of Marlborough, he's somehow behind this."

Explanations would be required, but his skin, his chest...she needed to touch him. Above her, Cyrus swallowed hard, nodding.

"Yes. I thought I'd lost you." His voice was thick

and uneven. "It hurt to ignore you, but I hope you'll forgive me someday. I promise to make it up to you."

Her head rested in the crook of his shoulder, the place where his arm and chest met. Her fingers grazed his chest, tracing the furrow between his chest muscles.

"You don't have to make anything up to me. I choose to love you, Cyrus. All of you."

His breath stalled and Cyrus's whole body relaxed. He needed her tender touch. She'd been determined to vent her spleen upon finding him; now she wanted to heal him.

"I love you, Claire Mayhew." He squeezed her, his arms big and enveloping. "It is my most unpleasant flaw that I want to do right by those I love. I take charge. Too much. I've always worked better solving problems on my own."

She tipped her head back, all the better to see his face. "Why did you leave me standing in the middle of Cornhill? Was it something to do with the salting?"

He told her everything—from Emerson's advice, to North's confession, to Marlborough's greed and threats. He held nothing back, even confessing his dislike of London. He wanted to go home to Stretford.

Cyrus talked, pulling the pins from her hair, and she listened. One by one, the pins came free, and her hair fell free.

"But why deed the shop to me?"

He played softly with a long, flaxen lock, sending shivers down her spine.

"Because I wanted you to have what you wanted

most." Tense lines framed his mouth, and he admitted, "The duke may still win. He has access to people and places I never will."

"You can't mean to marry his daughter?" she cried. "No."

She gripped his shirt. "And you think I want the shop more than you?"

He chuckled and kissed her forehead, a soft chiding kind of kiss. "It was in this very room you told me there were women in England who didn't want marriage to me or any other man. You convinced me about your wish to be an independent proprietress."

A pang settled in her chest, as she recalled her staunch words. "I don't want to be alone."

"You don't have to be." He kissed her forehead, and she felt his smile against her skin. "There's only one woman I'll marry. You, if you'll have me…someday."

She scrutinized him, as if seeing another facet of the man. She studied his eyes and strong nose, the square jaw that had been struck by too many hard forces, and the cleft that drove her mad.

"Yes," she said quietly. "But what will you do about the Duke and Duchess of Marlborough? They practically announced that you're engaged."

He pulled her close. "I've bought most of the duke's debt. That should give us enough leverage to move on with our lives."

A sweet tremor brushed her skin. Sunshine could've burst when he said those words. She burrowed in closer to him, listening to his steady heartbeat. "Keep saying that."

"Saying what?"

"Words like *us* and *our lives*." Her voice quavered and another tear trickled down her cheek.

He set her on the familiar cushion and wiped the streak of wetness. "Miss Mayhew, you are incredibly easy to seduce if a man can use simple words like *us* and *our lives* to sway you."

"You have me nearly flat on my back, sir." A lazy hand unloosed his waistcoat buttons.

She opened his shirt and spread her fingers wide over his chest. She found his heartbeat, the rhythm beneath her hand beating strong and true. Like the man. Another tear sprang free and another after that. He leaned close, an aching expression on his face.

"Shhhh..." he soothed her, wiping away her tears. "I don't want you to cry."

"I'm happy, Cyrus."

She sat up, sniffling, and his eyes widened when she pushed him back against the settee. "These are good tears," she said quietly, straddling his lap. "You make me very happy. But you must make me a promise."

She pushed her skirts high up her thighs, the wool making little snicking sounds. At the juncture of her thighs, she found what she wanted. His placket. Her hands freed four brass buttons.

Cyrus was entranced, his head dipped low to follow her progress. "Anything in my power to give...I will."

Their heads bent close and she unloosed one more button. Late fall sunlight flooded the other half of the study, leaving them in soft shadows. They had a small paradise here in this corner of the room.

"We will share our burdens." She eyed his bruised

cheek, her hand caressing the skin beneath the healing cut. "No secrets."

His pewter stare bored into her. "No secrets."

Cyrus pulled on the bow that tied her into her dress, working the lacing free one X at a time.

He reached for her hand, the scarred one and kissed the pink mark. "Did I ever tell you about the fairy tale that fascinated me as a boy?"

"I think you'll like it. There are lots of *us*'s and *our lives* in this one…"

And he regaled her with the finest tale of shoes and keys and forbidden fruit, a tale that lasted long past midnight.

Epilogue

Late Spring, 1769

"OF COURSE I HAD TO MARRY YOU. SOMEONE NEEDS TO take care of you. You keep leaving your clothing everywhere." His eyes glinted hot and tender.

"I like to think of those items as bread crumbs, leading you to me."

They walked through the grassy field, their fingers linked together.

"I need no leading to find you," he said.

Holding hands was a favorite part of being married to Cyrus Ryland, one of the pleasant surprises she had discovered. He welcomed daily garden walks, tucking her close to his side. Nor was he ever bothered to sneak away for a time and simply hold hands. Most interesting of all, Cyrus understood her need to keep the New Union Coffeehouse running well.

Today, he had surprised her with fishing poles and a basket lunch. They walked along the River Irwell, not far from Manchester, in thick grass, her hems dragging.

The time wasn't the best for catching fish but was perfect for being alone.

And perfect for sharing secrets.

"This spot," he said, pointing to a willow tree draping the bank. Green branches trailed the water like fingers skimming from a boat.

"It is perfect." *Like life when I'm with you.*

They spread a blanket, kicked off their shoes, and stretched out side by side. She untied his queue and ran her fingers through his hair.

"You know, love," she said, stroking his hair, "you've upset the balance of nature with your beautiful hair. If other women only knew."

He'd already shut his eyes, forgetting the fishing poles entirely. "My valet warns me there are many more gray strands this year." One lazy lid opened. "He claims it's because I'm a married man."

"Aging you, am I?"

The corners of his eyes crinkled from his smile. "Something is." He grabbed her hand and kissed her palm and the pale skin on her wrist. "But not you."

Peaceful moments passed, not measured by a clock but by birds singing and the river's flow.

His chest heaved, but his eyes stayed closed. "There's no place I'd rather be than with you, Claire Ryland."

"I feel the same about you. And? What is it you want to say to me?"

He chuckled, the sound coming from deep in his chest. "A man can hide very little from you, can he?"

She circled her finger on the skin above his nose. "This, among other signs, gives you away."

Cyrus sat up, brushing bits of grass that clung to him. He leaned an elbow on an upraised knee, staring at the meadow beyond.

"When I think of growing old, I know I face a good future because of you," he began. "But I want to grow old somewhere out here, not London."

"And this is what troubles you?"

His pewter eyes pinned her, his voice soft. "Because your happiness matters to me." A semblance of a grin stirred his lips. "The New Union… it's in London."

Her new husband was *that* concerned for her happiness. She sat up.

"Cyrus, you make me happy, not a place." She waved her arm over the beautiful, river touched meadow. "I'd be happy here."

He studied her as though checking for a fissure or a fault. They'd waited months before getting married. This was new. They were new.

She leaned close and kissed his cheek, her finger stroking the cleft on his chin. "People drink coffee in Manchester."

"I've heard they do." His voice was a pleasant rumble against her skin.

"Cyrus, I'll go wherever you want."

She found another bit of grass clinging to him and brushed it off. She liked taking care of him as much as he devoted himself to her.

"I've learned a few things, being married to you."

"Such as?"

"We never really lose our flaws. Being with the people we love smooths out those flaws, makes us better, but flaws?" She batted the air. "They are boon companions for life."

"And I'm better equipped at knowing my wife is about to deliver sage commentary for my benefit."

She laughed softly at his insight. "Cyrus, you will work for the rest of your life to take care of others. It's ingrained in you. But it's time you do for yourself... and as your wife, I expect it."

One brow shot up at her stern tone.

"Tell me that you want to leave London and get lost in the Midlands somewhere. That's what people do when they love each other. They share those wants and needs."

He reached up and pulled her down to his chest. Her head tucked perfectly against his shoulder, and he proceeded to tell her many things.

Acknowledgments

There are three people who left their mark on this story. Thank you to my awesome agent, Sarah Younger, who loves a good alpha male. What woman doesn't? Sarah's encouragement and curiosity about Cyrus is a joy. Even better, I appreciate her support and loyalty. My editor, Cat Clyne, deserves kudos for pointing out the good and flushing out the excess. I appreciate her championship of the Midnight Meetings series and her gentle words along the way. I could read Cat's smile via email. Lastly, thank you Brian Conkle, for being the man who stood in our kitchen and said, "It's your turn," and meaning it.

Meet the Earl at Midnight

Book 1 in the Midnight Meetings series
by Gina Conkle

❧

The Phantom of London. Enigma Earl.
The Greenwich Recluse.

*Half of his face, shadowed by gold and brown whiskers, showed
male perfection, but the other half, a bizarre pattern of scar lines and
puckered flesh. Lydia recoiled as much from the hot anger flashing
in his eyes as from astonishment.*

He's a mysterious recluse

Lord Greenwich is notoriously elusive. His tendency to hide
his face in public has earned him some choice monikers,
including "the Phantom of London." Is he disfigured? Mad?
No one is more surprised than Miss Lydia Montgomery
when she is betrothed to him to save her family from
penury. But if Lydia wants a chance at happiness, she'll have
to set aside her fear and discover the man hiding behind the
beastly reputation…

❧

"A refreshing Georgian spin on *Beauty and the
Beast*." —Grace Burrowes, *New York Times*
bestselling author of *Once Upon a Tartan*

For more Gina Conkle, visit:

www.sourcebooks.com

Kiss the Earl
by Gina Lamm

❦

A modern girl's guide to seducing Mr. Darcy

When Ella Briley asked her lucky-in-love friends to set her up for an office party, she was expecting a blind date. Instead, she's pulled through a magic mirror and into the past…straight into the arms of her very own Mr. Darcy.

Patrick Meadowfair, Earl of Fairhaven, is too noble for his own good. To save a female friend from what is sure to be a loveless marriage, he's agreed to whisk her off to wed the man she truly wants. But all goes awry when Patrick mistakes Ella for the would-be bride and kidnaps her instead.

Centuries away from everything she knows, Ella's finally found a man who heats her blood and leaves her breathless. Too bad he's such a perfect gentleman. Yet the reluctant rake may just find this modern girl far too tempting for even the noblest of men to resist…

❦

Praise for Gina Lamm:

"Gina Lamm writes excellent [time-travel romance] with humor and great storytelling." —*Books Like Breathing*

"Snappy writing and characters who share a surprising, spicy chemistry." —*RT Book Reviews*

For more Gina Lamm, visit:

www.sourcebooks.com

When a Rake Falls
by Sally Orr

He's racing to win back his reputation

Having hired a balloon to get him to Paris in a daring race, Lord Boyce Parker is simultaneously exhilarated and unnerved by the wonders and dangers of flight, and most of all by the beautiful, stubborn, intelligent lady operating the balloon.

She's curious about the science of love

Eve Mountfloy is in the process of conducting weather experiments when she finds herself spirited away to France by a notorious rake. She's only slightly dismayed—the rake seems to respect her work—but she is frequently distracted by his windblown good looks and buoyant spirits.

What happens when they descend from the clouds?

As risky as aeronautics may be, once their feet touch the ground, Eve and Boyce learn the real danger of a very different type of falling…

Praise for *The Rake's Handbook*:

"A charming romp. The witty repartee and naughty innuendos set the perfect pitch for the entertaining romance." —*RT Book Reviews*

For more Sally Orr, visit:

www.sourcebooks.com

Wicked, My Love

by Susanna Ives

❧

A smooth-talking rogue and a dowdy financial genius

Handsome, silver-tongued politician Lord Randall doesn't get along with his bank partner, the financially brilliant but hopelessly frumpish Isabella St. Vincent. Ever since she was his childhood nemesis, he's tried—and failed—to get the better of her.

Make a perfectly wicked combination

When both Randall's political career and their mutual bank interests are threatened by scandal, he has to admit he needs Isabella's help. They set off on a madcap scheme to set matters right. With her wits and his charm, what could possibly go wrong? Only a volatile mutual attraction that's catching them completely off guard…

❧

Praise for Susanna Ives:

"A fresh voice that reminded me of Julia Quinn's characters." —Eloisa James, *New York Times* bestselling author

For more Susanna Ives, visit:

www.sourcebooks.com

Married to a Perfect Stranger

by Jane Ashford

❦

Time and distance have changed them both...

Quiet and obliging, Mary Fleming and John Bexley married to please their families, but John was almost immediately called away on a two-year diplomatic mission. Now he's back, and it seems everything they thought they knew about each other was wrong...

It's disconcerting, irritating—and somehow all very exciting...

❦

Praise for Jane Ashford:

"Ashford captures the reader's interest with her keen knowledge of the era and her deft writing." —*RT Book Reviews*

"Ashford's richly nuanced, realistically complex characters and impeccably crafted historical setting are bound to resonate with fans of Mary Balogh." —*Booklist*

For more Jane Ashford, visit:

www.sourcebooks.com

Earls Just Want to Have Fun

Covent Garden Cubs

by Shana Galen

❦

His heart may be the last thing she ever steals...

Marlowe runs with the Covent Garden Cubs, a gang of thieves living in the slums of London's Seven Dials. It's a fierce life, but when she's alone, Marlowe allows herself to think of a time before—a dimly remembered life when she was called Elizabeth.

Maxwell, Lord Dane, is roped into teaching Marlowe how to navigate the social morass of the *ton*, but she will not escape her past so easily. Instead, Dane is drawn into her dangerous world, where the student becomes the teacher and love is the greatest risk of all.

❦

Praise for Shana Galen:

"Shana Galen has a gift for storytelling that puts her at the top of my list of authors." —*Historical Romance Lover*

"Shana Galen is brilliant at making us fall in love with her characters, their stories, their pains, heartaches, and triumphs." —*Unwrapping Romance*

For more Shana Galen, visit:

www.sourcebooks.com

About the Author

Gina loves history, books, and romance...the perfect recipe for a historical romance writer. Her passion for castles and old places (the older and moldier the better!) means interesting family vacations. Good thing her husband and two sons share similar passions, except for romance...that's where she gets the eye roll. When not visiting fascinating places, she can be found delving into the latest adventures in cooking, gardening, and chauffeuring her sons.

MARQUIS

Québec, Canada